THE SEA AND THE SAND

FINN ÓG

NOTE FROM FINN

Free novellas and short stories are available at www.finnog.com where readers can sign up to receive advance copies of new books.

Also by Finn Óg

Charlie

The Sea and the Sand

Too Close to Home

A Half of Penitents

The Carbon Collective

The Watcher Girl

For the oul' fella

1

The world is irritatingly small.

Sam stood on Grafton Street, watched the man go up in flames and cursed how approximate people have become. He sighed for a moment and watched the crowd part like a sea of red, the glow of the inferno flickering off their faces, horrifying and beguiling in almost equal measure. Sam shook his head, looked to the sky and stepped forward to douse the screams.

He'd grow to wish he'd let the man burn.

"Snap!"

Isla was cheating, as usual, in part due to a misunderstanding of the rules. At six years old the fun was more in beating her father to the draw than in stockpiling cards, and so she shouted before the face had even been flipped. It delighted Sam to watch how her little mind anticipated his hand movements, to see her excitement. It seemed like a normal, wholesome thing to do of an evening after all the wee woman had been through.

They were drifting, alone, across the Mediterranean in their fifty-four-foot home. Progress was deliberately slow, there'd been a lot of rebuilding to do and the work was far from finished. Sam wasn't sure whether his daughter's scars would ever properly heal but she was gradually becoming less afraid of bedtime and the potential horror that sleep could bring.

He'd made resolutions, starting with how he made a living. He wouldn't take on any more work that could possibly impact his daughter or his family. The last job he'd been embroiled in had done that and more. From here on in, Sam determined, any risks taken would be his alone, and even at that they would be minimal. He had a child to raise and she no longer had a mother to step into the breach.

"Daddy, you can have some of my cards," she told him, sliding a frugal collection to his side of the chart table.

"Thank you, darlin'," said Sam, the salt and the stubble tautening at a gentle reminder of his daughter's provenance. Isla's mother would never have seen anyone stuck; winning had never been Shannon's priority.

"What story do you want tonight?"

"Aw-uh, is it bedtime already?"

"Not yet, little lady, but in a while."

It had become part of the ritual to keep the imagery gentle: stories at night of normal life, of other girls, of school and excitement and toys and boys and the weird and horrible things they do. Sam's plan was to encourage Isla to want such things again, to grow the appeal of ordinariness rather than the nomadic sea-gypsy style they'd become accustomed to. Although the perpetual sailing suited Sam, and for a while it had seemed the best way to make Isla feel safe, he knew the time would come when she would have to swim in the real world again, so their grift when the wind blew them west, was aimed at Ireland once more.

By night Sam plotted the charts and the future and occasionally sailed. It allowed Isla to keep watch while he dozed by day in the cockpit. She'd become quite the little sailor, careful and clipped on at all times above deck, and he trusted her. Mostly they anchored or found a marina at night but they'd ended up further east and south than he'd ever intended and luxuries like safe harbours were thin on the North African coast.

Occasionally, when the notion took him, he stood at the helm and allowed his own healing. The breeze peeled back his grief and the anonymity and privacy of the sea enabled him to let the stream roll down his cheeks. Such moments kept his pain from Isla, avoiding her interrogation and worry. He'd never allow her to see him weep – it would upset her too much. She understood how much he missed his wife, her mother, but it would never be the same as it was for her. Isla hadn't just lost her mam, she'd held her hand as that beautiful life ebbed away. They'd spoken as she bled out. Isla had cuddled her and looked into the face of her killer, convinced she was next. Worse still, she'd believed it was all her fault.

Sam read to her until the flood and fall of her little body slowed, and curled his neck to make sure she was deep enough to extract his arm from under her. Then he waited for two full minutes, watching her eyelids for any sign of disturbance. Placated, he went on deck and indulged his maudlin currents, allowing himself to be swept back to better times and to lament his loss. That's when the tears came. Eventually he'd snap out of it and sail the boat, but for a while he would purge. It brought an odd sort of pleasure – the wallowing, the reminiscence.

He was shocked when Isla's little face appeared in the

companionway; the yellow light breaking his night vision as she came up the steps.

"What was that, Daddy?" she said.

"What, wee lamb?" Sam replied, scraping the tears from the crevices in his face.

"The noise – the whistle."

Sam turned his ears from the wind and stood stock-still but could catch nothing.

"There. Can you hear it, Daddy?"

"No, snugs, I think you better go back to sleep," he said, pressing the autohelm into gear and checking the radar screen to make sure their course was clear.

He was lifting her into her bunk when she said it again.

"There it is, Daddy. Why can't you hear that?"

"You're dreaming, wee love. You're still a bit asleep," he told her, tucking her in, keen to get back to the helm.

"I'm not, Daddy. I'm really, really not," she replied.

"Ok, I'll go up and keep an ear out," he said as he hugged her. He was worried she might not sleep now, and was anxious they were sailing with no watch above. "I love you so much," he said, and returned to the cockpit.

And then came the sound: high-pitched – audible to younger ears at a distance, older ones when up close.

And it was close.

Amid one hundred thousand square miles of sea, Sam and Isla were no longer alone, and every resolution he had made went over the side.

2

"Wasters," spat Habid, as he watched honest men haul nets out of the sea. The noise behind him was gradually increasing as the bumper-track of a city came to life with a relentless hammering upon horns. Not that Alexandria ever really slept, Habid was struggling to adjust to the relentless commotion.

His life had taken some curious turns in recent months. Habid had been a shepherd, of sorts, herding flocks through the sands of eastern Libya. Now he was amassing money hand over fist, more than he'd ever known. It made him rather pleased with himself – cocky, harder, less pleasant than his usual unpleasant self.

He wrapped up the bits and pieces, keen to get them cleared from the beach before the darkness disappeared entirely. But he afforded himself a few minutes to sneer at the fishermen as they stood thigh deep in their underpants and plucked the occasional wriggler from an otherwise empty net. What a lot of work for absolutely nothing, he thought. There were barely enough fish in their buckets to make a meal for each man's family.

He looked into his little bag – well, it was his now, but a few hours ago it had belonged to someone else. It was filled with pawn, of a sort. For extras. Other travel providers were at it, he thought, so why not? Airlines, rail companies, intercontinental crossings weren't cheap. Nothing was complimentary any more, even the basics came at a cost. Like water. Or sunscreen. Or a life jacket. Of course, his clients didn't have any cash left, so he'd been generous to take alternatives.

Habid hadn't a clue how long it took. He knew nothing about boats. He knew about dust and sand and living like a bloody Bedouin. The disruption in his own failed state had allowed him to abandon his post as a border guard for Gaddafi, but the sea was a mystery he had no notion of finding out about. That's why he hadn't gone himself. Not yet anyway.

"Get dressed and get your life jacket on," Sam barked below at Isla.

"What's wrong?" she shouted, reawakened from her sleep and instantly alarmed.

"I think there might be someone in the water," he shouted back. "Pass me up the flashlight."

Isla emerged from her cabin half dressed, reached for the lamp and handed it up to him as he worked the helm with his other hand.

"Now go and get warm clothes on and your harness and your life jacket."

"Ok, Daddy." She tore off.

Sam held the wheel and leaned as far outboard as he could, straining to hear the sound again, but it was gone on the building breeze. He must have passed it, whatever it was. He debated leaving it in his wake – it wasn't his problem, then he saw Isla coming and she put paid to that.

"We can rescue them," she said, excitement dancing in her eyes, and for a moment Sam saw her mother looking straight at him.

There was no question in Isla's mind about what they ought to do. None. And there shouldn't have been for Sam either, except that he didn't want anyone else on his boat, near his kid, for what would inevitably be days at sea.

Perhaps one day Sam would learn to trust his instincts.

Habid fancied a treat. A nice place to put his head down before returning to the dust. It was a risk, he conceded, to check into the Sofitel Cecil but it looked so sumptuous after his filthy journey across the desert. He imagined a beautiful shower, a soft, clean bed, a toilet that flushed. He had enough money, but there was no concealing what he was: a sun-dried Libyan blown with the sand by a Spring that had uprooted countless thousands across North Africa.

Except he wasn't seeking refuge from it – he was making his fortune from it, and he had a fake passport and a bag full of cash, so he strode in and acted like he owned the place.

"I can hear someone screaming!" called Isla from her vantage point above the spray hood. She was on tiptoes, peering into the dark, her little ears straining for sounds from the sea. The girth of the waves was increasing and the boat had begun to roll gently into them.

"What direction?" shouted Sam.

"What?" screamed Isla in return.

"Point to it!" he tried instead.

His little girl turned and gestured with absolute confidence.

Sam turned the wheel and headed as she directed. Eventually
he too heard the noise – a woman, he reckoned, yelling from
the surface. He leaned over again, glancing at Isla to make sure
she stayed well inboard. He painted the surface of the sea with
the LED beam but detected nothing.

"We're not close enough, Daddy. It's over there," shouted
Isla above the thunking draw of the diesel's pistons.

They carried forward. A high-pitched wail reached Sam
from the starboard side, just as Isla had indicated, and he
gently brought the boat around, conscious he could do more
harm than good to anyone flailing around beneath them. He
was also wary of any stricken vessel languishing in the sea. If he
hit something, they would all end up in the water.

His beam caught something and he stroked the torch back
to find it again, but it was gone in the swell. His mind reached
for the image – a black-clad human with arms in the air. In that
position they'd no doubt plummeted beneath the waves and
perhaps hadn't come up again. He coated the area again,
hunting as much for a boat as a person. As always, his primary
concern was his little girl; he wouldn't let their home sink for
anyone.

Then there was a slightly different tone coming from the
water, a new urgency to attract the beam. Sam jabbed and
swiped the torch like a dagger but couldn't find a face, which
must surely be turned towards the light. Suddenly two images
were revealed and he juddered back to catch a veiled woman
and a child. Of all the thoughts he might have mustered, his
first was pointless: why hadn't she taken off the niqab? The
child was clinging to a pathetic life jacket, half inflated; the sort
of useless article found under the seat in a passenger plane.

"Come and take the wheel, Isla," Sam ordered, confident in
his little woman's ability to hold the boat steady to a compass
bearing. He reached for a line out of the aft locker and tied it
around his waist.

"Keep the boat at zero-six-zero, darlin', ok?"

"Ok, Daddy," Isla said, half frightened, half excited.

He kicked off his shoes, tore off his fleece, stepped over the guardrail and dived in.

Habid lay between the fragrant crisp white linen sheets of the largest bed he'd ever seen and wondered whether the job had been done.

He took comfort from his surroundings as the wind rattled the shutters outside. He imagined the fuel must be close to exhausted as his cheek plunged deep into the spongy pillow. Habid hadn't cared about the outcome of previous trips – he hadn't given them a second thought, but this one was slightly different – if it worked out then a much grander plan could be put into action. So, try as he might, his thoughts prevented him from dozing off.

Sam pulled fifteen hard strokes before the line snagged at his waist. His strength in the water had been hewn long before his years in the Special Boat Service but that had its drawbacks: he swam face down. It had been drilled into him in childhood, during the 6 a.m. training lengths he'd hammered out every morning in a Belfast pool as one of his bleary-eyed parents gazed on from the gallery. Because of that he'd taken his eyes off the woman in the water and now had to relocate her in the moonlight. He needn't have worried.

Treading hard and breathing fast, he kicked round to confirm his bearings and find Isla but was gripped from the sea by a birdlike claw. He span in shock and was confronted with the menacing mask of the niqab and rabid eyes cutting through even the blackness of the garb. How the woman managed to remain afloat in the sodden shroud baffled Sam, but he barely had a second to ingest the image of the frightening figure before a girl of similar age to Isla was thrust towards him, unconscious, her head lolling back into the sea.

It took all the power in his legs to remain afloat in the waves as he extended the child, unfolding her like a tripod. He raised her head and rolled her slightly towards him. With his left arm curled all the way round her neck and over her face, he managed to pinch her nose and place his mouth over hers, forcing it open with his chin.

The woman immediately started screaming, slapping and grabbing at him in protest and Sam wished she would just succumb to the deep. He breathed hard into the tiny lungs and used his right forearm to bellow the child's stomach as if playing the pipes. All the time he was being scrabbed and punched by the woman, and it was after he'd exhausted his second lungful that he turned and pushed her back, lifting his legs to give her as hard a kick off as he could. But she had somehow caught the life jacket and the rope between him and the boat, so wasn't going anywhere. He'd no choice but to keep kicking and breathing for two. Every exhale was matched with a glance up towards the boat and Isla and at least two slaps or punches from the woman to his rear. He was about to give the effort up as hopeless when the child's body started to gently convulse in his arms. He raised her further from the sea and she vomited heartily all over his half-submerged face. The result quieted the mother and placated Sam until he became aware of an entirely more frightening risk.

He looked up at their boat, now thirty feet away, and saw another woman emerging from the water, up the bathing ladder towards where Isla stood, alone.

3

Despite the decadence, Habid couldn't enjoy his treat. It wasn't his conscience that prevented rest, he possessed little by way of guilt or regret, nor was it concern that events at sea may not have gone to plan – that would have annoyed him, but it wouldn't have surprised him. No, Habid was worried about getting caught. Not so much about being arrested, but the prospect of losing his earnings. He'd worked hard for his money and if some hotel worker alerted the police, the spoils would vanish. Baksheesh, they might call it. Corrupt wouldn't come close to characterising some police officers.

Deportation he could deal with – it was his intention to return to Libya and repeat the process anyway, refining nicely as it was. Losing the loot, however, wasn't attractive. He'd spent years taking border backhanders in the eastern desert, so he knew that capture would result in his money being pocketed by some low-level Egyptian official.

Greed got the better of him. He twisted around for a while and eventually sat up in bed, decision made. His clothes were still soaked from the wash he'd given them in the vacuous bath, so he couldn't just dress and leave, but in gazing at them hanging from the retractable line in the marble bathroom, his eye was drawn to a hatch above the toilet. Presumably an access point for the recessed spotlights.

Habid rushed to the main suite and looked at his phone and navigation kit but decided the cash was of more consequence, so he lifted the booty bag and stood on the toilet seat to deposit his wages into the ceiling.

"Daddy!" Isla screamed.

If anything, the woman on the boat was even more concealed than the woman in the sea. A burka clung to her body, shrink-wrapped and wringing. She moved with efficiency for someone who'd been struggling in the sea.

When faced with a choice: your child or someone else's, it doesn't need computing. Sam pushed the girl towards the woman who'd been attacking him and tore the line arm over arm as he drew himself towards his boat. As he did so the woman on board turned to face him, and although he couldn't see her eyes or face he sensed some indecision.

Isla kept her station but looked with alarm at the woman in the cockpit. She'd never seen someone in a burka before and was clearly afraid.

"Daddy, please!" she yelled, panic setting in.

Sam hauled harder as the woman turned towards his daughter. Even the adrenaline wasn't enough to launch him above the freeboard to grasp the toe rail, so he had to swim to the transom and mount the bathing ladder just as the woman had. He kicked his body from the water, but as he rose the rope snagged, holding him back. His eyes opened in panic as he realised what had happened. The drifting slack on the rope had caught the propeller shaft, and he realised it would soon wind the line back beneath the boat and pull him under.

"Knife, Isla!" he panted, as his numbed hands worked at the knot at his chest.

"What, Daddy?" she shouted, the wind and engine muffling her hearing.

"Knife!" he yelled, and she immediately ran to the life raft where they kept a timber-handled blade in a sheath. She drew it and ran in her little Crocs towards her father. At the same time Sam caught a feint from the woman in the cockpit, as if she'd been inclined to move or assist but had instinctively decided against it.

Isla presented the knife just as Sam's ribcage tightened and the rope began to draw him back into the sea.

"Stop the engine, Isla!" he yelled as he was dragged back.

The waves caught his breath. He became wedged against the hull and he tried to get the blade between the rope and his skin, but it was dug deep into his flesh. His body rolled with the pressure sucking him towards the slowly rotating prop. Under water he flailed for the rope tail that was now behind him, dragging him towards the centre of the hull. He lashed wildly and his hand hit the propeller, snapping the knife from his paw. His breath began to combust and he was forced to gently exhale.

Then came a dawning: *this is it.* His mind hummed and pulsed; his heart, straining for oxygen, beating like a bass. But then a switch flicked from disciplined calm to desperation. His thoughts shuttled through what his drowning would mean for Isla – left with the woman on the deck, the people in the sea. There was something wrong. He felt the prop hit his belt, his back, rip at his flesh.

Then slowly the judder in the hull stopped and the

propeller halted. Isla had strangled the engine. The realisation summoned a second chance, a last effort. He rolled as far as he could and forced his stomach towards the skeg in front of the prop shaft. The air was gone from his lungs and his chest began to whoop and buckle. The skeg wasn't sharp, designed only to prevent weed or sea debris from fouling the propeller, but with the vigour of what little panic was left in him he rubbed the rope against it, his face lacerated by the blade-like barnacles gripping the hull. His rhythm slowed as he asphyxiated and Sam didn't even get to see the rope part and his hands open as a priest's might during the offertory. What air was left in his bloodstream carried his spent body towards the surface.

They didn't knock. Habid didn't suppose they were obliged to. Egypt was a law unto itself these days – the Spring had seen to that. No matter how authoritarian any regime had been, the rising had wiped out the established order like a societal tsunami sweeping east; no matter how long any leader held power, nothing was stable any more. Rank and privilege had all but vanished along with any and all accountability.

That's probably why they kicked the door in. Because they could.

It fell like a concrete slab and landed at Habid's bare feet. Two suited men walked across as if it were a drawbridge. Each grabbed an arm. They dragged him into the corridor and down the opulent staircase.

Later he sat, like the fishermen he'd laughed at, in his underpants. His frame shook behind a rickety desk to which his hands were manacled as the two men – one small and one huge, took it in turns to reach across and slap or punch his face and head.

"Why did you come here?" they wanted to know. They'd

obviously worked out that there was a game in play. It didn't take much detective work, thought Habid, staring at the small Garmin handheld GPS they'd bagged and tagged and placed before him along with his phone. But they were confused. "Why not just use the coast of Libya?"

Habid held out for a short while until they went to work on his genitals, and then he pretended to crow like a cock.

"They're too expensive," he gasped, to save a testicle.

"Who are?" inquired the small suited man, his eyes slight as a snake's.

"The tribesmen. They charge to let boats through to the beach. And the others."

"What others?"

"Officials. The coastguard is difficult," he said. "The men at sea, they cannot be bribed. But their bosses," his voice tailed off, "too expensive."

"They're supposed to stop the boats."

"They do. This is the problem." Habid just shrugged.

Of course they were *supposed* to stop the boats, but why stop them when you could tax them? Everyone has to make a living.

"Where did you get the boat?"

Habid said nothing, so the skinnier one nodded to the brute who unlocked the cuffs and dragged him to the wall. Habid started to panic as his arms were raised to a hook and he was half hung to an inverted and painful dangle.

"We carried it," Habid said.

"I asked where you got it!" screamed the skinny suit, who found Habid's apex with a shiny loafer.

For some reason Habid noticed its leather tassels as he slunk towards the grimy floor but found himself dangling from his bloody wrists.

"A man, from Suez," he managed, as he was unhooked and shoes began to dance on his head.

When he came round he stared in horror at what they were

doing to him and more fuzzy details were imparted. He lied about organising long courier journeys from China and Bangladesh west to Arabia and beyond. He was asked about the process at sea. The suits didn't take any notes but wanted names and know-how, and Habid realised he was being fleeced for commercial rather than criminal information. He might as well have hosted a webinar.

They forced him to explain the plan, the route. He'd created a life based on dishonesty and disinformation and had no intention of changing now, so he reserved a lot and shared a little in the hope of retaining a bollock. They'd already deprived him of a finger and toe.

When he talked he conjured the hallucination that he and these cops might work together, these people who'd disfigured him. Despite the kicking he hunted for an opportunity. How else could they get the required flock? Egyptians didn't really want to leave their country, not yet anyway. Even if they did, they wouldn't possess the sort of money Habid was becoming accustomed to. He dealt with Libyans – and not just any Libyans either – taking them across the desert, the sands. Habid's happy place.

"How do they get out to sea?" barked Tassels.

"The boat comes with engine," Habid said, trying to impress them with the efficiency of his operation.

"Where does the engine come from?"

"Container. Stolen engines, from Europe. They are wrapped in the rubber boats. Then we collect and carry." Habid paused at his mistake, which apparently went unnoticed. "It takes only four people to lift the package to the sea, then it is pumped up." Habid made as much movement as he could with his leg to suggest a foot pump, but he didn't want to draw attention to his good leg with its complete complement of toes, lest he should be deprived of a digit.

"What about fuel, gas?"

"In plastic cans," said Habid.

Until this trip he hadn't ever checked and didn't really care how far offshore the boats had managed to get.

"So what happens when they get out to sea?"

"They keep going. They have compass, and moon and sun, north and west."

"They know how to do this – the people in the boat?" Tassels asked incredulous.

"We have ways," said Habid, shelling up, keen to keep some information for himself, conscious he'd already gone too far.

His reticence earned him a hammering – blows to the lower back, stomach and kidneys. When he could breathe again he was treated to a smack in the face.

"We put someone on board who knows the sea."

He then returned to lying while forging a plan of false information.

"But the fuel must run out?"

"Then they wait."

"What for?"

"For NGO or foreign navy to pick them up."

"But foreign navies won't always pick up refugees," said Tassels, his curiosity growing.

Habid felt he was drawing the small suit in.

"Ah," he replied, keen to show he had the knowledge. "This is where I can help you."

He got a slap for the suggestion.

"When they see lights, they must knife the boat." He thumped the table with his good fist.

"So they get rescued or drown?" said Tassels.

"Yes, makes it hard not to pick up."

"And they do it – the people? They destroy the boat? They go into the sea?"

Habid neither knew nor cared. In the past the boats had left his mind the moment they left the sand. This time was a little different though. This time there was another play. But he didn't tell the suits about that, or that the boat wasn't the only thing due to get stabbed on this outing.

4

A damp drape lifted up Sam's neck and chin as if he'd been stroked with a facecloth. He opened his eyes to catch a glimpse of the lithe neck of a woman before the flap of her head covering fell back as she righted herself. He could hear his daughter's forceful little temper.

"Get away from him!" she was shouting. "Leave my daddy alone!"

He scrabbled upright, seeking grip on the cockpit floor. He rose to find another, slightly broader, woman sitting beside the child he'd rescued. The smaller woman scuttled back to join them. He felt no threat from her but turned to Isla for some sense of what was happening.

"Daddy, they wanted to start the boat but I wouldn't show them how," she said, in a mixture of proud conviction and desperation that almost immediately gave way to tears. She threw her little arms around his neck.

"I thought you were dead, Daddy," she said into his water-logged ear.

"I'm not dead, darlin'," he said, wrapping her tight and

feeling a heavy pain in his right arm. He looked beyond her hair and saw that his hand was covered in blood – his own, he assumed. In fact, the floor around them seemed awash with the stuff. His back ached too, the slab of meat at his hip – a pain he'd never felt before.

"It's ok, wee love. I'm ok, I'm ok."

"No, you're not, you're cutted really bad and you're still bleeding and they just looked at you," she sobbed.

He wondered how he'd managed to get back on board but Isla was in no fit shape for explanations.

"Ok," said Sam, now only half caring about whatever had gone on while he was unconscious, "get me the first aid kit and we'll get sorted out."

Isla's muscles didn't flinch; she stayed clamped to his neck.

"Isla, come on, get me the kit and we'll get cleaned up."

"No, Daddy, they might kill you," she whispered into his ear.

"They're not going to kill me, Isla. They couldn't kill me," he said, looking at the two women and the little girl.

But then, Sam didn't see what Isla saw.

Two days in the dark and Habid didn't know what way was up. The throbbing had kept him awake. He'd tried to elevate his arm and his foot to reduce bleeding through the congealed stumps of his extremities, but he'd tired quickly. A chain had been clamped around his arm which prevented him from reaching a wall to rest his limbs against. Big Suit had wanted to clamp it around his neck but Tassels didn't want him hanging himself, which gave Habid hope that his usefulness wasn't yet exhausted and he might still strike a deal with these cops, or whatever they were.

In an office two cells away, Big Suit was asking stupid questions and Tassels was pontificating.

"I don't know what you want from this rat. Why can't I clip him until he tells us where the cash is?"

"Can you not see there is something else going on here? Why else would he risk crossing Libya into Egypt? If you're going to traffick people away by sea, why not do it from your own country?"

Big Suit sat silent for a while. Above the neckline his wheels span slowly. "Because Libya is a mess since Gaddafi got ousted?" he said eventually, looking at his senior for affirmation.

"Exactly my point. It's a bigger risk, isn't it, trekking across Libya. Yes?"

"I suppose so," said Big Suit, who was broadly aware of the turmoil traversing the cities of the coastal highway, west to east, Tripoli to Benghazi and beyond.

"And why here? If the rat really just wanted to avoid the taxes of the Libyan elite, why not launch the boats closer to the border? How many cities are there between the Libyan–Egyptian checkpoint and Alexandria?"

Big Suit looked into the space in front of him and imagined the map of North Africa: the straight lines down from the sea, the jagged horizontals. His head actually juddered and rotated slowly clockwise as he charted the Libyan coast, the border and then counted the towns on the way to his own.

"Ten maybe?" he offered.

"So why here? Why bring them all the way to a bigger place, with more police, with its own coastguard and soldiers?"

"Maybe he likes the posh hotels?" Big Suit ventured.

"That rat is not an idiot," said Tassels. "He came here for a reason and we need to know what it is."

"Why?"

"Because the time is coming when we may have to get out," said Tassels.

"Out?" repeated Big Suit, struggling.

"Of Egypt."

"Why?"

"Because the beards are coming. And when they do they'll probably stop thinking about Cairo and turn their attention to other cities, like Alexandria."

"The beards," spat Big Suit. "They never last. Eventually we will have a strong president again and we can carry on as before."

"You really don't see it, do you?" said Tassels, withering in his contempt.

"See what? The Arab world needs order. It needs strong leaders. Like Mubarak was."

"Mubarak was thrown in prison, you fool, and why was he put in prison?"

Big Suit had watched all the happenings from the television screen in the custody suite. Tahrir Square. The revolution. The sweeping clean of the cobblestones. His hero arrested and thrown in jail. Anyway, the army was still in charge. Much of the detail escaped him at the time, the rest had vacated his mind as more pressing information poured in. Like eating. And breathing. And sleeping. He shrugged.

"Why did the Arab Spring begin?" Tassels tried another tack, willing his muscle man to grasp the importance of what he was trying to say.

There was no response.

He pressed on. "Because people got tired of *this* – what we do. They'd had enough of corrupt governments, and Mubarak was corrupt. And the people were sick of it."

Big Suit's eyes were looking at Tassels but there was no ignition. He sat there like a truck full of fuel with no keys.

"Things are back to normal now."

Tassels tutted. "You think like an Egyptian, not a man of the world. Look at what happened in Tunisia."

"Tunisia is next to Libya, not Egypt," said Big Suit, as if his grasp of North African geography earned him an unexpected point.

"That's not the issue, you fool. The issue is what happened there and why it matters to us."

"I don't care about Tunisia or Tunisians. Nobody in Egypt does. That's not the way Arabs work," said Big Suit dismissively.

"You're right," said Tassels, which led to a proud buttock clench and a shimmy of the shoulders from Big Suit. "But what started it all and what did it create?"

"A grocer got cross and set himself on fire." Big Suit shrugged – no big deal.

"But why?" Tassels tried to lead his colleague to the obvious conclusion.

"Because he was sick of taxes?" attempted Big Suit, which was sort of correct.

"Because of people like us," said Tassels, "taxing and taking a cut, and because the government allowed it to happen. The authorities turned a blind eye – and probably taxed the corrupt collectors in turn. That grocer set himself on fire because he was sick of corruption."

"So?" said Big Suit. "He died. What of it?"

"What of it?" shouted Tassels. "What of it is that Arabs everywhere saw an opportunity! What of it is that the Tunisians took down a regime!"

Big Suit stared at the floor for a while. "What's that got to do with our thing?"

Tassels shook his head slowly. "Then it spread, didn't it? It came here and Mubarak's regime fell, then Gaddafi's. Then it spilled blood everywhere. Yemen – look at Syria!"

"But what's that got to do with the rat?" Big Suit shook his head.

"Is Egypt stable?" Tassels sighed, exasperated.

"It will be when we get another Mubarak."

"Mubarak's not coming back. You're an idiot if you think the people will stand for that type of government again."

Big Suit sat silent, admonished again.

"What happens in Arab countries when strong leaders fall?"

"Doesn't happen very often," Big Suit muttered.

"What happened in Iraq?"

"Mayhem."

"What happened in Afghanistan?"

Big Suit started to catch the drift. "The beards took over. For a while anyway."

"And what do the beards do?"

"They pray?" he ventured.

"They go back to another time. They force everyone back to another time. They take away opportunities for men like us – entrepreneurs. And what do they do with us?"

"They put us in jail?" Big Suit tried.

"They slice our throats." Tassels drew his index finger across his neck.

Big Suit shuffled. "The beards won't come here," he said.

"They're already here," said Tassels, "and when they get their day I don't intend to be here. You can stay if you like."

"Getting into trafficking, though, that's risky," said Big Suit. "Taxing criminals for protection and taking a cut of profits, that all makes sense – makes money, but with trafficking there are strangers involved. We should just keep taking a little bit off everyone. We will still do well."

"*If* we keep taxing," said Tassels, "but things are changing. Soon there might not be anyone or anything left to tax."

"So you say," said Big Suit, "but I don't know that the rising really changed anything."

"Then why did they call it the Arab Spring?" spat Tassels.

Big Suit looked stumped.

"Ben Ali fell. Mubarak fell. Gaddafi fell. Assad will probably go eventually. When strong leaders go they are always replaced by something worse."

"Not in Egypt," said Big Suit. "We won't have the beards. Not here."

"You don't see what could happen here – and so easily. The conditions are ripe."

"This is not al-Qaeda territory."

"Why do we never hear anything about the military offensive in the east?" asked Tassels. "It doesn't need to be Taliban – there are all sorts of beards. Madder, even, than bin Laden's bunch. They could make our way of life difficult. We could end up with no toes, trussed up in the cell down the hall if those bastards found out what we've been doing."

Big Suit shrugged. "Those religious nuts are better off heading to Iraq where there is no control of anything."

"You think like a city cop," Tassels scolded him. "Look at the Copts. Those Christians are getting killed quietly every day. Nobody cares. The Sufis – they're attacked all the time and nobody even knows about it. This is a revolution and it could be endless. Not every city is like Alexandria – even Cairo is different. The beards are still strong there and there are extremists in the desert."

"The desert," hissed Big Suit. "They eat camels in the desert."

"You've never even been east," countered Tassels. "Sinai – soldiers are wiped out there every day but you know nothing about it because there's a news blackout. The government doesn't want anyone to find out."

"I don't believe those rumours," said Big Suit. "That's just the beards trying to scare people, to make themselves look strong. There's nothing in Sinai but hills and sand and Palestinians trying to escape Gaza."

"You do not realise what is coming," said Tassels. "We need money, and soon. And we need more than that."

"What?" said Big Suit.

"We need a way out of Egypt when the time comes. And that greedy little Libyan rat can help us. That's why he's still breathing. For now."

5

Isla sobbed as Sam winced. He'd been forced to plop a few drops of iodine into tank water to clean his cuts, which were worryingly deep. He waited for his arm to dry before applying superglue to seal the flaps of skin back into place.

His arm was badly chewed but that wasn't his main concern – he could deal with that because he could see it – and mercifully he didn't think there was a broken bone, but the muscular pain was substantial and he was certain his ribcage had a few cracks. It was his flank which was the worry. It was still bleeding, and although he couldn't see his lower back he knew it definitely needed stitching and there was no way his daughter could do that for him. To add to the problem, the only kit to do it was a coarse two-inch sailing needle and repair thread.

"Can you help me?" he asked the women, holding the needle up and gesturing to his gaping back.

They recoiled when he turned to show them what he intended; the skinnier woman looking away to sea.

Sam knew the cultural problems, women touching men

and so on, but he'd hoped that by saving one of them and her kid they might have overlooked such sensibilities.

And so it was that his terrified little girl was forced to hold the mirror he'd unscrewed from the wall in the heads while he performed the painful and awkward reverse repair. He growled back what would otherwise have been screams so as not to upset his child. The job was a mess – he knew he was adding ugly scars to the patchwork of his torso. The field hospitals he'd been deposited in hadn't been graced with plastic surgeons, and while his body had occasionally been reworked by brilliant military doctors, their concern was to keep his heart beating and his lungs breathing, so another crazing on his skin was unlikely to matter greatly.

As he lay recovering, face down on towels on top of his bunk, he realised they'd a problem: it would take days for his skin to knit, so he couldn't swim under the boat to free up the rope from the propeller shaft. He estimated they'd been drifting south for five hours, towards Africa, which wasn't where he wanted to be. Sam was vaguely aware of the continued instability in Morocco, Algeria and Tunisia, and he never wanted to set foot in Libya again. He'd been there years before on an operation that had been successful but brutal and had no intention of returning.

His body wasn't really fit for sailing either. He wasn't even sure if he'd be able to pull a rope with his right hand, but there was no choice. He couldn't land in Africa and that was the way the wind was blowing them. He needed to get rid of the women and the kid and get medical help. That meant Europe, where an Irishman could be seen without the handover of insurance or money – one of which he didn't have, the other he was keen to keep hidden.

Wincing and weeping from his wounds, he lifted his body from the bunk. The only other option was to deposit the women on board a passing ship. The Automatic Identification

System was a handy tool but Sam rarely turned their signal on. AIS helped vessels work out whether they were on a collision course with any fast-moving craft, and it allowed Sam to plot a route well away from passenger ferries or commercial container boats. The system could also transmit a huge amount of information, like where the crew was headed, what they were transporting, where their journey had originated and their unique identifier from the International Maritime Organization – through which any large freighter could be traced to its owner. Sam loved and hated the system in equal measure. As a troll he got great use out of it, but he'd become increasingly reclusive and was careful to protect his own privacy and that of his little girl. Therefore their own signal remained firmly switched off.

Twelve miles east was a vessel that looked like it might do the job: a ship with a vast hold laden with animal feed travelling from Beirut to Morocco. Sam decided to wait until its course settled and then sail towards it. When in range he could call its crew on the VHF radio, explain what had happened and hopefully get rid of his own cargo.

Habid woke to excruciating pain. Big Suit had chosen to rouse the rat by standing on the stump of the captive's absent toe. Habid screamed in agony as the wound reopened, which pleased Big Suit as it would serve to frighten other inmates and make light work of their confessions. Big Suit didn't often get the opportunity to prune the prisoners but Tassels had allowed him to go to work this time meaning that his boss probably knew what way things would go for the Libyan. It seemed unlikely the desert rat would require fingers or toes in future.

He yanked the chain as if flushing a toilet and dragged Habid like a feral dog through the corridor and into the interrogation suite. The Libyan's slug-like trail of blood from his stump smeared the floor. Big Suit made a mental note to get him to clean it on his way back. If he made it back. Big Suit had slept well and was full of energy but he wasn't sure how much more the Libyan could take.

Habid's gaze rose to meet the smiling face of Tassels who directed that he was to be hooked up from the get-go.

Habid had prepared and so began his pitch. "Look, I realise you are businessmen and you are clever, so I have a suggestion about how we can work together for mutual benefit."

Tassels laughed. Big Suit decided that was worth a kick.

As Habid gathered air back into his lungs, he tried again. "You want to make a fair cut of this business – I understand that. I was once a border guard and I also made a fair cut of everything that happened at my post in the desert," he gushed. "Every man has to make money, it's understandable."

Tassels told Big Suit to get the bolt cutters.

Habid picked up the pace. "You need someone like me to find the people that want to leave."

He glanced at the GPS in the bag on the table and hoped that the two policemen would be unable to interpret the dogleg trace of his movements across the desert. It quite literally represented his route out of jail.

Tassels was snorting again. "There are people all over Africa who wish to get to Europe."

"Yes, but they are poor and cannot pay well. You need someone like me to find people with enough money to make it worthwhile taking this risk!" He began to shout. "The large boats – always intercepted. The wealthy people know that. They will end up in detention centres. But my service, what I offer, is different."

"How?" Tassels tried not to sound too interested.

"Better – smaller boats, select clients, with money. They need escorted across the desert. They refuse to leave from

Libyan coast because they know they will be caught or killed. Can you find such people – the ones who minimise the risk – fewer trips for more money? For that you need someone like me." There was a pause behind him and Habid didn't dare hope his suggestion had struck a chord. He filled the silence. "I can get the wealthiest, the people who were in Gaddafi's circle. I can bring you the people who can pay big money. They live as dogs now, underground and hidden from the militias, the tribes. I can find them for you, bring them here and they can pay you. And me," he ventured.

"If they're forced to live in the sewers, how can they pay?" Tassels asked dismissively.

"Because they kept their money in accounts in other countries. Many, many bank accounts in Africa, Europe, here in Egypt. That's how they pay me when they cross the border."

Tassels was mildly excited. He knew that much of what Habid was saying was true. The wealthy districts in Cairo were awash with foreign financiers – wealth managers in pin stripes.

Habid, however, was cautious not to give too much away. He'd taken some of the migrants across the border on the strength of big promises, only to find their accountants had snaffled the cash as soon as the Spring had sprung. Still, there were other ways to pay.

"The Libyan dinar is scrap now," Tassels probed.

"Ah, but think back to when it was converted and deposited – when the oil flowed and the world wanted dinar to pay Gaddafi for black gold. That's when it was turned to US dollars or Egyptian pounds. The value was taken out of Libya long before the leader fell."

Tassels felt a tingle and paused for a moment. "So where is this money you made? From the last group?"

Habid thought of the transfers – of the bag in the roof space of the Sofitel, but his greed was so great he couldn't bring himself to give it up. He remained silent.

Tassels tutted. "Thought as much." He swept his hand forward as if throwing sand to the wind: *proceed*.

Habid's heart sank. The cutters appeared, jaws open and menacing between his legs. He knew he was out of time, so he played his last hand. Well, most of it.

And then the bolt cutter retracted, its handler deeply disappointed.

"How did I wake up, wee love?" Sam asked Isla. "After I was in the water?"

Isla was busy applying gauze tape to his wounds and Sam thought it an opportune moment to question her while she was distracted. He couldn't work out how he'd been resuscitated. It was extremely unlikely that the women would have performed CPR on him. No Muslim woman who wore a full veil was likely to feel able to do that.

"One of the grown-ups pushed on your tummy," she said. "I made them do it. I said, 'You can't start this boat without my daddy!'"

Sam shook his head in wonder at the little woman's strength of character. It was as if Shannon was telling him the story. Isla was turning into her mother before she'd even turned seven.

"One of them pushed your tummy up and down and up and down," she said. "Then on your top tummy, right here."

He turned a little to see her place her palms against her chest.

"Then they turned you over onto your side and you puked all over the place."

He was mildly concerned about the possibility of infection. In his time in the navy he'd seen two strong men die, not from the ripping and tearing of their flesh and limbs, but from an unseen attacker carried on the air and visible only when it was too late. One of his sergeants was killed through something as simple as a nick on his hand, but he lost an arm in roaring agony before his body had been taken from him.

Sam began putting the pieces together as she worked on his flank. The CPR made sense but Sam was struggling with the rest of it.

"How did they lift me into the boat, Isla? They're not strong enough."

Sam weighed fifteen stone of lean steak. The propeller had severed his belt, he'd had no shirt on, nothing to grab. His body must have been as hard to grip as a fish, and breathless bodies tend to float face down.

"I don't know." He could sense her shrugging. "They just lifted you up."

"Right up onto the bathing platform?"

"Yeah," she said, as if it was no big deal.

"And they managed to drag me into the cockpit?"

"Yes, Daddy, I told you."

Sam thought for a moment. It still didn't add up.

"Isla, I don't think those women are strong enough to have done all that, wee love," he said gently, not wanting her to think he was doubting her but keen to get to the bottom of it.

"But the man is strong enough, Daddy."

6

"So how many people were actually in the boat?"

Habid could tell Tassels was developing a grudging regard for the line of business he'd created. "Ten," said Habid. "Always ten."

"Why only ten?" asked Big Suit. "Why not take more?"

"This is a premium service," said Habid with pride and indignation. "Besides, if you start sending dozens, hundreds of people to sea, you'll get caught sooner or later because you need a big boat."

"What do you mean?" asked Big Suit.

"The boats the amateurs use, they are much too large. They're maybe fifty, sixty feet long and cheap, pathetic, dangerous. There's only one thing such boats are made for."

"What?" said Big Suit, who struggled to keep up with basic conversations.

Tassels closed his eyes in bewilderment and embarrassment. "Trafficking," said the senior cop sighing.

"But he uses boats for trafficking?" said Big Suit, permanently baffled.

"That's the point," Tassels spat, which made Habid feel the

boss was siding with him a little. The big bloke might be handy but he was evidently as thick as bricks.

"If the authorities find such a boat," Habid elaborated, "it is seized and the courier thrown in jail forever."

"So you buy smaller boats," Tassels said – more a statement than a question.

"Yes. Manageable. To be carried by four people. That way they can be easily rolled up and hidden in a lorry, brought to Alexandria and carried to the sea."

"And who are the four people who help you carry it to the sea?" Big Suit chimed, oblivious to the collective opinion on his intellect.

"The people who pay for the privilege," said Habid with a hint of pride. It was rather like making a condemned man dig his own grave at the feet of a firing squad.

Tassels swung back on his creaky timber chair and stared at Habid. "And how can you be sure that passing boats or NGOs won't simply let your clients drown?"

"Well, you see, there is a way," said Habid, growing in confidence and erring a little too far towards the raconteur for the smaller cop's liking.

"Just get on with it," said Tassels as the front legs of his chair hit the floor and Big Suit's grip tightened with longing on the bolt cutters.

"Women and children. We take three men, three women and three children," he said.

"And the navigator is one of them?" asked Tassels.

"Yes," said Habid, and then froze at his mistake, stunned by what he'd said.

"That makes nine."

Tassels' head rose and Big Suit's eyebrows arched as he began to nod vigorously.

"Yes, so who is the tenth person?" Big Suit chipped in, only to be hushed by Tassels.

Habid sat stock-still and silent.

Tassels pursed his lips and raised his eyebrows.

Habid held out, and so the smaller cop opened his palm again, as if sowing seeds, and Big Suit set about clipping Habid's sweetmeats.

Sam burst two of his makeshift stitches as he bounded up the companionway and reached past the woman with the niqab and gripped the front of the burka on the second adult. He ripped it forward before realising it was all one garment, but despite the strength of the fightback from beneath he managed to get his fingers into the eye slot and tear it open. A black head of hair appeared first and Sam grabbed a fistful to turn the face upwards ready to strike it back down with his raised fist but was turned by the niqab-clad woman's scream. All thoughts of violence vanished when he saw the look on his daughter's face.

"Don't hit him, Daddy," she said, confused and terrified.

The woman had wrapped her salt-stained dress around what Sam assumed was her own child to shield her from the imminent beating.

Sam stared at the man's stretched face, then at his little girl, his left hand still gripping the back of the man's head. Isla couldn't comprehend what had triggered her father's sudden lurch from the bunk, brushing her aside to get above deck. To her, there had been no deception – she had no grasp of what the wearing of a burka signified and she'd obviously heard him speak while Sam was unconscious. Isla had no point of reference to understand the conceit.

Sam also struggled to compute what was going on, not helped by the fact that his judgement was clouded by the severe pain he was in. But one thing was plain; he couldn't allow Isla to witness a beating.

He dropped the man backwards with a thud. They stared at one another but Sam was utterly lost for words. He simply shook his head at the other adults in turn, demanding an explanation as the robed and curled form cowered beneath him on the cockpit floor. The palms of the man's hands were open, his arms bent at the elbows, his knees raised expecting an attack, appealing to prevent one. When none came he gradually, gingerly, allowed his posture to relax and he slowly edged towards the woman, keeping one hand raised in an appeal for mercy. Sam watched and rotated to mirror the man's progress as he reached towards the woman. She initially recoiled before relenting as he placed his arm around her. He babbled furiously in Arabic throughout – his free hand open in conciliation as his wrist flicked between himself and the woman with an occasional gesture towards the little girl. Then he clasped his hand to his heart and his eyes looked up at Sam, again appealing for understanding. Although Sam had spent considerable time in the Arab world, he only caught one phrase repeated over and over: "*Min faDlak, min faDlak*", which he'd always understood to mean a mixture of *excuse me*, *sorry* and *please*.

Sam watched the display for a few minutes and somehow drew the conclusion that the man was the woman's husband and the child's father. He turned to Isla. "I think he's saying he's the girl's daddy." He looked to his daughter for confirmation but she plainly had no idea what was going on. Sam realised that Isla was still confused as to why he'd been so angry. "Men aren't supposed to wear the face cover, darlin'. That's why I was cross. I thought he was being sneaky, trying to tell lies and fool us."

"Why can't men wear the mask?" she asked, which was too profound a question for Sam to attempt to answer in the circumstances.

"I don't know, Isla. It's their culture."

The man was still gabbling away.

"What's *culture*?"

"I'll explain later," Sam said.

"So why did he wear the mask?" Isla asked, which was a very good question.

Sam reached forward and clasped the remains of the head covering that hung limply like a hood around the man's neck. He shook it at the man. "What's this all about?" he barked with real anger.

That sparked a new series of gestures, none of which Sam followed. Then, noticing something, the man placed his palms in the air, apparently seeking some indulgence, and shimmied sideways, pleading again, appealing. He pointed at something to Sam's right.

"What's he looking at, Isla?" Sam said, refusing to alter his gaze or stance.

"I don't know, Daddy. I think it might be my colouring book," she said.

"Hand it to me, please."

Isla got the book and gave it to her father. Sam handed it to the man who then began to mime writing.

"Pass me one of the felt tips, Isla," Sam said, ensuring his daughter remained behind him and at a distance from the man who eagerly took the pen and began drawing.

Reluctantly Sam allowed his gaze to fall to the page where the man was outlining a rubber dinghy. He then drew lines shooting from a dot he'd drawn and blew through his lips, allowing them to smack together like a horse whinny.

"Oh, Daddy, I think he says their boat sank," said Isla.

"Yes," said Sam, who had worked that much out. He reached forward impatiently to shake the burka again, motioning the winding of a fishing reel: *get to the point*.

The man nodded vigorously and began a mixture of gestures and scribbles. He drew what could have passed as a ship and requested the bag of colouring pens. He selected a red one and drew a solid red cross on the side of the ship.

"Yes," said Sam, "I understand. You wanted to be rescued by the Red Cross."

"Red Cross," the man repeated, nodding endlessly and returning to his picture. "*Loo-joo*," he seemed to be saying, "*Meh-men*," was all Sam could grasp until he started hugging himself before gesturing to the woman and child. He then returned to the page and drew a man, a woman and a child but crossed the man out. He kept pointing to himself and shaking a finger like an epileptic metronome. He returned to the page to draw arrows from the woman and child in the dinghy towards the ship but kept crossing out the man and looking to Sam, seeking understanding.

"What's he saying, Daddy?"

"I think he's saying that women and children get rescued by ships but men don't," Sam muttered vaguely, "or that men don't get asylum."

With mention of the word the man became over animated, as if he'd just won a game of charades.

"*Ass-ee-lum, ass-ee-lum*," he kept saying, nodding and smiling.

"I think you're right, Daddy," said Isla. "What's *ass-ee-lum*?"

"Not now, Isla," he said, staring at the man and more determined than ever to get the passengers off his boat.

———

The screaming was disturbing. So much so that Tassels took a break and left the corridor of cells to stand outside and strike up a smoke. Acrid Egyptian-dried tobacco, sweepings off some grotesque, blackened floor. He'd found them in a drawer of the custody officer's desk. They rasped his throat like a wood file.

Three walls of separation plus thirty feet and he could still hear the whining. Big Suit was evidently having fun. That big ass better not kill the rat, thought Tassels, who sensed a real opportunity. He just needed more time to work out what was going on. This was direct policing, he mused: no faffing around with permissions and detection, just cut off a few balls and all will become clear.

Inside the interrogation room Big Suit stood back and began to panic. Blood was gushing down the rat's legs. He'd been overzealous; nipped and tucked tighter than usual. Habid began to fail. His legs jellified and his sway became a fall, leaving him hanging from the hook. Big Suit dithered. He knew he was in trouble. The options were unattractive: summon Tassels and receive a roasting, or wait it out and see if the bleeding stopped. He knew in his heart that the flow wouldn't cease of its own accord, so he dropped the cutters and ran outside.

"What?" Tassels coughed as Big Suit burst into the yard.

"He's weak – he can't take it," Big Suit blubbed. "I think we need to get him some medical help."

Grim and thick as he was, Big Suit had never actually managed to murder anyone before.

"What have you done, you idiot?"

"He's bleeding. He's losing consciousness."

Tassels ran inside and lifted Habid's head by the hair.

"This is your last chance – that donkey dick has managed to slice an artery," he said but Habid was barely able to listen. Life was draining from his eyes.

"If you tell me now what your scam was, I'll get you a doctor."

Habid had endured all he was prepared to. There was just enough blood left around his brain to do the calculations: if I tell them, I'll die on this hook like halal.

He mustered a few words. "Doctor first, then we cut a deal, then I tell you," he said, and he promptly passed out.

"Why don't you like the man daddy?"

Sam smiled as warmly as he could at Isla, but his brow was bunched tight.

"It's just going to take time to trust him."

"Why?"

"Because I don't know what he wants."

"I think he just wants to get to a nice country," she said.

You're so like your mam, he thought, but avoided saying so as he knew it would send her into silence and sadness.

"I'm just trying to understand what happened wee love."

"You got really cross, Daddy."

"I'm sorry darlin', I'm really trying not to get so cross."

"I thought you were going to punch his head in."

"Where did you hear that?"

"What?"

"Punch his head in."

Isla just shrugged.

"I don't really want to punch anyone's head in."

"Yes you do," she said, not looking at him.

"What do you mean?"

"Mammy said it was your way of minding us."

"When?"

She shrugged again.

"What did mammy say?"

"She told me you had seen bad stuff and it made you cross sometimes, but it was just your way of looking after us."

Sam stood at the wheel, slightly bemused that this conversation had taken place.

"Did she talk about the stuff I had seen, the bad stuff?"

"No, but I know it was in the army."

"Not the army."

"The navy then."

"What do you know about that?" he said, peering below to see where the migrant family was. Isla shrugged once more and looked out to sea.

"I'm working on it wee love."

"It's OK. But you can't kill that man, Daddy."

"I'm not going to kill anyone," he raised his voice, then immediately hushed it – despite the fact that his instinct was to do just as his daughter described. In the dark corner of his consciousness he could see the scrawny man being left in the wake of the boat before disappearing into darkness.

"You promise?"

"Isla, I don't just go round killing people," he said, incredulously.

She gave him a look he had never known her capable of, a searching yet soft stare. It was broken only by his need to look away, guilty at his half-truth.

"I'm just confused about what happened, Isla. I don't really know how or why he helped me on board."

"I don't know, Daddy," she said, confused and on the cusp of upset. He knew to leave her alone, she was too young to understand or explain.

He hunted for the positive and sought empathy for the man that, like Sam, was a father, a husband and someone who wanted – and strove for – a better life for his family. That, Sam could identify with. He resolved, therefore, to approach the man with an open mind rather than a hammer.

―――――――

Tassels stared at Habid, half-dead in the bed. Of course a hospital was out of the question – there no way of explaining how a prisoner had lost a thumb, a toe and a testicle while in custody. Even in Egypt that would cause consternation – even if the mutilated patient was a Libyan. Not that he looked like one now: white as a European, the blood drained from his face and arms.

Tassels had a cousin who'd been a doctor. The cousin had been sent for and had savagely cauterised the rat's wounds. The doc had performed the searing smoky procedure on Habid where he hung, peering up and stroking a soldering iron of sorts into the seething tissue.

Then there was the need for blood, and the lack of testing facilities, and the gamble they took syphoning Big Suit – the first part of his punishment – the proceeds of which were pumped into the rat. The kit the cousin possessed was far from sufficient but calling for medical reinforcements wasn't an option financially. The three men assembled a grubby ICU in the police station's 'infirmary'. The mood was intense, the care coarse and the unit a filthy former cell. Tassels became more agitated and angrier as the operation grew increasingly uncontainable. The outcome was inevitable. What should have been a two-way uneven cut of whatever scam the rat was running had now turned into a three-way split: the doctor and one-and-a-half cops. Still, Tassels suspected it would prove worthwhile, if the rat ever woke up.

The woman came to sit in the cockpit, the man followed. Sam found himself wanting to atone for his outburst, to show some hospitality, regardless of how inhospitable he felt. He looked at them, the salt crusting her niqab in the sun, grading her in salt beneath. The discomfort must have been enormous. He couldn't help hoping the man's balls were chafing.

"Do you want to wash your clothes?" he ventured.

She turned to look towards him, but he had no means of knowing what was going on beneath the veil. The man too stared at him.

Sam called below deck. "Isla, pass up the washing liquid please."

A bottle of Fairy was landed by a little arm on the step.

"No Isla, the clothes liquid."

The Fairy disappeared and was replaced by a small capsule of blue and green liquid. Sam began to point at their black garments, before making a gushing sound and a rubbing motion which he imagined conveyed the cleaning of clothes. The man began to shake his head. Sam ignored him and looked at the woman. He fluttered his fingers over his head, then pretended to hold a shower head and rubbed his armpits. He felt like an ape.

The man became more agitated and immediately sent the woman below. Sam shook his head at the bloke in wonder.

"You're not making it easy to like you," he said, feeling safe in the knowledge that the man could not understand him. "I don't know who you guys think you are."

The man stared, then turned away, but not in shame.

"You think she needs your permission?" Sam's anger rose again, but the man ignored him. "Do you think we're going to watch her shower or what? Do you think she'll pick up some western affliction off the soap?"

He tried to calm down. If Shannon had been there, she'd have ripped the man's head off. The man got up and followed the woman below.

"Why doesn't she say anything, Daddy?" Isla called up from below.

"Don't earywig, Isla," he snapped, cross that he had been caught out so soon after promising to be nice. He sighed. "What do you mean?" he tried to moderate his tone. Her head appeared in the companionway.

"The mammy. She never says anything. He's the only one who speaks."

"They do things differently," Sam tried.

"Why?"

"I don't know," said Sam, which wasn't entirely untrue. He'd spent enough time among misogynists, white, black, Arab and otherwise to have knowledge, if not understanding. Senior officers who commanded their wives like staff, Taliban who treated their women like slaves.

"You *do* know, Daddy," Isla said, "you're just not telling me."

Sam sighed and looked at his little girl brimming with determination and frustration.

"I promise I will explain it best I can when I'm better, ok?"

"Oh-kay," she said, slowly.

Little apples, Sam thought.

7

A lollipop was the first thing he noticed.

His gluey eyes sucked slowly apart, one after the other, although it took a while for his vision to find focus. When it did it conjured a maroon marker plonked directly in his sight line. Habid was sure it must be a piece of confectionery – red and purple and glistening with sugar. It looked like it ought to be licked.

It wasn't until a solid ten minutes had passed that he realised what he was staring at: his own toe, or half of it, bulging like a toffee-coated apple, burnt and bright. The realisation heightened his agony and he tried to scream but couldn't. His throat was so dry, his tongue carpeted and stuck to his palate. His airway had been blown through with a thousand sands, his body sapped of all moisture. His bellow exited like a dying gasp followed by a horrified choke as he raised his hand to his mouth and was reminded of what had happened his finger.

"Don't worry," came a voice from the side.

He tried to move his head but pain shot in all directions. He caught sight of an IV bag. Blood. He longed to swap it for a bottle of water.

"Your torment is over. We have removed your interrogators."

Habid realised he was in a different cell. One marginally more habitable than his last. There was a window, somewhere, high and behind him. His gaze fell again to his foot and he began to wretch.

"It's ok," he heard, as a small sponge pressed to his lips, its moisture immediately vanishing into the intensely dehydrated cracks. "They are gone. I am a doctor. I am here to care for you now."

"*Shukran*," Habid muttered, opening his mouth for more.

The hand waved the little stick with the sponge on the end and squeezed a little into his mouth.

"Let me go and get some more," the doctor said, and walked to the door.

Habid felt an overwhelming sense of hope. They'd kept him alive and he was about to get some water. He would trade anything for water – anything. Another toe? Take it. Just bring me the water.

The doctor closed the door behind him and came face-to-face with his cousin leaning against the wall in the corridor. Tassels raised his eyebrows for an assessment, which came by way of a whisper.

"He's conscious and craving. He needs fluids or he'll slip away soon and we may not get him back, even with an IV."

"Tease him," said Tassels. "Fluids flow with information. Make him believe you want to get to the bottom of what happened to him – that you're on his side. But you need the whole story. Get everything from him – the supply route for the boats, where he gets the migrants, how much they pay. We must get the details about the money."

"I am a doctor not an interrogator," said the cousin.

"You're an educated man," said Tassels. "You'll find a way. If you don't, you've been complicit in torture, haven't you? And I'm a police officer."

The cousin looked at Tassels. "I *am* an educated man," he said evenly, curtailing his anger at the implicit blackmail, "which means I'm smart enough to ruin you for what you have done here," he said, shaking mildly in an attempt to keep his voice from raising an octave.

"If I'm exposed, then you will be exposed too – you're clever enough to know that. Just remember why you're indebted to me, *doctor*," sneered Tassels.

The doc closed his eyes and shuddered at the shame of it. His cousin had forced home the grip he maintained over him.

"Those allegations went away because of me. The investigation could so easily be reopened," said Tassels leering.

The doctor's shoulders made a barely discernible movement and he looked up and to the right. He knew there was truth in what his loathsome cousin said. He exhaled loudly and was about to turn the door handle to tend to his patient once more when his cousin spoke again.

"One more thing. Find out who the tenth person was."

"What?"

"There were ten people on the last boat. Make him tell you who the tenth was."

Wash or don't wash, Sam reasoned, fresh water was a precious commodity at sea. It came from rainfall or the painfully slow water maker, so it suited him to save it. Trickier to set aside was the issue over names. Every movie Sam had ever seen in which language proved a barrier had gone the same way: hands on chest – say name; point to other person and they say their name. Yet the man steadfastly refused to acknowledge any understanding.

Sam went through the rigmarole hands flat against himself, "I am Sam." He even pointed at his daughter and said "Isla," then threw an appealing look. The man held his gaze and said something to the woman whose eyes caught Sam's then bolted downwards before her head turned and she looked away. Sam got the distinct impression the man had told her not to reply, then scolded himself for being ungenerous and again offered the benefit of the doubt.

Sam checked the AIS more often than a single thirty-something checks their phone. He willed the Morocco-bound ship closer but it was still over nine miles away – two hours at current progress. He was also irritated that as he sailed towards it he was headed in the wrong direction – east not west. With every course adjustment he doubted his decisions: to take Isla to sea, to wrap her up in his world, to shun – if only for a while – ordinary life. It felt as though every tack he'd taken since Shannon died had been wrong. The one person he really wanted to look after seemed to be constantly placed in danger by his actions, his impulses and reactions. Each time it happened he considered it his comeuppance, just desserts, for all the things he'd done – the role he'd played in scrubbing out humanity in places where the presence of people like him may have been required but was also at the very least questionable.

He tapped the screen of the plotter readout that tracked the ship and became increasingly agitated. He was sore from the stitches and the cuts on his arm, and his muscles ached every time he adjusted the sail trim. He refused to sleep while strangers were aboard but he knew he would be unable to keep that up. He had to get them off the boat and back to the routine he and Isla had come to enjoy. And he had to get west, to the European Mediterranean, and to a hospital.

"Ah-ah," the doctor scolded as Habid's chin stretched for the sponge, his parched lips curled like a camel's. "Easy does it."

Habid looked at the doctor with confusion.

"I need to know what happened to you," he said.

"In a moment," squeaked Habid, his neck again extending like a turtle's, craving moisture.

The doctor relented and offered him a swift wipe of the sponge on the stick, leaving Habid wanting more and more and more.

"Now, I need to know everything, please, and then I can fetch you an IV – get your fluids back to normal."

Habid stared at the doctor in amazement. Why?" he asked.

"So we may prevent this from occurring again. I see this too often," said the doctor.

"You give me water, I'll tell you what they did," said Habid.

The doctor dipped the cocktail sponge into a cup and raised it to Habid's mouth and paused. "I'll also need to know why they did this to you," he said, waving the sponge gently.

"Yes," said Habid, beyond caring why this doctor gave a damn. "Ok."

The doctor squeezed the liquid into his patient's mouth and began to build a plan of his own.

The wind warmed Sam's cheek as he sat on the port side of the cockpit, facing forward, working the wheel with his right hand. He'd spent longer on the port tack than he ought to because the position gave him relief; it didn't place strain upon his right flank where the stitches were tautening and he could expose his trunk to the salt air, speeding up the healing.

The rope fouled around the propeller prevented it from folding away, which he guessed was slowing them by about a knot but, still, they were making progress without the engine.

Normally he'd be in his element sailing reasonably fast, the boat heeled over and slicing through the waves at close to eight knots. Normally Isla would be at his side asking questions, taking her turn on the helm or simply pottering around, drawing, trying to read, building imaginary scenarios for her teddies. Instead she was below attempting to interact with the child from who knew where. In other circumstances Sam might have taken comfort from Isla's attempts to form a fledgling friendship. He'd often watched, baffled, as children managed to communicate. For the first few years they could barely speak, yet they seemed to crave one another's company. Then as toddlers they're drawn together, strangers waddling, by some kindred curiosity, their nappies in synchronised sashay as they circled like unacquainted dogs, sniffing interest.

He could see the two girls from where he sat. Isla was sharing tiny garments as they dressed her dolls. She chattered a little but there wasn't any response. The Arab girl seemed content or perhaps resigned to sitting at the table in the saloon watching and repeating his daughter's actions.

The mother sat across from them, still on edge. The niqab covered her head and eyebrows and the flap concealed everything below the bridge of her nose, so Sam's only point of reference was her grip on the built-in furniture. Her arms were splayed in an L shape, resting atop the cushions on the corner unit she'd wedged herself into. Her hands were tensed, talon-like, clawing the fabric as if holding on. It made Sam think of the scratches she'd inflicted on his face and body. He wondered briefly whether she might be nauseous with the swell of the sea but he couldn't tell whether she was pale.

The man, mercifully, was asleep. Sam could just make out his loaf of black hair through a small Perspex hatch on the bulkhead. So long as that particular stranger remained still Sam was content. It allowed him to concentrate on sailing as hard as possible towards the intercept. The sooner these people were off his hands the better. There were too many unanswered questions that Sam wasn't sure he wanted to resolve.

No matter how much he tried not to think about it he couldn't shake the notion that there might have been more people in the sea. Hours had passed since Isla had heard the shrill blast from the faded plastic whistle. He'd found it later, attached by a threadbare lanyard to the dilapidated life jacket. Where had the jacket come from – some old airliner? It looked decades old. Had this small family set to sea on their own? If so, what boat had they been in – had it sank? In Sam's experience it was hard to completely submerge a boat at speed unless it had absolutely no buoyancy or was overturned by a massive wave. The night hadn't been rough to begin with and the three people couldn't have been in the sea for long. The woman and child couldn't really swim – the failing life jacket was all that had kept them afloat. And why hadn't the man stayed with his wife and child in the water? Sam hadn't caught sight of him until the cloaked figure boarded their boat, which suggested he'd retained enough energy to propel himself through the sea. No, Sam concluded, whatever boat they'd been in had only just failed when he and Isla happened upon them. And what were the chances of that? Best-case scenario, they had been very, very fortunate.

Stupid, thought Sam, a stupid thing to think. It wasn't fortunate to end up flailing for your life one hundred miles from the nearest shore. He reckoned Crete has been the most likely destination, but without seeing what type of boat they'd been in it was hard to say for sure. He didn't even know where they'd come from, but then he hadn't tried very hard to find out. And what of the others, if indeed there had been any others. Had this family seen them drown?

Sam looked at the child and her interactions with his own. Her movements were minimal, her face blank. There was no animation, no enjoyment. She approached play in a functional manner, going through the motions. The longer he watched her the more persuaded he was that she was in shock, stunned beyond any display of emotion. Understandable perhaps given all she'd just been through. Maybe that's what was curtailing the child, why she didn't speak, why she was functioning but not really engaging. They must have spent days at sea in the sun. Sam couldn't even begin to imagine what had driven them to take such a risk. What drove a parent to take their child towards the horizon with no guarantees and odds stacked in favour of death by drowning?

He let it drift. Not his problem. His problem was making contact with the merchant ship, turning tail and getting to Europe before his wound turned green.

Big Suit's wingspan was enormous. He was able to reach both walls of the grimy corridor to support himself. His mind fluttered to images of soldiers in rehab reteaching their legs to walk, tears in their eyes. Betrayal was burning in his heart. It was like being dumped by a girl as a teenager; rejection in favour of someone more important. Even in the narrow confines of his mind he was able to work out what Tassels had been prepared to do: sacrifice his life in favour of the rat's. Big Suit knew he could have died on the floor as the blood was deliberately drained from him. Hours had passed since, perhaps days. He had no idea. And yet still he could barely walk, and that was just the physical.

He was hurt. Inside. He'd given Tassels everything the man had ever asked for: loyalty, respect, brutality. In return Tassels had drained him. He'd loved that man, been devoted to him. He'd attached himself to his mentor and answered every call with enthusiasm. And at the first sign of profit his boss had forfeited him without a thought.

"Vessel *Teetaya*, *Teetaya*, *Teetaya*, this is yacht *Tuskar*, *Tuskar*, *Tuskar*. Over." Sam waited.

"Our boat's not called Tuskar," Isla said behind him. She'd heard him use the VHF radio a hundred times.

"Well, I have to call her something and I don't want them knowing what she's really called."

"Why?"

"I just don't," he said, staring at the illuminated readout on the radio transmitter, the blocky number sixteen, the international hailing channel. He willed a response.

Sam had caught the glow of the merchant ship's lights, probably still two miles away, advancing slowly. He knew it was the ship he'd been waiting on from the AIS readout on the plotter.

"Vessel *Teetaya*, *Teetaya*, *Teetaya*, this is yacht *Tuskar*, *Tuskar*, *Tuskar*. Do you read me? Over."

"Why are you calling the boat *Tuskar*?" Isla's curiosity was insatiable, which Sam normally enjoyed but it often surfaced at the most inconvenient moments.

"It's a rock off the coast of Ireland. It's what I aim for when we're sailing home."

"I want to go back to Ireland," said Isla.

"So do I, darlin'," he said. "So do I."

The radio rasped into life with a crackle and hiss. Sam reached to turn the squelch down.

"*Tuskar*, *Teetaya*," was all the operator could be bothered saying.

The accent could have been anywhere between Turkey and Morocco. Good as Sam's ear was, he had no idea.

"Channel eight, please. Over," he tried.

"*Madha*?"

Sam couldn't remember what that meant exactly but he

knew it was Arabic, a language in which he couldn't count. He thought about North Africa, it's colonial past, and tried French.

"*Huit, s'il vous plaît?*"

"*Tayeb*," barked the radio.

Ok. Sam anticipated problems. Not least because the door to the forward cabin cracked open a little, the man obviously curious as to what was going on. Sam reckoned he'd heard the Arabic, albeit there were only two words. He clicked the dial down to channel eight and started again.

"*Teetaya, Tuskar*. We require assistance. Over."

"*La afham*."

Sam looked at Isla. Isla looked back.

"I don't know what he's saying," she said.

"I don't think he knows what we're saying." He shrugged to her.

Normally Sam would smile at her reassuringly but he wanted more than anything in that moment to get the migrant family off their boat. The door to the forward cabin creaked a little more and the woman emerged. She sat by the table in the saloon and looked in their direction.

"Do you know what he's saying?" Sam asked her, then sighed. "You probably do, but you haven't a bloody clue what I'm saying."

"Daddy," Isla scolded him for swearing.

He ignored it. "*Hablo Inglese?*" Sam tried into the handset, aware that he was now trying Spanish where he had just succeeded with French.

There was no response.

"*Vous s'appellez anglais?*" Sam hunted his head for the right phrase and realised he had just asked whether they were called English. Again, no response. He dropped his forehead onto the back of his wrist, the radio mic hanging limply in his hand.

"Daddy, what's wrong? Who are you trying to speak to?"

"I want to get a ship nearby to take the people we rescued off the boat."

For a moment Sam thought the woman's head shifted a little – a robotic, involuntary twitch. He noted it but was interrupted by a blast from the speaker.

"What you want, *Tuskar*?" A new voice, no less rude but at least in a language Sam understood.

"*Teetaya, Tuskar*. I have two adults and one child on board in need of assistance. They were rescued from the sea and need repatriation."

"Sick?" came the curt response.

"Negative, *Teetaya*," Sam said.

"Injuries?"

"None," said Sam without thinking, abandoning his radio etiquette to match the abrupt turn the conversation had taken.

He imagined a ship would be reluctant to take sick people on board and considered their health an advantage.

"Then why need off boat?"

Good question, thought Sam. "They are from North Africa," he tried. "You are going to Morocco."

"Where exact people are from?" the voice asked, more curious now.

Sam looked at the woman and sighed. "I don't know, they don't speak English."

"Where you going?" the operator asked.

"Ireland," Sam replied, and again caught a movement from the woman out of the corner of his eye.

"Take people to Ireland," the voice said.

"I can't." Sam's anger grew. "They're not European – they'll not get in. I need to get them back to where they came from."

"You not know where they came from," the operator remarked, and Sam's exhaustion and discomfort overtook him.

"You have an obligation to help distressed persons at sea. You need to send a rigid inflatable and take them ashore."

"You say they are not distressed. No sick. No injured."

Sam realised his mistake and cursed himself for not having thought the exchange through in advance. He'd assumed the crew would be willing to help but that flew in the face of everything he'd learned in recent years about the cut-throat world of commercial shipping.

"If you do not take them, I will report you to the authorities," Sam tried, knowing it was useless.

"Fuck-a-off," came the reply.

Sam ground his teeth and slammed the chart table triggering stabbing pain from his arm and side. "I have your IMO, I have your vessel's name. One day, you bastards and I will cross course again and I will fuck you up!" he shouted into the handset and threw it down, cackling laughter returning through the speaker.

He turned to find Isla staring at him with tears in her eyes and the black drapes of the woman disappearing into the forward cabin.

"What is your name?"

"You first," said the doc.

The rat looked at the cup of water swaying in the doctor's hand and gave in immediately.

"Habid."

The doctor pursed his lips. "You can call me *doctor*. Now, tell me what happened."

Habid didn't like that. "Tell me your name."

The doctor looked at his patient and deflected. "You should tell me what they did to you. Maybe I can stop them from doing it again."

"Who called you here?" Habid was lucid enough to try and set some ground rules.

"The police."

"The small man – with the tassels on his shoes?"

"Yes."

"Is he the chief?"

The doctor laughed. "No, he might have had the chance to be once upon a time but he is too dangerous."

"Corrupt," corrected Habid.

The doctor said nothing.

"Why did he call you?"

"Because I tend to the prisoners." The doctor noted how easily the lie had come to him.

"So why didn't you take me to the hospital?"

"You know why," said the doctor, gathering rhythm.

"If you help to cover-up torture, why would you ask me questions pretending you want to prevent it?" Habid rounded on his carer, keen as a fox.

"Well, Habid," shrugged the doctor. "You have me there."

"You are working for the police," said Habid. "You are the next interrogator."

"I am the man with the water, Habid," said the doctor, "and the morphine. That's all you need to know."

"No, what you need to know is this, if you want a slice of my business, I want a deal. And I walk from here with insurance."

The doctor stared at Habid for a moment, then leaned in and whispered as he swabbed the rat's mouth. "That police officer is a dog. He is my cousin. I detest him. I can help you, for a price."

Habid's head jolted back as he focused on the doctor. He had no choice but to whisper back. "What do you want?"

"I want passage to Europe. I want papers with medical qualifications. I want a new life, and I want money."

"You don't want much," scoffed Habid.

"You don't need much," said the doctor with equal sarcasm, "except medication, fluids, antibiotics to treat the infection and protection from the next round of interrogation when you refuse to talk."

Habid considered. "I have infection?"

"You will almost certainly lose a leg, perhaps a hand, and as for your family area ..." the doctor looked towards Habid's groin, "... it could fester. Very painful without drugs."

Habid's neck prickled with panic.

"Can you save the leg – the hand?" he asked, suddenly desperate.

"It is possible."

"How do I know this isn't just another means to get the information your cousin wants?"

The doctor thought for a moment, staring at Habid, weighing up the risk of trusting an inherently untrustworthy human. "There is no gain without risk," he muttered absently.

"What?" asked Habid, lost.

The doctor emerged from his distant musing. "My cousin must be removed as part of this arrangement."

It was Habid's turn to weigh. He rested his head back, closed his eyes and wished he was at his lucid best. "You could have him removed if you wish, but to achieve what you want – what I want – we would be wise to leverage his influence."

"What do you mean?"

"He can help us for a while. He can open doors, keep the police away from us. Until the time is correct."

"What doors?"

"Do you know how difficult it is to get people from Libya to Egypt without getting detained?"

"I'm looking at it," said the doctor.

Habid cracked a wry smile.

"It can be done, doctor. I made a stupid mistake – I went to a hotel, that is all. But with the police turning to look the other way, we can do more. Move extra people."

"There is more to this," said the doctor. "The risk is too great to cross borders."

"You are a clever man," said Habid.

"So what else is going on here?"

"All in good time," said Habid. "You show me you mean what you say and we will progress. Until then, small steps."

"So what is the first step?" asked the doctor, suddenly aware that the rat had managed to turn the table.

"We need the boats."

The doctor was keen to reassert some authority, conscious he was rapidly losing relevance. "I will help you get your boats, but you must make sure I get what *I* want. A new life. In Europe."

"You are a doctor. You could probably go to Europe anyway with your skills."

"Ordinarily perhaps."

"Why do you need me?" Habid's cynicism knew no limits, even in the midst of his misery. "What did you do?" he leered.

"Nothing you need concern yourself with."

"Bad choice, doctor – if you are still a doctor."

"I'm the man with the drugs."

"I'm the man with the ability to get you what you want. You see, doctor, we are dependent on each other. So, what happened?"

The doctor exhaled and lamented the cunning intelligence and stubbornness of the rat.

"I've been in the pay of my corrupt cousin for too long. I have, let's say, a questionable clinical record."

"You got caught," Habid asserted knowingly.

"Just as you are. Now you and I can help one another get out of the net."

Habid thought about the fishermen he'd seen slaving for nothing on the beach, the wriggling of the few fish that had been caught and the one that had escaped as a clumsy Yfronted man had fumbled it from the net. He wouldn't give up. There was always an opportunity. "If we do not collect the next boat, the supply chain will halt."

"What do you mean?" asked the doctor, a little too eagerly.

"If we do not collect, the supplier will assume we have been compromised and the arrangement will end. No second chances."

"So how do we collect the boat? From where?"

Habid tried to shift a little, the pain coursing through him. "Sinai," he said.

"You go to Sinai to get these boats?"

"Not any longer," sneered Habid. "That's up to you now or your evil little cousin. Now, what is your name?"

"Doctor," said the doctor. "You can call me doctor."

Sam almost ripped the chart as he tore it from under the lifting lid of the table and wrestled it open. He'd spent thirty minutes hugging Isla and apologising for being so cross. When she eventually spoke he realised he'd misunderstood the root of her upset. She'd been shocked by his anger, certainly, but eventually she explained it was more than that.

"I don't want her to go," his daughter said.

"Who?" said Sam, momentarily confused.

"My new friend," she said.

Sam looked down at her big brown eyes swimming in sadness and realised how much he'd deprived her of: friends, normality, interaction, play. His heart sank.

"Alright, darlin'," he said, and hugged her again. "But eventually we'll have to find somewhere safe to leave her ashore," he said.

"Why? Why can't she stay with us?" Isla pleaded.

"Because she has to live with her family and she's from a

different country and when we go to Ireland they won't be allowed in."

"Why?" Isla asked again. "Why in Ireland won't they let someone in?"

"It's complicated, darlin'. We need to leave her somewhere closer than Ireland," Sam said, looking at the door to the forward cabin, grateful for the language barrier that prevented eavesdropping. "So they can get the food they like and apply for asylum."

"What's that?"

"Safety," Sam said. "They must have been running away from something scary – like a war or something."

"Then we should look after her," said Isla, firm in her understanding of the important elements of the conversation and oblivious to the bureaucracy.

He might as well have been cradling his dead wife. "If we could, we would, Isla," said Sam, and half meant it. There was something about the kid that Sam admired. A stoicism or a steadiness in the face of adversity. "But we wouldn't be allowed to."

Isla remained silent but Sam knew he hadn't heard the last of the argument. His determined little girl was simply gathering her thoughts and working it all out. She would challenge him again, as she always did, with a logic he found hard to fathom and difficult to counter.

Tassels vibrated at the news, his excitement growing as the route was recounted. His cousin leaned nonchalantly against the door frame and explained with surprising conviction what he and the rat had concocted as truth. Tassels span on the dusty floor making a sweeping noise as he shuffled around building his plan.

"So if we get the boats, we can make the contact and create our own arrangement for the future."

"I suppose so," said the doctor.

"Good, very good," Tassels muttered distractedly. "Now go and see to him. Keep the information coming. And send that fat fool in here."

The doctor opened the door and nodded his head back towards the office. "He wants to see you," he said to Big Suit, who was perched on a precarious plastic chair, his head in his hands.

"It's about time you got up off your ass," Tassels barked into the hallway.

The large man lumbered weakly into the office and was coated feet to face with a disgusted look.

"You need to get on the road."

Big Suit's jaw muscles flexed, distorting his face.

"Get your car, keep your phone on. I'll let you know where as soon as we get the information from the Libyan."

Big Suit suspended his astonishment. He hadn't expected an apology but an explanation would have been nice. In the past Tassels' temper had often been followed by an arm-around-the-shoulder session, a rub of the back, assurances whispered of Big Suit's importance, the regard in which he was held. Almost fatherlike.

"I don't understand," was all he could manage.

"Of course you don't – you're an idiot."

It was as if Tassels had a new group of friends to play with and his old friend was no longer as interesting. It grated even more that the new in-crowd consisted of a disgraced doctor and a desert rat. The gruesome urges Big Suit had been pushing away resurfaced immediately but he suppressed them in the knowledge that he wasn't yet fit enough to finish this relationship to his liking.

"Where am I going?"

"East."

"Where *east*?" said Big Suit gasping.

"To a port. I'll let you know which one."

"Why?"

"We need to collect the rat's boats for the migrants. They must arrive by ship – there is no other way. If we are to take over his operation, we will need those boats. It will be a port – maybe Sharm."

"You want me to go into the Sinai?"

"I don't know yet, you fool, but I want you on the road and most of the ports are east. If plans change, I'll call."

"My phone is broken." Big Suit removed his handset from his pocket sheepishly, its screen crazed, battered and unreadable.

"How did you do that?"

Big Suit stared at the floor silent.

"You dropped it, didn't you? When you got too excited with the rat."

"I've never been to Sinai," Big Suit then tried.

"Well, here, take this."

Tassels tossed the little bag containing the seized GPS and the rat's phone at Big Suit who fumbled and dropped it. He nearly lost consciousness as he stooped to lift it.

"That phone may be useful in case the boat delivery person calls. Ring me, we'll get the rat's number."

Big Suit struggled upright, tadpoles swimming around the surface of his eyes.

"But Sinai?"

"Are you scared?" goaded Tassels.

But Big Suit wasn't scared. He was delighted.

Sam stared at the chart and reached for the parallel ruler,

glanced at the GPS and plotted the latitude and longitude coordinates across the paper to pinpoint their position. Then he cast around looking for the nearest land mass; they were almost equidistant from Cyprus and Greece. He didn't want to go to Cyprus – Larnaca was where his special forces career had ended and he had no desire to return. Besides, it was east and he wanted to make west – Crete it was. He drew a line direct to Crete and as there was little tide to speak of he grabbed the dividers, placed the pins on the side of the chart to measure ten nautical miles and began walking them along the pencil line like a child might steer a toy. Three hundred nautical miles.

He looked up at Isla and would have sworn again if she'd been wearing her headphones. With a good wind at their back and with constant work they might average eight knots, but Sam was still in shit shape. On top of that the engine was fouled meaning they couldn't rely on the iron sail if the breeze dropped. He planned an average of five knots, which was still hopelessly optimistic, and reckoned it would take them the guts of three days. And that was just to hit land. Finding a berth could force them to the western side of the island – closer to their ultimate destination but an extra day with their uninvited crew.

Sam was exhausted. The distance meant he would have to somehow teach the man to sail. Not an appealing prospect. He'd been through that language barrier before with Iraqi Special Forces and it had been painful. The only other option was to go south but that meant Egypt, Israel or Libya, and Sam had a chequered past with each. Anyway, his working assumption was that the migrant family had been escaping one of those places. He hadn't the energy for a battle and something inside Sam suggested that the family's risk ought to harvest at least some reward. To take them back would mean that their journey, and any lives lost, had been in vain. Plus, south was further from Ireland and at that moment he craved some stability for Isla. Her sadness at the suggestion of offloading the Muslim child had suddenly made him understand her loneliness. He settled on a course of two-nine-zero, climbed on deck, hoisted the sails and leaned into the breeze.

"You sent the blood donor to the desert?" inquired the doctor, who possessed just enough professionalism to be concerned. "We took a lot of blood out of him. He's not fit to drive – he's not fit for anything."

"He is a fat oaf and he had enough blood for three men," spat Tassels.

The doctor hadn't kept track of the quantities extracted from Big Suit but he knew it was pints. He was astonished that the larger policeman had even managed to walk to his car.

"Call him," said the doctor.

"Suddenly you're worried about someone's health?" sneered his cousin.

"He may run out of reception," offered the doctor, clutching at straws but desperate to make sure the supply route didn't close down. If Big Suit died, there would be no more boats and no European dream for a dodgy doctor.

Tassels conceded, dialled the new number and held the handset to his ear. "What does it matter? If he runs into a few mad militants, it just means all the more for you and me." Tassels' leery smile revealed stained teeth, a stump and a gap.

The doctor nodded back pretending to agree but was repelled by the exposure of his cousin's rotten cavity.

Tassels held up a hand. "Where are you? Forget Sharm," he barked. "The rat is talking. Turn east towards Nuweiba." Tassels looked up to the doctor, his raised hand paddling open in inquiry.

"Ferry terminal," gushed the doctor, recalling what he and Habid had agreed.

"Ferry terminal," repeated Tassels into the phone, before a long pause and some muted squawking. "Well, I've never been there either," he said. "Just get there and call me when you arrive." He pressed the red button and turned to his cousin with a smug look on his face. "Now we're getting somewhere."

The doctor nodded.

In his bed in the cell Habid cracked a small smile at an extra layer of deviousness.

8

The man was an imbecile – that much was plain. He had plenty of physical strength and was fit, but he was thick. No matter how many times Sam showed him how to load a winch with a rope, clockwise, he made a bollocks of it, so Sam opted instead to show him how to helm. He stood at the wheel and coaxed the man to feel the list and drive of the boat, allowing her to drift too close to the wind and gesturing at the decline in the speed readout on the instrument panel before correcting the movement to the show an increase in the digital readout. No. No concept and no understanding. Sam paused after a while and almost laughed at how ridiculous the situation had become. Here he was trying to teach an idiot in a woman's outfit how to sail in a different language. Who was the fool, he wondered, him or me? The dynamic was confusing. The man had been smart enough to dress in a burka in the hope of securing rescue, yet couldn't wrap a rope around a drum without direction.

Sam settled for a watchman. With binoculars in hand and increasingly impatient gestures, he impressed upon his new crew the need to alert him when any vessel was spotted. Sam attempted to apprise him of what the blips on the radar meant but realised the man may never have even seen a television and gave it up as pointless. Irritable, he pushed on the autohelm and sought the sanity of Isla below.

He found his daughter and the little girl stowed away in Isla's cabin. It was a tight fit for adults but the kids had managed to make plenty of space and a small den out of sleeping bags. To Sam's surprise he found them giggling merrily, taking teddies and dolls in and out, blethering away in noises rather than words, apparently understanding everything one another meant. Sam watched for a while delighted at Isla's evident happiness and the other child's apparent improvement. He boggled at their creativity – he could never offer the type of play this Arab child could, which fed his anxieties about how Isla would take their inevitable separation. Curious, he thought, how he could crave something that would upset the person he loved most. A reminder, perhaps, of how much he still had to learn.

The mother was in the forward cabin. Sam could hear her. The sobbing. It stopped as soon as the creak in the floorboard betrayed the presence of another outside the door. He didn't dare imagine what she'd been through. He didn't feel required to – he'd been through enough himself. Then he felt the boat fall into an unnatural sway and he knew a gybe was coming. Cursing the eejit he'd left on deck, he made his way to find out what the man had done.

Big Suit used the long drive to plan his next move. His 1987 Toyota Corolla possessed about as much grunt as a donkey, and a man of his intellect required time.

As darkness fell he shook his big bloated head in exasperation at the steaming lumps deposited on what passed for a highway. There was no warning, just instant life-threatening danger every time one of the mountainous gatherings loomed into the blaze of his headlights. He didn't know what they were or why they were there. Could it be camel shit heaped into pyramids and left on the road? Why would anyone allow that? The east, he concluded, was not Egypt as he knew it.

Headlights presented another alarming example of the oddness of the east. Big Suit couldn't understand why people drove at night on such treacherous roads without their lights on. In Alexandria there were street lamps and shopfronts and artificial illumination – no need for headlights there. Out here, though, his mind boggled at the madness of the carry-on. It wasn't as if the passing cars didn't possess lights – drivers flashed them in the split second before they swerved out to overtake him. A courtesy of sorts, to let him know they were there. So why not run them as a matter of course? How did they not hit these curious objects in the road? Why were bodies not littered along its crust all the way to Suez?

Big Suit had never been to Sinai – he'd never had the desire. The desert wasn't for him. Hell, he hadn't even liked Cairo on the few occasions he'd been there. A city by the coast had all he required, but thinking of home while hurtling deeper into the desert with its dangers darkened his mood.

Tassels had screwed him. Screamed at him. Embarrassed him. As soon as that posh doc turned up, Tassels had turned on him. His boss had become Mr Big Balls, barking at him and ordering him around, cursing him for being overzealous with the tools. Big Suit was still seething at his belittlement and of Tassels' words rattling around his vacuous head.

"Sit there and roll up your sleeves," Tassels had commanded. Big Suit had complied realising only at the last minute, as the needle was inserted into his arm, that he was to be drained. "Take as much as you need," his boss had said, as a small pump rocked back and forth exchanging haemoglobin and filling bags for the heart of a rat. He'd faltered and fallen, had been left to lie on the floor of the cell for hours as the doctor and his boss put all their effort into the Libyan, ignoring their fellow Egyptian.

Eventually Tassels had him dragged out and tended to, but not out of concern. He now realised he'd been saved only to complete work that ought to have been done by the rat. All of this for a boat. A dinghy, probably. He didn't even know if it would fit in his car.

As the miles clicked by he hurtled deeper into a fug of anger. He had an opportunity out here in the sand and his boss would, in the end, learn not to embarrass him again.

Sam wondered whether he could pay to have the family offloaded. He'd amassed a good amount of cash through his previous employment, but his stocks weren't inexhaustible. Frequently when he'd rescued a woman from a brothel or a bloke from a ship, he'd come across bundles of notes. Often he split them with the poor unfortunate he liberated, but that still meant he'd gathered a substantial safety net for him and Isla. He had it wrapped in bags and cellophane in the bilges of the boat. As such, he wasn't keen to be boarded – it would be difficult to explain where the money came from. Besides, it had allowed them to go sailing and leave the past behind as far as that was possible. He wasn't inclined to just hand it over, so he tried to think of another plan.

Big Suit was jumpy even before he caught sight of the glow in the distance. He fished for his own, battered phone in the well beneath the gearstick and wished he'd been as frugal as the other drivers and left his lights off, even in the dark. Whoever was up ahead was sure to have spotted him but he reckoned the fire was at least two miles away. He scrambled to shut off his headlights and then plugged his handset in for a minute to give it some charge. When it lit the glow through the crazed glass began to worry him as he hunted for an old contact. He found what he was looking for – listed simply as 777. His little brag that he knew powerful people in high places. He debated using the rat's phone to make the call, but then decided that an unrecognised number might go unanswered. He willed his own phone to have a good moment and not cut out. He hit dial and waited.

"Long time," said a voice at the other end.

"What can I say?" Big Suit tried to sound jolly. "I'm sorry, my friend."

But the man on the other end had no desire to be kept up to date with Big Suit's brutality. "You must want something?"

Small talk wasn't really this man's forte and Big Suit was grateful for his directness. "Sorry. Yes, Waleed. I want ... well, just advice."

"About what?"

"Are you still in, you know, the unit you were in?" Big Suit faltered, suddenly scared of his own shadow. The three digits stared out of the phone at him: 777. Why had he entered it as that? Why not simply *Waleed*? He looked at the numbers, instantly worried that the call might be tapped, or that by asking what he was about to ask his phone would be placed on a list somewhere for tracking.

There came a sigh at the other end. "I'm still doing what I did when I left the academy," his former friend confirmed.

Big Suit adjusted himself, grateful he had such a contact. He and Waleed had once shared a room. The superior intellect of the man had created a role model of sorts for Big Suit. Admiration flowed one way, benevolence the other. Big Suit had respected the man and would have done anything he asked.

Everyone at the academy knew Waleed was destined for much bigger things. He had leveraged Big Suit's brawn and used it to run his own fiefdom at the academy. Every leader needed foot soldiers and they didn't come in larger, more dense packages than Big Suit.

"Are you in trouble?" Waleed asked.

"No! No, no. I'm just, well ... I'm in Sinai and I wanted a briefing on what to expect or where to go. I hear bad things about this area and I don't really believe them but—"

"What are you doing in the Sinai Peninsula?" his friend cut in, edgy, almost angry.

"I've to collect something for my boss. I ..." Big Suit began to doubt the wisdom of his plan.

"You what?"

"I've got to collect it in Nuweiba. I thought, wondered really, it might be of interest to you. To your unit."

"Oh?" said Waleed.

"Yes," said Big Suit, encouraged by the semblance of interest. "But, you know, I'm in the middle of the desert."

There was a heaving grunt on the other end. "You came from Alexandria?"

"Yes."

"Through Port Said?"

"Yes."

"Where did you cross the canal?"

"Suez."

"Did you go south from Suez or are you on fifty?"

Big Suit looked at the jagged line on the screen of the rat's GPS. It made no sense to him whatsoever. "I went east. I was on fifty, I'm about to join fifty-five," Big Suit said. "It's the fastest route—"

"Are you armed?"

Big Suit's heart sank. "I have a revolver?" Big Suit offered. "What do you want?"

"I wanted to know how safe it is but I think you've already answered that."

"It's not an area to go driving around on your own, even for a man of your exceptional talents. Big fists are of limited use when you have people prepared to cut off your head."

"So it's true, about IS. They are here?"

His friend snorted. "And the rest. The peninsula is riddled with extremists at present – al-Qaeda, Hasm, half a dozen spin-offs, Ajnad Misr, I could go on. We're currently monitoring eight marauding groups in that area, mostly north of where you are, but the road is not safe, they want to kill soldiers and ..."

"Police officers," Big Suit finished the sentence for him.

"There is no way to negotiate with them. If they catch you, they will kill you. I assume you left your identification back at your base?"

Big Suit stared at his wallet in the thin moonlight on the dashboard. He was just about smart enough to know how stupid he was. "But I hear this area is swamped with soldiers and your unit?"

Big Suit didn't dare name it. 777 had an odd reputation. Decades previously it had been disbanded because of disasters dealing with hijacks, and nobody really knew for sure if it still existed but every soldier and police officer had heard of it. Big Suit knew his friend had joined it straight from the academy but didn't know what his role was or where he was based.

"If I were you, I'd turn around and go back. If you *must* collect this *thing*, go south towards El Tor and then cross the desert. The closer to Sharm you get, the greater the number of police to protect what's left of the tourist industry."

"I can see a fire on the highway. Ahead of me. Any idea what that might be?"

"Could be a checkpoint – military. Could be Bedouin."

"Good," said Big Suit.

"Could be militants."

Big Suit sniffed. "Do you think so?"

"Who knows? I've got to go. Turn back, it's no place to be on your own with only six rounds in your pocket."

"Thank you," Big Suit muttered, but the line had gone dead.

Big Suit fumbled with the gearstick to try and turn the Toyota. The night became black almost instantly as cloud covered the moon, drawing his eye to the glow of the fire in the ahead. Wide as the road was, he almost managed to drop off the edge, which could have been catastrophic for a car of the Corolla's vintage. He was just finishing the turn when lights flashed in front of him and a large vehicle loomed to a stop. Their bonnets faced one another, the monster truck bearing down on him. *Where the hell did that come from?* He cursed the practice of driving in the dark like Batman.

The doors of the large vehicle opened and two men dressed in black emerged from either side. Big Suit cocked the old Colt. One of the men took up a stance in the glare of the lights and placed an AK-47 against his shoulder. The other man came around and tapped on the windscreen. Big Suit had no choice but to wind it down.

"What are you doing?" asked the man, and Big Suit heaved a breath of relief as he spotted a beret wedged beneath the epaulette strap on the man's shoulder.

"I am police," he blurted. "I have decided to take the road south instead."

"Police, you say," said the soldier, as if beginning a fairy tale, "and why would a police officer be out here in Sinai on his own with only a revolver to protect him?" He gestured at the gun wedged between Big Suit's moistening broad thighs.

"I'm going to Nuweiba," he said.

"Phone," said the soldier.

"What?"

"You have a phone," the soldier's hand curled in an impatient beckon. Big Suit cautiously handed his wrecked unit over and looked on in horror as it was handed to another man and then placed on the ground before being smashed to pieces with the butt of a rifle.

"Why did you do that?"

"Why are you here, police officer?"

"Official business." He tried to conjure some authority into his voice but he was shit-scared. What if they weren't soldiers at all?

"Official business?" inquired the soldier with his sing-song sarcastic voice. "Which is what?"

"Can't say," said Big Suit.

"Oh, I think you will say," said the soldier, "one way or another."

The chart showed a harbour, probably a marina, on the southwest coast. Sam didn't have enough detail on his memory cards or his paper maps to say with much clarity as he'd never intended to go anywhere near Crete. Such luxuries were expensive and there was no point in buying charts for places he'd no interest in. He was also too far from land to use data to buy the e-charts, so settled for the miniature before him. There were offshore beaches marked, sandbanks, he imagined, but he needn't have cared.

Four miles out to sea, sweeping ahead with the binoculars for navigational hazards, he paused on a disturbance. A wash, barely perceptible but he knew what it was: a rigid inflatable, or a big, fast pilot boat. Sam reached down and booted up the radar that confirmed what he already knew – it was headed straight for them. It was doing more than thirty knots, which suggested a certain determination – or a petrolhead skipper.

Either way, not ideal. He reckoned they had twenty minutes before the Greeks arrived. He looked around thinking about what to prepare, then realised there was nothing to do but tell the truth.

———

How quickly the tide turns, thought Big Suit as he sat in the back of an enormous van, the headbanging judder of its motion telling him they had rolled off the highway and were stirring up dust through the desert.

His panic had subsided a little. When the men got him out of the car he'd realised they might not be soldiers at all but militants, jihadis, Islamic State extremists. He'd considered fighting but then the back doors of the van opened and revealed twenty armed soldiers all with AKM assault rifles, official Egyptian army equipment. They obviously weren't elite troops – the kit looked standard but was well beyond what any desert beard would have. They had proper helmets and goggles. He relaxed a little.

The two men in the front hadn't arrested him, nor had they bundled him into the back. They'd simply invited him to climb aboard. A gesture with a jag as there was no choice involved. He hadn't thought to ask why he was being taken away or what the problem was. He hadn't thought to offer his identification. They'd taken his old revolver from him, sniffing at it with disdain, but other than that he was treated reasonably. And so he sat, silent, unable to think of anything to ask the soldiers that wouldn't make it look like he was afraid. The soldiers showed no interest in him as together they rattled and banged deep into the featureless desert.

———

The VHF radio crackled first – a hail. Sam ignored it. He didn't want a repeat of the container ship fiasco and was determined to show his desperate cargo to the Greek boat and whatever brand of official had been sent to meet them. He imagined it was a coastguard or customs vessel of some sort, so he held his nerve and waited.

Gradually the drone of her engines increased and the boat's captain resorted to a loudhailer that was equally useless because Sam knew not one word of Greek. Eventually the woman opted for French and then English, at which point Sam raised his arm.

"Lower your sails and prepare for inspection," she called.

Sam waved back, tapped the autohelm, flicked the halyard trigger and went on deck to gather the tumbling mainsail. Returning to the cockpit he hauled the furlers for the two genoas, deliberately allowing his wounds to weep a little; intending the blood to elicit sympathy. Then he stood and waved the boat over, glancing at the useless idiot in the cockpit who appeared more nervous than at any other time in their journey.

The enormous RIB span a tight circle and aligned itself with Sam's boat. He caught a bowline before two armed men stepped aboard while the captain came amidship of her own vessel and addressed Sam in broken English.

"Where have you come from?"

"We rescued three people from the sea three hundred miles south-east of here. They need help. I am injured."

"Nationality?" she quipped, not unfriendly but not as sympathetic as Sam had hoped for.

"Irish. My daughter and I, we are Irish. I think the ..." Sam gestured to the man at his side, in a dress, and struggled for a description "... refugees," he tilted his head, unsure, "could be Egyptian. I don't know. I don't speak Arabic."

"You brought them to Greece – three hundred miles?"

Said aloud, it did seem a bit odd.

"I tried to get a container ship to help them, to take them from us, but they refused."

"Of course they did," she said, her hardened stare fixing on him as if he was a dope. "There are thousands of people coming."

"Are there?" asked Sam, genuinely surprised.

"You do not use radio, no? We tried to call you ten minutes, no answer."

"I'm trying to save power."

"And you have not seen them?" She had turned sarcastic. "Migrants. Floating. You have not seen anything, I suppose," said the captain, exhausted at what appeared to be a routine rigmarole.

"No," said Sam, surprise still in his voice.

"You are stranger to workings of the world at present," she stated scathingly.

"Deliberately. We have been at sea for a long time."

"Why?" she barked rather than asked.

"Long story," said Sam, and beckoned to Isla who was now on deck. "This is my daughter. Isla, go to the chart table and get our passports. They're reddy-brown in colour and have a harp on the front."

"What's a harp?" she asked.

"They're little books with our photographs in them. I need to show them to the lady," he tried instead.

She disappeared down the companionway.

"ID?" the captain snapped at the man.

He shook his head.

"He doesn't speak English," Sam said. "I don't know very much about him."

"Of course you don't. Where are the others?"

The captain's face fell to the passports Isla had retrieved.

"Get the woman and the girl, please, Isla. Tell them to come up."

"Is she going to take them away?" Isla's sadness reappeared.

"To safety," Sam said, to which the captain snorted and Sam realised things might not turn out as he had intended.

"You're European," the captain stated, "and you have ..." she paused as the woman and child emerged, the elder still entirely covered, and her face frowned in disgust, "Arabs of some kind. This does not look good for you."

"Why?" asked Sam, genuinely bemused.

"Did they pay you to bring them here?" she snapped.

"Of course not," he cut back. "Why would you think that?"

"You don't work for an NGO?"

"My wife used to," he muttered, then shook his head.

"Only three in the sea or the boat. Only three people?" she inquired.

"Only three who survived," said Sam becoming irate.

"So you *do* know their story?" the captain rounded, full of *ahah, got you!*

Sam shook his head in wonder at the line the woman was taking. The two armed men were rifling around below and Sam kept half turning to see what they were looking at. "I know nothing about them," Sam said. "We just picked them up from the sea, at night, a few days ago, and I'm trying to get them to safety. Here. Greece. Europe."

"Why not back to Egypt or Libya or Cyprus?"

Sam had no intention of getting into any of that. "Because we are headed to Ireland," he said, "and we are making west."

"Then you can take them to Ireland," said the captain, snapping the two passports together and lifting her head to receive an assessment from her crew. The captain and her men chatted in Greek for a few moments and then, to Sam's incredulity, stepped over the guard rail and prepared to cast off.

"I am injured, our engine is fouled, I have refugees and two children aboard and not enough provisions for them. What the fuck do you expect me to do?" he screamed as the engines readied for take off.

The captain stared at him and barked an order. A man emerged and threw a huge bale of water bottles onto the deck of Sam and Isla's boat.

"You will not be allowed to land in Greece. I shall put out an all-points communication. We have too many migrants already, and you, to me, look like a people trafficker. If you try to make land here, you will be arrested. Go home," she commanded as the RIB tilted and the throttle was gunned. Sam stared at its wake and couldn't believe what had just happened.

Betrayal. Perhaps the hardest emotion bar grief to endure. Big Suit was experiencing it twice in the space of two days.

He felt hurt, initially, then afraid. Then resigned. It was true what people said – a bully's greatest fear is being bullied. Big Suit was at moping stage by the time his former friend offered him the ultimatum.

"Just spell out the whole plan and you'll probably survive this, but you'll not retain your soft little number in Alexandria exploiting hard-working men for half their profits."

"I don't," Big Suit began to protest.

"You do. Not all your fault – you're easily led – mostly down to your horrible little boss."

"I hate him."

"Oh?" said Waleed. "He finally turned on you, has he?"

"How do you know him?"

"We know what you do in Alexandria and we won't think twice about meting out your kind of justice back upon you." He gestured around the poorly lit room with dust underfoot. "So talk, or we'll cut bits off you and throw them into the desert, and then we'll leave the rest for the jihadis and they can cut your head off on the internet."

Big Suit could believe what he was hearing but not who he was hearing it from. It was a compelling enough argument. He'd heard variations of it from his boss a few dozen times and knew what way it would go. Why lose a hand to prove a point when they would get what they wanted anyway? No. Senseless. His biggest fear, however, was how little he had to give.

"You don't need to torture me," he said. "I came here to tell you about it. I'm here deliberately."

"You're here because your boss sent you to Nuweiba," scoffed Waleed.

"Yes—no—yes, but as soon as he sent me I decided to find you and tell you."

"Of course. I believe you." Waleed was unaccustomed to sarcasm but it seemed a fitting moment to give it a go.

"I don't know much but, please believe me, I'll tell you everything I do know."

"Yes, you will," said Waleed. "Let's start with why you're going to Nuweiba."

"I think to collect a boat or boats."

"In a Toyota Corolla?" he said, tiring.

Big Suit had no answer.

"A boat for what?"

"Trafficking."

"Ah," said Waleed, "you're getting into the people move-ment racket now."

"We took a prisoner from the Sofitel in Alexandria. We just wanted his money really."

"Money from what?"

"Well, we didn't know. We had a tip-off from the front desk saying that a filthy desert rat had checked in, and we thought, how can someone from the desert afford the Sofitel? So we went to see him."

"And how did that work out?"

"Not that well. He was a tough little bastard. I trimmed him to within an inch of his life but he didn't give much away. I think they're still working on him at the barracks."

"So what are you doing out here in the desert?"

"I got from him that he was into people trafficking, and, well, my boss, he thought he would take a slice of that."

"Of course he did. Why stop criminality when you can profit from it?"

Big Suit nearly nodded then remembered why he shouldn't. "He sent me out here where we thought the boat and engine were being delivered for the next trip."

"To the desert?"

"To Nuweiba. But that's why I called you. I knew you worked in intelligence."

"Good of you to look me up but trafficking isn't really our main concern."

"Oh, ok," said Big Suit, disappointed. His head fell.

Waleed almost felt pity for the man but then grew angry at the inconvenience the distraction his former classmate presented.

"You think we have time for people trafficking out here?"

"I don't know." Big Suit's huge jowls slapped as he shook his hanging head.

"This is an antiterrorist unit." Waleed softened a little. "We hunt Islamic State and the like, their training camps. We try to stop them massacring people."

"I'm sorry. I shouldn't have called you. It's just that, with Gaddafi's people coming through, I thought you'd be interested."

"Gaddafi's people?" Waleed's tone changed.

"Yes, that's what the rat said. He's finding Gaddafi loyalists and making them pay."

"By killing them?"

"No, pay to leave – through the Libyan border, then by boat."

Waleed sighed with impatience. "Do they leave by boat from Egypt or Libya?"

"Egypt – Alexandria."

"Why Alexandria?" Waleed was very curious now.

"It's to do with money and bank accounts," was all Big Suit could muster. In truth, he hadn't paid that much attention. His interest in interrogation lay in the persuasive arts.

"So a Libyan is bringing ex-Gaddafi loyalists to Egypt, getting them to pay him in Alexandria and what – sending them to sea?"

"Yes, I think so."

"Do they have bank accounts in Egypt – is that why they go from Alexandria?"

Big Suit shrugged. "I think it's also because many people leave from Libya but get caught and sent back."

Waleed considered this for a moment and Big Suit felt optimism creep in.

"I think the rat is talking in return for his life."

"Where exactly in Nuweiba were you going?"

"Ferry port," said Big Suit. "My boss is to call with more information."

Then there was silence as his former friend stared at him before eventually raising the rat's phone and placing it in front of him. "This one?"

"Yes."

"We will wait for him to call then, with further directions."

"I guess so," said Big Suit. "That's all I know."

"You understand that if you're not telling me everything, I *will* find out, don't you? How do you think I got you here?"

"My own phone?" ventured Big Suit.

"Your own phone," agreed Waleed. "This is no place for an unprofessional thug like you."

Big Suit felt more hurt than surprised.

"We have real-world problems in this area," he said. "Corrupt officers like you make the beards look like they might have a point."

"What?" Big Suit stared in bewilderment at a man he continued to idolise.

"The reason there is all this trouble – the militants killing everyone they disagree with, the Spring, the chaos?" He gestured to Big Suit as if offering an opportunity to answer.

He received a confused look in return.

"People like you. Greedy fat pigs who want to take cash off hard-working people while sitting on your lard arses doing nothing."

"I work hard," he protested.

"You arrest the weak and then exploit them. You charge people extra money to do the job the state pays you to do!" yelled Waleed. "You tax the people who provide employment and if they don't pay – what do you do?"

Big Suit faltered for a response.

Waleed filled the void. "You find reasons to prosecute them for petty violations or things you and your snake of a boss dream up."

Big Suit's eyes welled with shame. Had this tirade come from anyone else he would have held firm, but exhaustion and weakness drew his head towards the filthy floor.

Waleed wasn't finished. "And what does it achieve? It makes people believe that the bloody jihadis might offer a better way. It makes them think the religious nutters will deal with you corrupt idiots. They find out the hard way, in the end, but not before their daughters have been raped and they're living in a caliphate watching executions every afternoon."

Big Suit sat in astonishment. He had no idea his former friend harboured such loathing for corruption, for anyone.

"And the worst of them all are the scum who send our

people to sea with no hope of survival. Fellow Arabs fleeing abuse and attack at the hands of IS or al-Qaeda or whatever other mad group. The victims trying to take their children to a better place currently floating face down in a sea they'd never even paddled in."

Big Suit just gawped.

"Now, when this phone rings, we will monitor what you say. You will stay here, on this chair, and you will tell your boss to fill you in on the whole plan."

"But he won't do that – he just won't. You don't understand. I never get the full story."

Waleed understood perfectly.

"Then you bring him here."

"Here? I don't even know where *here* is."

"To Sinai. Then we'll find out the plan for ourselves – the routes, the people involved."

"How? How will I get him to leave Alexandria?"

"There will be a way."

9

"You shouldn't say those words, Daddy."

Isla had managed not to cry this time; not in front of her new friend.

"Sometimes, Isla, those words fit the description," Sam muttered, still staring at the wash left by the customs boat, or the coastguard, or whatever it had been.

He began to run through his options: he could ignore the crabbit captain and land somewhere else on Crete, but there was radar and if she had marked him and he landed anyway, could he really afford the hassle to be arrested, to have Isla taken into the care, regardless of how temporary, of someone else? Since Shannon had died Sam hadn't trusted anyone other than Isla's grandparents to look after her, so the answer came swiftly enough: they would not be separated. He could keep heading west but they'd be fishing for their dinner soon. Only so many cans and wraps of dried pasta could be stocked on a boat their size, and protein was essential. His provisioning had been based on certain assumptions and he'd never imagined being denied berth in a European country.

He slowly climbed below and pulled out the charts, staring

at them, hunting for an attractive option. Italy was one, Malta another, but less so. If the Maltese refused him, it was a long way to the next stop. Whatever he chose he knew he was looking at over five hundred nautical miles, four days of sailing.

He looked at the Arab man, now staring back at him, and imagined how things would be if he were no longer on board, if the woman were forced to show her face, a bit of arm, a foot – and the child dressed like Isla. The next attempted landing might prove a hell of a lot easier. Life aboard might become a lot more tolerable. He allowed himself a few moments of resentment to imagine what their journey would have been if he'd let the family drown. It lasted no more than a minute before Shannon put a stop to it. Her influence was so strong it almost irritated him. She would never have thought like that, it just couldn't have entered her head. Of course his wife would have saved the family, would have starved if necessary to feed them, rationed her own to share all she had. She hadn't been a saint – Sam knew that better than anyone; she had persuaded him to kill to let innocent children live, but he could rationalise that. It made sense to him. His gaze fell upon his daughter as he pushed back the loss and gulped to free his aching throat. He would never want Isla to think as he just had. By hook or by crook he would get the family to safety. And off his boat.

Some people recover quickly but the doctor had never seen anything like Habid's healing: the speed at which the scabs appeared, the infection drifted back, the stumps repelled the infection. Even amid the detritus of his Egyptian prison cell, the rat had managed to convalesce at a remarkable pace.

"Any news from Sinai?" Habid asked, as the doctor's saucers poured over his abrasions, replaced dressings and tinkered with the syringe driver.

"Apparently he's gone off-grid," the doctor said. "My cousin cannot reach him."

Which was gratifying and disappointing at the same time.

"How far did he get?"

"Don't know."

"Well, where was he last?"

"Suez, I think."

"He's probably done a runner."

"Don't think so. My cousin sent him east across Sinai to the ferry port at Nuweiba, just as we agreed."

"We don't have long to get the boat. If it's not collected soon ..."

"I know. You said. The route will dry up."

"It took a long time to negotiate in the first place," said Habid. "It will take a long time to find another supply route. Word spreads fast. People will not trust us. They will think we have been turned, that we are working for the state."

"So," said the doctor, "we will find someone else to get the boat."

"You could go," suggested Habid.

The doctor looked distinctly uncomfortable at the proposition. "Who would look after you?"

"Then we need to send Tassels."

"Tassels?" inquired the doctor.

"Your cousin, the cop. He's got tassels on his shoes."

"Mmmm, he's unlikely to leave Alexandria."

"You will need to persuade him."

The doctor just grunted and raised his eyebrow.

But Big Suit was progressing Habid's wish all by himself.

Shuffling and tapping were the first indications the man had spotted something. Sam stopped working on his dressing and chuckled when he settled on *Sinbad* as the name of his watch-man. He could be from Baghdad, Sam supposed, relishing the irony – a more useless sailor he'd never encountered. The man had shown a certain bravery in taking to the sea in the first place, so Sinbad seemed fitting, if probably politically incor-rect. But Sam was an ex-marine and cultural sensitivity wasn't an immediate priority.

He twisted slowly out of bed, attempting to protect his tight-ening stitches, and looked at the brass clock on the bulkhead. Forty hours had passed since they'd – as commanded – left Greek waters. He had a rough idea of where they should be, provided Sinbad had managed not to knock off the autohelm.

Dancing a jig, he was. Bare feet slapping on the teak, binoc-ulars dangling from his scrawny neck, eyes alight with discov-ery. Sam reached out to prevent his expensive glasses bouncing off the stainless-steel binnacle, then choked the cord towards him angrily, forcing the man to calm down and remove the leather strap from his throat. Sam turned towards the sun plummeting into the west, and caught the shadow low on the surface. Land. At last. He checked their speed: four knots. A short age away, but still. He was filled with the promise of unloading the easterners, stocking up with food, fuel and water, and cutting a course for Ireland. He nearly danced a jig himself.

He had no idea how premature such a sentiment would have been.

Big Suit had a penchant for vacancy. Ordinarily he could sit and stare at a wall or a spider and remain clear of conscience and devoid of thought. He never mused upon the mutilations he'd performed and he never felt pangs of guilt. He was grateful for that. Yet today, or tonight as it may be, he was expe-riencing something new: panic. His old friend was going to finish him. And the absence of his boss meant he had to think for himself. Again, a new sensation.

There was a layer to Waleed that Big Suit hadn't noticed before, something else going on. That lecture about corruption was almost religious, as if he'd been driven by some faith. That flew in the face of all they'd done at the academy, but then Big Suit thought back to what actually occurred during training and what Waleed's role had been. He thought of the room they'd shared and realised, for the first time, that he'd never once seen his roommate pray. He guessed he'd put it down to rebelliousness and acknowledged that he'd admired that in the man. Waleed didn't give a rat's ass for any authority as far as Big Suit could tell, yet he excelled at everything. Why? In every class, physical or mental, he was streets ahead of the other recruits. It was as if he'd been through it all before.

His thoughts turned to survival. Big Suit's skills were limited. If he got expelled from the police, what could he do? How could he turn this around? What weakness was there – what opportunity?

He combed through their conversation but his mind wasn't even working at its usual pedestrian pace; the lack of blood in his system made him light-headed and dreamy. And maybe that's why the notion came to him as he drifted into sleep on the grimy floor. Waleed's hatred of the extremists, his disregard for the beards at the academy, his refusal to roll out a mat and pray – his apparent lack of a mat. Why didn't Waleed have a mat? Big Suit had never wondered about that before. He'd never seen Waleed at the mosque either. Why had nobody questioned that? And then it came to him as the blackout draped him: Waleed wasn't Muslim.

He was Coptic.

10

Valuable data was wasted forming a plan. Sam always felt better when he'd a plan but begrudged his allowance being used in satellite time to plot their passage. He preferred to save data as treats for Isla – a new movie download, maybe an audiobook or a game for her tablet, yet here he was hoovering it up and navigating via Google Earth. Not ideal. It grated badly for an ex-naval officer to use such a tool but there was no doubt it was good, and the charts and plotter cards Sam had aboard simply didn't have the detail.

Portopalo di Capo Passero, Italy. Sicily to be exact. The village looked fairly tired – pretty enough but also remote enough, Sam hoped, to be of little interest to the authorities. To the east was a channel facing a small town, but to the south was a harbour, a breakwater, and even a cradle lift for boats. That sealed it.

He looked at Sinbad's gnarly feet through the window beside the navigation table. He was sitting in the cockpit keeping watch with the binoculars. Apparently. Sam wouldn't trust him to look after a bowl of Rice Krispies if he'd any other choice, and he wouldn't leave Isla above with him. The man seemed reluctant to spend time below deck or with his wife. It seemed they only conversed when the going got tough. After the boarding by the Greeks they'd spent time in the forecabin talking, hushed but urgent. When the container ship passed, the man had stern words with his wife. Sam had heard them being delivered but was baffled as to what they might be, and he'd heard nothing back from the woman. He put it down to culture, of a kind.

Shannon would have struggled to hold her tongue. Sam's instinct was to avoid getting involved – they all had to sleep and he wanted his as undisturbed by threat as possible. Interfering in other people's marriages didn't seem like a wise course to him. He wasn't about to change centuries of subservience by remonstrating in an unintelligible language with a man who would only take it out on his wife at the first opportunity.

The man's toenails were inches from his face, separated by reinforced Perspex but repulsive all the same. Sam looked forward to the day, soon, when he would see those feet patter away up the quay in a Sicilian harbour.

His plan was that he would sail to within a few miles of the Sicilian shore at night with his AIS and VHF and all other instruments switched off. He would prepare the little rigid inflatable that hung from the davits at the stern and attach the twenty-horsepower outboard. He would show the man how to use the engine – steering was easy from the console in the middle, the throttle was a lever, the direction dictated by a wheel. Even an idiot such as his unwelcome stowaway could master that, Sam thought. He had, after all, managed to get his family far offshore once before.

Then it was a case of the man doing his thing. They would have landed safely in Europe, and as far as Sam could tell that had been the man's aim. His family would enter whatever asylum system Italy operated, they would be fed and watered and given shelter.

Sam sketched out an appreciation, a risk assessment, of what could go wrong and what he would do in the event of a disaster. The risks were many. First, the name of their boat. Isla and Sam had made it their home, and their home wasn't complete without Isla's mam, Sam's wife. Her death had left them with no prospect of full repair, but they'd decided, together, to name the boat after her. It did, after all, give them protection just as Shannon had. It was where they turned for privacy, solace, comfort and rest. It was the prospect of adventure and new things. They had settled on the Irish spelling *Sionainn*, but always referred to her as *Sian* or *Shan* – it avoided confusion when speaking to relatives or friends. The problem was the name was burned into the backboard of the rigid inflatable tender Sam proposed sending the Arabs ashore in.

Next was the evident ineptitude of the man. There wasn't much Sam could do about that other than sketch the plan on a piece of paper and hope he understood how to steer towards the lights. How they might get ashore undetected was largely up to the man himself but there did appear to be a sandy bank they could drive the boat up. Which presented the next issue.

Sam wanted their boat back. It wasn't a cost thing, although the boat was worth a few thousand, as was the engine; it was because the boat represented a safety net for him and Isla. The RIB offered an alternative to a life raft in the event of a major problem. If *Sian* hit a half-submerged container and become catastrophically holed, he and Isla had the option to get into the RIB under their own propulsion. Depending on where they were, that may be preferable to floating aimlessly without any control in a wobbly life raft hoping for rescue. Sam had two emergency grab bags stitched into the RIB and a sun cover in preparation for such an eventuality. He wanted the little boat back. He also wanted to avoid it becoming associated with trafficking. His working life after the Marines had been consumed with preventing people trafficking, so few things would be more repulsive than being charged with being involved in it.

He would have to land himself, but at a distance from the family. His idea was they would abandon the boat, he would saunter ashore a few days later like a salty sea gypsy and inquire after a missing dinghy. If the Arab managed not to drown everyone and get ashore as directed, the chances were high that someone would hand him the boat and ask no questions. Then, with luck, he would be able to pay a few hundred euros to get *Sian* lifted out with the travel hoist he'd seen on Google Earth and sort out the fouled propeller and engine without infecting his wounds.

It was a fine plan riddled with holes, and if it all worked out, Sam would eat his woolly hat.

Big Suit was woken with a gentle toe to the head. He was lying on the floor, a position he was gradually becoming accustomed to. The foot before his face was readying for another tap.

"Don't. I'm awake," he said, gathering his surroundings and predicament while stirring inside was a vague memory that something exciting had occurred to him. He struggled to remember what.

"Get up. Your boss is calling you."

Waleed. His former friend now his wake-up call.

"What will I say?" asked Big Suit struggling to his feet.

"Nothing, for now. Listen to what he has to say, then I'll brief you and you'll call him back. Tell him you stopped for a piss."

Big Suit looked at Waleed and rallied as his memory returned. He knew something about Waleed that Waleed wouldn't want anyone else to know. The sadness he felt that a man he admired was treating him like a dog turned to loathing. He ignored the proffered phone; a deliberate act of defiance.

"What is your real name?"

Waleed stared at him for a long moment. "What?" he spat dismissively.

"Your real name," Big Suit repeated, eager to discover whether he was correct and if so, find a way to turn it to his advantage. As usual, he hadn't thought it through. "You have no tattoo." Big Suit nodded towards Waleed's wrist, which betrayed him as he clutched it with his free hand. In that flinch Big Suit confirmed his suspicion. "Many Coptic Christians have tattoos on their wrists – crucifixes. Not you. Why not?"

"Because I'm not a Copt, you fat fool," Waleed replied with remarkable calm.

"Obviously," the now smug Big Suit responded, "because Copts are not allowed in the security services or intelligence. They're barely allowed into the police, so you can't be a Copt … except you are."

Waleed looked at Big Suit for a long while, curious that after all the years he'd managed to conceal his background a genuine idiot had worked it out. But what Big Suit had failed to work out was that by playing his supposed ace, he may well have condemned himself to a life in a forgotten cell in the middle of a dangerous desert.

"Call your boss back and say what is written here, then we will … negotiate."

Big Suit smiled in leering triumph. He looked at the paper he'd been handed, read what was printed and snorted. "He'll never do this."

"Just ring him back and read it."

Big Suit shrugged, selected the missed call and hit dial. His boss answered almost immediately.

"Where are you?"

"Route fifty. Stopped to pee. Sorry."

"Where on Route fifty?"

Big Suit looked at Waleed who was now wearing a headset, apparently listening in. He wrote on the piece of paper for Big Suit to read out.

"Near Nekhel," he said. "I think."

"The doctor thought you could be sick from blood loss but you sound fine. Keep going. I will know more when I call again."

Waleed nodded, and scissored the air with his palms. Big Suit took his lead.

"Ok," he said and cut the call.

"We will wait for information," Waleed said.

"You'll never get him to come here to the desert."

"Let's see what his plan is first. We will take it from there," said Waleed.

"It will give us time to negotiate," said Big Suit.

Waleed had no intention of being beholden to anyone. He leaned forward and plunged his thumb into Big Suit's left eye forcing him backwards off the seat, screaming.

Then the lights went off and the large, stupid torturer lay writhing in panic on the floor in full realisation that the deck he felt he was dealing was in the hands of someone else.

Exhaustion breeds hallucination, and anger. Sam knew that. He'd been exhausted plenty of times – often deliberately – during selection, special forces, during training, on operation. The key was being able to distinguish between what was real and what was imagined, and crucial to that was knowing when you were exhausted. And Sam knew. He was falling asleep as he spoke to Isla, curious at her father's insistence she be clipped onto him rather than the jackstays, as per normal. He kept repeating that if anyone came on deck she was to shake him hard until he woke. He had frightened her a little.

"If the man comes up, you wake me, understand? Shake me as hard as it takes – smack me if you have to, but wake me up, Isla."

"Oh-kay, Daddy," she said, looking at him as if he'd lost it.

"Anyone, Isla. If anyone comes up, you wake me. And you stay clipped onto me, and if anyone comes near us or your clip, you hit me hard, ok?" He was vaguely aware he was rambling and sounded daft but the point had to be made.

The darkness of sleep deprivation had conjured some pretty unwholesome suspicions about Sinbad and for some reason the image of his gruesome toes kept floating into Sam's head. He'd looked at the man not thirty minutes previously and saw him in an entirely different light. Sam had been at the helm coasting the cutter over the swell, driving forward at just under seven knots on a tight reach when he was aware the man was watching him. Sam didn't need to look over, he just knew he was being appraised, and instinct made him believe he was being scrutinised, learned from. Sam's addled brain threw those numbers into its busted calculator and came up with the notion that the man had been skimming him all along, observing how the boat and sails worked while pretending to be an automaton. But Sam had shaken his head, reminded himself that Sinbad couldn't even walk the deck without falling on his arse let alone grasp how the compass worked. Then he asked himself again how the man had managed to get so far offshore in generally the right direction if he really was such an idiot? Which led Sam to ideas about inflatable beach dinghies being swept to sea, and then inevitably to Shannon who would have helped the man regardless. Probably. So he decided the time had come to risk sleep, before he strangled an innocent man in front of his family.

He shut down. A plummeting sleep at fifty fathoms and

diving. He could feel the free fall and worried whether he'd ever resurface. It had been days upon days since he'd got more than twenty minutes at a time.

———

If Big Suit was in shock, Waleed was in a stunned state of his own. He'd just half blinded a man for whom he once had the kindling of affection – perhaps not, sympathy, maybe. That man had threatened him and all he had worked for despite being the least likely person in the whole of Egypt to have solved the equation.

Waleed sat in his desert office and contemplated the predicament he suddenly found himself in. He knew much of it was his own making – why had he ordered the detention of his former roommate? Why had he cared that the brute was rolling around Sinai with just a spud gun to protect himself? Why had he taken the hard approach with him – why not just turn the hulk around and send him back to Suez? Curiosity, in part, he supposed, dressed up as professionalism. He'd wanted to know what the big man had been up to, for sure, but in a way it was more that he'd felt a sort of nostalgic protection for the fool. Waleed had always known that his roommate was borderline educationally subnormal and easily led, and that any evil in him had generally been massaged to the surface by more manipulative elements. When the pair shared digs at the academy, he got to know the vulnerabilities of the boy despite his bulk. He had coaxed out the background – how he'd been bullied as a child and abused by his father and had grown a brutal shell to protect himself. Waleed could chart it and understand how it had developed: soft big lump learns to protect himself, toughening hulk of a boy begins to understand that the best way to avoid being attacked is to strike first, bulging teenager understands that other boys admire physical strength, youth learns that a tough reputation makes life easier and brings friendship. All of that, turn by turn, had led to him leaning on others in the same manner that his father had leaned on him. Waleed considered it learned behaviour and so tested it again and again to see whether he really was plain bad or whether there was something more in him.

He'd placed temptation before his roommate on dozens of occasions – opportunities to exploit other students, to get on the make when out and about in the local area, yet the big dope had only followed; he'd never led. Not once had he taken the initiative to grab money or dole out harm. Only when coaxed, prodded or ordered into it had the fool become involved, but when that switch was flicked everyone in his presence had to take a step back. It was as if some inner rage came to the surface, some muscle memory that fuelled the pummelling beatings he meted out, as if he were remembering his father, or the bullies, and all the kickings he'd endured as a kid. After-wards he seemed able to shrug it off as normal – one of those things. You told me to do it, I did it, it's done. Violence comes as no shock when you've always been served it for breakfast.

In the right hands he was harmless, and with the right guid-ance he was useful. The Egyptian Police could use a man like that. The army would have been a better bet but he hadn't applied. Waleed had considered using him for the finer arts, interrogation and the like, but he was just too thick to take on board the subtleties involved; the fine line between giving and taking during a protracted period of high-level questioning would have been lost on the big man, so Waleed had allowed him his space and let him drift off into a local unit.

Obviously that had been a mistake. Somewhere along the way, Big Suit had grown to enjoy his trade, to relish the abuse and the power. How he'd leapt at the prospect of blackmailing Waleed was a clear example. The large, slow unit that Waleed had once known would never have jumped to that option by himself. He'd obviously learned – probably under the influence of a user. Waleed decided to deal with the dope after he'd dealt with the dope's boss. Waleed's remit was to wipe out extremists in the Sinai Desert, but he'd watched with deepening sadness as a growing number of people took to their certain deaths at sea having paid for the privilege.

Sam woke with a yelp like an unexpected outburst from a nervous dog. Isla had tugged on the line between them, as she, with the diligence he had taught her, had kept watch. She was staring through the binoculars over the top of the spray hood.

"I can see lights, Daddy." She was breathy, not speaking aloud but conspiratorial.

"How long have I been asleep?" he asked her.

"Ages and ages," she said.

It was pitch-black and the auto-steering gear was working hard making adjustments according to the wind and set course.

Sam realised it was the first time Isla had kept watch at night. He glanced at the chart-plotter readout, then stood with her. He returned to the GPS and then the radar to make sure there were no dangers ahead. He must have been out for at least three hours.

"You must be freezing, wee love," he said. He'd never expected her to be on deck with him for so long.

"I'm ok," she shrugged.

Tough little nut. Like him, she struggled more with the heat than the cold.

The coast appeared clear with no ships or rocks blocking their way.

"Did any of the others come up on deck?" he asked his daughter.

"No," she said. "They're sleeping, I think."

He did the sums: forty miles from shore, visibility must be very good for the lights to be so clear and they were sailing at six knots. Not good. It would take them about six hours to get close enough to put his plan into action. By then the sun would be up. There were no circumstances in which he would make the same mistakes he had in Crete – no assumptions this time. He didn't imagine for a moment the Italians would welcome stray migrants or that their suspicions wouldn't fall on him as they had in Greece. He wanted the family off his boat and safely ashore before anyone realised where they'd come from. Then he wanted to retrieve his dinghy and fix the engine. Deniability was essential, so they had to land at night, which meant they were going too fast. Sam unclipped himself from Isla and reclipped her to one of the cockpit hoops. He took the furling rope for one of the headsails and began to pull it in, noticing how much better his back felt as he did so. The sleep had performed wonders and his muscles ached just a little less. They would sail around at forty miles offshore and get some rest while the sun shone, then make their way towards land a few hours before sunset. It would give him time to brief the family and demonstrate the dinghy and outboard engine to Sinbad. Sam's excitement grew as he relished the prospect of ridding himself of the unwelcome presence, but his anticipation was tempered with the inevitable backlash and sadness that the loss of a friend would bring to Isla.

Militants had been pouring into the Sinai Peninsula and he could see their rationale: it might be arid but its sands were not Saharan; there was rock and shelter and enough resources to survive; and there was next to nobody out there save for a few towns, disparate and unprotected. If a group wanted left alone to plot military campaigns, Sinai was hard to beat. Infiltration was impossible: anyone who joined the militants were brought in by the fighters themselves, vetted and transported from who knew where, so Waleed couldn't send in an undercover agent, and, anyway, this wasn't an area someone could simply wander in off a dusty road – there weren't any. Besides that the beards had so many rules, hang-ups, stipulations. Each group he looked at would invariably kill anyone suspected of being a different brand of Islam, never mind a Jew, a Christian or a Coptic for that matter.

The beards could be dealt with from the air, of course, but Egypt wasn't in the habit of shooting up settlements from the sky. Not without the proper intelligence, and that intel was hard to obtain without boots on the ground, in the camps. The Brits or the Yanks would probably blow them up with one of their drones if Egypt requested it, but that would require asking, and the country's leadership had changed so often in recent years it was difficult to keep track of who its allies were. The Israelis would have the capability in spades, and Waleed was of the view that Israel had most to gain from wiping out such groups, close as they were to the Israeli border. Yet, again, Israeli intervention in Egypt was a no-no, even in such unstable times. The peace accord between the two countries had to hold fast otherwise Israel would fall out with Egypt and Jordan and would once again have hostility on all fronts. So Waleed spent most of his days analysing satellite data, being briefed on movements and trying to guess which town, village or settlement was next to get the militant treatment.

Meanwhile the guilt built up as his former friend whimpered in a room down the hall. Big Suit's boss still hadn't phoned, which rendered Waleed's own plan far from clear. As the days passed, he grew to wish he'd never intervened and had simply left the idiot to IS or similar. He simply didn't have time to deal with people smugglers, much as he hated them. Waleed couldn't even leave Sinai – he was the senior commander in the dust and hadn't been home for forty-nine weeks, there was too much going on. If he'd left the big fool to the beards, it would've saved him having to confine his friend indefinitely, or worse, which increasingly seemed like his only option now that the hulk knew his secret.

"No, this is to rev the engine. It's not throttle - not power." Sam wanted to throttle the man, never mind the boat. "Once engine is running, then put this lever down. Ok? Then use this one – red button, to drive off. See?"

He'd been at it for thirty minutes and still the man was struggling. It was as if he couldn't hear the revs in the engine, the differences in high and low. Sam gave up and decided to try the woman instead. He called to the cockpit from the dinghy they were bobbing around in at the stern of the boat. Isla's little blondie head appeared, an open look on her face.

"Try and get the woman to come down here, please, Isla."

She shrugged and vanished from view. The impact was immediate. The man started shaking his head and made a rare vocal contribution.

"*La. La.*"

The decision was complete. He had evidently understood what Sam was intending and was having none of it. Chauvinist idiot, Sam thought. Can't do it yourself but won't be shown up by a woman.

The woman's clothed head eventually arrived over the stern above them. The man barked something at her and she promptly disappeared.

Sam again considered toppling the idiot over the edge and holding him under. Sinbad was no longer a joke of a name, it was appropriately offensive. He stared at the man, but the idiot just hardened his repose into a kind of trout pout. How West-ern, Sam thought.

"Get back aboard," he ordered, not one bit concerned to conceal his disgust. "If you can't work the throttle, I'll point you at the shore and you can at least steer towards a certain point. You can manage that, can't you?"

But Sinbad simply stared back, hardened, berated – embar-rassed, Sam hoped.

In the cockpit Sam looked at what he was about to explain to Sinbad and breathed through his nostrils like a bull. He had little confidence this fool could land his family in the neigh-bourhood of Italy let alone on a specific beach.

"We are here." He flicked an x on the chart in open sea. "Here," his pencil stroked another mark on the chart beside the Sicilian harbour, "is where you are aiming for."

Sinbad looked at him and nodded an agreement of the delusional. He seemed to be suggesting that he got it, now move on. So Sam moved on, suppressing a hankering guilt that he was casting them adrift and clearing his conscience all at once, and that he didn't care that much whether the idiot was understanding him or not.

He moved to the chart plotter, again showing first their current position and then where Sinbad was to steer towards. "Now," he said, "this is a light, and it flashes." He picked up a torch and held it upright, flicking it on and off. "Look, watch. Count – one, two, three, then stop." He paused for five seconds. "Then again – one flash, two flashes, three flashes," he said, and covered the bulb end. "Then stop. See?" But he didn't believe for a moment that Sinbad saw at all.

He pointed to the light on the chart plotter and counted off again, then looked up to the woman who was paused pensively on Sinbad's shoulder as if nervously eavesdropping. Sam hunted into the letterbox of her concealment and willed even a slight nod from her. "This could save your daughter," he appealed, pointing at the child. "*You* need to understand." Through the gap he imagined he'd seen a glint, a hint, that she at least got it. They had to hunt for the flash and drive to the light. That was all. It wasn't hard, surely, even in a different language? Yet what use was it that the woman understood? If the patriarch didn't, he would hardly listen to her anyway. He didn't seem the type.

Sam had one more option. He flipped open the laptop and raided Isla's data again. Google Earth. What use it would be in the dark he didn't know, but at least they would get a sense of what it was they were to point at. He could only offer them the street view but the light would look broadly the same from the sea. He started flashing with the torch again and abandoned a notion he'd had about giving them a compass with a bearing to follow. She might manage but Sinbad wouldn't. Losing a boat was one thing, losing his handbearing compass for no benefit was another.

Sam's frustration would wear off eventually.

He told the adults to get some sleep while Isla told the kid to "come on" and they gathered on different sides of the cockpit table to draw. Sam watched them for a while, growing drowsy again in the sunshine, warming again to the kid and her little gestures of generosity. The girls handed one another pencils, colours and Isla chattered away about how lovely the kid's drawings were.

"That's beautiful," she said, and the other child glowed, then stole a glance at Sam whose eyes were all but closed. The sway of the boat and the hot breeze coating him was taking him back to the garage for repair.

"I love your flowers," he caught Isla on the drift.

"Thank you," pricked a flicker of alarm in Sam, but it wasn't enough to bring him back from sleep.

"How likely is he to let me go?" Habid asked the doctor. "You know him, he's your cousin."

"Not at all likely. He will try to get the information from you, through me, then he will try to put all my talented work here to waste."

"You mean let me die?"

"Oh, no. He will want to kill you himself. He is evil to the core, that man."

"So he needs to understand that he requires me," said Habid, as the drugs that were saving parts of him were hooked up at his shoulder and applied through the cannula in his arm.

"Well, then you better have something else to tell him. He's an impatient man."

"You pair aren't screwing me, are you, doc?" Habid asked.

The doctor paused, looked at the wall and said, "At some stage, Habid, you're going to have to place your trust in someone. You know more about me than I would like you to but that is my risk. If you want to stay alive, I would suggest that I am your best bet."

"And if you want a new life, I am yours. But there are things you will need to know – which I shall keep to myself until you are ready to leave, things that could give you a life of luxury wherever you land."

"Really?" said the doctor, with his best effort at disinterested scepticism.

"Really," said Habid. "One day I shall explain what the tenth person on the boat is for."

The doctor paused a beat, a stiffening not lost on Habid.

"Ah, so your cousin has not let that query go then?" he prodded, knowingly. "You tell Tassels there are parts of my process that could make him a rich man but that shall remain with me until I am persuaded that this is a partnership and I will not end up dead on the banks of the Nile."

The doctor turned to face him. "Ok," he said, nodding.

Something about his acceptance gave Habid confidence they were on equal terms.

"We must ensure the next boat gets collected. Where is Big Suit?"

The doctor snorted. He'd grown accustomed to Habid's descriptions of his interrogators. "Somewhere between Suez and the ferry port, halfway across the desert."

Habid was silent for a moment. Priorities, he thought. Number one, keep the boats coming. Number two, get well enough to get out of bed. Number three, get released.

"Right, doctor, you can give him the next instalment."

"It had better interest him. His ability to concentrate is somewhat limited," the doctor mused as he tapped the fluids and checked the syringe driver, pretending not to be curious.

"Explain that you have got more from me, about the route and method I use, and that I have been given drugs in return."

"Ok ..."

"Tell Tassels that the people I smuggle from Libya have wealth beyond his wildest imagination."

"He already knows that – you told him during your interrogation.

"But he does not know how I get their money."

"How do you get the money? You hardly transfer it back to Tripoli?"

"I never do anything through Tripoli or Libya. Only a madman would bank in an Arab country in this climate."

"So how do you do it?"

"I keep bank accounts in Europe, of course."

"But how can you guarantee they will pay?"

"Ah," said Habid, "with absolute certainty. What is the one thing a wealthy person will take with them when they flee?"

"Their family?"

"Of course," said Habid. "But what *thing*?"

"Their phone?"

"Think, doctor. What would you take?"

"Cash?"

"On a boat?"

"Ok, the means to get my cash – a card or bank details."

"There you are, doc. You got there in the end."

"But why would they hand over their bank details to you before they leave? That would not make sense. They would have nothing left when they reached Europe."

"Oh, they don't hand it over before they leave, just a deposit," said Habid, his lips snarling. "That's what the tenth person is for."

Three hours before darkness fell, Sam began to narrow the distance between the shore and the boat. He aimed to shave almost twenty miles off the gap, leaving the family just one hour, at full speed, to get ashore. The little RIB was fast if the man could keep it in a straight line. Sam cursed the thoughts that passed through his head as he readied the kit. Not giving them life jackets, for example. His instinct told him that any rescuer or investigator would look at the decent gear they had on and conclude that they had come from a yacht run by people who knew what they were doing. The safety clothing Sam had was in stark contrast to the safety procedures adopted by the people who had helped the family set to sea in the first place. They'd been cast off with an old deflated rag of a yoke, probably robbed from the abandoned fuselage of a plane in repose in some African desert scrapyard.

Yet Sam wouldn't abandon the child – he couldn't. There was something quite lovely about her, about the friendship she and his daughter had forged. There was a gentleness, a caring in her, that Sam admired. Little wonder they had become pals. Sam may not care for her father, but the child probably did.

The boat slid through the night, fetching on her fastest point of sail. Sam's anticipation built as he neared his goal, his excitement tempered by the impact achieving it would have upon Isla. The chart plotter's estimated time of arrival at the waypoint he'd set ticked down fast, and he eventually shifted to make the final preparations.

He piled three expensive life jackets on top of one another and added water to the repository. He checked the little rigid inflatable, pumped air into the sponsons making sure they were rock hard. Eventually, he lowered the boat into the water, hove the yacht to, and turned to face the music.

Placing his hands on either side of the companionway he pressed his head into the saloon and said, "It's time."

The man looked at the woman who said something to the child who immediately began to sob. Groundwork had evidently been laid.

"What's happening?" asked Isla, alarmed.

"They've got to go, wee darlin'. They're going to safety, ashore, where they'll be looked after."

"No, Daddy, they can't." The distress rose in her voice. "They can't go in the sea again."

"They're taking the RIB, wee love, our dinghy. They'll be fine. I showed the man how to use it."

Isla looked at him, distraught and shocked but unsure what to say or do. The family stood, and the woman smoothed her filthy outfit and breathed a deep fill of preparation. Then Sam's heart nearly broke as the little arms of the two children reached out and hugged like they'd known one another all their lives. There's something particularly endearing, thought Sam, about watching kids behave the way they've seen adults do when they're touched by real affection. Both girls were crying now, not dramatically or petulantly but with resign, regret and deep sadness. On some level one knew the other was being dispatched into danger and was helpless to prevent it. Those wee arms, little hands. That hug nearly made Sam change his mind all over again. And then the man stepped in, offering Sam his limp hand, presumably in thanks. Sam took it, astonished by its lack of vigour, and then they swept on deck in a flutter of black cloth and urgency.

Sam fastened the kid into the life jacket, her mother watching intently and then copying. The man left his unzipped – Sam couldn't have cared less. He hardly noticed their clambering over the stern as Isla was gulping her sadness in heaves of tears, and Sam wrapped her up and felt his shirt soak as her anguish poured out. What am I doing? he thought, his daughter's distress almost too much to take. And then, to his amazement, he heard the engine start. The man had managed to get it going without assistance. He lifted Isla onto his shoulders to see them off, stooping and straining his stitches to untie the painter. And then the three black souls set off, the man at the centre console incredibly having managed to work the throttle. Sam turned to face the light and gestured his palm at their destination. Not a nod, not another look and they were gone as the man pressed forward the lever and the boat rose by the bow before eventually settling back down onto the plane. Glad as he was to see them depart, Sam was slightly bewildered at the speed of it all.

"He's driving that boat alright," he muttered.

Isla's wet face peeled from his neck to look after the wake of the boat as it tore into the distance.

"Go way," he said, as if against the odds the man had come up trumps. "He'll look after them, wee love, just like I look after you."

"What do you mean?" she said.

"Well, do you not think I look after you?" he asked, hurt.

"Yes, but what do you mean he will look after them?"

"Well, he's her daddy," Sam said, "and daddies look after their little girls."

What she said next changed everything.

Tassels stared at his cousin. "What did he mean?"

"I don't know," said the doctor. "That's all he said before he lapsed into sleep. Not surprising given the drugs swimming round his system."

"He's playing you," said Tassels. "He's just playing for time to get better, stronger. You need to lean on him harder."

"I think he's telling the truth. I think he's starting to trust me."

Tassels spat in contempt. "I don't even trust you."

"People do in situations like this. It's Stockholm syndrome – anyone who shows kindness in a time of great stress is often treated as a friend. The bar has been lowered so far that even a person the victim would normally hate becomes a valuable comrade."

"Do you think I am not familiar with the process?" said Tassels. "It's just good cop, bad cop."

"Except you prefer the bad cop, worse cop routine. And look where that got you," the doctor said, bristling at not being trusted even by a tramp like his cousin.

Tassels gloried in the jibe. "I want to know what he's talking about – how he get their bank details, and what is this tenth person all about?"

"It will be a while before he wakes but before he does there are things you haven't thought through, obviously."

"Like what?" Tassels rounded, offended.

"Like how you can possibly take over this operation. You can't very well tramp into Libya, find these wealthy ex-oligarchs and turn them into exiles, can you? You're going to need the rat for that."

"Ex-oligarchs?" Tassels' interest piqued.

"So he says."

"So they really are filthy rich?"

"According to him."

"Like those super-rich Russians?"

"Who knows, probably. Same resources – oil, energy – possibly. So how are you going to get that sort of clientele?" The doctor gently kneaded his cousin that he might rise later.

Tassels was thinking. "You leave the planning to me, medicine man. You just get the information and I'll decide what to do with it," he said, but he knew his cousin was right. He had no idea how he could get his hands on the money without the rat.

11

"That's not her daddy," Isla said with confidence – and confusion.

"Course he is," Sam replied.

Isla wasn't for arguing but she was convinced. "He's not."

"How do you know?" He was curious as to her reasoning rather than persuaded by her conviction.

"He's not nice to her," she said.

Sam considered for a moment and decided a little cultural education would do no harm.

"Just because a man has rules for his family doesn't mean he isn't being nice," he began, looking into the dismissive countenance of his daughter. "People from different countries have different rules, wee love. Like, where these people are from, sometimes the women walk behind the men. It's like, their ... way." Sam realised he was struggling to understand this let alone explain it to a six-year-old.

"I *know* that," she said. "Some women have to cover their faces except when they're at home. Girls don't have to – just adults. That's not what I'm talking about."

Sam gazed at his daughter wondering where she picked up

such things. She'd had very little contact with other people in months. Aside from the iPad, his brutal mug was about all the company she'd enjoyed.

"How do you know all that?" he asked.

Isla just shrugged.

"What really makes you think he's not her daddy?"

"Because she told me."

Waleed had often opened his rations tins with a pair of pliers. It made an awful mess – shards of metal, twisted, nicked, cut and torn apart, the uneven openings oozing the contents all over the place. That exact imagery came to his mind as he gazed at the stationary bus during rush hour in a sleepy Sinai city.

Arish: coastal, cosmopolitan, confused, dangerous. In any other environment it would have been a resort for the rich and famous, but it was close to Gaza – host to skirmishes, ripe for mad militants.

Sitting with his face to the sun was an older man who must have dozed off on his way to work. He looked peaceful, his feet outstretched beneath the seat in front, his belly clasped by the intertwined fingers of both hands through which his intestines were currently leaking. The press had turned up and were snapping furiously, arguing and jostling for position, as dust-suited men with blue gloves lifted fragments of flesh from the tarmac and surrounding shrubbery. Nobody on the bus had survived. Many had died from glass or metal shrapnel from the vehicle itself, others from whatever the beards had packed into the teenager's death vest. And the old man, probably not far from retirement, had known nothing about it. Waleed took a little comfort from the thought that he'd died in his sleep and not known the horror of the blast or the indignity of being turned inside out as the world gazed at his breakfast oozing between his fingers.

Of course it meant nothing but trouble for Waleed. Bollockings from Cairo, lectures on the importance of the tourism industry and the need to prevent such attacks. Lessons screamed down the line about how twitchy the Israelis were getting, how he'd failed to get on top of the insurgents. He'd heard it all before. He would be stuck in Arish for weeks now as his investigators tried to identify the dead by literally piecing together the parts of the bomber's story. All a waste of time, in Waleed's view. They knew it had been a teenage girl. Probably some poor, misguided volunteer or someone Islamic State had picked up on its travels who had opted for suicide over endless gang rape. Waleed would learn little from her, assuming they could jigsaw her body and background back together.

Yet this was his station, and it meant that his fat former friend had to remain confined to barracks back at Waleed's desert base where he'd be fed, but probably not well enough to maintain his girth. Waleed called his custody officer and ordered the prisoner be kept in isolation, that no record be made of his detention and no information offered should anyone come asking. That was one of the benefits of his unit – it outranked everyone else when it came to sharing or withholding information. Right now Waleed had bigger problems to deal with whether Big Suit knew his secret or not.

Sam tried hard to compute what his little girl had just told him.

"But they don't speak our language."

"Yes, they do," she said matter-of-factly.

"Did you hear them?" Sam struggled to understand how he could have missed what his six-year-old had picked up.

"Just Sadiqah," she said.

"Sadiqah?" Sam repeated, stunned.

"That's her name. My friend."

"Did her mammy hear her talking to you?"

"No," said Isla.

"Is the woman her mammy?" It suddenly occurred to him to ask, struggling to measure all of this in one gulp.

"Yes."

"Does her mammy speak our language?" Sam hadn't heard evidence of it but Isla was surprising him at every turn.

"I think she does but I didn't hear her speak," said Isla. "But the man knows what we are saying," she said with absolute certainty.

"How do you know?"

Infuriatingly, Isla just shrugged again.

"Listen, darlin', this is so important, how do you know he understood what we were saying?"

"After you were on the radio to the rescuers he got very cross with Sadiqah's mam, and when you went up to steer the boat he grabbed her and shaked her and said cross things to her."

"In English? In our language?"

"No, in Arabic," Isla said.

"How do you know what Arabic is?" Sam was utterly perplexed.

"I told you, Daddy, Sadiqah told me lots of things."

"Where did she tell you? This is a small boat, Isla!" It crossed his mind that the story might be a ruse to punish him for casting the family adrift. Then he felt guilty for doubting his daughter.

"She told me in my cabin when we were colouring. She's very good at colouring. I wish I was good at colouring like her." Isla's attention was shifting.

"And did her daddy hear you talking?"

"No, I told you! He's not her daddy. She whispers to me.

And she draws pictures for words she doesn't know in our language."

"Right," he said. "Right. But ... but that doesn't explain how you know he speaks our language, Isla."

"Yes, it does," she said.

"How?"

"Because he knew what you were saying to that ship that you screamed bad words at on the radio, and it made him cross until the ship went away. I was watching him," she said.

Sam found all this hard to argue with despite knowing he'd been hoodwinked where his six-year-old hadn't.

She was still a little cross with him and felt justified in hammering home the point. "That's how he knows how to drive the boat. He understood you the whole time."

Sam thought for a moment. "Why didn't you tell me he could speak our language?"

"I thought you knew," she shrugged. "You kept talking to him in our language."

The flaws were hard to find. "So who is he if he's not her daddy? Is he the woman's husband?"

"No. Sadiqah never met him before."

"Before what?"

"Before they went into the boat, in the sea."

"The woman didn't know him at all?"

"No."

"Shit."

"Daddy!"

"We've got to get them back, Isla."

Tassels paced, trying for the fourth time to call Big Suit. There was a connection every time, so he wasn't out of range, but there was no answer.

The doctor watched his cousin march back and forth down the dusty corridor and imagined a plan of his own. "Has he vanished?" he asked.

"He can't vanish," said Tassels wearily. "I'll order a trace."

The cop picked up a landline extension and barked orders at some tech, reading the rat's number from his own screen.

The doctor pressed the advantage that was forming in his mind. "What if he misses the pickup? Will you be able to get another boat?"

"Probably," said Tassels, but he didn't understand enough about what was involved.

"So you could miss the next trip and the income from it?" said the doctor, with no small measure of concealed self-interest.

"Not if you do your job and find out what exactly the delivery process for the boat and engine is. Why don't you just concentrate on that and we can move on from there." Tassels gestured to the door.

The doctor was happy to take his leave. He had an experiment to conduct on a rat.

The wind backed and eased through the night, making the going painfully slow. Sam was forced to tack back and forth to get ashore. When eventually they made land he discovered that the harbour didn't shield a marina after all, but the quay Sam tied up at was as robust as it was jammed. All sorts of fishing boats were laced to the eyes on the concrete walkway, yet the whole village looked redundant. It didn't make sense to Sam. From the sea it could be a potential paradise – ocean-facing, great climate, the fishing presumably plentiful and the views stunning. Why then, he thought, did the place feel so tired?

He'd kept an eye out for their small tender all the way to the quay, the rigid inflatable on which Sadiqah, her mother and the man had raced ashore. Isla had stood above the spray hood with the binoculars. Her little neck had strained with the weight, and Sam had watched and admired her determination as she periodically rested her arms and allowed the heavy glasses to swing on the lanyard around her neck. To her disappointment she'd spotted nothing, nor had Sam.

He made the boat fast and then reached up a mighty forearm to swing his little girl off the deck and onto the harbour. It was the first time their feet had hit dry land in almost two months and he was craving real milk for her. First things first, though, he thought, as they made their way to a little boatyard where a modern travel hoist stood, like everything else, motionless. It crossed Sam's mind that there may have been some sort of nuclear evacuation, such was the silence and apparent abandonment of the place. Granted, it was only six twenty in the morning, but he'd never been in a fishing port where there was zero movement at such an hour.

There was a host of perfectly serviceable sailing and motorboats in the yard, as well as some that had suffered neglect. After a thorough hammering on an office door, a bulky, unshaven Italian emerged.

"*Ciao,*" Sam started, referring to his phone and Google for translation, using up valuable data, and hoping to give a reasonable account of himself.

"*Che cazzo vuoi?*" growled the man, which Sam took to be impatient at best.

Sam typed 'can you help', waited and then began. "*Potete aiutarci?*"

The man shrugged.

"*Battello,*" Sam tried, miming a lifting motion as if he had a television under each arm.

"You look like a monkey, Daddy," Isla remarked helpfully.

Sam chose to point at the travel hoist, in which a small boat was already hung, like everything else, motionless.

"*Si*," said the man, becoming more accommodating, no doubt at the prospect of receiving some euros. "*Inglesi?*"

"No," said Sam. "*Irlandese.*"

"Ok," said the Italian. "What boat?"

Sam beckoned him over and the man, seemingly oblivious to the nails and metal shavings on the ground, strode out into the yard in his bare feet and shorts. Sam pointed at *Sian*.

"Big boat," said the man. "How heavy?"

"Sixteen tonnes," Sam replied. "Fifty-four foot."

"When?"

He was a man of few words. Sam quite liked him.

"Now?" he ventured.

The man laughed.

"Two hundred euro," the man said, which was heavy but Sam had no option.

"Can you do it now?"

The man nodded slowly. "Why?"

"Rope. Around the propeller shaft."

"Ok," said the man, understanding.

Sailing her into the harbour under jib had been manageable in the calm conditions behind a breakwater but Sam didn't want to be without an engine for long.

"I tow you over. First drop this boat in sea."

Sam shook his head. "I can sail her in."

The man looked at him as if he needed his head felt, then shrugged. "You damage crane, you pay."

Sam nodded.

"Money now, please."

Sam dipped in his pocket and extracted a fold of notes. He peeled off four fifties.

The man nodded and he and Isla set off back to the boat.

Isla stayed on the quay and began to unwind the warps while Sam unfurled the small genoa with one of the jib sheets.

"Ready?" he called to her.

"Ready," she replied, and he flicked the sheet around a winch and backed the jib, spinning the wheel against the force to bring the boat directly astern. Then he skipped onto the side deck and held out his shovel of a paw for Isla to grab and whisked her aboard.

"Good job, wee love," he said, and returned to the wheel.

Behind him he could hear the grunt of a diesel engine fire up and the grinding of steel wire as the barefoot man lowered the smaller boat back into the Mediterranean. Sam cleared the neighbouring fishing boats, then allowed *Sian* to come around into the gentle breeze as Isla readied the winch on the other side to gybe. She handed him the tail of the rope and as they passed through the eye of the breeze he drew it in armfuls and filled the sail on the new side.

"Tell me when the wee boat's gone, Isla."

"Not yet," she called back from the foredeck. "I've got the bowline ready, Daddy."

Sam furled the headsail again, allowing the way on the hull to propel her towards the dock.

"She's gone, Daddy!" called Isla, but Sam could see that himself. He liked to give her jobs to keep her involved and invested. It helped her learn.

"Where's the man?"

"He's leaning out of the crane. He looks worried."

I bet he does, thought Sam. If he got it wrong, the top of the travel hoist would be a write-off, as would their own mast. But then, Sam did enjoy a challenge no matter how trivial.

In the event the boat slid in gently and perfectly, and Isla threw the rope to the man as accurately as any deckhand might. The man shook his head in admiration at the little woman, then skipped around the wheel of the hoist to take a warp from

Sam. Within minutes they were dangling out of the water being driven towards the hard-standing area. The man stopped the crane, found a rickety ladder and rattled it up against the hull. Sam and Isla climbed down and inspected the mess of the shaft. The man stood beside them shaking his head, fashioning an opportunity.

"You want me to fix?" he asked.

"No," said Sam, producing the sharp knife from the life raft. "But if you can power-wash the hull, I will pay for that." He scraped at the weed growth, like a damp, soft beard, and chipped a barnacle or two with the blade.

"Hundred euro," said the man.

"Fifty," said Sam.

"Eighty," said the man.

"Sixty," chirped Isla, and the man laughed. The child had it.

The barefoot Italian strolled off and Sam hacked at the bound rope for ten minutes until it fell free of the shaft and skeg, before climbing the ladder to replace the knife. Then he and Isla strolled off as if they hadn't a care in the world, despite having a woman and her kid to rescue from a man who, for all Sam knew, had done away with them before they even reached the shore.

Habid's eyes flicked open the moment the door latch was fingered. He was able to push himself a little more upright. Lying back made him feel vulnerable and given the propensity for violence in the police station, he was reluctant to place himself at even more of a disadvantage.

"Doctor," he muttered with some relief.

"Habid," said the doctor, urgency in his voice. He crouched beside the rat as if tinkering with the meds and whispered keeping his back to the door and its inspection flap. "Big Suit, as you call him, has disappeared. He's not answering calls."

"What does Tassels think has happened?"

"He doesn't know."

"Do you think Big Suit has deserted – gone AWOL?"

"I don't know."

"Maybe he thinks he killed me."

"That would not bother him," said the doctor. "They probably kill people all the time."

"What then?"

"He may have crashed. He was very weak. He should not have been sent on a long journey – or any journey. We took a lot of blood from him."

Habid ticked through his options.

"We must get the boat. It is true what I said – the supply chain will close down if we do not collect."

"When is the next journey?" asked the doctor.

"It does not work like that," said Habid, "but the boat must be retrieved regardless."

"You are almost able to get out of bed but you cannot expect to drive or travel yet."

"I have no intention of either," said Habid.

"Well, I can assure you I am not going to Sinai," said the doctor.

"No," said Habid. "You are staying to care for me. To keep me alive. You must tell Tassels I have deteriorated and that if he wants a piece of my business, he must go and get the boat himself."

"He will not do that."

"Then he must find someone who will – and tell him that will come out of his cut."

"He won't like that."

"It is a choice. Simple. Either he is greedy enough to go or he takes a risk and brings in another person. I know what I would do."

"How much further?"

Isla was complaining. To be fair to her, for all the exercise she got through sailing the boat, walking wasn't something she'd been used to for weeks.

"Don't know, darlin'," Sam said.

"Well, check your phone," she suggested, exasperated.

"I'm trying to save data, Isla, so that you can watch films and *Scooby-Doo*. Just keep an eye out."

"We'll never find them," she said.

Isla was still cross he'd let them go in the first place. Sam could understand that, but he wasn't about to concede.

"Just keep your eyes peeled. We won't find them if we give up before we've even started. What do we say?"

Isla huffed and puffed like a teenager but said what he wanted regardless. "We never roll over, never, never, never."

"Never, never, never," Sam repeated.

It was important to him that she believed that. It had got him through so many tight spots. No matter how many times his life expectancy appeared to have expired, he had muttered that simple phrase, taken something from it and fought his way out. No matter how tight the corner, how stacked the odds, it had served him, and it would serve his daughter too.

"There's Mary," he heard her say, drawing him from his drift.

He looked up to see a shrine, right there by the sea. He wondered how three Muslims walking around the area might be greeted, given that one of them was a man dressed as a woman.

"People here must be Catholic," Isla said, but Sam didn't have the energy to inquire how she knew the difference.

He had spent considerable time avoiding any talk of denominations or differing religious beliefs. He had told her that God was God and loved everyone and had left it at that. Religion had played an enormous role in Sam's life, the wars he had fought, the operations he had been sent on, the surveillance jobs he had carried out. All of them had some genesis in opposing views on faith. He was happy to believe what he believed and not get involved beyond that. Shannon had modified that slightly when she'd been around. She had faith beyond his own, a belief that drove her every day. Not that she went to church much, or lit candles or believed in what some black-clad pontificator preached. But she had an inner peace and an absolute sense of what was right and wrong, and there was never any hope of persuading her otherwise. It was hard to be around someone like that without some of it rubbing off.

They covered four miles before Sam was persuaded that they had turned the wrong way. The terrain was getting flatter, the roads smoother, the buildings better tended. The area grew more in keeping with what he expected from a coastal Mediter-ranean town: commoditisation of the spectacular scenery, restaurants, shops, stuff to be sold. That's why he felt sure three Muslims would have avoided it. Too many folk, too many ques-tions, too many people in positions of authority. That's what Sam would have done anyway. His rule of thumb when arriving somewhere unannounced was to keep as low a profile as possible and move around only at night.

"Darlin', I'm sorry. We've come the wrong way. We're going to have to walk back."

"Oh-wuh, I told you to use your phone," she said.

"Isla, quit giving out. You want to find them, don't you?"

"Yes."

"Then give over and come on."

"Use your phone map," she insisted, the stubborn little tyke.

Sam made a rigmarole of producing the phone and switching on the data. He then lectured her on how she couldn't complain in days to come that she was fed up with the old TV shows downloaded on her tablet.

"Ok," she said and, as usual, she was right. As soon as Sam consulted the map, he knew where they would be.

Big Suit was starving. He began to kick the door of his room. It wasn't a cell – Big Suit doubted they had one – but it was basic: dirt floor, block walls with reclaimed windows at a height well above his head. The roof was flat but there were no air gaps. Attention during construction mostly appeared to have gone into the placing of a steel cross member that spanned the block walls. Red paint had flecked and fallen from a foot-long section in the middle. Big Suit knew what that meant: it had been used to tie something – or someone – up. It was above head height, so the pain endured by its victims must have been considerable. Big Suit had no intention of trying out the attraction, and if it came to it during interrogation, he would sing – it was the least painful journey. Not that he knew a great deal. Emptying his mind of information wouldn't take long.

He heard a faint sound and pressed forward to listen. A doorbell. A doorbell he'd heard before. Back at the station. The rat's phone – he'd heard it when his boss had tested the number. It was dinging quietly away in whatever room lay beyond the door. They must have charged it, he thought. At least someone is looking for me, he thought, and imagined his boss and the toxic atmosphere at the station. Big Suit grinned. There was hope. He leaned against the wall rubbing his back against the concrete blocks in a shuffling scratch as cattle might at a standing stone. He had barely quelled his sweat-induced itch when the sound came again, broadening his smile. He crouched against the wall by the doorframe willing the phone to ring again. His immediate concern wasn't torture, but dinner. He wanted food and water.

Eventually the chime restarted and was followed by impatient footsteps. The sound of the phone momentarily grew louder and was then cut-off. Big Suit strained to hear what was happening. There was silence for a moment and then a man's voice.

"Sir, the prisoner from the highway? That other phone he had, it keeps ringing."

There was a pause that Waleed was presumably filling on the other end of the phone call.

"Possibly, it was left just feet from the interrogation suite."

Big Suit worked out that Waleed wasn't in the barracks. He longed to hear what was being said at the other end of the connection.

"I was wondering whether I should switch it off?" There was a pause and then, "Nuweiba, sir? Ok, I could send it with a patrol headed east, but do I leave it switched on?"

After receiving a curt answer to that question, the conversation was finished. Waleed was evidently busy, or very firmly the boss. Or both. Big Suit listened with a plummeting resignation as the guard, or whoever he was, passed his frustration down the chain of command.

"Get a patrol together. They're going east, probably some distance. And tell the driver to come to me before they leave. I have something they've got to take with them."

From the road the roof of the building reminded Sam of a skateboard track – all swoops and jumps, or a Viking longboat designed to bend and roll with the waves. He and Isla looked down at it from a height as it faced the ocean, Egypt and Libya. Sam couldn't say what had brought him here but he knew he was right. If the woman and child weren't close by, they'd been here. Such notions seldom took him, but on the occasions they presented he had learned to trust them.

"What is that?"

"See that sign?"

"Uh-huh."

"What do you think that is?"

"A house with a big chimbly."

"Chimney."

"A house with a big chimney."

"No, it's not, it's a church." Sam began to wish he hadn't got all educational and had just answered Isla in the first place. "*Chiesa*," he read. "I think that means church. *Madonna di Eleusa*, that's what the sign says."

"What does that mean?"

"Dunno, darlin', but *Madonna* is Mary."

"Madonna is a singer," Isla said.

"How do you know that?"

"Mammy."

Sam smiled at the thought of Shannon's endless playlists and her dancing round the kitchen with their daughter. He packed in the explanation. "I think they were here."

"Why?" said Isla, suddenly interested.

"I'm not sure. I think it may be lit up at night – the cross I mean. The picture shows a cross at the front facing the sea. I think the man might have aimed the boat at the light. He probably got the lights mixed up."

"Good thinking, Daddy-o," said Isla in an American accent robbed straight out of *Scooby-Doo*.

"The church kind of faces Libya, where they maybe came from."

"They came from Egypt," Isla chirped.

Sam rounded on her. "Is that true, Isla? I need you to tell me the truth now, how do you know they came from Egypt?"

Isla reeled back a little, startled at her father's intensity. "Sadiqah," was all she said.

"She definitely said Egypt, not Libya?"

"She did say Libya," said Isla, getting confused. "Libya and Egypt."

Sam realised he'd startled her and crouched to give her a hug. "I'm sorry, wee love, I got excited. I just need you to tell me everything Sadiqah said to you, ok?"

"Now?"

"No. Now we've got to break into this church."

"Daddy!" she hissed in a stage whisper. "You're not allowed to break into a church – that's where holy God lives."

"Isla, you're not allowed to break into anything, never mind a church, but we have people to rescue from that man, so it's justified."

"Justified?"

"It's just … it's allowed, that's all."

"Doesn't look like a church," she said, staring down at the funky roof.

"No," said Sam, distractedly. He gripped the galvanised gate and hauled up and rolled over it, landing on his feet. He put an arm through the bars and hoisted Isla as high as he could, allowing her to grab the top, then he caught her on the other side.

"The police are going to get us," she said.

"No, they won't," he replied.

"Yes, they will," she said, and pointed. "Look, Daddy."

***

"He won't go," said the doctor, fresh from a screaming match.

"Then my supplier will terminate the arrangement – no more boats."

"There must be another way."

"It took months to set up. Months. There are people in Libya waiting to be collected. If we do not move soon, someone else will move in. End of business."

"He wants to know how you normally get the boats from Nuweiba and why we cannot use that supply chain."

"Because the person who saw to that left on the last journey."

"So how did you plan to get it?"

"I was going myself but I can't do that now, can I? Tell him that. Tell him if he hadn't cut my fucking toe off, he might have been able to sit on his ass and count his money. But now he will have to work for it, and it is his own fault!"

The doctor didn't need to relay the message. Tassels could hear it being screamed from his office.

There had been an accident. That much was plain. Sam turned to see the tail end of a dark blue car with a red stripe and writing up the side. As they walked down the slope he realised that, as usual, Isla had been quite right. There was rack of strobe lights on its roof. Aside from the carabinieri, which Sam vaguely recollected as being part military, part police, a coast-guard van came into view and his heart plummeted. Had he sent the woman and child to their deaths? He half crouched to speak to Isla.

"You're going to have to stay outside until I see what's happening."

"Has there been an emergency?" Her face was shaken with alarm.

"Well, there's no ambulance, so that's good," he said, which truthfully could be good or bad – ambulances didn't come for dead bodies. But if they were already dead and laid out in the church, he didn't want Isla seeing them. "You sit on that bench and I'll be out in a minute."

Sam placed his hand on the door handle under the sheltered pointed alcove, its prow aimed towards the sea and Africa. He lowered his head, said a prayer and pushed inside.

Nautical, he thought, as his gaze rose to the beams in the roof. It's a boat, a church boat. Made sense. How many from this fishing village had died at sea? It seemed as much a memorial as a place of worship; like the dozens of monuments scattered around the harbours of Ireland, names etched against the brutal winds, indelible carvings that only the weather could take, just as it had taken the humans who owned them.

Just short of the altar a woman sat wrapped in a foil blanket, glistening like a Christmas decoration. Sam's heart leapt a pace but he didn't recognise her, and he was grateful for it. She was being admonished by a man in a blue coastguard vest, her head dipped, enduring it. Sam muttered his thanks and turned to leave when he heard another voice, a tiny one, call out. He froze.

"Daddy?"

It wasn't Isla but he knew in an instant who said it and why. He turned to see Sadiqah sit up from a pew. She too was wrapped in foil, her hair like a bonfire, stiff with salt and all over the place. The woman's head lifted immediately and she began to sob. Everything became clear.

The coastguard turned and called out to two carabinieri who made towards Sam. He knew he was about to be arrested, that he'd allowed himself and Isla to be compromised, and that Sadiqah knew him only as *daddy*. He knew too that the woman whose face he had just seen for the first time had been his companion at sea for days, that she had clawed him to save her child, that she had been silent for some dreadful reason. And he could see for the first time her vulnerability, her fear and her beauty now that she'd been stripped of her niqab.

Tassels hadn't been in good humour, even before his cousin arrived.

"Well, did he say where the boats come from?"

"China. The network is intricate, hence why the rat says it took six months to set up. The boats are made in some far-flung province, transported to a port, hidden in containers and offloaded in Nuweiba away from the authorities. Then they are loaded onto a lorry and concealed. They travel west, taxes to pay, bribes. But he was clear about this – if one boat goes missing or is not collected, the deal ends."

"Well, we will pick up the boat, won't we?"

"I thought ... your colleague had gone missing?" the doctor almost referred to him as Big Suit.

"He'll show up."

"He'd better show up soon. The rat says the boat will be ready for collection. And if it is not collected—"

"Has it been paid for?"

"No," said the doctor, who had no idea whether it had or not. "Did you not give your colleague any money?"

Tassels ignored his cousin's question but the answer seemed obvious.

The doc pressed his advantage. "And is he driving a lorry or even a van? The rat says the boat won't fit in a car."

Tassels' head fell forward between his shoulder blades, his hands gripping his filthy desk. Eventually he sat. "He can get one when he gets to Nuweiba. He can hire one."

"So he has money?"

Tassels rounded on his cousin. "Look, just get all the information you can from that rat. You leave the details to me!"

The doc was dismissed. It had gone better than he could have hoped for.

―――――――――

Two police officers grappled Sam who had decided against flight. Isla was outside and he wouldn't leave her, but he cursed himself.

"I've got a child outside," he shouted as they tried to wrestle him to the ground, finding him much more solid than expected. "I'll be calm if you agree to bring her in here and look after her."

"English," said the coastguard to the officers.

"Irish, *Irelandese*, European," stated Sam as he allowed the men to slip a cable tie around his wrists. If necessary, he could twist and snap his way out in a matter of seconds.

"Ireland?" queried the coastguard.

"Yes, Irish," he shouted. "We rescued them."

The coastguard evidently had some English because he nodded sagely as if he knew what was really going on. "Yes, yes," he said. "And how much did she pay you?"

"Bring my daughter in. She's outside the door on her own. Bring her in and I will explain everything."

The coastguard said something to the police, who didn't appear to like the idea of taking direction from a coastguard. Whatever was said, it was the coastguard who walked warily to the church door and opened it, apparently cautious that he might be on the cusp of attack. There was a dreadful pause during which Sam struggled to turn to face the door but for no good reason was prevented from doing so by the police. He could hear the door close as a muffled, softer conversation was had. Eventually the door creaked open again and Sam breathed in.

"Daddy!" she called and pattered up behind him before

confusion set in. "Hey, let go of my daddy!" she shouted, and to Sam's astonishment she kicked out at one of the policemen, nipping him right on the shin bone with her little brown boot.

The policeman yelped and swiped at her but got lucky and missed. If he'd connected, Sam would have finished him. He stared at the officer who felt the full weight of his mistake as Sam's body tensed to the point of detonation.

"Isla, calm down, wee love. It's a mistake. They don't understand what has happened," he said as he held the cop's gaze.

"It is certain we understand," said the coastguard. "You are not first man to bring people from Africa."

"I brought them here for safety, not money" Sam said.

"Yes, yes, well, we have you now and you will be processed and so will these people. They will be sent home eventually." The coastguard seemed to know everything.

Sam looked at the policemen on either side of him. "And what are you two going to do? Are you going to jail me for helping someone?"

The two carabinieri were young, probably far from home and placed in the heart of Mafia land with no idea what to expect. They didn't appear to understand a word Sam was saying. The coastguard began an exchange with them, nodding knowingly before reverting to Sam.

"They will take you to the police station and then they will process the foreigners." He nodded at the woman and Sadiqah who were now huddled together just short of the altar.

Sam stared at them. "I know you can speak English." He directed his call to the woman. "I know she's your daughter and that man wasn't your husband. Isla told me. I know she is Sadiqah. Now, for the love of God, will you tell these men I am not a trafficker? Tell them what happened!"

She stared at him for a second and then, as a rooster crowed for the first time, he heard her speak.

"I never seeing this man before," she said.

12

The driver stared at the phone as it blinked its displeasure. It also offered a loud beep warning the three men in the cab that if it didn't receive some nourishment soon, it would shutdown.

"Have any of you got a charging cable for that thing?" the driver inquired. He knew he was on the hook to see through this curious command.

The two soldiers to his left shook their heads. Of course they didn't.

Twenty minutes later they were treated to another bleep and forty minutes into the journey the phone gave an exhausted I-told-you-so string of bleeps as it settled into deep sleep.

In Cairo a police tech dialled another mobile phone and in Alexandria Tassels answered at a snatch.

"Where is it?"

"It was stationary for a long while, then it was on the move for about fifty miles and now it is dark."

"What do you mean *dark*?"

"Well, it was in the middle of Sinai, which doesn't have

many phone masts for triangulation, so it could be out of range – maybe it went off the highway."

"He would not have left the highway," said Tassels, who in truth had no idea whether his colleague, with all his intellectual challenges, might have left the highway.

"The phone could just be flat?" said the tech.

"He has a charger in his car," said Tassels. "I've seen it."

"Hmm ..." the tech gave a doubtful grumble. "I can see you tried to call this number several times and he did not answer."

Tassels began to experience a mild sensation of panic. *Traceability*. He should never have involved the tech unit. They now know he was aware that his sidekick was in Sinai. If the big idiot was executed by extremists with that phone in his pocket, he would have a lot of questions to answer. He hung up his own phone without another word. Tassels closed his eyes at his own stupidity. He had to work things out, but one thought did occur to him: if you want a job done right, do it yourself.

The coastguard looked confused, Sam's mouth fell open, Isla was left speechless. The carabinieri to Sam's left tried to seize control but it was clear that everyone in a position of authority was unsure as to who was most senior.

The coastguard translated for the cop. "Migrants must go to detention centre. We find someone to take this child."

"Well," said Sam, a dreadful but familiar calm descending upon him, "that's not going to happen, chaps."

Isla instinctively stepped back and the coastguard made the mistake of grabbing her. The policemen holding Sam's arms were forced together as Sam lunged from their relaxed grip. They were too slow to react and the coastguard's face exploded. Sam withdrew his forehead, Isla moved swiftly away and the injured man fell back into one of the pews. He wasn't unconscious, but he wasn't about to get up either.

The renewed tugging on Sam's arms made it easier to release himself. He'd already twisted his hands in the cable tie giving the necessary leverage to open his wrists and snap the plastic shackle. The power in his shoulders was incredible – muscle memory from lugging GPMGs for dozens of miles, thousands of chin-ups and carrying a bergen for half his adult life. His strength had been topped up by winching and sanding and working above his head. The two young cops didn't stand a chance.

"Isla, turn away!" he shouted as he went to work on the two carabinieri.

They went down easily with only one broken arm and a possible snapped collarbone. Sam meant them no ill will – they were just doing their job. He tucked them up in their own cable ties, double wrapped, wrists and feet. Nicely packaged. The coastguard was out of his depth and scared. He too was trussed up, his radio removed and treated to a hefty boot in the chest for having reached at Isla.

And then there was a problem: what next? Sam fell to his knees and put his arms around Isla who was strangely completely calm.

"You've got blood on your head, Daddy," she said.

"I know."

"Don't get it on my t-shirt."

He laughed. "I won't, darlin'." In the moment he found it helpful but disturbing that she hadn't seemed fazed by the violence.

Sam then turned to the ungrateful bloody woman who had so easily forsaken him.

Habid watched the doctor's deviousness flourish with every visit. It gave him pleasure to see the doc's confidence build because it created opportunity: a cocky customer is ripe for the plucking.

"He is screwed," said the doctor, "the interrogator—"

"The butcher," corrected Habid.

"Big Suit," settled the doctor, "is still missing and Tassels does not know what to do. He's driving a car, far as I can tell, with no real cash on him, so my cousin is starting to doubt whether he will be able to pick up the boat or pay for it if he ever does turn up."

"Good," said Habid. "So Tassels thinks he needs another plan if he is to get in on the next trip to sea?"

"Indeed."

"When the time comes, tell him Nuweiba. That's where he can get the boat. At the ferry port."

"OK," said the doctor.

"And what about you?" probed Habid. "Are you ready for the next trip to sea?"

"As a passenger?"

"As a passenger," confirmed Habid.

"I think I am," said the doctor.

"Have you the money?"

The doctor faltered. "Money? You have the cheek to ask me for money after saving you and preparing the ground for you to be released?" he hissed, incandescent.

Habid cracked a menacing smile. "Don't worry, we have a deal, doctor. The money is not for me. It is for you when you get to the other side, to set up, to begin again, as it were."

The doctor calmed down a little. "Well, yes, I shall be fine in that regard."

"And your medical qualifications, they are in order?"

"Of course," said the doctor, knowing full well that they weren't.

"Then aboard you shall be," said Habid, affecting as eloquent a tone as he knew how, "provided you can get me out of here to make the necessary arrangements. I need to get others to join you, including your captain. It makes the trip more ... economical."

"You put a captain on board?"

"Generally a fisherman. Someone who knows the sea and boats. From Senegal. They are the best candidates – their rates are reduced slightly. They keep the process safe."

Which was true, up to a point.

"Why did you not just tell them that we'd rescued you?" Sam snarled in a barely audible hiss, livid with the woman.

She stared at him, cold. "You sent us away with *him*."

It struck Sam that of the two of them she was somehow the more angry. "I came back," he said dismissively, "as soon as I knew he wasn't your husband."

"What is difference if he *was* husband? You are seeing how he is treat-ed me."

"That's how it is where you come from."

She just stared at him, unable to speak further. He had seldom seen such rage in someone's face, the injustice of which incensed him. But he had to think, to find a way out of the immediate mess.

Sam and the police were way beyond the point of reasoning. How many of their colleagues knew where they were? What or who had brought them to the church and was that person still around? And when were these men expected back at their station? Sam had no control over so many variables – their radios or phones could be buzzing within moments, without answer. And where was Sinbad? He'd be happy to leave the woman and take the child, but they were an inseparable package. His boat was out of the water, and, in any case, it was built for endurance not speed. Any fast inflatable would be on them within minutes.

What were his advantages? Well, he reckoned, the cops had no reason to suspect that he'd arrived by boat. The coastguard's presence was an irritation but he calculated that the police would assume he was the collection agent for the migrants, not the delivery man. They were more likely, therefore, to determine that he'd arrived by car to take them to their next destination. So he thought that if he left by car, they would look inland. Only problem with that was he didn't have a car.

The disadvantages were that he'd told the coastguard he was Irish and he'd told the crane man he was Irish, and that wouldn't take long to piece together. He didn't want people crawling all over the boat. There was almost one hundred grand in notes in the bilge and he didn't want to have to explain where it had come from. He looked up again at the woman, which stirred her from thought and re-ignited the argument.

"What you know of where I come from?" she rasped in rage.

"I know husbands don't always respect their wives. That's what I thought was going on."

"What you know of how my husband treat-ed me?"

"Well, where is your husband?" asked Sam, exasperated, but even as he said it he instinctively knew the answer.

It came quietly. "His body was with me when you take us from sea."

"There are things I need to know, Habid," said the doctor, who had drawn up a seat beside his patient's makeshift bed.

"There are things you *want* to know, doctor, but that does not mean you *need* to know them."

The doctor was becoming familiar, exhausted even, with

Habid's superior tone. It was as if the rat relished his ability to hold officials at his mercy despite being mutilated and susceptible to their whim. If the doctor decided to cut the fluids or dose the rat, he would die. Infection, the doctor would call it, and nobody would really be able to counter that. Yet the rat had knowledge the doctor wanted, that Tassels needed, and which he had been prepared to take to his bloody grave with him. The doc stared at the invalid and decided he had to give him credit. The little Libyan had balls, well, one but it was big.

"So indulge me," said the doctor, adopting the florid language of his uneducated but street-smart companion.

"What do you *want* to know?"

"When I get on the boat and the Senegalese captain drives us to sea, what guarantee have I of being picked up?"

"None. No guarantee, but it is extremely likely you will be picked up," the rat paused, "one way or another."

"By an NGO, to go to Europe."

"Yes."

"What if it's someone else. The Egyptian navy might intercept us."

"Unlikely, but possible." Images of the doctor's corpse floating face down, arms flapping slowly to the rhythm of the waves filled his mind. "Some navy or customs boat could pick you up."

"And what would happen then?"

Habid saw an opportunity. "Well, you would be taken to a holding centre – maybe in Egypt, maybe in Libya. You would be detained indefinitely unless you have documents to show you are Egyptian and they see you are a doctor. If you carry your bank details, then maybe you can buy your freedom."

The doctor didn't like the sound of that but noted how the rat seemed to take energy from the suggestion as if it pleased him.

"And how many of your boats get intercepted by the authorities."

"None," lied Habid, "so far."

He had no idea what happened to the boats he'd sent to sea. His business was a work in progress refining all the time, which was why he'd altered the plan for the most recent journey – to get more bang for his buck, as the Americans might say.

"But the plan is to be picked up by a European boat?"

"Of course."

"And what do I do when I get to Europe?"

"Escape," said Habid, "as fast as you can if you have any sense. You do not want to enter the asylum system, do you?"

The doctor thought for a moment. "What is the alternative?"

"You need money and an identity. That is why I suggest you have access to money when you get there. Your cash card, your credit card, your bank details. You need to assume an identity of a doctor."

"Well, you see, therein lies a problem."

"I was waiting for this," said Habid. "You don't have your papers, do you?"

"I still have my original qualifications but any new employer will want a reference, won't they? They will want to call a hospital and confirm that I worked there. That I am reliable."

"And you are not reliable, are you, doctor?" sang Habid.

"I am a good doctor."

"Not the same thing," said Habid.

"So my question is, how do the other people you ... well, help, how do they create new lives?"

"There will be clever people looking for migrants like you. Spend a few pounds, ask around. The best way is to take a dead person's identity then move to the next country with their passport and driving licence and get the medical documents in order and begin again."

"But they will check references with the dead doctor's past employers."

"Then we will need to find you a doctor – maybe here in Egypt, maybe in Libya from my flock. A good doctor. Someone more respectable than you."

The doc thought again. "But any European employer will ask for that doctor's references and they will discover he is still in Egypt or Libya?"

Habid smiled his disturbing smile. "Not if the doctor vanished without trace. In that case the hospital will be glad to hear their missing doctor has turned up safe and well, albeit in Europe."

Sam favoured the police car – small and easier to fit into a garage or lockup, but he realised there was no choice. He had to take the coastguard van.

"Where's the boat, the one you came ashore in?" he snapped at the woman, gruff, grudging.

"Is over." She pointed at the rocks, seeming to have adopted a truce of sorts. That he didn't appear intent on leaving her to the delights of a detention centre probably helped.

Sam walked to the water's edge and stared down at his tender, banging precariously against the sharp outcrop. It was floating at least, which meant he could probably repair any damage. His calculations were done in an instant and he bounded down, stepped aboard and quickly spun off the turning bolts that secured the engine. He hoisted the outboard onto his shoulder and returned to the coastguard van laying the motor gently inside. Then he made the same trip with the fuel tank before, at the outside limit of his strength, heaving the boat onto his back. Sam stumbled and fell all the way up to the car park, but the boat slid into the van nicely.

The woman watched him, her foot jamming the door of the church allowing her to keep one eye on the captives. Sam walked in past her and wrestled the coastguard's coat and vest from him, re-securing new cable ties. The man didn't even attempt to struggle, which Sam thought pretty poor. He then helped all three men to their feet and using the tiny church as cover from anyone who happened to walk along the little road, pushed them into the back of the van.

"Isla, you're coming with me." He turned to the woman and her daughter. "You and Sadiqah stay here, in the confessional, quiet. I'll be back soon."

"You will not come back," she said.

Sam realised he was within earshot of the men and took his opportunity. "I am going to get the car, then we will make for the mainland and get off this bloody island." He stared hard at her, willing her to take on his deceit.

If she understood what he was doing, she didn't show it. "You will leaving us here," she said scornfully.

"I came here for you, didn't I?" he asked.

She appeared to have no answer to that. She just stared at him.

"Why would I do that if I wanted to just abandon you here?"

"Leave girl here," she said, motioning at Isla, "if you are true."

"There is no way I will leave her. That's just the way it is. Now, if you want to go into custody, fill your boots, love. Scream and shout and get me stopped. But if you want to get away from here, get in the fucking confessional."

"What is *confessional*?"

Sam all but dragged her inside the church, to the booth, where he flung the door open and told her to sit still and shut up. Then he marched outside, swept Isla up into the front seat and started driving up the coast. Once they were moving the men started kicking and making noise. Sam was curious as to what had suddenly got into them given that they'd been so unusually compliant up to that point, but he didn't care. The place was a ghost coast – there was nobody to hear them.

Four miles north he found a deserted beach with an apparently abandoned shack and drove the van some way onto the sand, turning it so that its inhabitants wouldn't be seen from the road. He slung open the doors and pulled out the little rigid inflatable, this time resting it on the sand and securing the outboard engine and fuel tank, which was less than a quarter full. The coastguard had what smelled like unleaded petrol in a jerrycan bungeed to the side of his van. It would have to do.

Sam lashed the men's legs to the cargo hooks in the base of the vehicle to prevent them rolling to the window or managing to get out of the van to summon help. Not that he fancied their chances of finding anyone – Sam began to wonder if the place had suffered some economic shock or nuclear leak. Perhaps it was simply evacuated outside peak season.

He and Isla trudged down the sand hauling the RIB behind them and eventually pushed it afloat. It took less than thirty minutes, full plane at over twenty knots of speed, to get back to the little coastal church, during which time Sam worked out his next few moves. The wind had shifted nicely, which helped him make up his mind.

He lashed the boat to a rock and piggybacked Isla up to the church. "Run inside and see if anyone's there. Don't say anything, just have a look, and if there is someone inside, run back out again just like you were only playing."

"Oh-kay," she said, unsure but compliant. When she came back out she was adamant. "There's nobody there."

Sam walked in and pulled the confessional door. He found the woman with Sadiqah on her knee.

"How did those men come to be here? Who called them?"

"I do not know," she said.

"Where is the man who was with you? The one I thought was your husband?"

"Is gone," she spat.

"I don't understand. How did the police know you were here?"

She shrugged.

"Where did he leave you?"

"He is driving boat to rocks. Then he take-ed what he want," she stared down at her torn clothing, "and he go."

Sam could see lace from a strap on her shoulder beneath the ragged cloth but he didn't have time to get into that.

"So what did you do?"

"We come here," she said, as if he were stupid.

"So how did the police come?"

"I do not know!" she hissed. "We are sleeping and then we are ..." she motioned her arms out as if pushing back and forth, "and they here look-ink at us."

This was as good as Sam could have hoped for.

"So they definitely don't know you came here by boat?"

"No." She shook her head confused why that might matter.

Sam was still struggling with the idea that she had been able to understand English all along never mind speak it understandably.

"Then why was the coastguard here?"

"I do not know," she said, exhausted.

"Ok," Sam said, "Isla and I are going to get the big boat. We are going to cast the small boat out to sea. It will drift off, slowly, then we will motor round from the harbour, pick up the small boat and come ashore and get you. Do you understand?"

"We can come now?"

"The big boat is out of the water on a crane getting repaired.

I can't have anyone else see you and Sadiqah. This is the safest way to get away without you being arrested."

She thought for a moment. "There is police car outside."

"Yes," said Sam.

"Someone will see," she said.

"Probably," he conceded.

"We should go."

"Then you will be seen. You look …"

"Arab. Muslim," she said for him. "Filthy immigrant."

That phrase had evidently been playing on her mind, Sam thought. She spoke with disdain, with hurt, with goading. Sam stared at her. He hadn't the energy for massaging facts.

"Get us cloth-es," she said. "Then we are look-ink norm-al."

"Just walk off and find a shop?"

"Take police car," she said. "Get it far from here."

He began to follow her drift.

Habid's sack nipped at the tuck the doctor had stitched into it. He'd been given baggy cotton trousers – a punishment for securing his continued inclusion in the racket. The fabric was of an alarmingly diaphanous quality, designed to embarrass, he suspected; Tassels' last salvo before he had departed. Well, he'd suffer for it in the long run.

The crooked cop had, as Habid had intended, headed for the desert in pursuit of his idiot subordinate. He'd ordered the *release of the rat* before he'd set off clutching a package the size of a brick – cash to purchase the boat.

Habid hobbled and yelped like a small dog abandoned. Gradually he regulated the pain, blinking the tears from his eyes. He stank. He looked foul. He craved warm water and privacy to lick his wounds and begin again.

He had demanded cash from the doctor to see him through.

A modest amount, enough to get him to where he needed to be. And so, like a dog returning to its vomit, he clicked and bumped up the steps of the Sofitel and made for reception. The young woman at the desk was perfectly squared away if somewhat lacking in modesty. Habid noticed her painted nails as she pulled her hands to her body in revulsion at the carcass that approached her.

"I was here last week," he said to her, his gaze concealing the calculation behind his dead eyes. A week, he thought, no time, yet an ordeal for which people must pay.

"Really?" she said. "What is ... eh, what is your name?"

"Get the manager," Habid barked. "He will remember me."

The woman sighed and with relief turned to the back office from which a man emerged a few moments later. His face morphed from curious to stricken in the course of two seconds.

"You made a mistake," Habid stated. "Time to apologise."

The manager snorted. "*You* made a mistake coming back," he said as he lifted a phone handset.

"That's right, make the call," said Habid.

The manager stared at him and waited for his call to be answered. "This is ..." he paused, not wanting to give his name in front of his visitor, "the Sofitel," he opted for.

There was a pause during which the manager's revolted expression turned to one of shame before the handset was replaced.

"How can we help you, sir? Would you like your previous suite?"

"After I receive a grovelling apology," said Habid, smiling a cracked and leering smile. "It seems the mistake was all yours."

This is mad, thought Sam, as he drove the little police car through the gates of the church and towards the town, Isla in

the back. He was wearing a coastguard bib and had absolutely no idea whether the community he was driving into
was tight-knit and talkative – and therefore dangerous – or as
abandoned as the rest of the locale. Not that there was
anybody to be seen, but he worried he might bump into a
relation of the coastguard who could identify another man
wearing his clothes. He was more worried, though, about
alighting from a cop car with no high-vis or official-looking
kit on, so he kept it on. The place may have been deserted but
it was an tightly packed little town. The streets were narrow
with windows overhead. He would have no idea if they were
being watched.

"I can choose clothes for Sadiqah," Isla chirped away
merrily in the back, happy to have something to apply her
mind to that didn't involve tying people up or beating them
over the head.

"Good woman," Sam said distractedly as he passed a small
shopping centre and craned his head around for somewhere to
conceal the car. He turned right twice and parked it in a side
street as far away from doors and windows as he could manage.
He got out and spun around, opened the back door and beckoned Isla out onto the street. They marched quickly, turning a
corner where Sam deposited the bib and coastguard jacket into
a bin. Within two minutes they were in a shopping mall.

"What size is she?"

"Same as me," said Isla.

"Not Sadiqah, her mammy."

Isla thought for a moment then went quiet. It was a trigger.
One that Sam hadn't touched in a while. He winced.

"Same as my mammy," she said quietly.

It was at such moments that Sam had to decide which way
to go – talk about his wife, Isla's mother, and face the pain, or
try to airbrush Shannon from their thoughts. They were under
time pressure but he refused to give in to temptation.

"Ok, fourteen on top, twelve on the bottom," he said. "What do you think mammy would choose then?"

"Sadiqah's mam needs different colours than mammy liked."

"Ok, well, you know I don't know anything about clothes, wee love, so you tell me what we should buy."

She tilted her head and hemmed for a while before chosing something utterly inappropriate.

"Oh-kay," said Sam, lifting the flimsy vest top from the rack. "I think Sadiqah's mammy would also like something longer that would keep her, like, warmer."

"Ok," Isla chirped, and pottered off with her hand touching the clothes as she passed.

Sam wandered towards the children's rack where he felt confident. If it was good enough for Isla, it would be good enough for Sadiqah. He was loaded up with stuff when Isla returned with a tracksuit and a jacket. The stuff was cheap but roughly the size they had agreed upon, so he just bought the lot and they walked back towards the church.

Habid stared at the ceiling hatch. There was no way he could get up to it in his present state. Still, there was no immediate rush. He padded and punted himself back to the soft, sumptuous bed. He was in pain but also in a good place in his head. It's all relative, he thought. The privations of the pharaohs, he imagined, compared to his surroundings must have been grim. In their day they'd been the richest and most elaborately cared for humans on the planet, yet they still defecated into fly-infested pits, and here he was dangling his damages into a porcelain potty with a flush and a fluffy hand towel. When he considered how his luck had turned in a matter of days, from the bacterial halls of one of the city's prisons to the penthouse of the poshest hotel in Alexandria, he felt as though those who had abused him were currently building his tomb to take him off to the afterlife. And he would have all his money with him. Perhaps the drugs were still addling his mind?

He had work to do but he'd been through a lot and would savour, despite the pain, the cleanliness and decadence of the room. His sutures forbade him climbing over the rim of the tub to bathe his battered bits, but as soon as he was able to negotiate the manoeuvre he would be ready for the sands once more.

Never one to waste time, he put his mind to process, aided by a luxury unavailable in Libya. His fatherland was dry in more ways than one, and so the minibar offered him a new kind of pain relief and an imaginative journey into sleep during which he could plot and crystallise his next moves free from inhibition. The best ideas came with hard liquor. He would temper the most outlandish in the morning, not that anything was particularly out of reach now that these countries were hurtling deeper into lawlessness. The opportunities, he thought, were endless.

***

The church was empty.

"Maybe they ran away," Isla suggested.

"Why would they run away?"

"Because you were scary."

Sam couldn't argue with that but he doubted the woman would have run off in her rags rather than take a chance to escape arrest.

"They are safe and well," boomed a voice, accented, confident, unafraid.

Sam span to find a man in black chinos approaching him, his grandad shirt open at the neck.

"Who the fuck are you?"

"Daddy!" Isla hissed, and Sam felt bad for swearing in front of her and in a church.

"I am the priest here temporarily."

"Right, father," Sam said, less startled. "Sorry about that. But where are the women?"

"Let us discuss *who* they are before we locate them, shall we?"

"Fair enough, father," Sam said, deciding that if the priest couldn't be reasoned with, perhaps God would understand if one of his representatives was tied up and gagged.

"Please, sit."

Sam noted how so many religious people he had met appeared to share a serene superiority. Isla sat next to Sam, utterly prepared to accept the priest's authority. Sam waivered and the priest noticed his indecision.

"You can talk to me with confidence," he said in perfect English.

"How do I know you're a priest?"

The man raised his eyes in surprise then drew a bendy white plastic blade from his pocket and snapped it into his collar, fastening the button at the front of his black shirt. He did look like a priest.

"What's your name?" Sam pressed.

"Most people call me Father Luca."

"Isla, give me the phone please."

"And your name is?"

"He is Sam," said Isla, handing the phone over.

Sam gave her a *bloody hell, Isla* look before typing *Sicily Father Luca* into Safari and waiting. He was sure the data allowance must be on the cusp of its monthly limit. The results petered through and he tapped 'images' and began to scroll. The load time was painful given the pressure Sam was under.

"You posed for a calendar?" he said eventually.

The priest laughed and shrugged. "There are many ways to help the afflicted."

Sam glanced from the image on the phone to the man at his side. They were definitely one and the same except on-screen he was holding a Bible, presumably at some cathedral, looking suave, handsome and a little bit suggestive.

"The Church is not what it was." Sam shook his head.

"You can trust me," said the priest again.

"You found the women? In here?"

"Yes, I was in a rush, I had come to get my things – my robe and a Bible and so on. I had an emergency. They were asleep and did not wake, so I called the carabinieri. I assume you know this woman?"

"How did the coastguard end up here?"

"It is not so polite to answer a question with a question," said the priest smiling.

Sam ignored it and pressed on. Time was ticking. "Father, why did the coastguard show up?"

"The police must have called them." He shrugged.

"Why would they do that?"

"I don't know," said the priest, curious as to why Sam was so concerned about the coastguard when the police should represent a bigger threat.

"Where were you when the cops arrived?" Sam pressed.

"There was a young man dying in the village. He needed last rites and I could not wait. I was not here when they came."

"Do you know where the women came from?" Sam tried to bottom out how much was known by the Sicilians.

"I think you need to tell me that."

"So you did not speak to them – that's why they don't know that you saw them," Sam thought aloud.

"Yes, but I think I should be asking the questions, do you not? Here you are in my church, from another country, the police are gone and the women are now silent. What has happened here?"

Sam stared at him, at the preacher, considering how to manage him, but he was running out of places to conceal people and out of time.

The priest seemed a little short on patience. "It is time you told me what is going on."

"Not here," he said, "in there." Sam nodded to the confessional. "Isla, wait here a minute, I'm just going to talk to the priest in the box."

"Why?" Isla asked.

"Not now, wee love."

Isla looked fed up but the two men settled in on their designated sides and Sam began.

"Bless me, father, for I have sinned."

The priest snorted, realising what Sam was up to, but had no choice.

"How long since your last confession?"

"Years, father, decades."

In actual fact Sam had been reared on the other side of the Reformation but busked along anyway in the hope that the priest remained true to his oath.

Luca sighed. "Go on."

"We rescued the women from the sea days and days ago."

"Where?"

"Off the coast of Egypt."

"What were you doing there?"

"Healing, father. My daughter and I, we've been through it."

"Tell me about that."

"I don't have time."

"You should make time."

"Father, I trust you will abide by the confessional. What I tell you here cannot be mentioned again?"

"Of course."

"Well, father, I have the two policemen and the coastguard tied up in a van parked on a beach four miles north."

"What—why?"

"They're fine, father, honestly. They're not hurt."

"This is not going as I had expected," said the priest, cool as an Irish breeze.

"I will need you to release them soon and to misdirect them for good reasons."

The priest suppressed a little snort. "These good reasons being?"

"We need to get the women to safety – the Arab woman and her daughter."

"They are safe here," said the priest reassuringly.

"We both know they will be taken to a detention centre. My daughter, she is the girl's friend, and, well, she hasn't had a friend in a long time, and that's my fault. And I let them down – the woman and her kid. I sent them ashore with a man who may have been ... abusing them in some way."

"In what way?" The priest bristled and stiffened on his timber stool.

"I don't know, but I thought he was the woman's husband, the kid's father."

The priest was confused behind the mesh. "I think you are going to have to start at the beginning."

"There's no time, father."

"There is no choice," said the priest firmly.

So Sam creaked the door open, located Isla and gave her the thumbs up. "Quick as I can, darlin', ok?"

"Ok, Daddy," she said sulkily, tapping uselessly on a pew.

The door closed.

"We were sailing at night," Sam started.

"No, go back. What were you healing?"

"Look, father, I'm not getting into that."

The priest summoned some seminarian authority and

spoke without compromise. "I will help you if it is the right thing to do by God, but all I know so far is that you have kidnapped three men and possibly a woman and a child. You need to explain."

Sam leaned forward, put his head in his hands, did the maths and sat back up. He didn't face the priest but spoke in profile. It felt less painful. "Look, father, in a nutshell, we're from Ireland. It's a long bloody story – sorry, father, but it is. My wife, Isla's mother, she got killed. Murdered in a fairly random incident. She was trying to do the right thing and some bastard stabbed her. Sorry again, father."

The priest nodded away the apology.

"Thing is, Isla was with her."

"Your daughter."

"Yes."

"When she died?"

"Yes. She was ... holding her. And she thought it was her fault."

"Why?"

"Look, father, there really isn't time for this."

"Make the time."

Sam knew he needed a significant diversion to create enough confusion to allow them to escape Sicily. He could really do with sending the police inland away from the coast, so he needed help, and to get it he spooled back into the damaged quarter of his mind where the dark stuff was boxed and stacked, requiring attention while being ignored. He span fast, unwilling and unable to give the words proper thought.

"A drunk man nearly ran Isla over in his car. She was on her bike."

"Ok."

"My wife was with Isla – they were out for a cycle. My wife, she was a strong sort of woman. A headstrong woman. Princi-pled, you understand?"

"I do."

"She drove to the man's house and stole his car keys to stop him driving. Then she went home, and Isla was playing with the keys – she was only small then, and she hid them in her wee bag."

"Ok." The priest was no less confused.

Sam began to talk very fast. "Well, through the jigs and the reels, the man turned up and demanded the keys, and he had a knife, and my wife – Shannon – she got scared for Isla and so she decided to give him the keys, but she couldn't find them. Then the man stabbed her in front of Isla and she died. And Isla thinks it's her fault."

"Dear God, forgive us," said the priest.

"Anyway, that's the gist of it."

"Where were you?" asked the priest.

"I was abroad working," which told the priest virtually nothing about Sam's life as a Royal Marine.

"What was your work?"

"You're better not getting into that, father."

"It must be tough work for you to disable three men."

"Well, I don't do it any more."

"You were military," stated the priest.

"Anyway," said Sam, "we were sailing and healing, and then Isla heard this noise from the sea, and it turned out there were people in the water – the woman, the kid and a man, so we rescued them, and to be honest, father, I've been trying to get rid of them ever since."

"But now you want them back?"

Sam was not oblivious to the irony.

"Not really, but I feel I should help them. The man, see, I didn't know he wasn't her husband, but Isla did, and she didn't tell me until I sent them ashore here, in Sicily."

"Why did your daughter not tell you?"

"I think she thought I already knew, somehow. It doesn't

really matter, but I didn't even know the woman spoke English for fuck's sake – sorry, father. She was silent for days, and she was in a burka yoke, I only saw her face for the first time when I came here to the church."

The priest thought for a moment. "So where is your boat?"

"In the harbour being fixed."

"It is damaged?"

"Look, father, that's not really the issue."

"And where is this man who isn't the child's father?"

"Fuck knows," Sam said, giving up on the apologies. "If he wasn't here when you found them, he must have scarpered."

"Scarpered?" Father Luca had, at last, come across a word he was unable to guess the meaning of.

"Fucked off, father. Now are you going to help me or not? Those cops won't stay tied up forever, and that woman and her kid won't stay out of a detention centre for very long if I don't get to sea soon."

He leaned forward and looked straight at the priest through the mesh. They were roughly the same age and both had the seasoning of lives lived in problematic parishes. They were old enough to have the confidence to break the rules and young enough to have the balls to get away with it.

"There is more in your head that you are not telling me. You would be best to let that out, to confess, to ask God for forgiveness."

"He'd be at it for years if he listened to my sins, father. Now – decision time."

"Something I need to know first," said the priest, "what did you do to your wife's killer, and what will you do with the women?"

"That's two things."

"Yes."

"I'll answer one."

"Ok," said Father Luca.

"I have no idea."

"I think you just answered both," said the priest.

"That's it?" Tassels asked as a large rubber roll was transferred from one lorry to his van. A hire vehicle which, on reflection, looked enormous.

"That's it," said the Jordanian who had transported it from who knew where.

"Well, how am I supposed to conceal that?" he asked, staring into the empty loading area of his own vehicle.

"Where are you going?" asked the courier.

"North-west. Port Said," lied Tassels.

"Risky," mused the courier unhelpfully, not really caring either way.

"Why?" asked Tassels.

"It's Sinai," he shrugged, as if that were explanation enough.

The Jordanian leaned forward and unfastened the ratchet straps holding the bundle together. The package fell apart like a bouncy castle inhaling before a kid's party. Inside was a large outboard engine that looked new.

"Four-stroke," smiled the Jordanian with pride. "No oil necessary. Very fast. Will travel long time, small fuel."

Tassels had no idea what he was talking about. "I'll need to find stuff to cover it with."

"If you want to deliver the rest of my load, you will save me money," said the courier.

"What have you got?"

"Four more of those," he said, pointing to the boat, "and rugs, Persian. Fine rugs."

"You have four more boats?" Tassels struggled to compute.

"Yes."

"With engines?"

"Yes," said the courier, confused.

"And where are you delivering them?"

"Suez."

Tassels bristled at the news. He could have avoided the treacherous journey and met the courier in safe territory.

"Who are they for?" he snapped at the Jordanian.

"Merchant vessels on the canal heading south."

"What?"

"Container ships, they come to Port Said from Europe, yes?"

"Yes," said Tassels.

"Then they go through canal, yes?"

"Yes, I get that bit, but surely the ships have their own small boats on these ships."

"Yes," said the Jordanian, who seemed to say *yes* a lot.

"So why do they need extra boats – why smuggle these ones?"

"Pirates," smiled the Jordanian conspiratorially.

"Pirates," repeated Tassels, none the wiser.

"Suez is halfway down the canal, yes? Many shipping companies pay for special soldiers. These men get on ships at Suez to keep crews safe."

"Ok," said Tassels, broadly aware of the pirate threat off the East African coast. "But what's that got to do with these boats?"

"When ships leave Red Sea, Gulf of Aden, pirates can attack. From Somalia."

"Ok?"

"Not at daytime – they stop daytime raiding because of Russian patrols."

"So?" said Tassels, adrift from the nuances of piracy.

"So, is at night special soldiers use these boats."

"To do what?"

"To sink pirate boats," said the Jordanian slightly frustrated at Tassels' lack of understanding.

"But why don't they just use their own boats from the ships?"

"Everywhere there are patrols. India, Russia – is combined task force."

"So they are safe – the ships?"

"Sometimes. Shipping companies are very greedy. They do not want pirates arrested, they want pirates dead."

Tassels shook his head. "So why not just let the special soldiers shoot the pirates when they get on the ship?"

"Pirates don't get on ship – patrols stop them most of time."

"So there is no problem?"

"*Sometimes* they get on ship. *Sometimes* they have ransom. Ship companies do not like this."

"So they send special soldiers to kill the pirates?"

"Yes."

"Then what?"

"Then they leave dead pirates in these boats," the Jordanian pointed at his massive rubber rolls, "take off engine, leave boat close to shore and stab the tubes so boat is useless. Families of dead pirates know someone is killing them. No more pirates."

Tassels stared at the deflated deterrents.

"So these boats are abandoned?"

"Abandoned?"

"Left in Africa?"

"Yes, left behind. Special soldiers are collected using ship's boats and nobody know of anything. Is necessary because all ships are checked when they arrive from Mediterranean at Port Said in north Egypt. They have all the small boats they are supposed to have and they get all-clear and travel south on the canal to Suez. Then they take on extra boats, smuggled so nobody can trace these boats back to the ship."

"I see."

The Jordanian nodded and smiled.

Tassels admired the sleeked plan. It was like passing

through customs with no contraband only to collect the illicit goods on the other side. The boats were sacrificial, avoiding audit from maritime checks. He imagined the pirates' bodies were mutilated before they were allowed to drift ashore – like heads on spikes or the bodies left by the roadside to deliberately decompose after Mubarak fell.

"So who collects these boats?" he pointed to what was left in the Jordanian's van.

"I do not speak to them. I just turn up on time and someone comes to collect."

"Did you expect someone to collect here, in Nuweiba?"

"One customer only. Libyan."

Tassels nodded. "I am here in place of that desert rat."

The Jordanian shrugged his shoulders. He didn't care, so long as he got paid. "If you take all of this west, you will be able to cover the boats with the rugs. It will be safer for you and I can go back."

"I will take them on one condition," said Tassels.

"What?"

"Next trip, you deal only with me."

The courier snorted. "I am just driver. I do not make arrangements."

"When you collect these boats, are there more? Can you buy more?"

"Perhaps if I have money."

Tassels reached into the cab of his van and pulled out the wad of notes.

"I will give you half of this if you return as soon as you can with more boats for me."

"This is not enough."

"This is a lot of money."

"Crossing Sinai is dangerous these days."

"I just did it no problem," said Tassels, who in truth had taken the safer and longer journey south, and had still needed to use his police ID on numerous occasions.

"Ok, if you collect here in Nuweiba and you take rugs and other boats to deliver in Suez, it is worthwhile for me. I can bring more boats. No problem."

Tassels shook the man's hand before exchanging numbers and arranging dates. He couldn't believe his luck.

———

"Listen," said Father Luca as Sam and Isla got out of his little Fiat. "Get in touch when you are back. Let me know everyone is ok."

Sam crouched down into the ridiculously small car and looked at him sceptically.

"You think that's a good idea, father?"

"I am not convinced any of this is a good idea, Sam, but my conscience is telling me that it is the right thing to do. I am trusting you. I want to know that trust is well placed."

"I am trusting you too, father," said Sam. "You're clear about what to do?"

"Yes. Now you must be clear too, Sam. You need to address many things in your heart and in your head. I can help you. When this is done, we can talk. Even priests have Skype." He handed Sam a sliver of paper with an email address on it.

Sam stared at Father Luca. He rarely made friends. Sam hadn't spent any real time with other men since he'd left the Marines, yet in the space of an hour he and an Italian priest had somehow come to an understanding and Sam found himself grateful and respectful.

"It'll not be on Skype, father," he said, "but, look, I'll be in touch eventually and we'll have a pint or two and we'll talk."

"I am not a pioneer." The priest smiled. "*Ciao*, Isla."

"Say bye-bye," Sam said to his little girl.

"Bye-bye, father," she said suddenly shy.

"Thanks, Luca," Sam said, nodded his sincerity, gently shut the door and tapped the roof.

He took Isla by the hand and began to walk towards the travel hoist. His spirits rose as he approached the boat hanging silent and imposing in the slings. The hull was washed smooth as an Italian tailor.

"Come on," he said to Isla. "I need you to sit in the cockpit while I put the boat back in the water." She climbed up the ladder.

"Ok," she called from above. "Can you drive the crane?"

"I hope so, wee love. I used to drive one years and years ago."

"When I was small?"

"No, darlin', long before you were even born. Before I met mammy, before everything."

Sam almost drifted off. Father Luca had somehow opened a few old wounds.

"When she's in the water, you start the engine and I'll jump down from the dock and we'll go, ok?"

"Ok."

He climbed into the open cab and stared at the levers. He didn't relish the experimentation he was about to perform while Isla was on board the boat hanging at his mercy, but there was little choice. The engine fired up and he looked around to see if the yard owner might appear. Nothing. He touched a few levers gently to get a feel for how the forward and aft slings were controlled, and with growing confidence and muscle memory gently tilted the correct two towards him to lift the boat off her keel about a foot in the air. Isla's head appeared above him.

"Sit down!" he yelled at her, "and don't move."

Her straggly hair swept behind her as she retreated.

Sam released the groaning brake and began to trundle the enormous machine towards the dock. He anxiously turned the massive wheel as the tyres found their tracks over the gaping expanse below, and eventually *Sian* dangled over open water. Four levers were pressed gently away from him and the boat began to descend into the tide.

As she floated twenty feet below him he released two levers using the front sling to keep her in position. The back sling could run off its drum as far as he was concerned. It needed to dive deep beneath the keel to allow them to reverse the boat out. He'd just switched off the engine when he heard a shout and turned to see the hairy boatman hobbling in his Crocs towards him. Sam had no patience for explanations. He climbed out of the cab just as he heard Isla fire up the boat's engine. Good girl, he thought. Then he leapt at the rigging and grabbed the first crosstrees. From there he shimmied like an ape to the mast, wrapped his legs around it and slid like a fireman to the lower spreaders. From there it was a gentle fall to the boom and a few paces to the cockpit.

"I've got to go!" he shouted up to the grisly yard owner. "I'll chuck you up some cash."

But the yard owner wasn't liking the departure or that his crane had been used, and plainly didn't understand what Sam was saying. He had clambered into the cab, started the engine and was starting to reel the rear sling in again.

Sam had seconds to act. He threw the boat engine into reverse, praying that the fouling of the shaft hadn't done any alignment damage or screwed the gearbox. *Sian* slipped quickly astern and rubbed gently off one of the dock posts as he turned her. The yard owner hadn't had the sense to pull in the forward sling, which would have contained them for a while, and was instead left swearing and swinging his arms from the dock as Sam turned the boat.

"Isla, get come cash from the bilges," he shouted, "quick!"

Up came a grand bundled in cellophane. Sam unwrapped it, handed more than half back to Isla to return below and rewrapped about three hundred euro in the cling film. He reversed the transom towards the fat man.

"Here, catch!" he shouted above.

The man had evidently seen what was was being offered and tensed himself as if he were about to grab a Fabergé egg from the air. Despite his unattended body he showed remarkable dexterity in retrieving the payment, which induced a pleasant bearing on his attitude: his scowl became a smile and he even waved them off. A week's wages in one day, Sam suspected, but worth it. He couldn't afford to have anyone call the police and betray their means of departure.

The fact that the coastguard had been called still niggled Sam but there were more pressing issues. Provided the priest did his bit, they might just get away with it.

Arish was a mess and Cairo was busting Waleed's bollocks.

He had taken the promotion against his better judgement. He knew it was pride that had driven him to accept the challenge to lead the desert campaign. It felt like a small internal victory – a Coptic at the heart of Egyptian intelligence, not that anyone else knew he was a Christian. He certainly didn't live as a Christian – his actions routinely strained the description. Regardless, he felt he'd achieved something against the odds.

And yet every day he had to deal with some general in Cairo screaming at him, demanding to know why the jihadists were able to strike with impunity in his area. It was all he could do to refrain from pointing out that "his area" was the size of some European countries. He was, in effect, supposed to secure over twenty thousand square miles with an inconsistently trained force. Waleed had some excellent, elite even, operators at his disposal but he also had an army of idiots more interested in money than following orders. Some could change direction with the sniff of a gnarled American dollar, like a kid to candy. Such men put smiles on smugglers' faces. Waleed had tried to stamp out that behaviour by imprisoning those caught taking baksheesh. The guilty were incarcerated in the incubator back at base along with his old classmate.

The big man's suit would be pretty grubby by now, Waleed thought, in the tin can in the desert. It was hot in there by day and very cold at night. He experienced a minor pang of guilt at having left his former friend to languish as he had but until the bombing was cleared up and all evidence extracted and analysed, there was no way Cairo would allow him to return to his headquarters. His bosses in the capital wanted to know where the explosives had come from, who had made the vest, which group was involved and how to strike back. The new president had a political point to make and make it he would. Some desert gathering would suffer as a result of the attack whether they had anything to do with the bombing or not, and so Waleed felt compelled to make an educated guess as to who had been responsible for blowing up the bus. It was the only means he had to prevent some innocent Bedouin tribe being incinerated from the air by the Egyptian air force.

And that meant remaining in Arish and fending off the colonels until he was as sure as he could be. And that meant leaving Big Suit under a hot tin roof many miles from home, and from him, until his job was done.

The chart just didn't have enough information. All Sam had to go by was the depth sounder, which indicted over one hundred feet of open water beneath them. They'd turned to port out of the harbour and motored towards the church. The offshore breeze was stiffening in their favour, which meant that the dinghy should be floating well off the coast by now. Isla had the heavy binoculars at her face hunting the surrounding sea for the little white RIB.

It was Sam who saw it first and turned *Sian* towards it. The plan wasn't without risks, but he left the engine running in neutral as he and Isla grabbed the small boat with the pole and hook and climbed down into her. He didn't want to drop the anchor – he didn't have time and he couldn't afford the possibility of a snag potentially leaving them like sitting ducks within view of the church.

They fired up the outboard engine and scudded across the waves. Just as they were about to reach the rocks he saw Father Luca emerge from the church with Sadiqah and her mother, both newly attired and, Sam imagined, washed – the mother's hair looked wet. Luca ran as if he had just alighted from a helicopter. They clambered over the rocks and into the little boat.

"Gotta go, Luca. I'm worried the big boat could run aground or hit a rock. I haven't got the right charts," Sam shouted as he turned the little RIB.

"God bless!" shouted Luca.

Sam pushed the throttle to settle the tender back onto the plane, the wind at their transom. Within a minute they were all back where they had started, aboard *Sian*. Sam hooked the little boat onto the davits and winched her out of the sea. Then he turned the yacht west, hoisted and unfurled all three sails, gunned the engine and made off quickly.

He settled behind the wheel and caught Sadiqah and Isla in the light of the companionway jumping up and down, delighted, before hugging. It gave him a great sense of peace to know he and his daughter had done the right thing and to see her so happy.

But there were stories to come and with them blew trouble.

The driver stared at the dying phone on the dashboard and called his boss directly. He'd never had reason to make such contact before and was nervous. He introduced himself as the man sent east with a mobile and GPS and tried not to inquire about the whole curious business.

"What are your orders, sir?"

Waleed sighed. He hadn't thought it through. In truth he'd all but forgotten about Big Suit's electronics. He'd been trying to throw a spanner in the works for any police officers who might be trying to geolocate him. The last thing Waleed wanted was a bunch of crooked cops blundering into his headquarters asking questions. On the other hand, with hindsight, he didn't particularly want them speeding across Sinai either or being picked up by militants and executed at the roadside. That would just bring more headaches.

That said, he needed to know what Big Suit had been up to, and the nasty business his former friend had got wrapped up in had to be stopped. Friends of Waleed's family had taken to sea at the hands of people traffickers – Copts fleeing moderate persecution never mind the extremist shit flowing into Sinai from Iraq, Syria, Saudi and Afghanistan. He felt the weight of that responsibility. To protect his people he had to stop the extremists. To stop the extremists gaining traction he had to help tackle the corruption they thrived on. The beards and their ideologies were only strengthened because so many officials in Egypt were on the take.

"Where are you?" he asked the driver.

"Near Nuweiba, sir," said the driver.

The eastern edge of Egypt. Waleed considered the facts: no ordinary plod would risk going that far – at least not for a colleague, it was just too dangerous. So to eliminate the phone and its signal there might well draw the matter to a close. If the phone went dark in Nuweiba, perhaps Big Suit's brave pals would conveniently forget about him and consider him lost.

"Ok," said Waleed. "Make sure the devices acquire a satellite fix or a phone mast then destroy them."

"Sir?"

"Just do what I say," Waleed barked. "Then get back to base and call me when you see the prisoner."

"The prisoner, sir?"

"The enormous man who we brought in at the same time as the GPS and the phone."

"Sir," said the driver who stared at the kit, glistening and valuable.

The phone was already dead. Nothing he could do about that. He stepped from the lorry and placed the handset in front of a huge wheel, clambered back into the cab and drove forward lamenting the loss in revenue. His attention turned to the GPS but he couldn't bring himself to repeat the process. Someone would give him a few dollars for that, he thought. He wrapped the cable around the device and went in search of a foreigner.

13

He stood malcontented at the wheel. A full day of frustration had fizzed close to the surface before Sam admitted he'd had enough. The more he thought about the risks he'd taken to retrieve the woman, the angrier he became. The jeopardy for Isla had been huge, something he hadn't given due consideration. His negligence spurred him to deflect the blame and march down the steps into the saloon to bang on the door of the forepeak.

"Hello?" he heard the woman say.

"It's time to talk. This isn't a cruise liner, love," Sam barked and marched right back the way he'd come. The kids were in their bunks and he could hear chatter and laughing.

In the cockpit he trimmed the sails and waited knowing she would emerge. He was accustomed to command after all. He was used to people doing what he told them, and he had, by osmosis, learned to deliver an order that would be followed. It took half an hour but eventually the woman climbed the steps and took a seat under the spray hood refusing to meet his stony glare. She looked angry, which only served to infuriate him further. He couldn't compute her hostility towards him given that he felt he had gone above and beyond to help her.

"So are you going to say anything?"

She had fashioned a headscarf from one of the tops he had bought her. She was wearing the tracksuit – the type that people who never played sport wore, which looked stylish enough on her, Sam supposed. It was the sort of tracksuit a young mum with loads of money would be seen in, and she carried it off well now that she was out of her sackcloth.

"You're just going to stay silent?"

She turned and stared hard at him but gave no indication she intended to speak.

"Like, seriously, what's with the attitude? We picked you up, saved your daughter, I got cut to shite in the process and you're refusing to speak to me?"

Her face darkened. "You are British military," she spat, livid with rage.

"What?" he said, suddenly on shakier ground than he had anticipated.

"You are army," she repeated.

Sam faltered. "I'm an Irishman sailing with his kid, that's all."

"You lie to me," she said. "Sadiqah told me. The children talk so much. You are SAS soldier."

"I am not SAS and never was," he said, glad to be able to tell the truth. Sort of.

She looked at him oddly, trying to distinguish fact from lies. Her head tilted slightly, then, by a tiny fraction, her eyes softened.

He decided to capitalise upon her subtle wilt. "What difference would it make anyway?" he said, a minor pang of conscience stiffening his neck as he deliberated on how much to tell her. He needed to know how the land lay before he allowed her any distance into their lives.

"Britain force-ed us into sea," she said, bitterness weeping from her. She looked up at him again, her eyes awash. "The cowards. Britain and America. They bomb us from sky. They driving us to civil war. All normal is gone, burn-ed by fighter plane."

"Hold the fucking boat just a minute here," Sam said. "Where are you actually from?" Although he knew instinctively from what she had said. And that was bad news.

The woman looked at him, the truth dawning. "You do not know?"

"I think I know, *now*. Now that you've talked about bombing." Sam made a mental note to listen to and trust every word his daughter uttered from now on.

"You not have guessed before?" the woman said, curious now.

"I stopped thinking about it. Why do you think I'm a soldier?"

"Because of job. Isla tell Sadiqah."

"Told her what?"

"Sadiqah say you are special soldier who taking peoples to safe places."

"And Isla told her this?"

"Of course. Children tell truth."

Isla was like a little sponge. She wasn't far off the mark.

"So just what is it you think I do – or am?"

The woman turned profile and stared out to sea considering her words. "Mercenary. You make-ed money from migrant."

"Seriously?" asked Sam, incredulous. "You think I'm some sort of trafficking bastard?"

"You are not?" she said, her tone suggesting that's exactly what she thought he was.

She turned to stare at him as the wash and motion of the boat filled the silence between them. Sam didn't know what to say. He struggled to make sense of the enormity of the misunderstanding and the length of time it had endured as they'd sailed together across the Med.

"Is that why you denied knowing me in the church?"

"I am not knowing you," she said matter-of-factly.

"Well, that much is obvious," he grunted quietly."

"You knew where we are. In sea. You finding us. Boat sinked then you come from darkness ..." she trailed off as she picked through her thoughts.

Sam just shook his head at her reasoning but didn't know what to do other than allow her to continue.

"Now I do not know. You have child. You love her, I can see. I do not know what you are. But I see how you move. I see *violence*. I believe you are British army. I believe that. You are very ..."

"Finish it," he prodded her. "Get it all out."

She flashed her eyes at him and used a word far out of keeping with her broken English. "Capable."

Sam stood silent for a long time but eventually allowed her one utterance. "I'm not *capable*," he said softly, "of what you're describing."

***

Pass a border crossing in one direction, prepare to face hassle. Pass it headed the opposite way, nobody cares. It amused Habid that his operation used borders to bring people together when their fundamental design was to keep people apart. It appealed to his twisted sense of gratification and justice.

There was always an imbalance: one side of the invisible line was better off than the other. If that wasn't the case, there would be little requirement for the demarcation in the first place; not where the people on either side spoke the same language and practised the same faith. It all came down to money. For as long as he could remember Habid had been deprived of cash by the very people who were currently paying for his wretched services. He was now accustomed to getting what he was due.

And so he strolled from Egypt into Libya without hassle through an official checkpoint as opposed to the line in the sand he had used on his outward journey. He nodded and smiled and nobody cared. And then he evacuated his bowels and bought enough food and water to see him though the seven-hour journey. He boarded a minibus, paid his fare and struck out for Benghazi. There he would retrieve his precious papers, his passport to wealth, his leverage, his loathing, his pension, his gold.

Sam's gaze fell to the horizon where the sun was languishing just before it flicked off the lights. He had tried not to think about it but seeing the blossoming friendship between his child and the rescued kid had nudged a worry given where these people were from, what had they seen and what that might mean for Isla.

Sam had believed in the notion of preparing kids to take care of themselves, but that was before Shannon had died. It worried him that the only person of her own age Isla spent any time with was a child who may have seen equally bad – or perhaps worse – stuff. The root of his concern was their point of departure. Libya was a place with which he was to an extent familiar. It was not a destination of mixed emotions for Sam. It was not like Gaza, which had been grim and wonderful in equal measure. He had, after all, met his wife in Gaza, amid horror. In Libya, he had met only horror.

Years had passed since his first visit. His superiors had largely kept him in the dark at the time. His orders had been both clear and vague. Clear in that he was to make sure an intelligence officer was safely delivered to a particular destination; vague about why he needed to be delivered at all. Sam had eventually been told what it was all about.

Sam had taken four good men and a spook from the sea deck of an aircraft carrier into one of the Special Boat Service's custom-built FICs. The Fast Interceptor Crafts were ideal for such operations because in the relatively flat waters of the Mediterranean there's no need for wave-cutting boats, which, although fast, have limited ability to launch other shore-going vessels. Besides, the Interceptors could pass undetected beneath most radar scans.

The bosses had relished the opportunity to deploy the FIC as opportunities outside training missions had been few, but, still, Sam couldn't figure out why the Security Service hadn't opted to fly the spook into Libya given that the place was awash with white European oil engineers. It was well above his pay grade to worry about it, though, and given that he'd only ever used the FIC in training he was as keen as anyone to get aboard and use it in anger.

After a spine-crushing three-hour blast at just under sixty knots, the coxswain rounded the boat's transom towards the Libyan coast and the inflatable Raider was launched. A skittery boat, not as easy to handle as its rigid-hulled big sister, but much less detectable and easier to carry across the sand than a solid craft. From there, the crew was down to three: Sam, a sergeant and a spook.

Ashore, the sergeant was left to conceal the boat under strict orders to extract if a predetermined time elapsed. Then Sam and the intelligence officer stripped to their crumpled underclothes and made for the shadows around the edge of the city. From that point on it was an intel op.

Sam was happy to accede responsibility. The spook was a fit-looking thirty-something by the name of Dyer. To Sam's surprise he'd turned out to be a Northern Irishman just like himself, and although they didn't talk much all the signs were that he was cautious and hard enough to get the job done. He took direction when command rested with Sam and through gesture and the odd smile betrayed his sensibilities. Sam had caught his eyebrow rising just a jot during the briefing as an overzealous and under-witted senior officer from an unidentified agency had tried to impress upon them the consequences 'for Her Majesty's Government' should things go awry. Sam felt at ease when the operation reverted to Dyer. If things went bad, he was confident they could make a fist of it together.

Her face was set. Stern. Dignified.

They sat for hours. The only movements were Sam's carving the boat through the waves making west, almost thirteen nautical miles in absolute silence. Sam's hands instinctive on the wheel, it spinning and adjusting as he lessened his grip allowing the hull's shape to do its job. The air hadn't cleared but it was thinning, and he allowed some hope that the anger would eventually lead to some form of truce. They refused to look at one another all that time, which helped each formulate their thoughts. The breakthrough came with a distraction.

"Daddy, how long till we stop again?" Isla's raggedy head appeared at the companionway.

"A long time, Isla. Don't start asking all the time. We won't stop again until we run out of food or water." Things Sam had intended to sort out while ashore until events had rather overtaken him.

"Well, what can we do?"

Sam was instinctively frustrated by the question, then turned it to his advantage. "You can put on your harness and life jackets and teach Sadiqah how to sail. You can teach her mammy too," he said, not glancing at the woman. From the corner of his eye he could see her shift slightly, her feet shuffling on the lip of the locker she had wedged herself against. The suggestion stirred her to speak, to verbalise something she'd evidently been thinking about.

"You can call me by my name now, I think."

"Ok," said Sam, relieved she appeared to be extending an olive branch.

"Alea," she said.

"His name is Sam," said Isla, earning her another look from her father.

Sam deliberately tested Alea straight away by extending his hand. He knew that if she took it, the niqab had simply been part of the escape. No committed burka-wearing Muslim woman would touch a man.

She waivered, looked up at him and then rolled a little to place her small fingers in his enormous paw.

"Pleased to finally meet you," he said, looking directly at her.

"How do you do?" she replied slowly with a rote response, which suggested to him that English had been learned in one of Libya's finer establishments.

"Get Alea a life jacket," he told Isla, who scuttled off below.

The thaw had begun but there was clearly a lot of hard frost to chip away, and Sam knew only too well that it wouldn't be until the ice melted and the cracks uncovered that the real damage would be revealed.

Benghazi had been beautiful. Once. Something else to thank the Italians for, thought Habid. In scooping migrants from the sea they'd made his operation possible. They had persuaded those who could afford it that their dip in the ocean might not end with certain death. News of those rescued by the Italian navy inevitably bled through more often than news of those who had perished. When migrants drowned, most sank without trace. Occasionally bad news of biblical proportions made it onto state television but more often than not the headlines were about the pressure on Italian and Greek islands, and their governments' attempts to deal with those who had made the crossing.

Habid swaggered along the seafront and looked at its scars. Gaddafi had terrorised the Americans, who blew the place to bits with the help of the British. Confusingly for most Libyans, Gaddafi later set about compensating the Yanks and the Brits for his bombings, and then the US had paid reparations for theirs – fixing Benghazi before blowing it up again. It was like Mediterranean Monopoly. Madness, thought Habid, utter, incalculable, ridiculous madness. Yet the whole debacle had generated cash, and he would have some of that.

To hide something precious in a town like Benghazi was impossible. Libya's fortunes could turn on the head of a firing pin; no alliance was worth a wink – for the nod that followed could destroy it in an instant. His papers were so important they couldn't be entrusted to a vault or a bank where nefarious forces could bribe and insist their way to seizure. And then there was incineration. Habid was in no doubt that further air attacks and bombings were inevitable. The only question was: which country was next in the queue to blow Benghazi to bits?

And so he had sought a fireproof hiding place for his plunder. Inspired by the remarkable preservation of the Dead Sea Scrolls, Habid's cunning mind turned to the tide as an option. The scrolls hadn't been concealed under the sea, but Habid imagined that was simply because there hadn't been watertight containers back then to guarantee safety. But what better way to prevent fire damage than to submerge his papers in water?

Habid had no knowledge of the sea – he was of the sands

where desert storms and tsunami-like floods could shift geography and make almost anything disappear. It was no place for a hide. Habid was a believer in history. He had made a remarkable discovery, one that would make him rich. He had taken his valuable bundle to the bay in Benghazi and asked himself what invaders don't destroy. And it came to him: they never ruin ports, for the ports are what they use to remove the wealth from any country. They need the ports to shift the oil they guzzle from the ground. Even during the Second World War, the ports were untouched.

With glee then, Habid rolled up his scrolls, capped the ends of a watertight tube and concealed them in the one place he was convinced they would survive. Not a dead sea, but a living one, from which he would eventually extract his fortune.

Sam had met Dyer years later in the way that operatives do – by blanking one another. To begin with.

The heat had been intense, the hospitality gratuitous. A consular reception for NGO staff at a colonial retreat in the Caribbean. Enormous fans were recirculating warm air as Commonwealth subjects poured wine for guests from the old country. Sam watched his wife struggle to hold her tongue as they were lavished with canapés and plonk while the local population struggled to rebuild after yet another bloody hurricane.

Sam had been about to go on leave when Shannon had been deployed, and he'd rerouted his flight home at his own expense to get some time with her. His plan had been to swim a bit, maybe dive a little, and then eat with his wife in the evenings. Instead she had lined him up for heavy lifting, driving water bowsers around the island, chainsawing fallen trees and a healthy dose of carpentry, which, he admitted, he thoroughly enjoyed.

But it had begun with a thank you from the high commissioner on the island. Sam and Shannon were duly introduced to an eminent midget, and it seemed to Sam that the man was just lonely and craving company he could relate to, but Shannon didn't care about his solitude among those he failed to find synergy with. Her role, as ever, was in disaster relief. She was disgusted at what she determined to be a decadent waste of money that ought to be decanted elsewhere. Sam found it mildly amusing, which earned him a frozen shoulder.

He'd seen Dyer the moment he walked through the white clapperboard door. Sam hadn't really packed the correct attire for such a gathering, and so he stood out sufficiently for Dyer to immediately take note of him too. The spook's broad shoulders filled out a linen sports jacket – Sam's inflated a poorly ironed shirt, taking at least some of the bad look off it. Shannon had been defiantly unperturbed by his get-up.

"Shower of stuck-up feckers," she'd muttered. "Do them no harm to see how workers dress when they come here to do a proper job."

Dyer and Sam locked eyes for the briefest of moments – neither issued a twitch. The inevitable handshake elicited no betrayal of their past acquaintance, and as the boozy night carried on they pressed flesh and talked small, evading questions as was their want.

Much later Sam sat alone, feet up on a wicker chair amid sprinklers watering the thick grass – while the fresh homeless outside the fence craved libation. He'd investigated the work involved in diverting the supply and had resolved to set to it the following night. He knew it would please Shannon.

"Well?" he heard from behind.

"Mr Dyer," Sam had replied without turning.

"I assume you're not here on official business, lieutenant commander?"

"Nobody ever called me that," he laughed, "and I'm a lieutenant commander no more," said Sam.

"Sounds like we have lots to discuss."

Dyer fell into the seat, his hulk straining the sinews of the wicker.

"I'm here by accident really," said Sam. "I had some leave and my wife got deployed to sort out the relief programme here. What about you?"

"I've been given a tidy wee number for a year."

It was soothing to hear the Northern Ireland accent. It negated the need to enunciate clearly for the benefit of comprehension.

"You must have got yourself in some more tight spots if you're being rewarded with the Caribbean."

"Something like that," Dyer replied. "If you're retired, why do you still get leave?"

"I didn't say I was retired. Got busted. Bad behaviour," said Sam.

"Didn't think you were the type," said Dyer genuinely surprised.

"Bad behaviour for good reason," said Sam, and left it at that.

Dyer withdrew a quarter bottle of Havana Club from one of his side pockets. And then drew another from the opposite pocket.

"Half 'un?"

"Aye," said Sam, falling into speak he hadn't had the luxury to use in months.

"Where've ye been?" asked Dyer.

"Helmand," muttered Sam. "I'm back to a bootleg."

"Right." Dyer breathed in, absorbing the implied news that Sam's fall from grace had been substantial. "Still, must be plenty of young Marines glad to have someone like you leading them about the place."

"You know, there's something not too bad about that side of it, but I'm getting tired. I've been in that kit for a long time. Most of the rest have checked out."

"I know well," said Dyer.

The pair appeared to be in similar places. Sam looked at the big Northern Irishman as they swigged from their dumpy bottles and took his turn to ask a question – he knew he'd be offered nothing otherwise.

"You not ready to get out? You've done your years, have ye not?"

"Twenty next year," said Dyer. "I've a few loose ends."

"Out here?" said Sam, asking a question without really asking a question.

"No, this is decompression."

"Must've be working, judging by that tan." Sam smiled.

"It's not a tough station."

"You sail?"

"Nah," said Dyer. "Like boats though."

"My wife, Shannon, she seems to have a fair bit lined up for me, but I've a plan that might earn me a pass for a day and maybe we'll get on the water."

"Dead on," said Dyer, a phrase Sam hadn't heard for a long time.

"I need a hand to do something that might land you in bother with that wee ambassador, but."

"He's only a commissioner, and he's a gobshite."

"Right, well. See if you can find us a set of spanners or shifters and we might get to go sailing tomorrow."

By night he heard Alea scream, which was an achievement

given the noise and banging of the boat as she sailed, and the distance between the cockpit and the forecabin. He assumed she was yelling in her sleep. It disturbed him because he imagined the children could hear her too, but they didn't mention it.

She and Sam had adopted a not-uncomfortable peace. Most of the time he just dozed as she sat in the cockpit and read voraciously through his stockpile of paperbacks. There was no deliberation, she simply peeled the next one off the shelf in the order they were stacked. He wondered how much she was able to understand and noted her incredible appetite for knowledge. Perhaps there was no better way to learn English – to prepare for life in the west, to be able to hold conversation, to better understand what was going on.

Occasionally she took a break and skipped up onto the deck, gripped the stays and gazed into the warm breeze, her hair blowing out behind her. Barefoot and lithe, Sam banished the flutter of a thought as he watched her, guilt edging it away. She only did it when he was asleep, and she always adopted the same pose. Sam often caught her as he stumbled out of a dream.

"You turn your face to the sun a lot," he said, not really intending to verbalise his thought.

"Mmm."

He couldn't work out whether she was annoyed at having been caught. "It's like you miss the sun on your face," he tried, happy not to have been ignored.

She turned her head to her shoulder, her back to him, in deliberation.

"It has been long time," she said.

"Why? The one thing Libya has, besides oil, is sun."

"Not all places," she said, her tone hardening.

Sam had a choice: pursue the dialogue or let it drift. He'd never learned to take the easy option.

"Why, where have you been hanging out?"

She turned, and the stare came back. Alea fixed him for a moment, then rotated again to the falling sun.

"Hiding from tribesmen."

"What tribesmen?"

"Any of them. All of them."

"Why?"

"We do what you do. Protect ow-er child. Keeping her from fighting."

"The Spring?"

She stiffened again. "There is no *Spring* before your planes arrive-ed. Is small revolt. Benghazi only. Then you take-ed chance to remove-ed Gaddafi."

"Will you quit with this *you* and *your country* carry on. I told you before – I am from Ireland. I am not American."

"You speak both sides of mouth," she stated, not inviting comment or rebuttal. "You fight for Great Britain."

"I fight for no one. Not any more."

"So is true. You have been army."

"Not really army."

"Then what?"

"I was in the navy."

Then she said something curious. "Why not have tattoo?"

"Tattoo?"

"You not have," she said, and Sam remembered she had seen him pretty much naked, which meant she had seen the scars – which perhaps explained her conviction that he had been in the military. "I believe men in navy have tattoo."

"Just like all Arabs are filthy?" Sam retorted.

She snapped him a stare until she realised he was being ironic.

"Anchor," she said absently.

"Excuse me?"

"In movies. British navy men have anchor tattoo on arm and hand. Like Popeye."

Sam laughed and she almost smiled.

"You think I should look like Popeye?"

"No, I thinking you *do* look like Popeye." She tried to suppress a curl at the edge of her lips and looked away.

"It was a while ago," he said, "that I was in the navy."

"Did you come to my country," she rounded, the smile replaced by seriousness, "when you were in *navy*?"

Her question was suddenly laden with suspicion. Sam was reminded there was deep damage and he would need to tread softly.

"Once," he said.

"What to do?"

"It was to do with my country. With Ireland, with Northern Ireland. There was a man – an informer, who had information, and I was sent to get him. I was never involved in any airstrikes, and I was never on a carrier where an airstrike was launched. I was gone before all that happened."

"It happen many times," she said. "It happen when I was same age as Sadiqah. They come in night-time. They kill my mother."

"They bombed your house?"

"They bomb neighbourhood. Many house. Many dead."

"The Americans?"

"You all the same – Americans, British, French. Same thing. Someone pull trigger, thousands are dead. You have fight with one man – Gaddafi. You kill everyone *except* Gaddafi."

Sam thought about that for a moment but had no way to counter her assessment.

"You grew up without a mother," he muttered eventually – not as a question but as a kind of explanation. He thought of Isla, then of Sadiqah and understood the risk Alea had taken to make the migrant journey.

"Ronald Reagan kill her."

"I was a child then too."

"You not child when Britain bomb Libya."

"So I am to blame for you going into hiding?"

"Your country is blame."

"I am Irish."

"Does Ireland have special soldier? I have read your books. Ireland is neutral country."

The books. The reading. The children. Sam reflected on how much was going on aboard this small boat under his nose without him noticing. Alea had obviously been vetting him, silently, working out who she was at sea with. He imagined she had probably been priming Sadiqah to extract answers from Isla.

"We're back to me being an SAS trooper, are we?"

"You are not simple Irish sailor," she stated, "and you are more than navy man," she said snorting. "*Informer*. Navy does not send simple navy man to Libya to get man out of country."

Sam knew he couldn't fool this woman. She was arguing and beating him and she wasn't even speaking her first language. "Well, do you want to have this out?"

"Have this out?"

"Cards on the table. You tell me who you are, I tell you who I am. All that stuff."

She gripped the vertical wires that held up the mast, elbows bent and pushed against them like a bow. She arched her back and allowed the sun to pour down her neck as if she were showering in the glow for the first time. Then she stood at ease, turned and walked slowly towards the cockpit.

"Very well," she said. "We put card on tables."

Shannon would have gone ballistic if she'd seen Sam swimming with the sharks. He'd been 'released' for the day, like a good boy who'd done something nice, to mess around with his new friend. Sam didn't tell his wife he and Dyer had known one another in a way that welds men to secrecy. As far as Shannon was concerned they'd bumped into one another at the party, got a bit pissed and re-rigged the consulate's irrigation system. The pipes were now pouring drinkable water through a hose they'd diverted outside the fence of the protected property. Nice work, she'd said. You can go and play today.

Not with sharks though. Not that it was any more dangerous than his day job, but extra risks were frowned upon regardless. He and Shannon were trying to start a family and she had no desire to be a single parent.

Dyer was as chilled as the beer in the boat above them. Sam hadn't managed to acquire a sailing yacht or even any diving apparatus. The two men were flicking around in flippers and snorkels in a place they'd been told to avoid. The sharks there were a variety that could easily eat both men as if sucking steak through a straw. The key was in the calm: if the sharks felt as though the men were supposed to be there and sensed no fear from their presence, then they stood a good chance of leaving the sea with their limbs.

Later they sat on deck with the buzz of having done something edgy and the tingle brought about by heart-pounding exercise. They chugged a few beers and nibbled the fat. Unexpectedly, it was Dyer who raised it first.

"D'ye ever wonder what that was all about?"

"What?" said Sam, knowing full well.

"Libya."

"There were loads of Libyas," said Sam.

Dyer looked put out, as if what had happened was of no consequence to his ... friend? Person he liked, certainly, respected – for sure.

Sam caught the creasing of his colleague's eyebrow. "I don't mean what happened. I mean operations that we were told next to nothing of the background. If you dig too deep, you end up going mad."

"So ... you don't care?"

Sam had to concede Libya had been different, so he made an admission. "I care. I care about that one because of what happened. So, well, I made it my business to find out what had been going on."

"Oh?" said Dyer, probing without probing.

Sam didn't care enough to be on his guard, and suspicious as he had become in recent years he didn't suspect that Dyer had been sent to find out how much he knew. The oddities of their reunion were too random.

"I asked a man about a year after the op. He hooked me up with another bloke who knew what was going on."

"Where?"

"Back home. Sure the whole thing was about Northern Ireland. I know that much for certain." Sam was letting Dyer know not to blow smoke about.

"Just so you know, Sam, I didn't have all the details back then either – and to be honest, I'm still not sure I have them all."

"Sure that's how they like us, isn't it? They tell us just enough to get the job done, and the rest they keep to themselves and their Machiavellian plotting."

"My agency is excellent at that."

"No shit."

"So what do you know?"

"Tell you what," said Sam, "for a change, why doesn't the spook go first and then you can hear from the oily rag."

"You're no oily rag," said Dyer grunting. "You were an officer, the one special forces *chose* to lead the thing. You also got us out of there."

"Was pretty messy though."

"Aye." Dyer glazed over a little, and then after a while, "Ok, Sam, I'll tell you what I knew."

"Oooh, MI6 secrets," said Sam, and pinged a few more lids off the local brew.

Dyer ignored the goading. "It *was* about home. I was told that a high-level asset had been discovered by the ESO."

"Libya'sMI6?"

"The External Security Organisation – so pretty much. Thing is, though, they were friends of ours at that stage."

"I'd believe almost anything of your crowd," said Sam.

"It was after 9/11 and the Yanks and Tony Blair had decided that Gaddafi was of great value in finding out about the jihadists, so they cuddled up to him."

"Right. You needn't go into the geopolitics, just tell me how that ended up in a bloodbath."

Dyer breathed deep and sucked on his beer. "Well, as you know, the asset was in jail and my bosses were worried that the interrogation would lead to him talking too much."

"About what?"

"About Ireland, Northern Ireland and his contacts there."

"Sure, what did that matter? I've never understood that bit."

Dyer regarded Sam curiously. "Well, why don't you tell me what you know and then I'll see if I can fill in the blanks."

Sam was impatient and a little looser after four beers. "The man I met was from West DET."

"A detachment – a military detachment?"

"Yeah, in the south-west."

"Of Northern Ireland?"

"Yes, where else?"

"Right." Dyer was clearly surprised.

The DET was a specialist surveillance unit deployed in largely autonomous teams around the country and made up of a mixture of special forces, intelligence agents, highly trained troops, mechanics and technical signals experts. Some of them had proved incredibly adept at gathering information. Sam neglected to mention that he himself had been seconded to the DET in the past.

"This bloke told me about an IRA man who was shagging some DET agent out Fermanagh direction. I'm guessing late 80s or early 90s. She was a right hard nut and had a key to this RA man's house. Anyway, she was lifting his post before he got it and giving it to her DET handler who was reading it and feeding it up the chain."

"She was a good get for the DET."

"Aye. And some of his post was coming from Tripoli."

"Right," sniggered Dyer, clearly impressed.

"So this RA man turns out to be the point of contact for the Libyan arms that Gaddafi sent to Ireland."

"Bloody hell," said Dyer.

"I don't know a lot more than that except that the Libyan who was writing to this IRA man was the same fella we lifted out of that prison."

"You sure?"

"No," said Sam firmly, "but I'm not an idiot. My DET contact reckons the same bloke knew who the high-level informers in the IRA were – who was really working for the Brits, and that worried your lot."

"Well, it would, wouldn't it? That was the start of the talks that led to the peace process. If the IRA found out that some of its senior people were working for the Brits, then the whole thing would have fallen apart."

Sam pushed his friend. "What I can't figure out was how a Libyan found out who MI5's agents within the IRA were."

"Sure, that's simple enough," said Dyer. "If he was making arms deals and British Intelligence found out, they'd have done two things." Dyer counted on his fingers. "One – they'd have turned him, and two – they'd have directed him to deal with *their own* agent within the IRA – wouldn't they?"

That made sense to Sam. "But wouldn't the IRA would get suspicious if he started dealing with someone else?"

"Not if his original contact got lifted."

"Ah." Daylight dawned. "Funny enough ..."

"That's what happened, aye?"

"That's exactly what happened. He was arrested and got nine years."

"Then a senior IRA member – who is also working for the Brits, suggests he takes up the Libyan contact himself. The Brits know the arms route, the secret silos within the IRA's quartermaster operation are exposed, MI6 is seen to help MI5 and we have a happy outfit."

"So," said Sam, reasoning it out. "It *is* possible that this Libyan – the bloke we were sent to get – knew who the top British agents in the RA were?"

"Or one of them, I reckon."

"And that was enough to send us in like that?"

"Yes, Sam, if he'd been caught by his own and was interrogated by the ESO, there would have been a problem cos of Bush and Blair and their cosy relationship with Gaddafi's intelligence services. All of that information was being fed to the CIA. Now, seriously, we might be friends but there's no way MI5 or MI6 wants the CIA to know who their high-level assets in the IRA are."

"Ok," said Sam, prepared to accept that as fact. "So we extract him under the noses of the CIA?"

"Sure, Sam," said Dyer, "that's why they fought so fucking hard. That's why it became such a bloodbath. And that's why the informant never made it to your boat."

"Right," nodded Sam, realising that they hadn't been sent to retrieve him. They'd been sent to execute him.

14

Plucking dollars from the air. That was what he'd done as he leapt around the exercise yard, undignified, inglorious, greedy and ridiculous. Years had passed since Gaddafi had been ousted, yet it seemed like weeks. And still the information had currency.

Habid often thought of what now led him to slither down that ladder. It had been forged into the wall of a Banghazi quay and largely forgotten for almost three quarters of a century. Its rust had left it vulnerable to knocks and thumps – various vessels had taken the top of the rungs with them as they'd arrived and departed. Habid had found it through due diligence and a pair of field glasses during his meticulous research. He'd scoured harbours hunting for an undercut after being inspired by the scrolls, and thinking of Judaism it occurred to him to find a gap in the stones. In his head was Jerusalem's Wailing Wall into which he'd watched Jews place papers – prayers he imagined, but he hadn't cared enough to clarify. Could he hide his papers in such a wall?

One thought had led to another and to him locating the half ladder and scaling the harbour stone face to reach it. Once on the rusted rungs he clambered down further and further until the water lapped his chin. One deep breath and he pulled himself beneath the surface, his body's natural buoyancy surprising him and he was forced to propel himself down the ladder deeper into the sea. When there were no more steps to be taken he unfastened a stainless steel chain from his belt and opened his eyes to the salt. The light was poor and his chest began to heave at the lack of air replenishment, but his hands didn't fumble his invaluable deposit. The steel links and the exterior padlock were clipped tight against the bottom of the ladder, and Habid took extra effort to roll the canister behind the old frame, wedging it tight into the wall. Satisfied with his work, he felt the ladder's uprights and allowed nature to float him to the surface, too afraid and inexperienced to expel air as he rose for fear of exhausting it before he broke cover. And then with a bellow and a suck he heaved oxygen into his lungs. Smug and soaked he reversed his motions and worked through what he would do with his treasure.

It had all happened by chance. As a border guard he'd been obliged to interrogate those attempting to leave Libya. That meant he occasionally identified enemies of the state – it wasn't hard, they were issued new intelligence images of people who had fallen foul of the regime on a daily basis. Never one to miss an opportunity, Habid often accompanied such miscreants to Tripoli or Benghazi for further interrogation and incarceration. That way he stood to exploit the unfortunate by offering to let them go for a fee, which he duly extracted. Then, regardless of the ransom, he betrayed and delivered them as directed to jail. Nobody cared that he had made a pit stop to gather cash. In those troubled times such behaviour had been expected and admired.

The last such occasion had been different though. As he and his fugitive neared Benghazi, the scale of unrest had become apparent. Never before had he believed it possible that

Gaddafi could be deposed. The leader had been too strong and been there too long. Yet the rumours they'd heard in the eastern desert proved true – Benghazi was once again returning to a pockmarked shell of itself, a cratered ruin of Aleppan proportions.

Habid had driven up to the prison entrance to find the gates ajar. He'd nudged them with the bull bar of his Isuzu truck, driven through the covered alley and out into the open courtyard where once a fortnight prisoners were permitted a solitary stroll. He gazed up from under the sun visor at the curling and fluttering above him and drew the jeep to a halt. His captive was equally mesmerised by the show, as swirls of air caught the leaves and bellowed them upwards, before the outside breeze lipped the sheets and sent them back to the soil.

Habid alighted and hopped to catch an A4 page. On it was a photograph and a description – a name and an intelligence assessment. His eyes widened as he realised what was in his hand. He turned to retrieve more of the documents, like a desperate contestant in a ridiculous television show. His sandals flopped and fell off but his energy was boundless as he stuffed the papers under his oxter and began to fill the glove box in the pickup. For an hour Habid ignored the shouts of his prisoner pleading to pee as he skimmed each page before stuffing it in safety. He refused to let so much as one document escape for that could be his passport to wealth.

Eventually every page was in his possession and he sat in the driver's seat and read greedily, ignoring the hiss of his prisoner's piss. What a story he had stumbled upon. What a glorious repository. Habid felt the moisture of the urine beneath his toes and turned to his charge with anger.

"You will be in here," he told him, brandishing the papers. "And then I shall know your real crime."

The man stared back at him, exhausted, dejected, defeated.

The Arab Spring was giving up Libya's secrets and a rat from the eastern desert had managed to obtain most of them.

"I was in the Special Boat Service when I was in your country. It is a unit that performs missions mostly at sea."

She stared at him.

He waited but had to shake her out of her fix. "Your turn."

Alea adapted to the format carefully. "I working in bank. My husband was banker. We had good life. Your turn."

"Then why did you leave?"

"Ah-ah," she wagged her finger, "you tell about you. I tell about me. No questions."

"Ok," said Sam. "Well … well, what do you want to know?" He was suddenly at a loss. Talking was not his strong suit.

Alea sighed. "Who you really are."

"I am a dad," he said, "and I am a widower, I suppose," which was the first time he'd ever acknowledged that in words.

"I am a mother and I am widow," said Alea looking stunned at what she had just said.

"It seems we have something in common, so," he said softly.

"More," she snapped at him, shaking herself from hurtful thoughts.

"I have been sailing on and off since my wife was killed."

She gathered pace as if spitting it out would make it easier, like ripping off a plaster.

"I am wanted better life for Sadiqah. We were living in hole in ground." She fixed her stare at the horizon. He could just make out the sheen on her left eye as the light faded.

"I wanted Isla to heal, but I went about it the wrong way. I took her away from other kids. I was being selfish. I wanted her close to me. I didn't want to lose her too."

"We were rich. We were rich and other people poor. They

hated us. When Gaddafi killed, they hunted us. We lived like animals. In filth. In yards. We could not keep living like this."

Sam didn't know what to say without a prompt. Conscious of the rules he resisted the urge to ask a question.

"You did the right thing for Sadiqah. You got her out."

"I got my husband murdered," she said, which seemed an odd phrase to use for drowning but Sam could just about see the logic.

Although the light was gone he knew she was weeping. He reached out to place his hand on her shoulder but she drew away and eventually went below. He knew he wouldn't see her again that night.

It didn't take long for Habid to work out what had happened. His gluttonous imagination allowed him to envisage it unfolding.

The sky had been peppered with rounds from reckless runts and their trigger-happy Kalashnikovs. Dozens must have died as gravity dictated – a law lost on idiots issued with rifles they have no idea how to use. They would have besieged the jails hunting for their comrades – enemies of a state that was crumbling around their ears. Gaddafi was on the run, the Jamahiriya was over. Prisons doors would have been rammed and the guards would have fled. The inmates would have wrecked and ruined as they left, destroying the fabric of their incarceration. Furniture and filing cabinets would have been tossed from the landings, fires might have been set. But above all, they would have groped for the gates, for freedom, for open space and their families and revenge.

They would have hunted the wardens, their torturers. They'd have beaten them to the ground, seized their weapons and summarily executed them in a frenzy. Then they would have streamed into the streets, kicking up dust, jubilant and ignorant of the papers they'd left coasting in the breeze at their backs.

And then came cunning in the shape of Habid, a man able to play for both sides and none, with no ideal greater than himself.

"Let me go," he pleaded. "The regime is collapsing. If you show me mercy, I shall tell them you are to be spared."

Habid lifted the butt of his rifle and swung it into the teeth of the moaning prisoner in the back. He laughed at the notion. He knew it was over – that anyone with a whiff of the opulent scent of the leader and links to the regime would be dragged out and slaughtered. It was convention. Saddam, the Baathists, dug up from the dirt and swung by the throat. It would happen to Gaddafi's men too if they were lucky. The man in the back could identify him in such a manner, so he hauled the wounded wretch from the jeep and bundled him into the prison searching for a cell far from the front entrance where cries wouldn't be heard. Inside he found cage doors thrown open, defecation smeared on the cell soles. The escapees must be ripe, he thought, as he plunged deeper into the darkness. They found a staircase and descended slowly, a sixth sense cautioning them. There was no noise, no reason for alarm, yet Habid and his prisoner adopted the same approach, their instinct being to creep, alert to movement. They were afraid of attack but neither knew why.

Down corridors they padded as silent as their moist sandals allowed. The stench came like steam barrelling towards them – a mixture of faeces and decomposition. Their heightened senses insisted they turn but Habid's greed drove him on. He had an opportunity like no other and he wanted no loose ends. The prisoner could not be allowed to share his story.

Yet Habid had not the appetite for killing. Not directly. He didn't care if people died, so long as he was in the clear. If he

just did what he was told, then he was fine: he had delivered
the accused to prison – no problem. He knew they would die
there but not by his hand. He had been in a firing squad once
but hadn't pulled his trigger. He'd felt nothing for the victim yet
ensured his prints weren't on the corpse.

Similarly, he had chosen not to dispatch the prisoner in the
yard. He would leave him in the bowels of the jail and his questionable conscience clear. Death, if it came, would be natural,
not of Habid's doing.

Then a shuffle, like a dog on a chain, alerted them to the
presence of a stranger. Habid froze and his prisoner stiffened
beside him. They stood in silence for a full minute hunting for
confirmation. Had they heard metal links drag? In the unlike-
liest of alliances, prisoner and guard looked at one another
bound by a predicament in which a greater enemy might unite
them. Habid took his hand from the man's arm and gently
reached out to undo the cuffs. The prisoner's jaw had been
badly broken by the rifle butt – he was unable to speak, yet he
looked up with gratitude. Habid doubted his usefulness in a
fight but if their enemy was animal, surely it would attack the
weaker target first.

A whisper came to them, a ricochet off the corridor wall.
Habid relaxed. Their foe was human. He had feared the feral
dogs used in the prisons. He called out.

"Who is there?"

"Help us, please. They have locked us up. We have children
here. Please!"

The voice was a woman's and she was immediately hushed.
He heard a whimper of a child and then a man's voice.

"Whoever is there, please release the women and children.
They have done nothing wrong."

The logic of what was happening appeared to Habid like an
epiphany – his intellect so keen that he moved immediately to
cash in. A fast turn with a raised elbow rattled the prisoner's

hanging jaw unnecessarily ensuring his silence. He reattached a cuff to one wrist and dragged the mute man into the darkness.

"I have a man here, a filthy dog," he called, willing his instincts to be correct but hedging his bets. If he'd got it wrong, he'd require some wriggle room.

He edged closer to the noises and eventually came to a cage door. It was hard to make out but there were a dozen shapes inside, some huddled, some tensed, all utterly contained.

"Who are you?" said Habid.

A man stepped forward from the gloom.

"We are ordinary families taken from our homes by Gaddafi's men. They beat us and brought us here. We do not know why."

Habid's instincts had been correct. He'd stumbled upon payday.

"What men?" He sought confirmation.

"From the regime."

Habid's eyes narrowed in knowing suspicion. "If that is true, then why were you not released when the others escaped?"

Even in the gloom the man could be seen to shift uneasily. "They are like a pack of rats," was all he managed.

"Why would they leave you here? You and women and children? Why would they not take you in the excitement of the Spring? What is different about you?"

The man stood silent while others turned away. That was enough for Habid. All the pieces fitted.

"You were of the regime," Habid stated, "but Gaddafi turned against you."

The man in the cage came to the bars and stared at him, a silent confirmation.

Habid pressed on. "Now you have enemies everywhere."

"How can you say that?" asked the man.

Another adult stepped forward as if to hush their

spokesman but the man held his arm behind him, his palm flat to stop the advance.

Habid sneered. "Because I have found your papers in the yard outside. I have read what people like you did."

The second man in the cell could hold his tongue no longer.

"So what did we do? What is it that we have done to justify this? We have not eaten in days. We have been tortured, beaten."

"That is what Gaddafi has always done to informers – you must have known that."

The first man held his stare, the second turned away.

Habid secured his position. "I have read arrest papers," he riffed, speaking to the second man's back. "Information to the Americans." He tutted, mock scolding as a teacher might a child.

The man rounded, incensed. "Shut your face, you do not know what you are speaking of!"

A woman whimpered and Habid suddenly realised that his confirmed suspicions had come as news to some in the cell. The prisoners' families had been unaware of their menfolk's offences.

The first man held up his hands again, appealing for calm. "What we did, we did for Libya," he said, uneasily. "We needed free of the leader. He was destroying our country."

"What you did was pass on information for airstrike targets," said Habid. "Little wonder the other prisoners had no sympathy for you. Little wonder they left you here to die. It is one thing to depose a leader, it is quite another to work for America and direct the slaughter of civilians."

Habid's tone was pragmatic rather than critical, which the first man sensed. He tried to appeal to Habid's better nature.

"So what would you do with us, with our families?"

"You were well placed in the regime once upon a time," said Habid – not quite a statement but not quite a question either.

"Yes," the man said.

"So you have money?"

"Not in Libya but, yes, we have money."

"And you must have had a plan to escape if you got caught?"

"We had prepared but we have no way of leaving. Not any longer. Now the tribes have taken over they will see us as people of the regime and will kill us. They will hang us in the streets and leave our bodies to rot."

A woman behind him wailed at the description.

"There are others?" asked Habid.

"Many more," said the man.

"Where is the money?"

The man stayed silent until a woman behind him rasped orders. "Tell him. Pay him. Get us out of here."

The man took his gaze to a distant nothing and began to speak.

"The money is everywhere – Europe, Uganda, Egypt. We spread it to keep it safe."

"How can you access it?"

"Not from Libya, but outside, yes. From a bank."

"So," Habid said with a little bow, "I can help you. I shall become your travel agent. Your very expensive travel agent."

15

They needed a plan – they couldn't just keep sailing west. They needed to know where they were headed to plot a course according to the weather forecast and get there before their food ran out. Feeding four wasn't like feeding two, and Sam couldn't afford another Sicilian escapade. There would be no unnecessary stops because under no circumstances could he afford to be boarded by customs. He was wary that a radio call may well have been issued seeking a yacht carrying migrants intent on depositing them somewhere in Europe. He knew any such alert would include critical information – the length and type of boat they were sailing, the description of the adults and children, the fact he was Irish.

Sam set the autohelm and began banging around the cupboards and bilges recovering every tin and packet they had stowed. He drew up an inventory and checked the water maker. Twelve days, he reckoned, of iron rations. He sat at the chart and realised how tight the whole thing would be. Although he hadn't yet acknowledged it to himself, he knew where they were going. He needed people he could rely upon, not nutters and strange priests – trustworthy as he felt Father Luca to be.

He plotted a worst-case scenario based on the wind fore-casts. As usual the breeze looked to be funnelling straight towards them from the Strait of Gibraltar where the Med met the Atlantic. It was a place he loved and hated passing through. On the way into the Mediterranean it often meant build-up and preparation for something dangerous; on the way out it repre-sented a return home, to his family, to Ireland.

Eight days. Assuming they hit no seriously bad weather. He snapped a pencil in frustration, realising he had stabbed the needles of the navigation dividers right through the chart and impaled it on the table. They would be forced to sail through any storm – he couldn't put into port and risk them all being sent to jail. When it was just Isla and him bobbing about, he'd avoided any and all foul weather. They simply found a harbour or marina and rocked it out tied up behind some breakwater. His anger at having to place her in a precarious situation grew, and he thought yet again about how his decisions had led him to a place where Isla's level of safety, not just his own, was reduced.

The worst of it was that they needed to sail two full days into the Atlantic before they would get fair enough weather and wind direction to turn for Ireland. Three hundred nautical miles, he reckoned, of hard, brutal, bow-banging graft. Then they could bear north for an endurance run of nearly nine hundred miles with the breeze on the beam, sailing fast but rolling – a further six days.

It was no way to treat children – he didn't want this for Isla. He wanted to cruise slowly off the coast of Europe, tying up every night, eating fresh fish not tinned curry. He wanted to hug the coast of Portugal, to throw down the anchor and row ashore and explore. To give Isla time to swim off sandy beaches, to savour every moment with her. He wanted a short dart across the English Channel to the Scilly Isles, a meal on Tresco, a last night in blue water and then a hop past the Tusker Rock and a spin up to Dublin. Instead they'd have to battle past the Bay of Biscay with its notorious seas and storms and rattle every bone in his little girl's body. On current stocks they'd have to aim for Cork – Crosshaven probably, Kilmore Quay at best.

And the children would get sick out there in the Atlantic. The swell and the need to keep them below decks so much would take its toll, he was sure. So Sam was pissed off – angry at the world, at the weather, at their rations, at Alea for being angry with him, but most of all with himself for taking Isla and hiding her away, for not ignoring the screams in the water, for headbutting the cops, for not leaving the woman to the care of the Italians.

But he knew somewhere in the back of his conscience he had done what Shannon would have done. Despite his frustration and irritation there was that whisper in his ear.

It will be ok. You're doing the right thing.

Habid had poured through his beautiful papers every chance he got. They were a fascinating, beautiful, intriguing and beguiling mix of information: who had done what, their confessions, their misdemeanours, their betrayal. It was all leverage. To a man like Habid it was cash.

He'd laid them out on the floor of an office in the prison while he worked out what he would do. He'd calculated that the safest place in Benghazi was the jail because nobody would want to return there, and the establishment of civic control was a short age away. He guessed this from the noise beyond the walls – the gunfire, the screaming vehicles, the shouting. There would be no prisoners, he concluded, not for a long time. Enemies of the new reckless and lawless state would be contained in the ground not the jail.

Gradually he built up

a picture by laying the rap sheet of the most senior at the top and cascading to the lowliest. It was quite a network. Among those working for the Americans were some of Gaddafi's most senior men in security, in finance and, of course, in resources: oil. What the west was really interested in. The papers revealed how each informer had been recruited – some through blackmail, some with cash, all with the promise of a life outside Libya when the time came. Ohio, Florida, San Francisco were all listed in their interrogations as places they'd been promised homes for their families with an education and a solid job; the Americans had offered a life in the soft sun far from the desert sands.

And then something curious. The revelation that one man kept appearing in the accounts of the informers. An Englishman. Careful, precise and polite, this man was consistently present at *debriefings* where information was downloaded into the minds of the American handlers and fresh promises made or cash handed out. Not that these men required cash – they were at the very top of the regime, well paid and living comfortable lives.

How had they been caught? The question preoccupied Habid. There was no reference in the documentation – but of course there wouldn't be. Gaddafi's interrogators knew how they'd been caught and the prisoners were unlikely to dwell upon such matters, not while their dangly bits were wired to a twelve volt battery. It intrigued Habid because it was a key part of his research. If he was to become rich as a result of his discovery, he would need to avoid similar pitfalls. He had no intention of ending up in prison. And so he marched back down the black corridors of the jail to demand answers. What he was told was more than a little unnerving.

"Africa," she said slowly, in awe, mesmerised by the view.

Alea hadn't seen land for several days. She'd spent most of her time with the girls below deck, playing, drawing and creating. Isla literally looked up to her, eyes like saucers, captivated. Sam wondered what was going on in his daughter's head, whether she viewed Alea as a mother figure or more of a teacher-type. He had dark moments where he imagined Isla might be jealous of Sadiqah because she had a mother instead of a father. He was under no illusions, given the choice a little girl would opt to keep her mum. It was natural. He'd have chosen the same. If he could swap places with Shannon, he'd do it in a heartbeat.

Alea emerged on deck just as the sun rose to reveal one of the planet's most beautiful sights.

"Turn around," said Sam, curious to see how she would react. "Look what's on the other side."

Alea did as she was bid and rotated gently. "Europe?" she gasped. "We are leaving Mediterranean?"

"We're going to take you to our country."

"Ireland?"

"Ireland," he repeated, savouring the thought.

"Why Ireland?"

"Because, to be blunt, nobody else wants you, and I have a friend there who may be able to help, and because I don't know what else to do."

Her face darkened. "Your friend will send us back."

"Maybe," he said honestly, "but she will do her level best not to."

"Level best?"

"This woman will do everything she can to help you."

His certainty on the matter made her thoughtful.

"Why?"

"Because that's what she does. She helps people. People who have been, well … treated like you have been treated."

Alea smarted and stood more erect. "How you think I been treated?"

Sam took a deep breath. It was plain that Alea was about to get contrary again and he didn't feel comfortable with the way the conversation looked likely to head. He'd just shown her the Strait of Gibraltar on a haze-free day at sunrise and she was already preparing to bust his bollocks.

"Eh?" she pressed. "Tell me how I been treated."

He hadn't the energy. "I don't know."

"You think you know," she said dismissively, "but you refuse-ed to say."

Sam couldn't help but rise to the bait. He was tired, irritable and the weather front ahead was making him anxious. "Well, I know how women are treated where you come from."

"You *think* you know," she said again.

Sam struggled with her hostility. Here he was trying to show some empathy and she was goading him.

"I know how women are treated in some Islamic countries," he conceded.

"What Muslim countries have you been?" She shot him a look, piercing, probing, accusatory.

"Afghan, Iraq, Palestine, Saudi, Yemen, Lebanon, Jordan," he said, trailing off.

"Libya," she poked.

"Libya," he agreed, "I already told you that."

"For why you are really going there? Not for fighting for oppress-ed women."

Sarcasm had never impressed Sam.

"No," he said.

"Then what?"

"I told you. My job," he said firmly, attempting to finish the conversation.

"Is strange job if navy takes you to dry and dirty places far from sea."

"All of those countries have a coast," he said.

"Not Afghanistan."

"No," he admitted. "But that was a different job."

"Is no need for imaginings what you doing *there*."

"How about we talk about what *you* were doing in the sea then? Or why you were running away from Libya?"

She stared hard at him. Sam sulked a little, hurt by what he felt was her ingratitude. He loathed the childishness of his emotions and tried to bring himself round but failed. His exhaustion poured out of his mouth before he had time to think it through.

"You know what I don't get, Alea? Why you are so consumed with my old job. Like ..." he paused searching for words in his sleep-deprived mind, "all I've done since we lifted you out of the tide is try to help you and all you've done is fire me flack."

"Fire me flack, I do not know."

"Give me grief. You're hostile. You're angry. You hate the British and the Americans. I get that. They blew up your home. But *I* didn't. Isla didn't. We saved you and your kid and you're just giving me shit all the time. I don't get it."

"You were army."

"I was not bloody army, but put it like this, if the roles were reversed – if you were Taliban, I'd still have rescued you."

Sam thought about this statement and wondered whether it was true.

"Rescue me so you could change me – make-d me like Western women?" she said, still nipping at him.

"Rescue you because life is the most important thing," he said, thinking aloud. "Anything can happen if there is life. If you're alive, you make up for your mistakes. If you're dead, there's nothing you can do about anything."

"You are speaking of you, not me, I think," Alea said.

Sam couldn't disagree. But then she pressed too far.

"What mistakes you are guilty? You save us to make-ing up for mistake, perhaps. To feel better?" Her lip curled in a snarl.

Sam's heartbeat rose with his voice. "I get that you're grieving, Alea, I really do. Your husband is dead, but, seriously, I didn't know he was in the sea beside us because you didn't tell me. And, for what it's worth, I know what grief is. I've probably seen just as much death and violence as you, and I live with it, I sleep with it, I eat it for fucking breakfast every day. Now why don't you go below and leave me alone until you're able to hold a civil conversation."

Alea stared up at Sam, the hardness draining from her. The admonishment had been unexpected. He realised she had wanted him to repent, to apologise for bombings he'd had no part in. He hadn't tried to justify events in Libya – that would have made her fight back harder, seizing an advantage to keep him on the back foot. Instead, she'd been told to shape up. They were what they were – products of their respective places. That wasn't going to change in the confines of a cockpit in the middle of an ocean. They just had to get on with it.

Alea did as she was told without histrionics. She gently rose from her seat and backed down the ladder into the cabin. She glanced briefly at Sam before she turned, a soft look with her big brown eyes, the tiniest hint of an apology.

"It was the Englishman," said the first man – the foreman of the informers.

The second man nodded his head in agreement at his back.

"The Englishman," repeated Habid, flat and without conviction, his tone designed to convey his scepticism.

"It must have been."

"Why? Why would an Englishman turn you in to Gaddafi if he was getting information from you?"

"The Englishman was different to the Americans. He was – he was silent, almost always."

The second man nodded. "He asked questions only when the Americans were finished. Very few questions – sometimes none at all. He just ... he just watched."

"Yes," said the foreman, "he never took notes. He just stood, back to the wall, in the dark sometimes. We could hear his voice sometimes, but mostly we could barely see him."

"I still don't understand why you think he was the person that betrayed you to Gaddafi."

"It is complicated," said the foreman.

"You think I am incapable of understanding?" Habid bristled, leading to an appeal from the second man.

"No, no, no, please do not think that." He stood up in the cell.

Habid felt the power coast through him – their liberty was within his gift.

"My friend was just explaining that there was a lot happening back then."

"When?" Habid's eyes moved to the foreman.

"When Tunisia began to explode."

"The revolution? What has that got to do with your betrayal?"

"I believe there was a plan. The British wanted to keep Gaddafi in power but the Americans wanted him gone."

"Why?"

"The Englishman must have been from British Intelligence. The Americans must have been CIA—"

"I had managed to work that much out by myself, thank you," said Habid.

"Yes, of course. The CIA wanted to know where the Gaddafi targets were – his home place in Sirte, his bunkers and compounds. They wanted to take him out."

"Is that not what the Englishman wanted?"

"I don't think so. I think he wanted information only about people in the regime. He wanted to know who liked who, what alliances there were. He did not care about locations. He wanted to know what would happen *if* Gaddafi was killed not *when* Gaddafi was killed. I think he wanted Gaddafi to stay, to be alive. I think the Englishman was one of Gaddafi's allies."

Habid thought for a while. "What do you mean, *allies*?"

"Ever since UBL destroyed the Twin Towers, the attitude has changed. America and Britain saw Gaddafi as a friend in the fight against extremists."

"Gaddafi hates the Islamics." Habid nodded.

"They tried to overthrow him many times. He defeated them always, and they ran to all parts of the world, but the Americans became more afraid of them than Gaddafi, so they turned to the leader for information on the militants."

"I see," said Habid, not sure that he saw at all.

"So Britain, especially Britain, started to rub Gaddafi's back. They asked him for help and he gave them it – they got their information. Then when they found the Islamics in different parts of the world, they sent them to Gaddafi for interrogation."

"Because they don't torture people – the CIA?" scoffed Habid.

"The British. They do not like to be seen to torture. They cannot be seen to torture, so Libya does it for them – they get the information."

"I still do not see why you think the Englishman told Gaddafi you were informers?"

"I think he wanted to offer them a reward for the information they passed on about the Islamics. And it also meant we would be taken out of the way – that there would be no evidence."

"And then you were arrested?"

"Yes."

"But Britain and America both still bombed Libya? They

did that together. If Britain wanted Gaddafi to survive, why would they join the CIA and bomb our country?"

The foreman shook his head in despair. The second man appeared behind him and spoke.

"Just because a president and a prime minister want something does not mean that their intelligence chiefs want the same thing. Just look at us."

"You were Gaddafi's intelligence chiefs," sneered Habid, shaking his head. "Slim pickings."

The second man said nothing.

The foreman took up the narrative. "The Spring was too well-advanced. They could see that Gaddafi might lose, so they took away evidence – they removed the risk. They threw us to the dogs to die so that we could not tell the world what they had done."

Habid was more confused than ever.

"What exactly had you done?" he asked, trying to remember what he had read in the papers. "Given them a few coordinates for aerial bombings?"

"Oh, no," said the second man, "we gave them the information to bring Gaddafi in from the cold. We were the people who brokered the deal to pay-off the victims of Lockerbie, to end arms smuggling, to make the leader acceptable to the West again."

Habid nodded slowly. He could see why the Americans and British might have cast them adrift. Which got him thinking, nobody liked loose ends. Least of all him.

***

"I thought you were a part," said Alea.

"Apart from what?" snapped Sam, eight hours later, cold and no less pissed off.

"A part of route." She pronounced route as *rowt*, as if she'd been watching American TV.

The kids were in their cabin. Alea had cooked, or more correctly heated some unidentified carbohydrate with wet meat from a can. Sam had inhaled it.

"Look, Alea, you're going to have to spell this out for me. I don't know what you're talking about." Sam was in no mood for another barney. The swell was building to the point that autopilot was a poor option, which meant that someone had to sail the boat through the heaving sea.

"I thought you waiting for us. When we were in sea."

"When we rescued you?"

"Yes."

"Why?"

"Because you are coming from nowhere," her voice rose in justification. "Like man is waiting for you to arrive-ed."

"What man?"

"Man we pay for journey. Trafficking man. Man who was on *this* boat."

"Why would you think that?" Sam couldn't follow her logic.

"Was long time we are in boat. Many days."

"I understand that bit."

"The man, he keep checking time," she said, motioning to her wrist. "He is waiting."

"What for?"

"For you, I think."

"Why do you think that, Alea? I don't understand." Although it was beginning to dawn on him.

"When is dark, he move women and children to front of boat."

"Ok," said Sam, unsure.

"He sit back of boat with men."

"How many men?"

"Two men."

"So three men in total?"

"Yes, three men. Seven women and children."

"Fuck," said Sam, realising how many had perished.

"Yes."

"But what has that got to do with me?"

"Captain of boat is fisherman. He can use engine. He can use ..." She pointed at the compass on the binnacle.

Sam nodded.

"He see your light."

"Yes, our mast headlight," said Sam, pointing upwards.

"This captain he jumping. Very, very happy. The traffick man get very cross. He tell captain *sit down*! Captain is shouting at light and then traffick man ... he stab-bed captain."

Sam was stunned. He stared at her but said nothing.

"He push captain into sea. Then he stab-bed my husband here." Alea pointed to the side of her neck and began to shake. "I screaming, Sadiqah screaming. We very afraid." The woman's eyes filled with tears but she didn't break down. She had something to say and she steeled herself to say it.

"What did he do then?" asked Sam, gently.

"He tell me, get bank papers from husband body."

"Your husband had his bank statements on him?"

"To pay man when we get to Europe. Was deal. But he make me give passport and papers."

Sam wasn't interested in that. He was worried about what became of the other women.

"Then he women take off cloth-es."

"You and Sadiqah?"

"No, other women. They take off full veil then he stab them dead."

Alea was convulsing now. Sam thought she was about to be sick. He wanted to move towards her, but instinctively knew it would be the wrong thing to do. He let her continue as her sobs grew louder.

"Sadiqah see everything. *Everything.*"

She placed her hand over her face and began to cry hard. Sam left her for a few minutes until the shudder abated.

"What did he do with the dead women?"

"They have papers. He take all papers and keep them inside his clothes in bag here." She gestured at her torso. "Then he push into sea."

Sam sat still for a long while waiting for her to recover.

"Did he push you into the sea?"

"No."

Sam just waited, unable to press her any further.

Alea blew her nose and then looked at him. "He stab boat." She began a sweeping motion as if she had a dagger.

"He let the air out before we were close?" Sam asked, surprised at the level of risk the man had taken.

"You were so close," she said. "I could see you."

"The boat must have sunk fast."

"Air is all gone. The water so cold." Alea began to cry again. "Sadiqah, she is panic, the sea in her mouth."

"The man was in the sea – could he swim?"

"He has preserver," she said, pointing to Isla's buoyancy aid. "When in sea he says blow." Her gesture was similar to that of an air hostess demonstrating how to use a whistle on a life jacket located under a seat.

"A whistle," Sam said.

"Whistle," she repeated. "Then you are in sea and Sadiqah is dying and you take us onto here." She opened her hands.

"And you thought I was there by appointment?"

"Is what?"

"You thought I had come to collect you – to pick you up."

"Of course."

Sam knew there was a flaw in her reasoning but it took a while to work out what it was.

"Alea, why would the man let you live when he killed the others?"

"This I do not know." She slowly shook her head, at a loss.

He realised she had thought about this but hadn't worked it out. Sam tried to reason it out. "Well, what did he need most?"

"Money?" she shrugged.

"Money is no use if you are dead."

"Safety?" she suggested.

"Rescued."

"Rescue." She nodded in agreement.

"So what's the best way to get rescued when you're not a migrant at all but actually a murderer and people trafficker?"

"*Aintihal*," she said, hunting for the correct phrase. "*Tazahar*."

Sam frowned.

"Make lie," she tried.

"You pretend to be a woman," Sam said.

"Pretend!" She seized the word. "Yes, he pretend."

"But why? If it was for money, he had already taken your passports and bank statements."

Alea thought about that for a while. "He need to say he is owner. At bank. He need to ..." She rubbed her fingers together.

"Verify they are his?" Sam ventured. "Prove it?"

"Prove it." She nodded in satisfaction.

"So he needed *you* to pretend that he is your husband."

"Yes," she said, then frowned. "But he take veil and dress as woman." She was at a loss.

"Don't you see?" Sam said.

Alea just looked at him.

"He didn't know who was picking you out of the water. I reckon he just wanted to make sure he got to safety. Maybe he decided that a woman had a better chance of being rescued than a man."

Alea shrugged as if it were a possibility. "Perhaps is simple. He want to get to Europe, then when he get he run away."

"Maybe he realised that the veil would be lifted eventually – that someone would see he was a man, and then he would need a backup. Maybe the backup was that he was your husband. Maybe you were his passport to asylum. Single men are less likely to be granted asylum."

"Maybe he need us for money from bank," she said dryly.

He couldn't fault her scepticism. "Yeah, could be," he conceded. "Whatever it was it seems to have worked, in part at least, but I'll tell you this for nothing, Alea – I had nothing to do with it."

The tears cascaded down her face and she eventually began to nod. "I am sorry," she said. "I am sorry, Sam."

16

It felt peaceful to be back in the barren stone-strewn desert. Habid, his staff in hand and with a scarf wrapped tightly around his face, struck out for his hidey-hole halfway between Benghazi and Tobruk. He chose to travel on foot for the roadsides were riddled with rival tribes attempting to assert their authority. It was hard to imagine how but it had never been easier to get shot dead in Libya.

Habid couldn't help congratulating himself. He'd retrieved the next batch of papers from his underwater hideaway and had them tucked safely into his belt. He'd selected the next group of travellers and would announce their names as if they'd won the lottery. They would emerge pale but grateful, their eyes batting in the sun – and they would do whatever he told them. There was nothing like a few months in a hole in the ground to instil discipline, even among those more accustomed to giving orders than receiving them.

He had held their feet to the fire from the moment he discovered them. Habid smiled at how clever his instincts had proven. Had he simply demanded a ransom for their release from that Benghazi jail, they would have known they were going to die and been unlikely to pay up. Anyone who chose to take that risk would part with money only once. Habid wanted security amid the madness into which his country was free-falling. He wanted repeat business, and the only way to get it was to supply a good service and receive recommendations so that others might present themselves for extraction. His wasn't the sort profession one advertised on Facebook, so he had offered the prisoners something – a carrot to informers more familiar with a stick. It was something they couldn't get anywhere else.

Hope.

Hope that they might one day live free again as the CIA had promised them but failed to provide. Hope in exchange for money that was useless amid their own detritus in the colon of a forgotten jail.

They were scared of everyone – of being caught by the militias, the tribes, Gaddafi loyalists, Egyptians, anyone. It made them subservient to Habid. He could ask them to strip naked and run barefoot over the rocky ground and they would do as they were bid.

Of course he had the expertise and the contacts – friends and colleagues at the border crossings who would let his little flock flow through. He knew how to pay enough but not too much. He knew to mix it up to prevent using the same checkpoint each time, which kept the border guards hungry for the little they got rather than cocky enough to ask for more. They too were glad of his business and eager to provide passage.

And it just got better and better. His deal with Tassels may have been forced upon him, and it was early days, but it was working well – so far. Months had passed since they'd first met and the dynamic between the two men had changed utterly. The few runs they had collaborated on had thrown up unexpected advantages – when Habid's little caravans reached Egypt they were guaranteed a police escort, no less. Not official, not in uniform, but Tassels let everyone know he was a police officer and was there to help them. Habid delighted at the awe in which the flock held him when they heard that. They gazed upon Habid as if he were Moses leading them to safety across the sands.

And then in Alexandria they entered a bank and make the transfers. Habid always allowed them to make their calls to other exiles in Libya with enough cash to make a similar trip. Later, when he was sure the boats were in place and that Tassels was not about to stroke him, he extracted a sum of cash and shared it with the loathsome little cop. Placated, the jumpy Tassels then arranged to have him driven back to the border to begin all over again.

Yes, he mused as he struck out from Benghazi, it was a fine plan that refined like oil – added value and accumulated interest. And the best bit of all? Tassels was at his beck and call.

The weather forecast for the trip ahead was favourable – no storms, no floods. The desert was a dangerous place when the wind rose or the rain came. A person could end up swimming in the sands – drowning even. Most people refused to believe the speed at which rivers could be created from nothing but Habid had seen it many times. The gushing flow created by a downpour, the stones from the desert surface swept up - barrelling at shins and feet, wreaking damage, inspiring infection.

Habid looked at the stump of his own toe sticking out of his sandal like a beacon. The infection had passed but the pain hadn't. He thought of Tassels and the deal they had reached. Then he thought of Big Suit and wondered where that thug had vanished to. And as his anger rose he again resolved to cut them out at the first opportunity – while causing them as much pain as possible.

Blind panic. It was a look similar to a first-time flyer's face when their aircraft hits violent turbulence. Alea remained silent but her mouth was open and her eyes enormous as she stared askance at Sam pleading for confirmation they weren't about to drown.

"This is how it will be for a few days," he shouted. "It will be tough but we have to sail through it."

"Days?" she yelled back, incredulous.

He just nodded, making wild adjustments to the helm to keep the boat on her feet. He'd reefed her down hard, two slabs and a storm jib, yet *Sian* was still on her ear, heeled hard over, riding the waves slowly, plummeting down the far side and hitting the trough with a shudder and bang.

Alea was reliving her hell. "Turn back," she screamed.

"You will get used to it," Sam assured her.

"No." She shook her head with certainty. She moved to turn back into the cabin.

"If you feel sick, come up here," he said. "You will feel better up here," he yelled, but she was gone.

Sam had the engine running. He was confident the wind strength would carry them home when he turned, and even if they did run out of diesel, he would prefer to get through the hard part as quickly as possible. Besides, the batteries needed a good charge – without them the iPad would go flat and the children would go mad with boredom. That would also mean he'd have to navigate the old way because his screens would dim and he'd be compelled to spend long periods dead reckoning their position and down below at the chart table. Not good. At least the movies and games would distract the children while the boat was hurled all the way towards Biscay.

The previous day had been disciplined: Sam had laden his crew with information. He needed to be confident they understood his directions. He'd walked them around the boat, explained that they needed to clip their harnesses on at all times. He had shown them the life raft, the trigger line, how to cut its tethering straps and throw it into the water. He had stood Alea at the wheel and made her sail the boat for two solid hours, gently explaining how the sails worked, how to tease the boat closer to the wind and when to bear away. He wasn't confident she had fully grasped the science of it – only time could teach her to feel how the boat behaved – but she was intelligent and the time wasn't wasted.

His deepest fear was injury – not just to the girls or Alea, but to himself. If he got hurt, they would all be in real danger. As a leader of young Marines it had been Sam's job to identify risks and threats and mitigate wherever he could, and now it was his job to keep those kids safe. As a consequence he found himself running through scenario after scenario, identifying dangers and flaws and loading Alea and the girls with instructions on what to do if A, B or C occurred. It had frightened them a little, he knew, but it was for the best.

Almost anything could go wrong in such a sea: the rig could come down potentially damaging the boat in the process; hands could get trapped in winches and under such loads fingers could get lost, blood spilled; catastrophic bleeds; concussions for those hurled about below deck; and the constant threat of being swept overboard were all real dangers. He'd tasked Alea with watching the radar like a hawk, another reason to get the batteries as full as possible. Sam didn't tell her but he knew that in weather like this merchant ships routinely lost their cargo. Semi-submerged metal containers as big as their own boat could be hit at speed, which would send them to the bottom in seconds. Sam wanted to maximise the chances of spotting anything ahead of them.

As the hours passed they settled, uncomfortably, into a routine. He would call out once in a while and Alea's hand would appear, acknowledging that she had consulted the radar screen and her thumb up indicating all was clear. If that changed, Sam would adjust course immediately then run below to the chart table to take a look. The girls were tucked in behind their lee cloths, full of Stugeron seasickness tablets. Sam was rotating them between Kwells and other brands, dosing them slightly beyond the recommended limits. He hoped they would sleep through as much of it as possible but the noise was atrocious. His approach was to act with confidence in the hope that his ease might spread among the others. In truth he was addled with guilt, seething like the hissing sea, that Isla was once again in danger because of his decisions made in haste.

Tassels resented having to collect the strangers. They went on the trips with the arrivals from the desert, but they certainly weren't prisoners. They arrived all sorts of ways – by train, by road, even by sea. The rat had refused to explain where they came from or what their role was. Some were African, some could have been European – or Albanian perhaps, maybe even Bulgarian or from somewhere in the former Yugoslavia. He couldn't tell because they refused to speak. They had the air of seasoned men ready for work. They had bags slung over their shoulders and were the only people permitted luggage. Each one of them declined the offer of life jackets.

Tassels didn't like it one bit. They ignored him as if they'd been briefed to give him a wide berth. Worse still, they didn't appear to pay. Tassels suspected the rat was doing back-door deals cashing in on extras while cutting him out. It infuriated him but he had no choice. Somehow he had become dependent upon the desert rat and he couldn't quite put his finger on the point the wind had changed.

Tassels had become irritably familiar with his role, his routine. He took a little comfort that he had created his own sideline. As far as the rat was concerned Tassels collected one or two boats at a time and ferried them across the sand sea of Sinai at reasonable risk. Tassels did indeed collect in Nuweiba, but he was now accustomed to the purchase of six or seven boats at a time, five of which were transported to Suez. For this he marked-up the cost charged by the courier and then bartered with the commercial shipping reps who seemed awash with cash. He had bundles of American dollars now, unconverted and ready for his next life; like a pharaoh stock-piling for an imagined re-incarnation. From Suez the going got easy. His police ID saw him through the rest of the journey and only occasionally was he required to part with a few green bills to ease his progress. It was the Egyptian way, he thought: add value, get paid.

There were two loose ends, well, one loose one, one fat one. Big Suit's disappearance still troubled him. If the beards had abducted the big man, they'd have beheaded him on the internet by now. If the army had him, Tassels was sure he'd have heard – probably through his own arrest.

The other irritating unknown was the doctor, his cousin. Tassels accepted that there had been little choice but to bring him in on the racket, but the doc was yet another intelligent individual who could hold him to the heat. Between the rat and the doc Tassels was compromised. They knew what he had done and they could and would exact their price, just as he would do himself if the roles were reversed.

The last issue to keep him awake at night was Alexandria itself. It never slept. As Egypt had plunged deeper into an economic depression, every idiot, his wife and children had taken to trying to feed themselves from the sea. The Spring was starving some Alexandrians and they would gather at all hours to cast nets. Folk were strung out along the beaches many miles from the town's seafront. Thieves had taken to stealing the precious nets at night, so sentries were posted – often the eldest child in any family, to keep an eye out for robbers. It had forced Tassels and the rat to venture further and further from the town and increased the possibility of being spotted. They had become more and more furtive as they prepared to cast the migrants to the sea, occasionally having to part with cash to ensure the silence of some wide-eyed observer. They opted against violence, for violence bred bitterness, which made the recipient talkative.

Not that Tassels ever saw the boats off. He was ordered to stand guard beyond sight of disembarkation. It was demeaning, but it allowed him to disassociate himself if they did get caught. Yes, the process was functional and lucrative, yet Tassels was haunted by the prospect of discovery. He worried that it was all too good to be true, that it would fall apart and he would end up as many of his prisoners had – wired to the mains, juddering and salivating like a feral dog.

There are few things worse than seasickness, Sam knew that from bitter experience. He had been a sufferer. In fact, at the start of a journey he could still become ill if he spent too much time below deck peering at charts or plotters.

Thirty-nine hours of beating into the forty-knot breeze had, remarkably, not disturbed any of his charges. They'd seen it through with a fortitude that made him proud of each of them. But as he turned further north the pitch of the boat changed to a sideways, uncomfortable roll – a yaw that turned Alea pale, then green. She sat in the cockpit with her back to the cabin heaving nothingness into a bucket, all life drained from her.

Sam had placed the children on shifts at the radar. Isla knew a little about what the instrument panel was telling them, and as he explained it all to Sadiqah he became aware of how much English the child appeared to have subsumed in the short time the girls had been together.

Sam had unfurled one of the big jibs and it was drawing them forward at about eight knots. If they could maintain that sort of hourly rate, they would shave considerable time off their ETA. They would also have enough food to get there – Alea's consumption was nil and Sam struggled to even get the pills into her. He knew the sickness stood a reasonable chance of passing before she became so weak that he had to worry and that many people eventually adjusted to the sea and her ways once the shock had worn off.

The pills, for the children, appeared to be working well though. They pottered around and chatted and clutched at items as they fell from shelves. The only hassle was cooking. Sam was running on vapour, awake only because he was too scared to sleep. The boat warbled so badly that he was reluctant to boil water and the flask had long since been emptied of coffee. He poured stodgy bolognaise into a pan and heated it a little. He and the girls ate it directly from the pan, ladling it down their throats, legs apart, wedged against the furniture. The smell turned Alea into a retching fit but they had to eat.

Fifteen more hours, Sam reckoned, before the sea would calm a little and he could get her back on her feet.

―――――――

The doctor was getting antsy and it was making Tassels angry. The constant pestering like that of a child.

"You owe me," he kept saying.

"I am aware of this," Tassels replied, "but you must wait."

"How hard can it be?" his cousin persisted. "There must be a doctor among these refugees. They have doctors in Libya, you know. Gaddafi must have had a personal doctor surely."

Tassels had rounded at that. "So you want to subsume the

identity of Gaddafi's physician?" he mocked. "How comfortable do you think your new life will be with that hanging round your neck? You'll be thrown in a European jail and forgotten about."

"Another doctor then, so long as they have papers. Qualifications."

"Like you once had?" sneered Tassels.

"I just need a reference. A real reference. Find me a doctor and your problem goes away."

"What problem?" Tassels narrowed his eyes, staring his cousin down.

"The problem you have in me," said the doctor, shakily but gathering courage. "The problem that I know what you did and what you are doing."

Tassels stared for a long while, then spoke as he turned away.

"There are often many ways to deal with problems."

17

The silence gave Sam time to think, and the more he thought the more he was sure there were things needing to be discussed.

He stared at Alea who was gradually gaining colour. As the swell eased he had found renewed confidence in the kettle and taken to making her hot black tea, spooning sugar into it to give her some energy. Her head still hung between her shoulders, swinging as if on gimbals. She was just beyond that state associated with prolonged seasickness where the sufferer no longer cares whether they live or die. He wasn't sure she would ever be fit for questionning, so he reckoned now was as good a time as any.

"Alea?"

Her head lifted. Her paleness exacerbated by her jet-black hair made her look skeletal. She bid him speak without making a sound.

"I need you to tell me. The man. The trafficker. When he took you into the cabin, did he harm you in any way?"

"You mean did he rape me." She stated it. She didn't ask.

"Yes," he said softly.

"What does it matter?" She shook her head slightly as if to say that Sam didn't care one way or the other. "Are you afraid he raped me on your precious boat?"

"What?" he said, disgusted.

"Are you scared that man took me on one of your beds?"

Sam looked away.

"Mmm," was all he heard, as if him looking away had confirmed her thought.

Perhaps that was his thinking. Sam thought about why it was important to him. He wrestled with the genesis of his inquiry. There was some truth to what she said. This woman appeared to understand the worst of men. His mind flashed to the violence of what he had suggested, the idea that it had happened in the confines of one of the cabins his daughter played. Where she, on occasion, slept. He wanted to believe that the selfishness of such thoughts hadn't been a factor in his question but he couldn't even persuade himself never mind Alea.

"Did he rape you?"

"No, at least you save me from this."

"I saved you – how?"

She was silent for a while, her head hanging. "He can see your body. When you lie. Not waking. Here." Her hand struck out, a finger pointing at the floor of the cockpit.

"When I was unconscious?"

Her head nodded, barely.

"How did that prevent you being raped?"

"He knows he not able to beat you. Or stab."

"How?"

He heard her sigh. She wanted to be left alone to her sickness. "My husband," she said eventually, "the other men in boat. They small men. Not strong. You are strong. He can see. When you lie there. He can see."

"Why did he not stab me when I was unconscious?"

"He cannot sail boat. He cannot start engine. Isla not show him. Very fast everything, no time. He already kill only man know how to use boat. He *need* you."

Sam paused while Alea heaved breaths in, fending off the gag reflex. Eventually she looked up.

"Did he try to rape you?"

"I see he is thinking he will force me. I tell him if he touch me, I scream. I promise him I not speak to you, to Isla in English, but if he touch Sadiqah, if he touch me, I scream, I tell you everything."

Sam thought for a while. "But you thought I was working with him?"

"Yes, but ..." She shrugged.

"You still thought I would protect you?"

Her eyes narrowed, brow creased. "You have daughter. I have daughter," was all she said.

But Sam understood. He understood that her alleged mistrust of him was not quite as she had explained it. He understood there was more to this woman than she was willing to share.

Big Suit considered escape, fleetingly, but he was too exhausted. He was too unfit to lumber across the desert. He was too lazy to try. In the back of his mind remained the notion that his old friend wouldn't allow any serious harm to be bestowed upon him. Big Suit was regretting calling Waleed out as a Coptic. It had taken time but he realised now that it had been a mistake – that in discovering Waleed's secret and voicing it he had compromised only himself. The dim bulb in his head flickered from time to time as he struggled through the likely scenarios: Waleed could take the view that the implicit blackmail had to be taken on the chin – that he would have to release his old friend and hope for the best. Alternatively he could vanquish the threat and bury it in a very wide hole in the desert. Big Suit thought this unlikely, though. Waleed had protected him, in a way, back at the academy. He was tough enough to have been selected for a special military unit but there was a decency to the man, a natural justice. Big Suit couldn't articulate that properly in his mind but he recognised it nonetheless. Worst case, he calculated at great length, was that Waleed would leave him to his suit and his sweat to rot it out in the desert tin can. To a man of Big Suit's intellect that prospect was at least unchallenging, if perhaps unwelcome.

He sat undernourished and unwashed and imagined calling a guard to tell his tales: *Your boss, he's a Coptic*, he might say. *Really?* Might come the reply. *Well, I'll tell my superiors.* And what then? Would the superiors act? And if they did sack Waleed, would that mean they would release Big Suit? Well, they'd need to find out why he was being detained and for that they would need to care. And they wouldn't care, just as he wouldn't in their place.

And so eventually it became clear to Big Suit that there was no advantage to spilling his guts. He willed his mind to think as his boss would – or that rat who had turned near death to his advantage, but his big toad-like head just shook in despair. Save for an act of grace from an old acquaintance he would probably die.

"Who is friend?"

"How do you mean?"

"You friend. In Ireland. Who can help us."

"Who will *try* to help you," he corrected her.

"Who is she?"

"She's a woman I used to work for."

"In Navy?"

"No. After that."

"What doing?"

"Helping her. Helping her help people."

"What people?"

"It's a long story."

"Is long journey." She wasn't for giving up.

Sam preferred Alea when she was being sick and silent. She had rallied significantly and had eaten some plain pasta.

"So is ok you ask me am I raped, but I not ask you what job you do for woman who is helping us?"

She made a fair point.

"I used to get people, well, women mostly – I used to get them out of Ireland."

"Get out of Ireland?"

"Yes."

"Why?"

"Because they were being used."

"Used how?"

He stared at her. "Used for sex," he said, his tone harsh, hoping to end her interest.

"And now you help us *into* Ireland," she said, the irony not lost on her.

"Not through choice, Alea, I can assure you."

"How did you get them out, the women?"

"Over my shoulder mostly," said Sam without thinking.

"You carry?"

"Sometimes."

"Just women?"

"No, anyone really who was in a shit shape."

"This I don't know."

"Anyone that my friend said needed help. She would call me and I would go, get the person, take them to the docks or the airport or whatever, and she would pay for them to get home."

"Why did you do this?"

Sam sighed. "Look, Alea, I didn't ask a whole lot about it. I just did what she asked and she paid me. Most of the time."

"Sometimes you do without money?"

Sam ignored the question. He wasn't about to tell her that he often shook down the pimps and madams who ran the women. That he considered the fleecing of shipping companies or gang masters as reward for risk.

She looked to sea, musing. "What is her name?"

"My friend?"

"Yes."

"I call her Charity."

Tassels stood at his desk his head hanging between his shoulders listening to threats with a resigned endurance.

"If you do not find me someone soon, this racket is over. I will expose you."

Tassels lifted his face to give his cousin a long, hard stare.

"I have nothing to lose," the doctor went on. "My license is already gone, I have no job, I can't even work the black market because nobody in Egypt can get any drugs or medication. You need to honour your agreement. You need to get me out."

"I have been looking for a doctor, you know that."

"You have not been looking hard enough. There have been dozens – maybe hundreds of migrants coming through. You have seen them all. You should have been checking their papers."

"It's not that easy," said Tassels, frustration creeping into his voice.

"Why?" pressed the doctor.

"Because I do not have as much control as you think."

"You are running this racket," said the doctor dismissively. "You told me they come with papers."

"They do, but the rat – he keeps the papers."

"They leave Egypt without them?"

"I do not know," said Tassels. "I do not know."

"You need to get those papers," said the doctor. "You need to find me a doctor I can swap places with. You need to find me someone whose identity I can take. Then you need to deal with that person."

"*I* need to deal with that person?" said Tassels, incredulous.

"Yes," said his cousin. "I am not in the business of taking life. My line of work is to save life."

Tassels scoffed. "Then why are you not a doctor any more?" he sneered. "You betrayed your oaths easily enough in the past. You just don't have the stomach for it."

"Perhaps," said the doctor. "But *you* do. I have seen evidence enough of that over the years. And evidence is what I possess, so find me a doctor and do what you agreed."

The doctor turned and slammed the door.

Something was bothering Alea. He could see her below, moving around, pausing as she tidied, placing things back on shelves, grabbing them as they rolled around the floor. The debris of sailing through a storm. He felt sure she was going to ask him straight out but on the occasions she'd glanced at him she became distracted by another job and moved away from his line of sight. She played with the girls and fed them and listened to music. She pretended to read but seldom peeled a page. At least her body had become attuned to the perpetual movement of the boat. Eventually she came above and sat in the cockpit. The going was steadier and Sam had both headsails out and had shaken the reefs from the main to keep up the speed as the breeze had eased.

"What is it?"

"Is what?" she said, but she knew what he was talking about because she declined to even look at him.

"You might as well just ask."

She waited a few minutes before beginning. "What if Charity not help us?"

"I told you. She will try. I promise you she will do her best."

"What if she not able?"

Sam realised they were slowly getting to the root of the issue. "Why might she not be able, Alea?"

"Europe has laws. They not like migrants. Nobody want Arabs. Nobody want Muslims. They think we all are bin Laden."

Sam hadn't the energy to disagree. There was some truth to what she was saying, he imagined. Not that he kept close tabs on society's opinions, or much cared for that matter.

"She'll try," was all he said.

"They will send us back to Tripoli," Alea said, resigned, staring at the darkness.

"Well, if they do, at least you'll be alive."

"Maybe not for long," she said.

"Alea, what are you not telling me?"

She gradually turned to look at him, her eyes sparkling with emotion, with fear. And then, slowly, she began to speak.

Habid's mouth hung open. It looked to Tassels like saliva might drop from his lip at any moment. He was leering, loving every moment of the conversation.

"You need to help me. If we don't find a doctor, my cousin

will disrupt this whole flow of business. He will go to the authorities and have us arrested."

Habid remained silent. He was almost quivering with joy at Tassels' pleas. The bent copper had no choice but to press on.

"Can you not see that this is dangerous for us? That doctor knows who you are – he can identify you. He knows me, he knows that big idiot who interrogated you. He has even tended to some of your Libyans. I mean, what he is asking for *is* possible, isn't it?"

Habid's expression didn't change. His eyes were alight, his return stare almost ravenous, as if he'd been deprived and was staring at an indulgence.

"So will you help me? Will you help us?"

Habid suddenly snapped out of his avaricious imaginings and focused on his former torturer.

"The doctor will receive what he is due, assure him of that. As will you – that is a promise."

Tassels could barely swallow.

"You cannot understand," she said, "you are military man. Gaddafi was your enemy."

"Alea, Gaddafi was everyone's enemy. I'm not pretending to know a whole lot about it but he didn't even get on with the other leaders in the region – other Arabs, not really. He was a total rocket."

"A rocket?" she said despairingly, lost as to what he meant.

"A maverick, a loose cannon. Totally bingo."

She stared at him in bewilderment.

"He was mad," he tried.

"Yes," she accepted, "but he kept control."

"He armed the IRA and they killed kids in Ireland. The IRA used his guns and his Semtex to kill people, including their own. He blew up passenger planes. Didn't he rape and abuse people in his big fuck-off tent?"

"You can never understand. Country like Libya needs strong leader."

"A rapist and murderer?"

She looked away again.

"No," she said, "but when the leader in power, people had chance. Now it raining bullets from sky in Libya. Mad men everywhere, shooting in air, killing each other. One *katiba* fighting another."

Sam was familiar with the phrase; it meant battalion or military unit. He took her to mean the tribesmen battling for supremacy.

"I know you don't want to go back there, especially with Sadiqah, but surely it's got to be better for women than it was under Gaddafi?"

"You think we are all like al-Qaeda," she spat. "For women – when Gaddafi there, life is OK. I go to work every day, no coverings. I can drive, I can study. But now," she said, "now is not possible. Islamists try to change things so women cannot do these things."

Sam had no point of reference and no argument to make. If what she was saying was true, then he could well imagine that the lifestyle of a widow and her child could be grim.

"There is more to it than that, though, isn't there, Alea?"

He let that hang in the air for a while.

"What you mean?" she said eventually.

"For you to return it would be particularly dangerous, wouldn't it?"

She didn't flinch, apparently ignoring his remark.

He pressed. "Your husband," Sam said, "he wasn't a banker, was he?"

Silence.

"Did he work for Gaddafi?"

She refused to reply.

"You had to hide because you were known Gaddafi loyalists, weren't you?"

"I was not," she said eventually, "but my husband was a part. But not always."

Sam didn't really need to know any more than that.

"I don't know if that information would help or hinder your asylum application in Ireland," said Sam, "but if I were you, I'd keep it to myself."

If Alea understood, she didn't acknowledge it. She seemed defeated. Eventually she rose and went below and Sam shook his head again at the incredible twisted mess he had landed in.

Waleed stared at the rotten flesh assembled on a stainless steel table. There were fragments of clothing, a buckle, some shrapnel. A pathologist was explaining that as far as he could tell this was all that remained of the suicide bomber. All Waleed could think about was what the parents of the girl whose remains were assembled like a flea market jigsaw would think if they could see her now. Most pieces were missing. Some hair had survived. Her gender had been confirmed only by eyewitnesses who had seen her climb aboard the bus.

Arish had returned to normal. The blood had been washed away. The deformed bus had been dragged off to a holding shed.

His investigation was pointless. He knew what must have happened: IS. Islamic State. Daesh. ISIL. It had plenty of names and plenty of people. They swarmed like locusts devouring all in their path, including young women who were put to work, raped, sold, whipped, killed. Waleed had read all the intelligence reports – dozens of accounts. They'd been headed his way, so he'd taken an interest. He looked again at the lumps assembled on the shiny table and imagined the young woman before IS had arrived in her town. She had probably been subservient to the men in her family and she may well have spent most of her day covered, but at least she'd have had some degree of freedom. When the glorious fighters had arrived to instil their ideology on her village she would have been taken from all that she knew, probably all that she loved. Her father may have been shot; her brothers probably executed.

Iraqi Special Forces had liberated towns and cities and forced these revolutionaries west and south. They had taken women with them and left old folk to tell the tales of genocide. Conditions for this girl had most likely got so bad she had willingly volunteered for the operation. When faced with the choice of heaven or being handed about like a shisha pipe, Waleed wasn't sure he wouldn't have done the same.

One hundred miles offshore Sam swept around inside the hood of the chart table for something he hadn't used in a long time. Eventually his fingers ran across the smooth screen of the smartphone Charity had given him. He pulled it out and plugged it in to charge before taking a staple and popping out the SIM holder. Wrapped in a piece of Blu-Tack and stuck to the timber bulkhead in front of him was the SIM card she'd supplied him with. He wondered whether she'd kept paying for the account given that he hadn't been in touch for months.

He snapped it all back together and the phone came to life. He waved it around with little expectation – they were still too far from Ireland to catch any service. That didn't stop him checking it far too frequently though, as he ruminated on what he might say to her. He wondered if Charity was upset that he had just disappeared. The last time they'd spoken he'd left her with quite a mess to tidy up. He reckoned she would understand that Isla was his priority, and if she didn't get that, well, that was just the way it had to be. But there was something about the woman that made him regret treating her as he had – being out of contact for so long without even telling her they were ok.

In truth she'd not been out of his mind much as he'd tried to make her so. He declined to allow her to form part of his imagination, yet she came knocking anyway. He refused her the space, reserving it for Shannon, who still whispered to him, who guided him, who still made him cry at night. But he and Shannon spoke less often now and he hated that; that she was drifting, that the smell of her perfume was wearing off the T-shirt he kept in the drawer beside his bunk. He'd put it in a plastic bag to try and prevent the perfume being replaced by the aroma of teak from the boat's furniture, yet still it weakened. He was scared that one day there might be no scent there at all.

The rat unfurled a page as if he were a courier in ancient times about to make an announcement. He stared at his document, plucked at random from his shallow sea scroll and scanned the list and descriptions. His gaze fell upon one name and he paused for a moment, deliberating. He peered into the darkness of the shelter behind his desert hole and called for the man to come forward. There was a shuffle and a patter of sandals, and a ragged head emerged from the gloom.

"You are a doctor?" Habid inquired.

"I am," said the man.

"A medical doctor?"

"Yes."

"You have references?"

"References?"

"If you go to Europe, can you get work as a doctor?"

The man looked wary and confused.

"Can a hospital call your employers and confirm you are a doctor?" Habid rephrased.

"Of course, but my former colleagues, they hate me."

"Because you worked for Gaddafi. Well, keep that to yourself for now. When you get to Egypt there is a man who will ask you questions. You do not need to tell him your references are ... questionable."

"What is this about?" asked the man, excitement building that he may be the next person to be extracted.

"You do not need to know," said Habid. "Have you got credentials? Have you got something to prove you are qualified?"

"I have a medical card. It gives me access to the hospital, or at least it did. And I have my certificate at my home."

"Address?" Habid barked. He had become accustomed to the process of rummaging through the houses of his charges. If their bank details could be found, they made it across the border. If not, they remained in the desert.

The man duly obliged.

"I'll be back," said Habid, "if I can find your proof."

"It was on the wall in my study," said the man, pleading. "Whoever lives there now, they may have taken it down. Please look everywhere."

I will, thought Habid. I will.

———

Twenty-five hours, Sam reckoned. Five knots of speed, just under one hundred miles, and any amount of uncertainty ahead. His options were many: he could aim for a small harbour and hope to approach unnoticed, but the chances of that working out were slim. Irish Customs had proved pretty

efficient in recent years at checking sailing boats. He had bene-
fitted from their diligence after all. The yacht that was home to
him and Isla had once been a drugs boat bought for cash in the
Caribbean, laden with cocaine and sailed across the Atlantic.
Customs, whether acting on US intel or on their own initiative,
had intercepted it, thrown the crew in jail and unceremoni-
ously ripped the boat apart. At least he had managed to pick it
up cheap at auction.

Crosshaven was his preference as he knew it well from his
days working at boats, but Cork Harbour was one of the
island's major ports and approaching vessels were likely to be
picked up on radar and stood a good chance of being intercepted for routine questioning. Sam didn't fancy that. He'd
spent a lot of time disrupting people traffickers and he'd
given the notion of being considered as one a whirl and it
wasn't appealing. Besides, he was reasonably confident his
past behaviour would be recorded somewhere in a law
enforcement database and arrest was a prospect he could do
without.

Sam dipped the diesel tank confirming they'd be sucking
air soon. They had enough food to see them through two more
days, but the wind was dropping and he didn't fancy a drift
around the south coast. Isla eventually broke his dithering.

"Daddy, can Sadiqah come and live with us?"

"What? No," he said, without thinking. "No, love, there's not
enough space on the boat."

"I know but we could live in a house when we get back to
Ireland," she said, rolling her tongue around the landmass as if
it were now unusual and exotic to her.

"Houses cost a lot of money, wee love."

"There's lots of money under the floorboards," she pointed
out unhelpfully.

Sam mused at how little he could conceal from her as she
became more alert, more worldly-wise. Boats weren't places fit

for secrets unless – it appeared – the secrets were being kept from him.

"Not enough to buy a house," he said, which was almost true.

Sam didn't rate his chances of getting a mortgage for the remainder given that his means of income was invisible and a tax investigation would do him no good at all. But the conversation served to confirm that they couldn't afford to put in at any major port. They'd be much safer going somewhere small, somewhere sleepy. He asked her to bring up the chart of the Irish south-east coast.

"How long?" Alea looked up from the galley. She'd gradually added an extra piece of clothing every day since they'd left the Med and he'd caught her shivering a few times.

"One day. Nearly there."

She climbed the steps of the companionway. "Then what?"

"Good question," said Sam, taking the map Isla offered from below.

He'd noticed how his daughter had declined any opportunity to get between him and Alea when they were speaking. He wasn't sure why. Any other time a stranger spoke to him she'd been right in the middle of it interrupting or sucking in every word.

"Where your friend take us?" Alea asked.

"Dublin, probably. That's where she lives."

"And what then?"

"Honestly, Alea, I don't know."

"You don't care, is true."

Sam thought for a moment, realised she was right and lied.

"I do care," he said, "but I have my own child to look after, Alea."

Sam got back to the chart. He could get Charity to meet them further west – Baltimore, Unionhall, Skibbereen. They were attractive destinations in that fewer people meant fewer cops, but it also meant that new arrivals were more likely to be noticed, particularly exotic-looking women and children no matter how Western their attire. Such places were also further from where Sam wanted go with Isla. His plan was to head north and east not south and west. He followed the coast in the desired direction – Youghal, Dungarvan, Tramore, Dunmore.

Kilmore was familiar to him but he remembered a bar brawl there, a village teeming with fishermen if not fish, each of them fairly hostile to sailors. Those who made their living on the sea tended to have little regard for those who took their pleasure from it, and there were often minor battles when yachts tied up alongside commercial vessels. Sam recognised that the fishermen often had a point – some yachts people acted like they owned each place they visited. For them the sea was a playground; for the fishermen it was a workplace. Each tended to look down their noses at the other and Sam could do without the hassle, so he ruled out Kilmore and Dunmore, and as far as he could remember Tramore was a sandy beach with little or no harbour. Dungarvan was unfamiliar but the pilot books suggested it was no longer a fishing port, so he set a loose course for it. He looked again at Alea, softening with the knowledge that he had a plan.

"Look, Alea, Charity is a good person, a really good person. This is what she does all the time. You'll be in good hands, you and Sadiqah."

"Who are the people she helps?"

Alea had obviously been working through scenarios. Sam plumped for the truth.

"Sex workers mainly. People who thought they were coming to the UK or Ireland to do other work, as far as I could see. They'd been promised cleaning work or whatever and they ended up being used for sex."

"I am not hooker," said Alea disgusted.

"Well, I know that, and *you* know I wasn't suggesting you

are a hooker," Sam's exhaustion wasn't up to any protracted discussion, "but the fact remains that my friend has expertise in helping women who need help – foreign women. That's all."

"And you and Isla will just sail away."

"Yes, Alea, yes, we bloody well will. I mean, do you think we owe you something?"

Alea plunged into bitter silence again and stayed there until Sam's temper rose once more.

"What? What do you think we should do? Stand by until we know you're in the asylum system and in a house somewhere?"

Alea turned to stare at him.

"You have dead wife. You are left with child. I have dead husband. I am left with child. Is good for you to be a man. You are in *your* country. Is good for you. I am woman. I am Arab. I am alone. I have not money. I have not home for my child. You have boat. You have money. You can go everywhere you wish to go. I am left with woman I not know."

For the first time Sam put himself in her place. He was stunned. He couldn't fault her. She was looking out for her kid just as he was looking out for his. She was fighting for her survival just as he had on countless occasions. But she made him recognise what he'd always taken for granted: he had skills few others could call upon. She was right. He could just leave them on the quay, turn his transom and forget about all he had left behind. He had cash, he had a floating home, he had independence, freedom and his tiny family. She had Sadiqah, which was her love and her fear, and she had a terrifying unknown ordeal ahead of her. She was being expected to rely upon a woman she'd never met, and she knew that with all likelihood she would face hostility as a Libyan in Europe.

Sam had been used to responsibility – the weight of taking kids to war regardless of how well-trained they were. When he'd led his Marines or his small SBS units, he had felt every ounce of their expectation – that they were in the hands of a seasoned commando, that his call would be correct. But since he'd left the navy,he'd stretched and cracked as the crush of that responsibility had been lifted from him.

And here it had returned. The same expectation; the same demand.

Help keep me safe for I am scared.

18

The hotel was one of the most frequently attacked on the peninsula yet still they came – wealthy tourists, Russians dressed like hookers, even Israelis on occasion but they booked less frequently nowadays. It was literally a stone's throw from the border crossing with Eilat, which made it within winking distance of the Red Sea, Israel and Jordan.

The man Waleed had tasked with destroying the GPS and phone recovered from Big Suit's car was sent to carry out a routine inspection. It was always good to have a man with a machine gun walk the perimeter of such establishments. It had the curious effect of making guests feel safe: nothing like having a heavily armed guard show up. It was one of Waleed's routine orders from Cairo: keep the tourists coming at all costs. It confused him. How holidaymakers could take comfort from such sights was a mystery. Surely, he thought, it would remind them of the intense threat they were under? Less than a few years had passed since check-in had been disrupted by a bomb-laden lorry that had barrelled through the lobby windows and exploded. No man with a machine gun was going to stop that.

In the same foyer of the rebuilt hotel the guard sidled up to the car-hire clerk perched at a small office desk amid leaflets with images of tired old Japanese saloons. The guard knew most of the vehicles didn't even have locks, which was fine because car theft wasn't an issue in Egypt. Even in cities cars were left unlocked to allow parking attendants to wheel them about to create space. Besides, many people couldn't afford fuel. But the guard's advantage was in the age of the hire fleet – no fancy inbuilt navigation systems in these vehicles. They barely had blowers to circulate the stifling air.

"Hello," he said to the bored man at the desk.

"Hello," the man said back, suddenly transfixed by the machine gun across the guard's chest.

"How much will you give me for this?" he said.

"The gun?" asked the baffled clerk.

"No, this." The guard furtively gestured to the GPS and cable in his spare hand.

"Oh ... ehm ... it is old," said the clerk.

"How much?" pressed the guard furtively glancing around him, keen to do business and move on.

"I need to call my boss," said the clerk.

The guard gathered up the kit and moved off. "Hurry," he said, "I'll come back in five minutes."

He wandered outside and took a tour around the swimming pool, soaking in the tits and arses of the privileged tanning team. Satiated, he headed back to the shade of the reception, approached the clerk, took the first price offered and went back to his vehicle.

An uncharacteristic fluster.

"This is Sinead. Leave a message."

Then calm. Sam tapped red. He seldom left voicemails and wasn't about to start now. Paranoia. He'd seen how easy it was to hack a phone. But at least the call confirmed that they had service, intermittent as it was.

"Daddy, who are you ringing?"

"A friend."

It was almost a shock to hear that voice again, even on an answering service. He had to stop calling her Charity. He owed her more than that.

"Who?" Isla asked.

"Charity," Sam muttered absently.

"That's not a name."

"Sinead," he said.

"A woman?" Isla seemed surprised.

"Yes," said Sam, unwilling to elaborate.

He could see the cogs turning in his daughter's mind. She had watched his odd stand-off with Sadiqah's mother and no doubt heard the frustration in those conversations, and here he was phoning a woman Isla had never met while out of sight of land. Sam wondered what she was thinking, and yet he didn't want to know because lurking somewhere behind it all was a sense that there was some inappropriate thought, some subtle betrayal, as the scent on the T-shirt weakened.

"Can Sadiqah and I go to the cinema when we get back to Ireland?"

Thank the Lord for the attention span of children, thought Sam.

"Maybe," he said, doubtful whether Dungarvan had a picture house and of the wisdom of taking such a liberty given the risk of being stopped and questioned.

"That means no," sulked Isla.

"I'm sorry, wee love. I need my friend to come and help Sadiqah and her mam as soon as we get ashore."

Shock crossed Isla's face. "You're sending them away again?"

Her eyes were like frisbees, as if he couldn't have done more to disappoint her.

"Not like last time," he said. "This time they'll be properly looked after and be safe."

"With Charity?"

"Sinead."

"Who is Sinead?"

"Sinead is Charity. Charity was just my nickname for her, my friend. I shouldn't have called her that."

"Why?"

"Just cos. Never worry about it."

"Charity's not a bad word, Daddy," Isla said, teacher-like.

"No."

"Then why—"

"Look, Isla, it doesn't matter. Sinead is going to help Sadiqah, that's what matters, and we'll keep an eye on them. We'll go and visit them for play dates. Honestly."

Sam caught Alea turning her head slightly. Her back was to him as she sat below but she'd obviously overheard them.

"Where will Sinead take them?"

"To Dublin, darlin'. They'll be safe there."

"We can go and visit them and stay in a hotel!" She fizzed with excitement.

Sam and Shannon had once taken Isla on a trip to Dublin. The family room had provided great excitement for Isla and the grandeur of the hotel lobby had made her feel like she was in a movie.

"Ok, Isla," he said. "I promise we can do that."

And he meant it at the time. He was sure such a simple request would be achievable.

At the time.

Habid was adamant – no easy outs. If someone had to die to

give the doctor what he wanted, then the doctor had to do the deed.

Tassels was happy with the plan. His cousin had become a serious pain in the arse, nagging and threatening him at every opportunity. He'd considered having the doctor knocked off just to get some peace, but Big Suit's absence meant he'd have to carry out the dirty work himself and in that regard he and the rat were remarkably similar.

Habid had called Tassels and explained what was to happen. He would bring a new batch of migrants across the border and expect to be met by a police escort in the normal way. Tassels would drive the minibus and deliver the expectant, filthy rabble to the banks where they would make their transfers and Tassels would get paid. They would then be offered a free medical with the doctor before making their way to the beach. The final person to receive an examination would be a man identified by Habid.

And so the doctor sat in a plastic chair and examined the small group one by one, waiting to meet his salvation, his passport, his victim. Because the victim was a fellow physician, the doctor had been forced to plan the process well in advance. The man was unlikely to allow himself to be injected, so Habid had settled on a seasickness remedy, gambling that the chances of his quarry being a seafarer in his spare time were few and that unfamiliarity with the sea would encourage the physician to swallow the pill. When he had taken the vitals of each of the migrants with his usual negligence, he sweated gently and waited for his new identity to reveal itself.

Habid had chosen wisely. Before him stood a man of equal height and colouring, haggard, for sure, but in age they could have been similar had the Libyan not spent the past few years in a hole in the desert.

"Hello, how are you?" he began.

"Fine," said the Libyan suspiciously.

"I need to check you for dehydration and make sure you are ready for the trip – the sea is a serious place."

"I am fit and well," snapped the Libyan, nervous that the examination could result in his exclusion. "Nothing wrong with me. I am a doctor, I would know."

"Ah, a doctor?" he said, eager to learn more about his future persona. "Where did you practise?"

"Tripoli, in a hospital and I had private patients too."

"Anyone famous?" asked the doctor, probing.

"You obviously know I had a famous patient," snarled the Libyan, "otherwise you would not have asked."

The doctor shrugged. "Gaddafi cannot have been an easy man to look after."

"No," agreed the Libyan, softening.

"What was your area of expertise?"

"Cardiac," said the doctor. "Angioplasty. The leader was highly strung."

The doctor sniggered. "We could tell. Even here in Alexandria we could hear him shouting."

The Libyan relaxed a little as the doctor listened to his chest and peered into his throat, ears and eyes.

"Your own heart is strong and your BP is fine," concluded the doctor. "Now, take these – they will help with any seasickness. You would be advised to avoid illness on the boat as the skipper has orders to drop dead weight into the water."

The Libyan had expected little more. This was a mercenary business and every man for himself. He popped the pills offered without querying it further.

"Now," said the doctor, "join the others and I wish you safe journey."

By dusk the group had assembled on the beach and the Libyan physician was dead. There was gentle sobbing from two women who had grown attached to him while in the hole in the desert. Tassels' cousin had joined them, examined the body and declared life extinct. Habid took control.

"This man was selected because he was a doctor. I do not want you to go to sea without his skills."

The rat's deviousness knew no bounds. He somehow managed to make his business sound benevolent while twisting every turn to his advantage. Alarm rose on the faces of the migrants. They felt their opportunity slipping away with the life of the Libyan physician. They began to plead with Habid to allow the journey to go ahead regardless. By arrangement Habid looked to the doctor.

"These people wish to go to sea, doctor. I cannot allow that without proper care. They have paid handsomely for the privilege. Will you take that man's place?"

"What?" feigned the doctor. "Leave – now? Just like that?"

"Please!" wailed the women, lighting on the idea.

"Where would I go? I cannot start a new life just like that. I do not even have any papers!"

Habid looked to the women and then to the dead man and then began a body search. The women whimpered – not so much in grief as in hope. Habid hoisted a sheaf of documentation aloft theatrically.

"These may help!"

The doctor took the papers from Habid and examined them.

"But – these men and women know I am not the man referred to in these papers."

Habid looked to the assembled group questioningly.

"We will say it is you." They all began to nod. "We know him well. We can tell you all about him. You can become him!"

Desperation delivered the plan better than the doctor had hoped. He could not resist laying it on thick.

"And you really want me to come with you, to keep you well?"

"Please," wailed the women.

One of the men fell to his knees in appeal.

"Ok," said the doctor reluctantly, turning to Habid. "I will go with them."

"Hurry on then," said Habid, disgusted at the doctor's ad-libbing.

Habid watched the dinghy warble over the waves, listening to the rev and fall of the outboard engine. He hoped against hope that the doctor would drown.

"Will you look who it is, fuckin' Houdini."

"Shut up," he heard Charity hiss. Sinead. He made another mental note to stop calling her Charity otherwise Isla would drop him in it when they met.

Sinead's sister ignored the request. "So to what do we owe the pleasure?"

The troublesome sister, as useful as she was irritating. He pitied the man or woman who would end up sharing her sarcasm daily.

'Will you please be quiet," he heard Sinead say.

Sam realised he hadn't yet said a word.

"How are you, Sam?" Charity assumed control. Sinead. Sinead assumed control.

"You have me on loudspeaker," he said.

The drone of a vehicle suggested the pair were on the road and he was patched through the Bluetooth.

"Yeah, but I'm not listening to ye," snarked the sister.

"Áine, would you ever just give it up?" Sinead snapped. "Sam, give me a second."

He heard a snap and a bang and Áine complain that you shouldn't drive while using a phone and then Sinead was back.

"Where are you?"

"At sea," he said.

"How are you?"

"Grand," he replied. "How are you getting on?"

"Busy," she said. "It's good to know you're ok. How's Isla?"

"She's here, she's good. Getting big."

"Ah, stop," she said, as if she was all too familiar with growing children, which he'd always assumed she wasn't. He found himself wondering, for the first time, whether she had any kids. It confused him – why he hadn't considered it before. It unsettled him but he didn't care to admit why.

"Are you too busy for a wee job?"

"You're asking me? I've had jobs coming out me pores and I've been trying to reach you for months, and now you ring me asking if *I* want a job."

"Sorry, Sinead." It was the first time he'd ever actually used her name.

It wasn't lost on her. She was silent for a moment. "You're grand," she said, as he somehow knew she would. "What's the job?"

"Can you come to the south coast?"

"It's a long coast, Sam. Where?"

Sam didn't like to give too much away on the phone. He knew a lot about interception due in no small part to the sarcastic sister sitting beside his friend.

"Well, where are you now?"

"Dublin, strangely enough."

The pair lived in Dublin together. Unfortunately. He thought again about why he'd imagined she had no children and wondered if their living arrangement had led to the assumption.

"About two hours from you. I'll ping you the place in the usual way."

Sinead's twin had set up the process: a message through an

encrypted app which the authorities hadn't yet gained permission to monitor – at least officially.

"When?" asked Charity. Sinead.

"Soon."

"We're on our way to see a band," she said.

"Not that soon, but after," he assured her.

"Ok, so. Will I come on my own?"

"I would be enormously grateful if you would," he said, swiping away images of Áine, the talented torment of a sister. He just did not have the energy.

"Right," she said.

"Sinead?"

"Yeah?"

"It's nice to speak to you."

He cut the call.

Waleed didn't like frayed edges. They nagged at him, festered in the back of his mind. Waleed was an organised man. He liked to tick things off in short order because he knew more tasks with new pressures would arrive at any moment. IS was taking care of that. His responsibility was enormous, his jurisdiction unmanageable; all he could do was hope to contain the militants, and through it all was the nagging knowledge that an end as loose as the trousers on a malnourished former friend needed to be dealt with.

Ordinarily he'd have formulated a plan of action by now because so much time had passed since the oversized thug had presented himself in Sinai. Waleed was rarely short on options; his position was one of power in a country where consequences for stepping outside the lines were few, yet Big Suit had somehow managed to prick a nerve. It was unfathomable how such a stupid man had managed to identify a secret that Waleed had successfully kept for twenty years.

He worked through the options. As a senior commander – and a young one at that – in an elite Egyptian unit, Cairo would surely be reluctant to lose him, but then the rules were quite clear: no Coptic Christian had a place in the intelligence services. None. It had never happened before and the policy was unlikely to change. Even if his bosses deigned to overlook the revelation, his men wouldn't. They were likely to turn against him. Sectarianism was seldom spoken of in Egypt because Copts were such a minority but that didn't mean it didn't exist.

Waleed decided to wrap up the Arish investigation as quickly as he could. Then he would try to clear his mind of the irritation languishing in the desert jail. How he would do that remained unclear but one way or another he had to keep his secret and he had to deal with the cumbersome problem. Quickly.

———

Sam couldn't see the gust approach in the dark but he felt it building. An instinct – a breeze before the breeze that any seasoned sailor can detect – a sense, a change in pressure, a whisper in the air. For the first time in days he felt his tightened stitches complain as he moved to shorten the sail. He hauled and furled in the big genoa, his lacerations whining with the winch. His wounds had become accustomed to the sedentary hours since the gale had passed through and he didn't relish the prospect of more expenditure of energy, more forceful stretching of thin skin. The wind hit them just as he was calling the girls to tuck in. Immediately the boat heeled and items lazily discarded started to tumble onto the floor.

"It's ok," he shouted, "just get in behind the lee cloths. We're nearly there anyway. Alea, pass me up my oilskins, please."

She did as she was bid but not before the sweep of rain hit him on the face with a ferocity that would ensure his discomfort for the next twelve hours. He flipped on the peak cap that was tied to his life jacket. It would keep the rain out of his face and allow him to see the instruments – the GPS, the radar, the chart plotter and wind indicator.

A few hours wrestling with the wheel broke the darkness. Sam could just make out the gloom of the Comeragh Mountains as the clouds barrelled into them and split around them, forced forward by the building easterly that was rising with the grey sun. And then the rain: deafening. Wet rain, Sam's grandfather would have said. Curious how some rains left barely a damp patch, others saturation.

The approach was tricky. For Sam to shift his head in either direction was a challenge. The cold breeze had seized his limbs and his movement was robotic and slow. He hadn't the heart to make any of the girls come on deck to help, so he opted for an outer harbour wall where he tied up with less diligence than normal before clambering back on board to consult the phone and open the app.

Confirmation. She'd sent the last message as she was leaving, two hours previously. He tore open his ocean jacket and held his fingers under his armpits trying to coax some movement out of them. The screen often failed to register his touch, not least when his fingerprints were geriatrified by overexposure to moisture, raisin-like and unidentifiable.

We're here, he managed to tap out eventually.

Where? came back immediately.

Are you here?

Statue in the square.

We'll be up now, he hammered. "Right, ladies, get your stuff, we gotta go."

He couldn't have hoped for more. He wanted no "Parting Glass", no maudlin gathering. Speed, he hoped, would distract his daughter. The downpour and what was left of the darkness only added to the urgency.

He watched them gather the little they had into a bag he'd stitched from old sailcloth. Alea brushed her hair and went into the heads, presumably to consult a mirror. Despite the available excuses, no woman would ideally meet another after two weeks at sea. She emerged almost radiant. Sam had no idea what she'd done but in the low light of the cabin he noted how well she looked regardless of her nervousness.

And then Sam's jaw began to ache as he watched his little girl approach her friend. Isla held a package wrapped in tissue paper. She presented it with bashfulness, nothing said, her eyes averted. Her lower lip was gripped taut and Sam knew she was one word away from tears. He doubted again the wisdom of casting these women adrift but he didn't know what else to do. Sadiqah did the crying for Isla. She received the parcel and set it aside, reaching for her little pal and hugging her for a full two minutes. Sam and Alea just stood and watched, unsure whether to make a similar gesture or what message that might convey. Oh, to be a child again, thought Sam. Alea eventually looked up at him. Those eyes. And the ache again. She smiled a sad, sad smile.

"Your friend, she is here," she stated.

"Mmmm."

"Let us go now, Sadiqah."

Despite the unholy hour there were a few rum-looking teenagers kicking about the square, gathered for shelter around a single cigarette. The locals probably called them knackers. The youths' eyes followed every move of the little troop, each stooped against the lashing, headed towards Sinead's car exhaust. They lit up in the red glow of her rear lights. The only heat in a windswept town.

She emerged from the car, tall and handsome, turning her collar up, her head tilted forward – through nervousness or against the rain Sam couldn't tell but her eyes looked up at him, gentle, inquiring, vulnerable.

"Sinead," he almost whispered.

"Ah, Sam."

"Thank you."

"For what?" she said gently.

"For coming," he said.

"You knew I'd come."

He turned quickly before he allowed himself to read too much into that.

"This," he paused, "is Isla. Say hello, darlin'."

"Hello," she said, her little nose dripping.

"So *you* are Isla," said Sinead. "Do you know that you are the apple of your daddy's eye?"

Isla smiled bashfully.

"You're a beautiful young woman. I love your coat."

Sinead appeared to know how to talk to children. Sam wished he did.

"This is Alea," he said, "and Sadiqah."

He gestured them forward. They had walked behind him the whole way. Alea pushed back her hood a little, sodden, but still stunning.

"Pakis!" shouted one of the youths from the doorway.

Sam tensed and turned but Sinead placed her hand on his arm. It was Isla, though, who spoke the words of her mother.

"Don't get involved, Daddy," she said.

The maturity of the comment astonished him.

"Let's get going," said Sinead. Familiar with Sam's skill set, she was keen to avoid a confrontation with the natives. She opened the rear door. "Alea, why don't you jump in the front and we can have a proper chat."

Alea appeared confused at first. Sam looked at her and she

at him. Sinead copped the awkwardness and looked a little flustered by it, put out even. She turned away with a surprised look on her face and chose to help Sadiqah buckle in.

Alea looked straight at him, no hint of a tear. "You are complicated man. Yet simple."

Sam stood silent, unsure whether he was being complimented or criticised. He let her carry on.

"I am grateful. And I am sorry."

Sam stared at the freshly widowed woman and then dropped his gaze to shake his head at her fortitude, her strength of character, her submission to the unknown. He hadn't the words. "Take care, Alea," was all he managed.

And then the car doors slammed, Sinead turning to Sam one last time. "This time keep in touch," she said brusquely, and he knew then her feathers had been ruffled and that the tide between them had ebbed as quickly as it had flooded.

He was confident that the car journey between the women would correct any misunderstandings. "I'll call you when we're settled. You know, see how they are."

"See how they are," she repeated, her eyes boring into him.

"And how you are. How ... you've been."

"That would be nice," she said, although he couldn't be sure she meant it.

And then they were gone and the Angelus called, and the wind howled, and not a tear was shed.

An end, he hoped, to an encounter he could have done without.

A fitting departure. From Dungarvan. In the rain.

PART II

CHAPTER 19

There was no screaming, which Sam struggled to understand as he beat the man out with his good offshore jacket. Despite the seriousness of the act all he could really think was, *this is my best sailing kit.*

His instincts were telling him to turn around and walk away. Don't get involved, as Isla would say. Let the man burn. But he couldn't because he'd recognised the man the moment the liquid had ignited. He'd spent a few weeks in his menacing company, after all. Perhaps that's why he was able to hammer the flames with such vigour. The fire was out in moments thanks to the beating. Every cloud.

And then there were guards and questions and denials from Sam: no, I don't know him. I was just passing. He set himself on fire, so I put him out. Grand. And then Sam melted into the crowd, charred jacket in hand.

"What the hell has happened to you?" Sinead asked.

"I'll tell you in a minute but why don't you fill me in on your bits first?"

The pair had been meeting every few weeks as Sam fulfilled his promise to Isla to keep an eye on what was happening with her little friend.

"Well," said Sinead. "Alea has had a better week. Sadiqah – not so much. After what they saw and what they went through there's a lot to get out, and Alea's determined to keep moving on because of Sadiqah but she's also really worried about her."

"Have you made the asylum application yet?"

"Not yet. I've been looking into it. I don't know the system that well because – well, I'm more about getting women *out* of the country, which now looks to be easier than getting them *into* the bloody place. I'm told that as soon as an application is made they could be taken to Mosney."

"Mosney?"

"Did you never go to Mosney when you were small?"

"No, what is it?"

"It's like a Butlin's holiday camp. Not a great place for kids, or anyone for that matter."

"Sounds ok to me," said Sam.

"No, it *used* to be a holiday camp. Now it's a detention centre by the sea."

"Oh, where?" Sam's interest piqued.

"East coast, above Dublin. We used to go there when we were children. It was fun then. Now – not so much."

"So it's for migrants?"

"Yeah. They're kept there until their asylum claim has been dealt with."

"I can imagine what goes on in there."

"Exactly. It's not where I want them to wait this out, so my plan is to keep them with us in sheltered accommodation until the counselling is finished and then start the process – unless I can think of anything better for them. But they're safe, that's the main thing, thanks to you."

She looked at him, searching for a reaction, receiving little more than a grunt of dismissal.

"You did, Sam. You got them away from that terrible man."

"Funny you should say that," he said as she gazed at him with something close to admiration.

"What?" she said, moderately alarmed.

"Well, the man who killed her husband – the bloke on the boat who wanted to rape her."

"Yes, the trafficker's brother."

"What?" asked Sam, new to this tidbit.

"Apparently he was a brother of the man who organised all the trafficking."

"Really?" Sam again realised how little he'd learned about the whole process.

"According to Alea."

But Sam's mind was racing. "I gotta go, Sinead, sorry," said Sam.

"Not a fucking chance," she suddenly hissed at him, careful not to disturb the other customers in the café. "This time you'll sit and you'll tell me what you're doing."

He rested back in his seat suddenly aware of his capacity to irritate her. He boiled down his story as quickly as he could.

"On the way here, on Grafton Street, a man set himself on fire."

"Sure, I know."

"How can you know? It was less than half an hour ago." Sam was incredulous.

"Somebody Facebook Live'd it."

"You're joking?"

"Look."

Sam gazed at her phone, which showed a bundle of firefighters and paramedics crowded around someone. Sam wasn't in frame.

"What's it say about him?"

"Who?"

"The man who went up in flames."

"Funny enough, it says he's an asylum seeker who burned himself in protest after being told he's to be removed."

"Removed?"

"Deported. Sent back."

"From where?"

Sinead scrolled a little. "Everyone's posting about it. They're pretty sympathetic."

"They shouldn't be," said Sam.

"What are you not telling me?"

"You'll not believe it if I do."

"Try me."

"That's him – that's the man. The bloke from the boat. I dunno how he got here but that's the bastard who skipped in Sicily."

"Go 'way," said Sinead, genuinely shocked.

"I've just hammered out the flames on him – see?" He showed her his blackened jacket.

"What the f—"

"Look again. Where is he gonna be deported from?"

"Well, I'd say he's off to hospital."

"He's not too bad. He didn't burn for long and he used lighter fluid. His skin was ok-ish."

Sinead kept tapping and swiping.

"Well, seems he'd been detained you know where."

"Butlins – what did you call it again?"

"Mosney."

"Right," said Sam, whose mind had slipped its lines and was headed to sea again.

"Looks like you're off again," Sinead said.

"Looks like it," he said, and did something he'd never done before. He reached forward and gave her a kiss on the cheek.

———

The best things come to those who deserve it.

Feet and faeces. Toes and arse. The doc gagged. The man next to him claimed he wouldn't notice in a few weeks.

"Soon you will smell just the same."

"A few weeks?" asked the doctor, incredulous.

"I have been here seven months. No one has ever left unless they were dead," said the man, who exposed festering bedsores as he rolled over to resume his sleep. For there was nothing else to do, not in this detention centre – this room, this oversized shipping shed now crammed with unsuccessful migrants.

The doctor lamented his luck but knew he'd got what he was due.

They'd spent less than twelve hours at sea. The skipper, whoever he was, had motored west, too far west. Because of the sea state, he'd said. The doctor had challenged him and so the African had changed course to prove his point. Immediately the women had begun groaning as the slop of the swell hit the rubber boat side-on and bile bubbled up throats. Reluctantly the doctor had acceded to the African's seamanship and the boat had been turned again to face the swell, making the going at least consistent and uniform if still like a roller coaster.

The crew had quietened as the journey went on. The thrum of the outboard, its occasional tonal changes as a large wave plucked the propeller momentarily from the sea. They crouched, resigned, tensing their muscles at the top of each wave, bracing against the plummet into the trough. Routinely the helmsman had to replenish the fuel, a precarious proce-dure during which petrol was spilled into the bottom of the boat. It swashed about with the seawater they were compelled to bail and soaked into their garments, inducing dry bokes and eventually headaches. The wind took to their rear treating them to the exhaust fumes of the engine. The doctor knew nothing of the sea and couldn't understand how waves could come towards the boat while the wind came from behind.

Night lifted to day and still they made west and north, the African consulting his little compass and gazing at the horizon. As the afternoon crept towards evening the African's agitation increased, although the doctor didn't understand why until the engine began to cough and splutter.

When it stopped the helmsman simply stared at the sea.

There was nothing to be done. They were alone, adrift, at the mercy of the wind, the waves and the sun.

Nobody asked, "What now?" Everyone knew it was time to wait for a boat to rescue them, to take them to the promise of Europe, to Italy or Greece, or maybe even Spain, because that was what had been promised. You pay premium, you get top-dollar service.

When night came the sobbing started. Fear crept over hope and promises were exposed for their emptiness. The wind built and the sickness returned. Mothers clutched their children consumed by fear. The boat stretched and contracted over the mounting sea terrifying all inside, including the skipper.

And so when salvation came it was greeted with relief despite it not being what had been hoped for.

The beam froze them in its ferocity. They shielded their eyes and dropped their heads jubilant at its presence, stunned by its sudden appearance. From nowhere came their rescue.

And they were grateful to step aboard a steadier ship, to be given water, blankets, orders. The direction was welcome until the dawning arrived that their Samaritans spoke their language and had guns and aggression.

The engines roared and the boat moved away. They

watched as their own tiny vessel was set alight and committed to the deep.

Within six hours they were back on the coast they had left, processed and marched into sheds by the port of Tobruk. After two years, a desert crossing and the depletion of every cent of savings, they'd arrived back where they had started once again bereft of their freedom and with all remaining dignity and hope expired.

***

Mosney was an easy nut to crack. Sam considered getting to it by boat but such fun exploits proved unnecessary. There was any number of ways in and out. It was all but signposted by a woman who stood at the end of what, in most states, would pass as a country road. She was plainly punting for business. African-looking women in miniskirts and knee-high boots weren't a common sight in County Meath, so he knew he was on the right track.

He tried the beach approach first but the shore was crammed with dog walkers and there was a fence of sorts. In the end he went at it from the car park just outside the gate and walked straight in unimpeded.

The huts had seen better days but Sam had been to much worse places. The whole thing didn't look too bad. It was the people who would cause problems not the infrastructure. Sam knew that while the vast majority of those being housed there would be genuine folks escaping war or worse, there were some who would turn the concentration of people to their advantage. The Nigerian woman on the roadside was testament to that. Whatever was going on there, that line of business wasn't generally voluntary work.

He asked around for the infirmary and was pointed in the direction, but when he got there the cupboard was bare. Empty beds – all three of them. He paused for a moment and thought. He'd ask some more, try to find out if an Arab man had made any friends. As he strolled about looking for other Middle Eastern folks he was treated to a break. From behind came the rumble of a heavy diesel engine and he turned to see an ambulance moving slowly towards the sickbay. It stopped outside, the doors opened and the ramp lowered and out was wheeled a bandaged body upright in a chair.

"Sinbad," muttered Sam to himself.

The GPS seemed a bargain but when the clerk's boss swanned into the hotel and actually looked at it he was less than impressed with his purchase. He had imagined he'd be able to charge a little more for its inclusion in any of his aged cars and that it would pay for itself within two journeys. But it was old and he couldn't understand what it was telling him. There was no map as such, just a squiggly line. He plugged it in to the computer but it immediately demanded a download of an update. The boss clicked his way through the on-screen directions using the hotel's Wi-Fi and overcame the frustration to bring his new toy into the modern world on modern roads with modern warnings.

"Ok," he said to the poorly paid clerk at the desk, "for foreigners charge ten dollars every time someone asks for GPS. Don't give it to locals."

Then he strolled out of the hotel for a look at the ladies. He had no idea of the global chaos he had just caused.

Sam turned the scorching on his jacket to his advantage.

"Hello, sister."

"Oh, I'm not a sister," said the woman. "I'm a healthcare assistant."

Sam wouldn't have cared if she'd been an alchemist or a soothsayer, he just wanted in.

"I'm sorry to bother you but that man in there, he was burned on Grafton Street in Dublin, yes?"

"Who are you?" The woman was Spanish or Portuguese Sam guessed.

"Sorry, should have said. I'm the man who – well, put him out." He held up the jacket and showed the melted holes in it.

"You saved him?" said the woman in wonder.

"Well, I put the fire out," he said, almost bashfully.

"Oh," she said. "You want to see him, yes?"

"Would that be ok?" he asked, his hopes rising that he might get in on such an easy ticket.

"Yes, yes, of course," she said, and ushered him into the little room. "Would you like a cup of tea?"

"No, thanks," said Sam. "I won't stay long. He's been through a lot." He feigned sympathy knowing that the man was about to go through a lot more.

"It's ok, no rush," said the woman and left him to it.

Sam couldn't believe his luck.

Waleed listened to the operation on the radio. He'd requested a patch through from Cairo and, with reluctance, the air force had agreed. It was utter devastation.

In the end they'd forced his hand: tell us what to target or we fly sorties, identify our own and incinerate whatever we think is out of place. That was politics in Egypt these days: be strong – be seen to be strong. The uprising and attempts at democracy had come to nought. After trying out a Western system, Egypt had elected the Muslim Brotherhood, which had been promptly overthrown for perceived incompetence in its administration. The people had tried various things including fresh riots, and the military had responded with typical ruthlessness. After countless thousands had been interred in the ground the country was back to where it had begun – with a notionally democratically elected leader of military pedigree who would surely become a dictator in everything but name. Mubarak was out of jail but not back in power. His replacement, however, struck an uncanny resemblance.

So when the demands came Waleed had been forced to give direction. He knew where the extremist camps were, what he didn't know was who was in them. His hunch was there were hostages or prisoners – innocents like the girl who'd been sent to blow up a bus in Arish. Waleed didn't want such people targeted but what choice was there? If he didn't offer coordinates, then some other entirely innocent settlement would probably be annihilated.

What he could hear on the radio was the pilot talking to command, confirming target acquisition and firing. What he could hear in the distance were occasional rumblings of the explosions. What he did silently throughout was pray for forgiveness for his part in what was being done.

If Sam had possessed clamps, he couldn't have opened Sinbad's eyes any wider.

"We need to talk," he said, "and I'd advise you not to fuck about."

The man had plainly been too busy burning to notice who had extinguished him in Dublin. He couldn't believe who he was looking at. Sam could barely believe it either.

"And just for the record, I know you can speak English and I know you can understand me, and I know about Alea and Sadiqah and what you did."

The man's face looked more and more disturbed as Sam went on.

"So here's what I want to know. What you are doing in Ireland, how the trafficking route works and who is behind it. You have about ten minutes to explain everything and then I start to twist your burnt bits, which will be pretty sore."

"Ok, ok, ok," said Sinbad, who had presumably thought through the wisdom of shouting for help and opted against it. There was only a small woman in the infirmary hut. If the roles were reversed, Sinbad knew he would simply slap the woman into submission, so he assumed incorrectly that Sam would do the same.

"Why did you set yourself on fire?"

"They lock me up. Here. I cannot have asee-lum. They say they send me back. I want TV to say, 'Look at him. He is needing help.'"

"Worked out brilliantly," said Sam. "Did you really intend to burn so badly?"

"What?" asked the man, confused.

"Did you think you would be injured?"

"Is not matter. Is better not to be sent back." Sinbad shrugged his bandages. "I thinking someone will help fast and I think fuel's only burning clothes."

Sam wondered if he'd been right about Sinbad's intellect all along.

"Right. What are you doing in Ireland?"

"I looking for Alea."

"Why?"

"She has something belongings to me."

"No – why Ireland?"

"I thinking you take-ed her here."

"Why?"

"Nobody else is allowing you. I seeing you leave from Sicily with her and child."

"You were watching?"

Sinbad fell silent, looking down.

"You came back when you realised she had whatever it is you wanted."

He shrugged. "Pier-haps I do not find her, pier-haps I find you instead."

"What, and you reckon you were going to persuade me to tell you where they were?"

"I have no choice."

"Well, whatever you want from them it must be bloody valuable. What is it?"

Sinbad hesitated, so Sam hit him with a flick slap on his most heavily bandaged bit. The man yelped in agony.

"If that nurse comes in here, I'll have to tie her up, and then you'll be alone and I'll skin you, understand?"

The man chewed the inside of his cheek as the pain ebbed.

"What has Alea got that belongs to you?"

"Information."

"About what?"

"About bank."

"About her bank accounts?"

"Yes."

"So? What she has is hers not yours."

"We make deal. We take her to Europe, she pay."

"Who is *we*?"

The man stared at Sam.

"You and your brother?"

Sinbad's shock was obvious.

"Yes, my brother."

"And where is he?"

"Home."

"And where is home?"

The man cocked his head, curious that Sam was short on this snippet of information given that he knew so much else.

"Libya," he said.

"So you are Libyan?"

"Yes."

"And you are a people trafficker?"

Sinbad's head wavered as if he were saying "kind of".

"I'm not the police, I'm a whole lot worse than that," Sam hissed.

"Yes."

"And you think Alea owes you money?"

"She owes me money. And more."

"What?"

"She has taken from me."

"Taken what?"

"I tell you, information – about bank."

"What are you talking about?"

"On boat with you I make her keep papers. Information, about bank."

"Why?"

"I think on boat you are going to attack-ed me maybe. And if you attack-ed me, maybe you tear clothes. And then you see information under clothes."

"But you knew I would not attack Alea," said Sam.

"She is Muslim woman."

"So you got her to hide the papers."

Sinbad's head began the dither and warble again. Sam pressed on.

"Why did you not take the papers from Alea when you got to Italy?"

"I did take, but was dark. Papers are in plastic, tape-ed to body. I take from her."

"And then you left her, you prick."

The man just stared at Sam who gestured that he was to elaborate.

"But she not give me all papers. She has taken many papers from plastic and keep-ed them for herself."

Clever woman, thought Sam, but his admiration also brought questions.

"There must have been more than her bank details in the papers," said Sam.

Sinbad moved uneasily in the bed but said nothing.

"There were also the details of your other victims – maybe even passports. The people you killed in the boat. The people you stabbed."

Sinbad closed his eyes in defeat and then opened them slowly.

"Correct?" Sam asked, reaching as if to pain his captive again.

"Yes," he said softly.

"The people you killed must have had a lot of money in banks if you came all the way to Ireland to get the papers."

"Yes," said Sinbad.

"Who were they?"

"They deserv-ed everything. They were evil people. They were Gaddafi people."

"What do you mean?" Sam pressed.

"They were richest people in Libya. Rich from oil. Rich from the leader. They were his circle, his chiefs. Military. Business. They lived in gold and silk."

"And Alea? Did she deserve what she got?"

"Her husband. He deserve."

"Why?"

"He was Gaddafi's man. His chief of spy."

"What do you mean?"

"He was rich, and he was bad man. He was torture. For Gaddafi. Then for America."

"What?" Sam couldn't quite put it together. "He was intelligence?"

"Yes," said Sinbad, grasping the word he'd been hunting for. "He was intelligence. Intelligence chief."

"For America?"

"For Gaddafi. Later for America."

"Are you sure?" Sam couldn't equate Alea's hostility towards America if this were true.

"Yes, sure. My brother, he discover the papers. The proof. This is how he get rich people to use our service."

"Your brother found intelligence papers?"

"Yes, I believe he find. I not see, but Habid tell me. A little."

Sam filed away the name Sinbad had let slip and thought for a moment. Something was still coming up short in his story.

"So you had some bank details but not all bank details?"

"Yes, some. The woman – she keep-ed the rest."

"And these were important enough for you to come from Sicily to Ireland to chase them down?"

Sinbad began to look even more uncomfortable and Sam knew he was on to something.

"They are important to us because they make us payment," he stressed, a little too desperately.

"There's something you are not telling me here, and now I'm going to have to rub salt in your burns."

Sam wrapped his big hand around Sinbad's arm and began to apply pressure while raising one eyebrow at his charge, intimating that it would only get worse. Sinbad stared at the hand and began to babble.

"Yes, yes, yes," he began, "ok, ok, ok, it not matter now anyways. I be removed soon back to Libya."

"Well hurry up," hissed Sam.

"Is papers, my brother's papers. Is plan to come to UK. To Great Britain," he said.

"What do you mean?"

"He is my brother, yes?"

"Yes," said Sam.

"So he is trusting me, yes?"

"I wouldn't," said Sam, "but carry on."

"He place-ed me in boat. This not normal. Normal is only fisherman to drive boat to sea."

"So what was different about this trip then?"

"This is trip with Gaddafi man. Spy man. How you say?"

"Intelligence chief."

"Yes, yes, intelligence chief."

"So what?"

"So my brother, he know exactly who is who in documents. And he want to use information about intelligence chief for new life in UK, so he can spend money he make from traffick business."

"So he sent a woo-woo like you to do that?"

"Yes," said Sinbad, oblivious to the insult. "He send me to find accommodation to stay in Europe, then UK, for him to come. He want me to take woman and child, and then he come and use documents to allow him to be big man in UK."

How naïve, thought Sam. Whoever Sinbad's brother was he appeared to think he could blackmail American or British Intelligence.

"And he thought MI6 would go for this?"

"He has more document in Libya. Very big papers."

"Leverage," muttered Sam.

"I do not know this," said Sinbad, shaking his head like a beaten dog.

"Doesn't matter," said Sam. And then something else occurred to him. "Why did he want you to take Alea and Sadiqah but not the intelligence chief?"

"I do not know," said Sinbad. "I think maybe he is wanting to take place of intelligence chief. To pretend."

"To impersonate him?" said Sam, incredulous. "To take his identity?"

But Sinbad did not grasp the meaning.

"Does he not know who he's dealing with here? MI6 will have pictures of every intelligence chief in every rogue state in the world. Did he really think he would get away with that?"

"I do not know," said the brother again. "I am told small story only. Just get woman and child to Europe. Kill Gaddafi men. Find house. Seek asee-lum. Nothing happened with plan."

"Nothing went according to plan," corrected Sam.

"Is fucking mess," conceded Sinbad, and Sam nearly laughed.

But there was one more hole in the history.

"So if you were to take them with you, why did you leave Alea and Sadiqah behind in Sicily?"

"What?" asked Sinbad.

"Why did you abandon Alea and Sadiqah in Sicily? Why did you go when you left the little boat? You just fucked off?"

"No, no, no," he said shaking his head.

Sam gripped his forearm tighter again.

"Is true," he pleaded. "I no leave them."

"Then what happened?"

"She see yellow light and she run a screaming at yellow light."

"What?"

"There is car, for official person. Car with yellow lines and light," Sinbad said, opening and closing his hand.

"A flashing light?"

"Yes, flashing light. Yellow, like sun."

Sam considered.

"A coastguard vehicle?"

"I do not know," said Sinbad.

Sam guessed someone had seen them struggling on the rocks and had called the coastguard, which would explain a lot.

"She run so fast and is screaming. I have no choice. I run other way," he said.

Well, well, well, Alea, thought Sam. You have courage indeed. He looked over Sinbad's head and read his name scrawled in dry marker on a whiteboard above the hospital bed. *Mr Halassi*. His gaze fell to a cabinet, the drawer slightly ajar. He reached around the hapless burn victim and pulled it out.

"*La, la!*" shouted Sinbad.

Sam grabbed a few scraps of paper from inside the drawer and stuffed them in his back pocket. The noise had caused the woman to peer in the window of the door and she made to enter, but Sam had got all he'd came for, so he stood up and left as fast as he could.

CHAPTER 20

Isla was tucked up with his folks, and given that Sam was in Dublin anyway, he looked up an old friend. They met in the back lounge of O'Donoghue's. The tourists sat out the front listening to the music and tall stories from the locals, and anyone who wanted a chat or a game of cards went down the back.

"You've been quiet this long time I thought you were dead," said Fran with a smile as wide as the mouth of the Liffey.

"Not dead yet," Sam laughed. "Not a million miles from it at times, though, Fran."

"Sure, don't tell me, ask me," he said. "Two fine glasses and a follow," he ordered.

Sam hadn't had a drink in a long time. He knew the effects would kick in quickly and he didn't want to get loose tongued in the long grass, much as he trusted Fran. He'd stick to a few and then get a train north.

"Have you been interfering with any ships recently?"

Fran's job was essentially to unionise the crews of container vessels and look after seafarers. Occasionally that meant extracting them from under the noses of abusive captains or oppressive on-board regimes. That was how the pair had met. Through a referral from Sinead, Fran had asked Sam to help him rescue more than a few crew members in tight situations. Sam's background had been ideal for such work – leaping on and off ships undetected, often with a forlorn Filipino over his shoulder. He enjoyed the little Dubliner's roguery and his commitment to comforting the afflicted while afflicting the comfortable.

"Ah, sure," said Fran. "You know the score, brother. The people that would cause trouble for honest-working men are everywhere. What about yourself? Have you been having any rows with wayward skippers since I last saw ye?"

"Funny enough," said Sam.

"Ye have an' all." Fran's eyes were twinkling.

"I did have a little barney with a man on a ship. Big boat called *Teetaya*."

"Let me write that down, brother," said Fran, who drew a little notepad from his breast pocket. "Spell that for me?"

Sam rattled out the letters.

"IMO?"

"Can't remember," said Sam, who had taken a note of its designation. "I have it written down on the boat."

"Sure, text it to me when you can and I'll have a look into its history." Fran smiled. "Maybe if it comes our way, we can perform an official inspection."

Fran had curious powers. His modus operandi was to leverage union membership among stevedores, who were essential to the off-load of any ship's cargo. He seemed able to persuade them to down tools and refuse to permit any vessel to unload. This meant that harbour masters were reluctant to allow a ship on which there was a dispute to land at any of his berths; time was money and quay space was valuable. In the meantime, Fran could board a ship at sea, occasionally with the assistance of the harbour master who invariably wanted a quiet life and any issues resolved *before* the vessel tied up to his berth. Once aboard, Fran demanded the crew's papers. If the ratings hadn't been paid or had been kept at sea beyond their contracted time, he'd get them reimbursed or removed. Some sailors hadn't seen their families in years. His take on it was that he was fighting slave labour.

"What did this ship do to annoy you?" asked Fran.

"Refused to take people in trouble to safety," Sam replied, with a coyness Fran was alive to.

"Say no more, brother." The case obviously appealed to him. "I shall discover all that my fine organisation has to offer on *Teetaya* and I shall relay it forthwith."

"Good man, Fran, thanks," said Sam. "Another wee drink?"

"Be civil, you two," said Sinead.

Sam looked at the sister and lied. "Nice to see you again."

Which was more than she did. "Wish I could say the same." Áine smiled sarcastically.

"Don't start." Sinead wanted to get on with other things. "What's going on, Sam?"

"Whatever it is, it's bound to be safe and wholesome," Áine chirped like a smoke alarm short on battery.

Áine had helped Sam in the past in his clandestine business, Charlie, and as a result had got into a few scrapes because of the nature of the work. It had all been unintended but she resented that her twin had been placed in danger as a result.

Sinead moved to quell the sister's vitriol. "That's all in the past. Now give it a rest, I want to know what's going on."

Sam explained what had happened on Grafton Street in greater detail. They weren't surprised at what he'd done – they were used to him by now, but they were baffled at how he'd happened upon Sinbad by accident.

"So you're telling us you weren't following him?" Áine was, as usual, sceptical.

"I wasn't – I didn't even know he was in Ireland."

"Right," said Áine, "and I came up the Liffey in a Comanche kayak."

Sam had learned to ignore her, despite her usefulness. He fished in his pocket for the scraps of paper.

"I don't know what any of this says – it's in Arabic, but that's definitely a number. Possibly a phone number. I'm guessing the area code is Libya."

"Big place," snapped Áine.

"Well, Triploi would be a good place to start, and after that maybe Benghazi, and then perhaps Tobruk."

"You seem very familiar with Libya and its towns. Maybe you've been there before?" she goaded, always pushing, always suspicious. Like many Irish people, the presence of British military – ex or otherwise – still grated a little.

"Can you trace the number?" Sam deflected.

Áine was employed by one of Dublin's tech multinationals. She seemed to have a new job with a new firm every six months. She was skilled and read code like Sam read trouble.

"If it's a phone number, then it can be traced, but sure this could be a nuclear warhead code knowing you."

"Do us a favour and look it up. Please."

"I'll get back to ye."

He'd only just settled back aboard when the phone rang. Not the old work one but the one he actually paid a contract for when he was north of the Irish border. It was his mother-in-law asking if Isla would like to go to Alton Towers.

"How long for?" he asked, nervous but knowing full well that he couldn't refuse. Isla's grandparents missed her terribly when Sam took her away and each time she left them was another reminder of unbearable loss.

They settled on a week, which made Sam antsy and irritable. He'd picked her up just a few hours before from his own parents and now he'd just two days with her before she was off again. She, of course, was delighted at the prospect of a week at a fun park.

Sam let her go to pack her bags and turned his attention to what he might do to occupy his mind in her absence. The answer pinged through on the other phone – the work one. He listened to the voicemail.

"Gimme a call, brother. I've the whole diddly dory on your rogue vessel."

Sam shook his head. In the world of shipping Fran was connected beyond compare. He was evidently excited too because he picked up on the first ring of Sam's return call.

"I've located this wayward freighter," he began immediately, "and it has a poor pedigree, my friend. A very grim boat on which to be a crew member." Fran's patter was nothing if not eloquent.

"Really?"

"It's been detained no fewer than fifteen times. If it ever comes to Irish waters, I guarantee you it'll not leave again. Fissures in the hull, lack of lifeboats, lack of supplies for the ratings – although note that the officers were all well fed and watered. Lack of an agreement in place, fire hazards, lack of fresh water—"

"I get the picture, Fran. Who owns it?"

"Greek at origin, flagged wherever it lands. They've changed it that many times it's had more colours up its pole than the summit of Everest. Currently Belize but by the next port – who knows."

Flags of convenience, which allow shipping companies to cloak their questionable work practices by adhering to the law of the country under which the ship's listed – or flagged. Unsurprisingly, many ships flew the canvas of states with questionable human rights records, some of which were even landlocked.

"So is it coming to Ireland any time soon?" Sam knew that Fran had the capacity to find out such detail through his network of trades unions overseas.

"No, brother, I'm telling you – we're too good at this here. They know that if they land in Irish or British waters, they're fucked."

"Well, where's it for next?"

"Tomorrow, Yemen."

"Lovely spot."

"I dunno. For those into public executions ..."

"Then where?"

"Then Saudi."

"Then?" Sam somehow knew what was coming.

"Egypt, then Sudan, the canal, then the Med. I dunno if it has sorted its cargo beyond that. Will depend on how efficient the owner is."

"Where in Egypt?" asked Sam.

"Well, if you fancy diving and cocktails on the Red Sea, you're out of luck, brother. Place called Nuweiba. Looks like a kip on the east coast."

"Alright," he said. "Can you text me the timings?"

"For where?"

"For all the ports, please, and thanks a million, Fran. I appreciate it. Let me know if and when it comes closer to home. I'd love to pay the skipper a wee visit."

"No bother, my friend. Talk to ye." And the colourful little Dubliner was gone.

The phone sat silent for all of ten seconds. Sam had been at sea so long it startled him every time it made a noise. He lifted it and saw *Charity* appear. He made a note to change that in case she ever saw it.

"Sinead," he said, "how are you?"

"Grand, grand," she began. "Alea's doing well, Sadiqah is improving too. It will take time, you know the story. How are ye and Isla?"

Sam loved that she never forgot to ask for Isla. Even before Sinead had met her, she'd inquired after his daughter.

"Not so bad," he said. "Isla's off on her holidays without me."

"Ooh, you'll miss her."

Sam was, well, touched, that she got it.

"Mmm. How's, eh, how's Áine?" Sam felt compelled to ask by return.

"Well, that's part of the reason I'm ringing. She's got a location for that number ye gave her."

"She's quick."

"Piece of piss, she said. I'll just read you exactly what she wrote down on a note for ye. I haven't read it yet, so don't take offence if she's herself. You know she's only messing."

"Go on," said Sam, although he wasn't at all sure she was *only messing* when she slagged him.

Sinead began reading: "Tell that gobshite that he got something right – it *was* a phone number and it *was* a Libyan mobile. But – for whatever reason, it's not in Libya any more. At least the last time it pinged a cellular mast it wasn't in Libya. It was in Egypt." Sinead paused. "Make sense so far?"

"Yes," said Sam, tension building at what he knew was coming.

"Last known location, eastern Egypt. Can track it from Alexandria across Sinai Desert with patches of nothing until ... I can't make this out."

"Does it begin with *N*?" he asked, his head in his hands.

"Yeah, how'd ye know that?"

"Sound it out," he said – just as he made Isla do with her reading books.

"What am I, like five? Nu-wi-ba," she said.

"Nuweiba," he repeated.

"Weird." Sinead dismissed the incidentals and got back to the note. "It went dark closest to a town called Nuweiba. Tell him to ..." Sinead trailed off for a moment then came back. "Well, that's the gist of it."

"Tell him to what?" he pressed.

"The rest is just nonsense really."

"Go on, some nonsense might cheer me up just now."

"No," she said, unusually firm.

"Go on," he giggled.

He later imagined her set on a path before being nudged by him towards wavering. It had been a big decision.

"Come on, Sinead, what else did she write?" he asked.

He heard her take a big breath and then dive in.

"Tell him to make a decision about my sister and stop fucking with her head. She's been through enough dickheads already."

There was a deathly silence for a few moments. There was no point in denying anything. They were grown-ups and they'd both been around the block. Sam eventually spoke.

"I don't mean to mess with your head, Sinead."

"I know, Sam," she said. "I know."

"I'm sorry."

"Forget about it. It's not an issue. But ... I'm going to go now, ok?"

"Ok," was all Sam could think to say.

And she was gone.

He sat for a long while thinking about things he didn't want to be thinking about. All he wanted was a bit of time with his daughter, alone. But that was going to have to wait, so he hunted for a distraction and wondered about Shannon and what she would say.

She'd ask what the bad guys had done. He'd tell her they were people trafficking. She'd ask what he intended to do about it – not *if* he intended to do anything but *what* he intended to do. He'd talk her through possible scenarios, toning down or ignoring the violence. She'd weigh it all up and opt for the hard road. If people are harming children or women, remove them. She would have no problem with that.

So he fired up the Wi-Fi and searched for flights to Egypt.

CHAPTER 21

"Irish Ireland, Irish Ireland. Passport office."

First impressions: Middle Eastern mayhem.

There were chickens running about being chased by headless Arabs, their scarves bound round their skulls to stave off the weather. Ancient Mercedes estate cars were three-storey stacked with mattresses, furniture, old square television sets, and Sam even spotted a dog kennel. He thought he'd seen it all until a pickup emerged from the ship with what appeared to be a bundle of sandy rugs in the back. He thought little of it until the rig opened its eyes, bore a jaw full of enormous teeth and he realised he was staring into the face of a camel. Like, seriously, who brings a camel across the sea in the back of their car? And what shipping company lets them?

He was enjoying Nuweiba very much indeed, despite the ferry crossing during which men had unashamedly squatted to shit on the decks and piss against the life-jacket holds. Sam doubted there were any life jackets in them anyway. He had thought on more than one occasion that if the ship was to sink, he would be the sole survivor.

The route was far from ideal. Sam was spoiled for passports, and all of his passports were spoiled. He had two Irish issues and one British – all legit and a by-product of the happy circumstance of being born in Belfast, where the Good Friday Agreement provided for possession of both. A person could be Irish, British or both in the new Ireland. A person could identify as a box of chocolates as far as Sam could care.

Sam's intention had been to enter Egypt as undetected as possible, but he had Israeli stamps on two of his passports. That could prove a problem for Arab border guards, many of whom were hostile to the Jewish state. Besides, his travel history was so murky he could well be mistaken for a mercenary or special ops soldier and be sent back or scooped. Being arrested wasn't an option – given Isla – so he had to travel clean.

To compound the complications he couldn't say for sure that he wasn't being actively sought in that state, given the work which Shannon had given him shortly after they'd first met. Israelis were exceptionally good at questioning new arrivals.

Because of the strife in Egypt no commercial carrier was flying to Cairo, so he decided to get to Amman, get through Jordan and catch the ferry at Aqaba, which was why some clown in an Egyptian customs kiosk was reading his passport, word by word, over a tannoy.

"Irish Ireland, Irish Ireland, please come immigration," echoed over a crackly speaker system. In his distraction Sam only picked up on the Ireland bit. He seldom heard his surname used. He would have to go back to his pre-officer days to remember a time it had been routinely used to his face.

He left the madness of the arrivals terminal and eventually found a small hut in a vacuous loading bay where his passport was returned. He'd been reluctant to hand it over on the ship – expecting some bloody backhanded fundraising activity to be behind it – but there was no other option. Kick up a fuss and maybe have to buck a few people over the side, or hand it over peacefully and hope for the best.

And the best had prevailed. His third passport remained Israeli-stamp free and he exited the ferry port exhausted but strangely elated to be back in business. He was about to get stuck into something he was good at as opposed to parenting – in which his skill level still rested with the jury.

He walked one mile north, found a beach, dug a hole in the sand and slept to the sound of the sea while he waited for his ship to come in.

Sam looked up at her, imposing, dangerous, full of menace – and smiled in the sure knowledge that few people would imagine him capable of what he was about to do.

Teetaya. Her name was plastered on the transom. He toyed with the notion of shimmying up the lines tying it to the harbour, but he wasn't confident in his own fitness having been at sea for such a long time. It had meant virtually no walking, and save for a bit of habitual core work and winching sails in and out, he'd done no exercise and was softer than usual.

In the end he didn't have to do anything so exotic. He simply strolled up the walkway and punched the man standing at its top in the face. He took the man's radio and phone, kicked him down the steps and swung the walkway away from the quay.

He worked his way below and found a fire axe right where it should be. Deeper again he identified the enormous seacocks that allow water in and out of the ship. Every vessel sucks seawater – to flush toilets and, more importantly, cool the engines. Sam merrily swiped the metal fixings with the axe as he passed, pishing water in at a furious rate. Within minutes he was wading around just below knee level.

Sam started to climb the steps in search of the real workers

– the ratings. He found some running about trying to identify why the alarms were going off.

"Sinking," he barked at them. "Get off the ship immediately!"

They turned and ran up the metal rungs. He cleared each deck as he rose through the bowels of the boat, kicking or throwing open doors to make sure nobody was left behind. Up and up he went until eventually he made it to the bridge where all hell was breaking loose with buzzing and beeping and the wailing of sirens.

"Who is the radio operator?" he screamed as he burst onto the floor.

A man Sam assumed to be the captain turned towards him and began with a barrage of questions in a language he didn't understand.

Sam ignored him. "Radio operator!" he screamed again, and in their confusion at this axe-wielding apparition two of the four men present pointed at a burly chap by a window.

"I am from the yacht *Tuskar*. Remember me? You refused to give us help," he said, his voice more even as he lowered his heart rate.

The burly man's eyes widened in sudden understanding. He made to move from his seat but Sam caught him with a well-aimed hurl of a small fire extinguisher. It left the operator nicked but not out.

Sam turned to the others. "Refusing to help a fellow seafarer in distress is an incredibly serious issue, gentlemen. The punishment for such a transgression," he somehow found himself adopting Fran's flowery prose, "is a spell in Davy Jones's locker."

"What?" spat the captain, evidently understanding the reference.

"To the seabed, my friend, but first you must give me the sea books of your crew."

"No!" yelled the captain, so Sam chased down the radio operator, opened the bridge's side door, dragged the man a few feet across the walkway and swept his feet from beneath him, depositing him over the rail and into the harbour below. Then he returned to the bridge and surged for the captain.

"Moment, moment, moment," shouted the skipper who made for a large chart table and crouched beneath it.

Sam was wary and stayed tight to the captain's back in case there was a gun in the ship's safe. The captain rooted around and came out with a clasp of passport-sized brown booklets and held them over his shoulder.

Sam nodded and took a step back. "Vessel *Teetaya*, you are currently sinking. That is why the alarms are screaming. This is because you refused to help people who were in trouble and because you have abused your crew for years. You can leave the ship by walkway for another few moments, or if you prefer to wait, you can test your dodgy lifeboats. As you are at dock in this fine port, the ship will not go under but will remain here clogging the place up. I am quite sure that this will cause your employer some anger and distress – and you will deserve every bit of what is coming to you."

With that Sam gathered the books for the ratings and left the bridge to its wailing commotion.

Living life impulsively might be fun in short bursts but it always leaves a low when the excitement is over.

Sam returned to his hole on the beach and realised he had very little to go on and nothing to do next. Around him sat a few circular beach huts, all abandoned. There was a dilapidated backpacker's retreat nearby with no customers but little else. He decided to take up residence, and stock of his situation, in the shelter of a straw mud hut.

What had he been thinking? That this people trafficker could be traced in a town just because his phone had last been here? That he would somehow find this man, batter him and return to Ireland with a job done? Sam's darkness crept over him. He had been distracted of late, had had purpose and direction – across the Med, to Ireland, getting Isla back to routine. When she'd gone on holidays he'd leapt at the first opportunity to avoid thinking, and he'd applied himself, as usual, one hundred per cent, but that was finished now and he was flapping around like a hooked mackerel in a bucket. The high of sinking *Teetaya* and wreaking revenge was wearing off. He needed a lead but he didn't even have a sniff to follow. So against his better judgement and fearing the awkwardness of the call he dialled Sinead.

"I didn't think I'd hear from you for a while," she said sheepishly.

"I mean it. I am sorry. I'm just not there. Not yet anyway."

"I get that," she unhooked him, her generosity boundless.

"But that doesn't mean I don't want to be in touch with you, Sinead. If that's not an annoyance."

"You know it's not."

"Thank you."

There was an easy and long silence between them, a peaceful understanding.

"You're on the boat, I take it?" Sinead asked.

Sam laughed. "You would not believe where I am, Sinead."

"Where?"

"Egypt. I just sank a ship with a hatchet."

"Fuck off," she said, which surprised him as she seldom swore.

"Serious."

"Why?" Sinead was struggling to make sense of it.

"When we were at sea with Alea and Sadiqah I called a

passing ship and told them I'd people on board who needed help. They told me to fuck off. It made me cross."

"Bloody hell, Sam, remind me not to make you angry."

"I feel better now."

"Did anyone, like, drown?"

"No, no, I just sank her in the dock. She's lying against the quay wall clogging up the harbour, but on the seabed all the same. Most of her is above the waterline."

"You're unbelievable."

"So are you."

And there was silence as he computed how that had managed to come out of him unguarded.

"So are you in that place, Noobia?" Sinead broke it.

"Nuweiba," he said. "Yeah."

"Are you going looking for this trafficker then – the fella who sent Alea into the sea?"

"I'd like to but I don't know where to start."

"Well, what was your plan?"

"I didn't really have one."

"Unbelievable."

"You said that before."

"This time I meant it," she sniggered.

"Maybe you could rub Alea up for me a bit. See if there's anything she can remember that would help me find this fecker."

"Like what?"

"Like what he looks like or what he wore or his kit, or whether he was the type to rough it or if he drove a pimped-up wagon. Anything like that could give me a start."

"I can't believe you went all the way out there and didn't have a clue what you were going to do."

"Well, Isla's away, so I've got a week and I might as well be at something useful."

"I'll give it a go with Alea. I'll call you soon as."

"Thanks, Sinead."

"And Sam?"

"Yeah?"

"No pressure, seriously, but do you think you might ever *be there*?"

Sam paused for a long moment looking at the waves and the sunset and gave an honest answer. "I don't know, Sinead. I really don't know."

Waleed looked in the rear-view mirror, closed his eyes for a brief moment and kissed Arish goodbye. Four months he'd spent in the town. Useless months during which he'd discovered no more than the little his instincts had told him the day he'd arrived. Regardless, the air force had carried out seven air strikes on known terrorist locations in Sinai and there were unconfirmed deaths in the hundreds. Egypt's latest leader looked decisive, the security situation had momentarily stabilised and Waleed had been ordered to return to his Sinai outpost to continue intelligence gathering.

Until he got a call to say there had been another attack.

"Where?"

"Nuweiba, sir."

"A bombing?"

"No, it's ..."

"Hurry up," Waleed barked, irritated at yet another distraction and keenly aware he had another matter to deal with back at base. An enormous matter in a grungy suit.

"They've sunk a ship, sir."

"What?"

"The harbour is completely blocked. The captain claims some terrorist came aboard and scuttled his ship while it sat in port."

"Terrorist or terrorists?"

"Well, sir, just one, apparently."

"One man sank a ship? Where was the crew?"

"They were all on board, sir."

"Then why didn't they stop him?"

"They say he was armed."

"With what?"

"Ehm, an axe, sir."

"An axe. One man sank a ship in front of its crew with an axe."

"That's... that's what they say, sir."

"Did he chop through the ship's hull with the axe?" Waleed was struggling to understand.

"I don't know, sir."

"And why do you think it's a terrorist incident?"

"Well, the captain says it was terrorists, sir, and, well, aren't all ports getting tighter security?"

Waleed sighed. It did sound like an attack, which was positive in a way. That an axe was used rather than explosives suggested the Islamist groups were low on resources.

"There's one more thing, sir."

"What?"

"The attacker – apparently he was a white man who spoke English."

"Right," said Waleed, thinking about the countless recruits IS and others had managed to attract from England and elsewhere. He struggled to remember one who had been white, though.

"What do you want me to do, sir?"

"Secure the area," he said. "Monitor all mobile phone activity in the vicinity and get Cairo to track any unusual comms. I'm on my way."

"Ok, so," Sinead began. "He's small, Libyan, gnarly and his hair is black."

"Hello to you, too," said Sam.

"Yeah, sorry. Hello."

"So this is Habid."

"You know his name?"

"His brother gave it away – the bloke in the detention centre."

"Right?"

"Anyway, tell me what Alea said. What about his habits?"

"I didn't ask about habits – you didn't ask me to ask about his habits, but you did tell me to ask about kit."

"Ok, ok, well, what does he use?"

"He's got a phone, as you know, which Áine tried again and still can't find. She says it's probably been destroyed. And he had a GPS."

"Did he now?"

"Yeah, so we tried to find out what type of GPS it was."

"Good girl," said Sam.

"Girl?"

"Woman," he corrected himself. "Sorry."

"You're grand."

"So was she able to say what type?"

"Kind of. We showed her loads of pictures on Google and finally she found one on eBay. It's a really old yoke, Sam, with a twisty aerial that sticks out the side."

"What make?" Sam asked, feeling like this was going nowhere.

"A Garmin. It took us ages to find it. It's really old – from the nineties."

"Right," said Sam with a sigh.

"Hold on, Sam," said Sinead, detecting his ambivalence. "I'm going to put Áine on."

Sam's resignation got deeper as he waited for the sarcastic sister to start.

"Hello?" came the curt voice of Sinead's twin.

"Áine," said Sam.

"That the GPS is so old is actually an advantage."

"How come?" he asked, refusing to brighten.

"Because," said Áine, mounting her high horse, "nobody ever tries to update the software on obsolete devices, do they?"

"Haven't a clue, do they not?"

"No, Sam," he could almost see her expression, "yet somebody recently did just that on a device similar to the one we're looking for."

"And how does that help us?"

"Well, Sam, it doesn't help *me* one bloody bit. It's *you* that's looking for the help, so perhaps *you'd* do well to be a little less dismissive."

"Alright, Áine," he said, "how does that help *me*?"

"It helps *you* because the software was downloaded at a hotel not a million miles from where you are."

"Serious?"

"Serious."

"How do you know?" he said.

"I could tell you but Neanderthals like you would never understand, Sam. It's all to do with whizz-bang computers and stuff."

Sam had to smile. "Thanks very much," he said, feigning offence.

"Well, I'm told you just sank a ship with a hatchet. You'll be off to paint your remarkable personal development on the inside of a cave this afternoon. You know, how you've evolved so far in the last few years from trained killer to, oh wait, trained killer."

"Nobody died, Áine."

"I take it all back," she said. "You've clearly become culti-vated. Make sure you capture that in your cave art."

Sam shook his head in wonder at her relentless hostility, but he'd learned to firewall her jibes and could hear Sinead hissing at her sister to ease up.

"Will you text me the hotel details?"

"Fine," she said, and hung up before he could speak to Sinead again.

In a rare display of efficiency, Cairo came through before Waleed had even made it to Nuweiba. His phone buzzed on the dash and he punched the answer button on the Bluetooth, anticipating yet another distraction.

"Yes?"

"This is a secure line from central," a woman said.

Waleed was no stranger to such calls. They came from the GID, the General Intelligence Directorate, known to most as the Mukhabarat. His own position was an extension of that agency, although more military than spook. The two wings were rarely without tension. He went through the security checks and confirmed his staff credentials and passwords.

"We have information regarding your inquiry this morning."

Such conversations were always formal, the operator gener-ally permitted only to relay what was written in front of them.

"Yes?" said Waleed.

"I have instructions to ask whether this is connected to a similar inquiry from the police in Alexandria."

Immediately Waleed's antenna shot up. Big Suit was a member of Alexandria's police force.

"What inquiry do you have from the police in Alexandria?"

"There is a similar request to track phone signals last positioned in your jurisdiction," said the operator.

"A specific phone?"

"I have no further details, sir."

"Can you not tell me whether the request is to track unusual calls or a phone unit itself?"

"I have no further details, sir."

Waleed thought for a moment. He was tired and didn't have much capacity to play this information.

"As far as I'm aware, my inquiry is not connected to the Alexandrian police in any way. However, as head of military intelligence in this area I would like to formally request sight of that monitoring in full."

"I shall relay your request, sir," said the operator.

"So what of my own inquiry?"

The operator began to read. "You requested notification of any unusual cellular phone communications in the area of Nuweiba and Nuweiba Port over the past twenty-four hours."

"And ongoing," Waleed chipped in.

"Noted, sir. We have a record of two unusual calls being made. Notification of the calls came through a cellular mast six miles north of the port at Helnan."

"Who made them and to where?"

"The calls were made from a phone registered in the United Kingdom to a phone that connected in the Republic of Ireland."

Waleed sighed. Tourists.

"What type of place is Helnan?"

"Sir?"

"You are in front of a computer, yes?"

"Yes, sir."

"Get on Google and look up Helnan. What type of place is it?"

"I'm not sure that—"

"It's ok. I shall explain to anyone asking – or listening – that I'm ordering you to take a look for me."

He could hear the operator typing. Then a pause.

"It is a resort, sir."

"A beach resort?"

"Yes, sir."

"Is it an upmarket beach resort or a downmarket beach resort?"

"Ehm ... I do not know, sir. There are images of huts on the beach and, eh, it looks *quite* nice."

Waleed breathed out in frustration.

"How much does it cost to stay there?"

He heard the keyboard batter.

"Ok, sir, I see what you mean. There is a backpacker's hostel there that is cheap."

"So what does that suggest to you about the phone call that was made?"

"Perhaps the call was made by a backpacker?"

"Perhaps it was," said Waleed, trying not to take his irritation out on a lowly operator who was just following a script. "Can I kindly request that we monitor *unusual* phone signals from the area?"

"I believe, sir," he could sense her bristling, "that this is the *only* unusual phone signal that was made. And the description of the Nuweiba Port attacker was that he was white and English, which is why I think this was noted and relayed to you, sir," she added curtly.

Waleed adjusted himself in the seat. The operator was clearly bright and ballsy. He quite liked that.

"Ok, you make a point. Please see what you can determine from the content of the phone call."

"Perhaps, sir, someone may have already made that assessment."

Waleed tensed. The operator's tone had changed a fraction.

He got the sense she was telling him something. Waleed thought on that for a moment but his mind was cluttered with questions. He'd come back to it.

"Can you do something else for me quickly?"

"Yes, sir," the woman said.

"Look up Islamic jihadists in Ireland, please."

"On our database?"

"On Google, please, eh … what is your name?"

"Tiye, sir," the operator said, unsure as to whether she should be saying anything beyond her notes.

"Ok, Tiye, I don't have a computer as I'm driving, so if you could look that up for me we'll see if you might be right about this being significant."

"I don't know if I'm authorised—"

"You're smart, Tiye," Waleed cut in, "I can hear that. So have a look for me, tell me what you find."

Waleed heard the woman hammer at the keyboard. He waited on the line for a few minutes listening to her breathing and reading, and then typing some more. He didn't think she was taking notes, which was wise, as there would no doubt be inspections of their workspaces and searches of their bags as they left. The GID was nothing if not cautious about possible infiltration.

"Ok, sir?" she began, checking Waleed was still there.

"Go on, Tiye, I'm listening."

"There have been only two arrests for Islamic jihadist-related activity in Ireland, and one loosely related case. There was a woman from Northern Ireland, which appears to be part of the United Kingdom, who is related to a jihadist, but she moved to England many years ago."

"Ok," said Waleed, dismissing it as unlikely. "Go on."

"There was a man arrested ten years ago for researching how to make bombs. He was sent to prison. Again, Northern Ireland."

"And the call that was made from Nuweiba was to the Republic of Ireland, wasn't it? That's kind of a different country?" Waleed wasn't entirely sure.

"Yes, sir, that's correct," said Tiye.

"So is there anything from the Republic of Ireland?"

There was another long pause as Tiye read.

"Sir," she said, frustrated and unsure. "There is really very little. One half-Turkish man was convicted recently of raising a few hundred euro for Daesh, but that's all. There does not seem to be any sort of radicalisation happening there. No indication of it anyway."

"Ok," said Waleed, his mind drifting away from any notion of a complicated plot. He thought back to the hint that Tiye had given him earlier and decided to press his luck.

"Tiye, can you elaborate on the calls made from Nuweiba – is there any further information on record?" Waleed formally stated to help the operator out in case the call was being monitored by her superiors.

"Sir, let me seek authorisation," she said.

Of course she has to, Waleed realised. Why his own agency wouldn't volunteer everything at first ask remained a mystery to him. As usual it felt like some sort of insane control freakery.

He was placed on hold for an interminable period before Tiye came back.

"Sir, I have authorisation to play you what we have of the second call. We do not possess the conversation in its entirety."

"Why not?" Waleed asked, although he was eager to hear the audio.

"We do not have capacity to record all calls. Where an unusual communication is detected, it can take a few moments to place a track across the transmission."

"Ok," said Waleed.

"Stand by, sir."

There came a thump and a click and then – relayed through

two poor speakers – Waleed could make out a woman and a man speaking in English.

"... *sank a ship with a hatchet. You'll be off to paint your remarkable personal development on the inside of a cave this afternoon. You know, how you've evolved so far in the last few years from trained killer to, oh wait, trained killer.*"

"*Nobody died, Áine.*"

"*I take it all back. You've clearly become cultivated. Make sure you capture that in your cave art.*"

"*Will you text me the hotel details?*"

"*Fine.*"

Waleed was astonished at the recording. His English was good but not good enough to catch it all. It seemed like an odd conversation.

"Can you send me that file please, Tiye?"

"Yes, sir."

"Did you understand it?"

"Some, sir. I have some English."

"What were the accents?" he asked.

"I do not know, sir. Ireland, maybe?"

"Yes," said Waleed. "Maybe Ireland. You know what I want now, don't you, Tiye?"

"Yes, sir. I shall make contact again when that information becomes available."

Sam stared at the map. He didn't like it one bit. There was only one road to the place he needed to get to. Either side of that, nothing – sand, stones, sunshine and exposure. Nowhere to hide, he imagined. No cover. No water. If he became compromised on the short trip north, there would be few options beyond a fight, and he was ill-equipped. He hadn't even kept the hatchet. Still, the journey needed to be made otherwise the whole trip was largely pointless, so he looked around for a car to break into but discovered that such deviant behaviour wasn't required. Apparently nobody locked their vehicles in Egypt.

Sam found an old Merc at the edge of the port sitting among others identically dusted and exhausted. He chose a silver one because its tyre pressure looked better than the others, which meant more speed and less chance of accidents or punctures. There were a few people around, handing over goods, blethering at a million miles an hour. With the exception of one they all looked preoccupied.

Against a white Toyota van leaned a man who looked as shifty and out of place as Sam. He had a crisp white shirt on with smart trousers creased down the front. Those two elements would have been enough to distinguish him from the bartering sandal-footed Arabs to his left and right, but his shoes put the lid on it. They were fine slip-on articles with small tassels, handmade. Sam generally had no time for people who wore such shoes. In his experience they tended to be exceptionally posh and dismissive. Whoever this bloke was, he wasn't some Arabian version of the white van man. Sam remained wary of him, suspecting him to be a police or customs officer. He stood and watched as the man's eyes darted around the port apparently hunting for something. Sam began to worry that the man may be looking for him – after all, someone had sunk a ship in the port in recent days, so additional security was inevitable.

Sam kept his distance, observing the van. After about fifteen minutes the man straightened his back, his eye having caught something. The crisp shirt was dusted off as a larger van trundled towards him. It drew to a halt, nose first, amid a following fug of dirt and dust. The driver didn't acknowledge the man in the shirt but went immediately to the rear of his vehicle and began, Sam imagined, to lower the loading door. Sam struggled to see what the cargo was but caught glimpses of carpet between the two vehicles. He was losing interest until he caught a familiar name: AVON. A piece of rubber languished out the end of a rolled carpet bearing the name of an old but well-respected manufacturer of rubber dinghies. Sam had seen hundreds of such dinghies in his years working on boats but none recently. The 'O' in the logo was a red dot and so distinctive that he was absolutely sure that the carpet had been wrapped around an inflatable boat.

Of course, that didn't amount to a row of beans, Sam reminded himself, but that the boat had been concealed in a carpet intrigued him. Seconds later the van and the lorry drew away in opposite directions leaving Sam in peace to pinch a Mercedes.

"Sir, we have the text message as ordered."

"Requested, Tiye, requested."

"Yes, sir, requested." She almost giggled.

"Well?"

"The hotel is named as the Hilton in Taba, sir."

Waleed's heart plummeted. He knew it well, at least he knew *of* it. It had been all but destroyed some years ago in a terror attack that had killed a few dozen tourists. The bombing had been instrumental in his own deployment to Sinai. He'd been appointed in the aftermath to shore up intelligence gathering in counterterror. Bad thoughts began to float through his mind: was this Irishman about to attack the hotel or was he just seeking a place to stay? The recording of the phone conversation had been far from clear on any matter other than that the man had been responsible for the sinking of a ship and was, apparently, a trained killer.

Waleed had only just arrived in Nuweiba after a long, sweaty drive. He bought a bottle of water, took a long piss against his own rear wheel and set off again north, to Taba; the edge of Egypt where his country met its nemesis, Israel – and its troublesome cousin, Gaza. On the way he called in reinforcements and ordered the hotel to be surrounded with a ring of security. There would not be another attack there, not on his watch.

CHAPTER 22

Sam couldn't find the handbrake. He'd never driven a
Mercedes before, so he just left it in gear and made the
last leg of his journey on foot. The hotel hadn't been
hard to find, although Áine's text had been typically curt:
Hilton, Taba. He'd thought a little about her hostility towards
him on the drive north and knew that much of it derived from a
protectiveness of her twin sister. He could almost admire that,
but it was exhausting nonetheless.

Sam had no idea what he would do when he got to the
hotel. All he had was an indication that a GPS device similar to
the one used by a known people trafficker had undergone a
software update on the premises. Sure the locations matched a
broader picture, but as leads went it was as flaky as week-old
sunburn.

In the event, he needn't have worried about deciding his
next move. Ten feet from the gate he found himself surrounded
by soldiers.

Sinead was pacing. Her sister was reassuring.

"He'll be grand. He's always grand. He's kind of ... inde-structible."

It was probably the nicest thing Áine had ever said about Sam.

"Then why can't you find him?"

Áine was staring at a computer screen. Her sister had asked her to track Sam's phone, which had gone dark five hours before.

"Maybe he ran out of battery or switched it off to get some sleep," she said.

"Don't do that," Sinead said.

"What?"

"Try to make me feel better by pretending you can't track a phone even if the signal's down. Sure, I've seen you do it before, remember?"

Áine sat silent. What her sister said was true. Even if a phone was powered down – even in some cases if its battery was removed – the tech existed to keep an eye on its where-abouts. Some agencies had the capacity to listen to what was being said in such a handset's vicinity, regardless of its security settings.

"He's a big boy, he'll be ok."

"He's got a daughter to look after," said Sinead.

"And the rest," muttered Áine, who was heard but ignored. "Sure, you know what sort of a fella he is. He'd fight his way out of a firing squad."

But there was no way to fight his way out of the circle of shit he'd landed at the centre of. At all points of the compass stood a man with a rifle, invariably a Kalashnikov. Sam could tell from the way the soldiers rested their fingers along the weapons that they weren't trigger-happy excitable idiots. These were calm, well-trained professionals, possibly part of a special unit. What was more, they knew to address him in a broken, faltering but educated English, which told him immediately that they knew he was coming.

"Lie down, lie down," barked the leader.

Sam did as he was bid.

"Hands back to air."

Sam got the gist of the orders and was cuffed. He was struck by the nervous nature of the soldiers, as if they were confused by him. The body search was correspondingly cautious – they had scissors to hand and cut the back of his T-shirt, gently peeling the cotton away as a nurse might the bandage of a wound. The men seemed preoccupied with his torso but, eventually placated, they patted him down and checked his legs and stomach and lifted him to his feet. His phone was gently taken from his pocket, as was his passport, which wasn't examined but handed back to him.

Something very strange was going on.

They took his pack of gum, handling it as if it might pose a danger. In reality it simply passed as Sam's travelling tooth-brush. He was shuffled into a rather opulent hotel lobby and guided to a small room behind reception where chemicals were stored on one side and the accoutrements of room service on the other. He was told to sit on the floor and secured by a second set of stainless steel handcuffs to a painted metal pipe.

There he spent two hours alone panicking that he wouldn't be home in time to collect Isla from her grandparents. He wondered how on earth he would explain to them that in the space of a few days he'd managed to get arrested and jailed in Egypt while they'd been on a roller coaster.

Finally a dishevelled man entered the room. Despite his creased appearance and two-day growth, Sam was immediately aware of his authority. This was a confident leader accustomed to having his questions answered. Sam somehow felt he was dealing with an equal, which could be an advantage but could be a disaster.

"You sink-ed a ship," the man stared down at him, speaking in clearly understandable but sketchy English.

Sam saw no question, so offered no answer.

"What is name?"

"Sam."

"Two names?"

"Ireland."

"Not country. Name."

"My second name is the name of a country. It's a bit odd."

"You name is Ireland, and you also are from Ireland? Passport?" he said.

Either this bloke was good with accents or he was good at his job. Sam saw no point in lying, and rolled to his right. "Arse pocket."

The man flipped through the pages of the passport but didn't look up as he spoke. "Why you sink-ed ship?"

Sam felt that was a fair question but it also alarmed him. How did the man know so much about him – that he was Irish and he'd been to Nuweiba? Sam opted for silence, so the man held out Sam's phone and shook it a little in demonstration. He then withdrew his own mobile phone and tapped the play button on the screen. Sam heard snippets of the conversation he'd had with Áine.

"Is you, yes?" The man's question wasn't really a question – more of a statement. "You are terrorist in Sinai to attack hotel." The man gestured to the salubrious surroundings of the storeroom.

"What?" Sam asked baffled.

"You are here to attack-ed hotel," repeated the man.

"No? No!" said Sam, shaking his head furiously. He

suddenly realised that the soldiers had been frisking him for an explosives vest.

"Then why sink-ed ship?"

Sam realised he was quite deep in the shit, so he had no choice but to talk. He knew that if he didn't, the likelihood was that he would end up forgotten in an Egyptian jail and Isla would suffer.

"The ship's captain was abusing his crew. Also, the ship was dangerous."

"Is now very dangerous. Is sink-ed in harbour. Is not possible to move."

"Good," said Sam.

"You coming from Ireland to sink-ed ship?"

"Yes," said Sam.

"Why you coming to hotel?"

"To stay. Before leaving."

"I am not believe-ed you. This woman on phone – she tell you to come to hotel."

He had a point. Sam sighed. "Another job," he conceded.

"What is another job?" said the man.

"What is your name?" countered Sam, teasingly, as if with give and take he might talk.

The man stared at Sam for a few moments, then his forehead creased and his eyebrows arched a little. "Waleed," he said.

Sam looked at Waleed, cool as a breeze, well informed and full of natural authority. He took a risk. "It's nice to meet you, Waleed. I'll tell you what I am here to do because you seem like the sort of person who might understand."

Waleed stared at Sam, curious. There was something about this prisoner, manacled to the floor, that intrigued him. His understated confidence, perhaps. He shrugged, gesturing for Sam to try him.

"I'm here to find a people trafficker."

Waleed snorted and shook his head – not dismissively but in serendipitous recognition. Of course you are.

And in that one shake of his captor's head, Sam saw a chink of light.

The doctor had some cash and decided to use it. In preparation for the journey to Europe, he'd exchanged what he could for euros at his bank in Alexandria. The bank hadn't held a huge stock and so rationed them to one hundred per customer, but like many things in Egypt sticky processes could be lubricated with moderate financial reward.

He approached one of the guards during his allotted exercise time in the yard outside the holding-centre warehouse.

"If I pay you, can you make a call for me to Egypt?"

"No," said the guard.

"Why?" asked the doctor.

"No," repeated the guard.

The doctor walked on in his circle until he passed the static guard again.

"I have one hundred euros," said the doctor.

"No," said the guard again, whose vocabulary was either limited or his dedication to his job absolute.

The doctor performed another tight circle.

"Two hundred euros?"

"Who do you wish to call?" asked the guard.

"The police station, Alexandria," said the doctor as he wandered beyond earshot.

On the next loop it was the guard who spoke.

"Three hundred and I will provide a phone for a short time."

The doctor nodded.

Waleed had brought one of his men into the room and ordered Sam be uncuffed from the pipe and sat up on a chair. He was wary of Sam's physique, so he left the shackles on his wrists behind his back.

"Why come to Taba hotel?"

"It's a bit of a long shot."

"I do not know what is this," said Waleed.

"The reason I came here. It is ..." Sam struggled to explain, "not likely to work out," he tried.

Waleed shrugged his lack of understanding.

Sam filled the silence. "There is a man who is sending people into the sea. He is a people trafficker. People pay him money to escape to Europe."

"I know people trafficking."

"Right, well, I was sailing – I sail. I live on a boat with my daughter. I picked up some of his victims. They were drowning."

Waleed's interest appeared to grow.

"Where you pick up?"

"One hundred miles north-west of Libya approximately."

"Ok," said Waleed warily.

"I took them to Ireland and this woman, she told me about the man who sent her to sea. For money. I am looking for him."

"You take to Ireland?" Waleed couldn't hide his surprise.

"Yes. Long story."

"Long journey," Waleed said dryly.

Sam was starting to like him. "You have no idea, Waleed. One of the longest of my life – and I've had a few brutal marches."

"Why you here in Taba? Why at hotel?"

"That's the long shot," he said. "This man, he had a device. A Global Positioning System. Like a phone, really. A GPS?"

Waleed visibly stiffened, which distracted Sam a little.

"It was an old yoke."

Waleed shook his head.

"It was – like – out of date."

Blank look.

"Anyway," Sam continued, "I have a friend in Ireland," he overstated the relationship immeasurably, "who can tell – from a computer – that a device just like it was updated on like a computer right here at this hotel."

Sam watched Waleed grow angry, which was confusing and worrying – something he was saying was touching a nerve and he couldn't understand what that might be.

"I know," he tried to placate his darkening captor, "it was a long shot."

"Long shot is gamble, yes?" Waleed finally spoke.

"Yes," said Sam curiously, "exactly."

"Pier-haps not so much long shot, maybe."

———

It didn't take long to identify the culprit. Waleed stomped outside and got on the phone. He spoke to the duty officer in the interrogation suite back at his desert headquarters. The man told him which military unit had been sent to Nuweiba. From that information Waleed was able to call the unit's sergeant, who told him exactly who had been ordered to drive Big Suit's kit east and destroy it. Waleed told the sergeant to send a photograph of the offender. As he spoke Waleed paced the marble floor of the foyer, passing the various tourist excursion desks that advertised day trips. None of them was doing any business. He had cruised each twice by the time he finished the call and was readying to return to the Irishman when he noticed the car-hire desk to his right.

"How much for a car?" he asked.

"For how long?" the clerk perked up from his boredom.

"Depends. Can I have one with a GPS?"

The clerk did all but breathe on his knuckles and rub them against his lapel.

"Yes, sir. You *can* have a GPS—"

"Show me," Waleed interrupted.

The clerk pulled open a drawer and with pride revealed Big Suit's device. Waleed's phone vibrated in his pocket and he ripped it out to view the picture message he'd just received. He turned the screen towards the clerk.

"Did this man sell that device to you?"

The clerk stared at the image in fear – fear of having the GPS confiscated and what his boss might say to him as a result. "No," he lied.

"I am head of military intelligence," said Waleed, which he rarely had cause or desire to tell anyone but he was in a rush, "so think carefully. If you lie to me, you will struggle to imagine what might happen to you."

"Yes, that's the man," said the clerk in a gush.

"Did that man also sell you a phone?" Waleed revealed his real concern.

"No, sir, no."

"That could be a life-changing lie," warned Waleed.

"It is not a lie, sir, really. It is true."

"Did this man *offer* you a phone?" he asked instead.

"No, sir, just GPS. This is all."

"Did you update the software on this GPS?" Waleed asked.

"Yes, sir, but still nobody wants to rent this. It is so old. It is not for vehicles really. It is for travelling across mountains or the sea."

Or the desert, thought Waleed. "Give it to me," he said.

The clerk relinquished the device willingly. "Please, sir, can you give me a receipt for my boss?"

"I will send a man to issue you a receipt," Waleed said.

He took no pleasure from discovering this lead. His real worry was that Big Suit's phone was still at large, and trackable.

The Egyptian burst into the room, quietly furious. He placed the old GPS on the table.

"Is this what you look for?"

"Could be ..." Sam began, utterly confused. "It's the right make, the right sort of age."

Apparently that was enough for Waleed. He walked around behind Sam, who assumed he was about to be attacked and braced. Instead, he felt his handcuffs being unlocked.

"Come with me, Meester Sam Ireland," said Waleed.

Free for the first time in hours, Sam was cautious but happy and curious enough to shrug his big shoulders, shake his heavy arms and tag along.

For one whole hour Sam sat at Waleed's side feeling the heat of the man's rage emanate from the driver's seat. They said nothing to one another but Sam listened intently as Waleed made call after call on his mobile phone. It was clear that Waleed was a leader, and an effective one at that. He could hear both sides of each conversation through the Bluetooth system in the car and each man on the other end was subservient and respectful and Waleed didn't need to shout or scream to get his answers. Every call was in Arabic, but other than a tiny clutch of pleasantries Sam couldn't follow what was being said. Finally there was a conversation with a woman called Tiye, and Waleed's conversation took a softer tone and he offered all the thank yous.

Sam stared at the road. He could tell from the sun that they were headed west. Whatever the perfect snake beneath them was made from, it appeared able to endure the heat as it slithered through the rocks and dirt of Sinai – the surface of which was garnished with only an occasional brittle shrub surviving against the odds and craving libation.

When Waleed spoke it came as something of a surprise out of the silence.

"I am not arrest-ed you."

Sam thought for a moment, but only one question came to mind. "Why not?"

Waleed laughed gently. "You can hel-ep me," he said. "Pier-hap-es I can also hel-ep you, Meester Sam Ireland."

Sam quite liked Waleed's use of English and was mildly amused at the constant use of his full name.

"So *how* can I help you?" Sam inquired.

"I have responsibility here," Waleed gestured around him, "in desert. ISIL, Daesh, militant, jihadi, very strong here in desert."

Sam took that at face value. He decided just to shut up and listen.

"You from nowhere come to my jurisdiction and are problem. I no have time to deal-ed with you."

Sam tried not to get excited or worried about what that might mean.

"I also have other problem. Many peoples, they are attack-ed every day. No one care."

Sam stayed quiet.

"In Cairo, in Alexandria, here in desert. Many innocent peoples. Immigrant, Sufi, Copts. They attack-ed."

Sam knew next to nothing about denominational politics in Egypt, but he was Irish and as such had at least a point of reference for groups that to the outside world seemed identical but could find no end of issues to dispute behind closed doors.

"These are peoples who want leave Egypt," Waleed went on. "They want be safe for families and go look to refuge."

"I understand," said Sam.

"Some peoples, they go to sea. They are desperate peoples. They pay for men to take to Italy, to Greece. Some peoples they come from Jordan, from Iraq, from Syria, from far away. Then they pay money and go to sea and they die."

Waleed was becoming increasingly agitated and expressive as he ranted about the problem. Sam watched his gesticulations head towards anger and decided to try and inject a tone of sympathy, of kindred experience.

"Has this happened to people you know?"

Waleed shot a hard look at him and Sam began to worry he had taken the wrong tack.

"Because I have direct experience of this," Sam scrambled a little, trying to keep his tone moderate. "I used to help people who had been trafficked."

"How?" Waleed snapped back, curious.

"I used to rescue people. Women mostly, sometimes men from ships. Who were being abused. Used. Made to work for no money. People who had paid bad men to take them to better places for a new life and instead were made to work as prostitutes or slaves."

"Hookers?" Waleed asked.

"Yes," said Sam.

"Exact-ally!" Waleed slammed his hand down on the wheel. "Many of my people pay money and leave-ed Egypt."

"Do they?" Sam inquired, and earned himself another icy glare.

"Egyptians," said Waleed oddly, after a long silence.

Sam let it slide, but Sam got the impression there was more to Waleed's story than he was prepared to discuss. Not that Sam was one to care. All he wanted was to finish what he'd come to do, avoid arrest and get out of Egypt quickly. "I just want to stop this bloke," Sam said, his palms open in an *easy, boy* sort of a gesture.

"I no have time to deal-ed with traffick problem."

"You're some sort of boss out here – a military commander?"

"I am head military intelligence in jurisdiction." Waleed swept his hand as if brushing away a butterfly, without pride or fanfare. Sam liked that. "Is difficult bloody job," he remarked, arid as his beat.

Sam laughed. "It sounds it," he replied.

"Every day, more problem from jihadis. Every day, more problem from Gaza. Every day, more problem from tourist. I think you know this."

"How would I know?" asked Sam, genuinely curious.

"I think-ed you are solider some time."

Sam was silent, which Waleed took as confirmation.

"I am think this man, he sink-ed ship, steal-ed car. This man can tracking GPS from other country. This man he thrown person into harbour and scare-ed crew of big ship – solo. This man travel alone from Jordan. So this man, may be army."

"Not army," Sam corrected, remembering the *trained killer* comment from Áine.

"Pier-haps in past," Waleed grunted, which Sam took as a reference to his vintage.

"Not army, though."

"Intelligence?"

"No," said Sam firmly.

Waleed sat quietly for a while. "Sailor." He nodded to himself knowing he had put the jigsaw of Sam's previous conversation together.

Sam said nothing.

"Special sailor, pier-haps." The name of a unit was on the tip of Waleed's tongue, but it just wouldn't roll off.

He was quiet for a while and Sam had no intention of jumping in.

"You said I could help you," said Sam, happy to divert the flow of conversation. "What can I help you with?"

Waleed took a deep breath as if preparing to tell an irritating story. "I have prisoner. He is idiot."

Sam laughed aloud.

"He is also dangerous. He is corruption but was not always. He is involve-ed."

"Involved in what?"

"People traffick," said Waleed, as if that much ought to have been clear to Sam by now.

This sounded like good news.

"He is also police officer."

"Right," said Sam, slightly surprised.

"I am not knowing what to do with him," said Waleed, as if confessing a weakness to Sam. "He is too stupid to organ-ise. But he has boss – also police. Bad, bad man."

"Ok," said Sam, "and how do you think I can help you with this man?"

"I think-ed he can hel-ep you."

"How?"

"Am think he can hel-ep you find traffick gang."

"That sounds like a hell of a reach," said Sam. "I'm not looking for any old people trafficker, I'm looking for one particular man."

Waleed turned and smiled.

"This is strange, Sam Ireland. I am think we are look for same man."

CHAPTER 23

"Your boyfriend's a dickhead," Áine seethed as she came in the door from work.

Sinead had arrived at the flat they shared just ahead of her.

"What?"

"Sam. He's landed us right in it again."

"What're you talking about? Have you been speaking to him? And by the bloody way – he's not my boyfriend," she said with unusual force before softening. "Is he ok?"

"I'm sure *he's* fine. It's *me* you should be worried about."

"Why? Will ye tell me what's happened?"

"I've been sacked," Áine said.

"What?"

"And hacked. Sacked and hacked. Well, hacked first, sacked after that."

"Áine, for the love of—will you just calm down and tell me what's after happening?"

Áine accepted she was making no sense, bailed into their sole sofa and began a measured rant. "So I get in from lunch and plug-in at my workstation and the whole fucking system is going cracked. Someone had proxied into my terminal and was raping the whole network."

"Well, that's a security issue, isn't it?"

Sinead knew very little about tech firms but Áine had been headhunted half a dozen times by the bluest, chippiest firms in Dublin, so she imagined their firewalls, or whatever, would be fairly robust.

"Eh, duh," said Áine, still seething.

"Don't do that."

Very little really annoyed Sinead, but that expression made her mad. Áine relented a little.

"I plugged my laptop into the network to help your ... colleague?"

"*Colleague* is grand."

"And I started trying to ping that phone again – the one that went dark in Egypt."

"Right," said Sinead, not understanding what all this had to do with anything.

"Then I went to get a blaa."

"Thought you were off white bread."

"What the actual fuck?"

"Sorry, but it was you who brought up your lunch."

"I nearly did get sick when I got back. The whole system was compromised, not just my personal laptop."

"And you think it's something to do with looking for this phone? For Sam?"

"I don't *think* it, sis, I *know* it. Our head of information security shut down the network – which is a major fucking call for an organisation like ours. It was down for one hundred and forty minutes. Nobody could do any work. Do you know how much that costs?"

"How much?"

"Fuck, Sinead, I don't know how much but it's a hell of a bloody lot, alright?"

"Alright," said Sinead, hands up at the onslaught.

"And the security team analyse what the source of the information attack was – and guess where they land?"

"At your laptop."

"At what I was looking for on my laptop – which was a phone – in a desert – in Egypt, for your bloody—"

"He's not my fucking boyfriend!" Sinead all but screamed.

That shocked Áine. Sinead's mouth was over ninety per cent cleaner than her sister's, so such outbursts tended to have a silencing quality.

"Sorry," she muttered.

"Who would have wanted to know about this?" Sinead tried to bring her own temperature down.

"They say it's at, like, government level."

"What? Serious?"

"Serious."

"Because you tried to find this phone."

"Seems so. But, like, what do we even know about what Sam's doing or who owns this phone? Look where we ended up last time. We were being tracked by a network of fucking paedophiles."

Sinead hauled air into her. That was true. Sam had sorted it all out in the end but there were a few days the previous year when it looked like they were in genuine danger.

"I don't know," said Sinead. "But before, last time, that was partly my fault. That job came about as a result of a referral from me."

"Not this one, though. This time it's to do with that woman and kid he plucked out of some Arabian sea."

"I'm really sorry, sis. Will this be a mark against you? Will you be able to get another job?"

"I dunno," said Áine. "It depends what the fuck is going on and who's looking for what. It depends on what your—" she paused and reconsidered her terminology, "what Sam's got mixed up in."

Four thousand miles away Sam remained dangerously unaware of the interest his exercise in emotional distraction was generating.

––––––––

"Why do you think I am looking for this police officer you have taken prisoner?"

Waleed had turned to face the road once more.

"You arrive-ed in desert from Jordan."

"You checked passport control?"

"Of course."

"But that's not got anything to do with anything."

"You are tracking GPS, yes?"

"Sort of." His head rocked from shoulder to shoulder. "Yes," he then conceded, "trying to, anyway."

"We are finding GPS in hotel in Taba, yes?"

"Possibly," said Sam, who suspected the device was the one he was looking for but had no confirmation.

"This GPS, it was update on computer."

"When?" asked Sam excitedly.

"Two days maybe."

"Two days ago?"

"Yes. Maybe."

"But that still doesn't mean it is the device I am looking for."

Waleed realised there were missing elements of his story that needed to be relayed.

"My prisoner – the police officer – he is sent by superior to desert for people trafficking."

"Right ..." said Sam, trying to follow the logic.

"He has same GPS. Same one. I take from him when he is arrest."

Sam's mind was up and running and jumping over shit but clattering most of the hurdles along the way. "I don't follow," was all he said.

"I make my men take policeman GPS and mobile phone to the east. I keep-ed prisoner at interrogation cell."

Sam sat silent.

"I order men destroy GPS and mobile phone, but they sell it. Bastards," he spat.

Sam decided to disregard the elements he didn't need to understand – like why Waleed had sent the kit east and why he wanted it destroyed. Instead he focused on what seemed relevant to his own job.

"If they sold it, how did you find the GPS again?"

"Is luck. You trace-ed to hotel in Taba. You tell me. Then is luck. Not important."

Sam shrugged. If Waleed said it wasn't important, Sam wasn't about to argue.

"But why do you think your prisoner is the man I am looking for?"

Waleed thought for a moment.

"GPS is same."

"Similar," Sam corrected, reluctant to pick holes in Waleed's argument.

"Is one you come look for or not?"

"I can find out if you let me have my phone back."

Waleed fished in his back pocket and threw Sam his phone. Sam tapped in his code and took a photo of the GPS sitting on the dash between them. He sent it to Sinead with accompanying text: *Urgent. Please ask Alea if this is the device. Ta.*

Sinead's phone pinged as she stared at her sister, not knowing what to say. She took it out of her pocket, saw the sender's name and went into the kitchen to read it.

What's going on, Sam? Áine just got fired for trying to track that phone.

While she was waiting she sent another message to the manager of the refuge where Alea and Sadiqah were staying.

Hi. Please ask Alea if this is the right device. She will understand. Let me know asap. Thanks hon.

Sam's neck muscles tightened at the response he received. He hadn't expected anything to come through so quickly. He tried to understand what it meant – why would Áine have been sacked?

"Waleed, is there anyone else who could be tracking the policeman's mobile phone?"

Waleed darted him a look.

"How you know this?" he barked. Tiye had asked him exactly the same thing.

"There was a man, in the sea, the night of the rescue. It's complicated but he gave me the mobile phone number of the man behind the trafficking gang. My friend, in Ireland, she was trying to track the number."

Waleed went quiet and Sam filled the gap.

"She has been sacked from her job, which seems very weird."

"Someone else is tracking this phone," Waleed said. "I do not know who."

The two men ticked over their own ends of the same story. Nothing appeared clear.

Fifteen minutes of pointless musing was interrupted by a message to Sam's phone. *Charity* appeared again on the screen.

She says, yes, it's the same device. Sadiqah recognises the missing button.

Sam snatched up the GPS again and saw what he'd paid no attention to before. The rubber cover on the top right button had been torn off.

"It's the same device," he said to Waleed.

"What?"

"The GPS. It is almost definitely the one used by the trafficking gang."

Waleed slapped the wheel, happy at the breakthrough.

Sam's phone pinged: *Charity. You need to tell me what's going on, Sam.*

He started writing. *I promise you, Sinead, I will. As soon as I know. Really sorry about Áine. Will try to fix any damage done. Thank you for this. Sam.*

"Gamble," said Waleed.

"What?"

"Was gamble, no?"

"I suppose it was," Sam acknowledged, distracted.

Waleed was now convinced that Big Suit was the man Sam was looking for. In the back of his mind a solution was presenting itself as to what he might do with the big fool.

"What you tell me about man you look for – the traffick man?"

Sam thought for a moment, thinking about how Alea had described Habid.

"He is small, Libyan and cunning."

Waleed's hands gripped the wheel until his knuckles went white. His jaw muscle flexed through his skin.

"Does that sound like your prisoner? What's he like?" asked Sam.

Waleed was quiet for a moment, then sighed. "He is big, Egyptian and stupid."

That explained Waleed's white knuckles.

There was silence for a long while until Waleed shifted gear to deal with a gentle incline.

"Is possible you speak to prisoner. GPS is strong link. This device," he gestured to the unit on the dashboard, "is not for vehicle. Is for desert. We speak to him, we see where is going." Waleed nodded, trying to build confidence in himself.

Sam kindled a gentle hope too. Waleed was right. The GPS in front of him wasn't for mapping roads – it was for tracking across oceans or open land. It was ideal for, say, desert-border crossings – the kind Alea had described. He lifted it and gestured to Waleed – *do you mind?* Waleed shrugged.

Sam had seen similar units on boats when he'd been a teenager but had never used one properly. It gave a track, a spidery line of where the device had been, and offered coordinates. It seemed that on land anyone holding the device could retrace their footsteps accurately. The advantage for Sam was that it told him where the device had been in recent months. He had next to no power left in his phone. It would blink itself to sleep shortly, but he looked at Waleed's smartphone in its holder.

"Waleed, can I use your phone?"

"No," he replied.

Sam felt berated, as if put in his place. Waleed noted the effect.

"You are not prisoner, Meester Sam, but I cannot give you phone. You are suspect still."

"Ok. If I give you some GPS coordinates, can you punch them into your phone?"

"We are in Sinai. Signal here very, very bad."

"GPS might work," Sam pressed.

He was keen Waleed felt they were working together.

The vehicle pulled up. There was no hard shoulder, but then there was no traffic either. Sam read out the most frequently used coordinates from the GPS. Waleed tapped in the numbers and held the phone up for a few minutes. He turned his head towards Sam, surprise on his face.

"Libya," he said.

"Bingo," said Sam. "Let's go talk to your prisoner."

Big Suit had taken to removing all his clothes by day and replacing them at night. It was his only means of regulating his body temperature. Daytime, the sun outside was splitting the rocks, by night it was freezing. He was lying with his upper body on the inside lining of his jacket in his soiled, moist underpants when the door opened and his old friend appeared. Big Suit scrambled to his feet, embarrassed at the way he was turned out. He automatically cupped his genitals and tried to hide his man boobs with his arms.

"Get dressed," Waleed barked.

Another man followed Waleed into the holding area. He was slightly above average size, fit looking with Western outdoor clothing. His face had the weather of a thousand sand-storms. Big Suit could tell he'd never seen the cell before because he gazed around the surroundings registering every detail. He was deeply tanned, so Big Suit was surprised when he spoke in English to Waleed.

"Is this where you might have imprisoned me?"

"There is still time, Meester Sam," Waleed replied wryly.

Big Suit had no idea what they were saying.

Stinking trousers hoisted, Big Suit stood to something like attention. He'd lost track of how long it had been since he'd seen Waleed.

"This man is here to ask you some questions. If you want to get out of here, then answer him honestly and quickly."

"Yes, Waleed," said Big Suit eagerly.

Waleed stared at the big goon and wondered what he might

do with the secret information he had miraculously stumbled upon if Waleed chose to release him. His lurking hope was that the Irishman might take him away to find this trafficking gang, and that Big Suit might somehow disappear in the process.

"Why does he call you by your first name?"

Waleed frowned as if the memory pained him. "We trained together at the academy, many years ago. Our lives have been very different since."

Sam turned to the captive. "Is this yours?" He held up the GPS.

Waleed snapped out a one-word translation. Big Suit turned to Sam and shook his head, talking in Arabic.

"He says no." Waleed listened while he spoke. "He says his boss give it to him. He says it taken from desert rat they arrested at hotel in Alexandria."

Sam was interested. "Describe him."

"He is little man. He is wearing Bedouin clothes. He is dark, darker than most Egyptians—"

"Where is he from?" Sam interjected.

Big Suit seized the chance to show willingness.

"Libya," Waleed confirmed with an arched eyebrow. "And he is injured."

This was news to Sam. Alea had made no mention of an injury.

"How is he injured?"

Big Suit's eyes fell to the floor, almost ashamed. He spoke defensively, and through his former friend spilled his guts.

"He has a foot injury and some other problems," Waleed said, as Big Suit gestured at his nether region.

Waleed then asked a few questions to which Big Suit shrugged in acceptance and admission. Waleed nodded knowingly.

"The injuries happened during the interrogation. This fat fool has grown to enjoy questioning people with tools."

Sam caught the gist. He imagined the interrogation had happened after Alea and Sadiqah had been sent to sea.

"Where is this Libyan now?"

"I do not know," Waleed relayed.

"Why did you have his GPS?"

"His boss sent him to Sinai. He was to collect boat for sending people to sea," Waleed explained. "The GPS was given because he never been here before, but he is too stupid to use."

"Where were you going to collect a boat in the desert?" asked Sam, but the answer was slowly dawning on him.

"Suez," repeated Waleed. "Then his boss call him to send him to Nuweiba instead."

Sam's neck was bristling.

"So you and your boss arrested this man – this rat – for people trafficking. And instead of charging him, you decided to get in on it?"

Waleed looked at Sam with narrowed eyes, confused. Sam tried again.

"He and his boss, they took over the business? The people trafficking business?"

Waleed nodded and put this to Big Suit.

"This is what his boss is want. He want take over rat's business to make money. But this man," he gestured at Big Suit, "he is arrested by my men out here. He is not knowing what happen-ed afterwards."

"He failed at the first attempt."

"Yes," said Waleed, not bothering to put it to Big Suit. "I tell you, his is not genius."

"Ask him what his boss looks like."

Waleed and the prisoner exchanged gestures and words before Waleed turned again to Sam.

"He is liking nice clothe-es. He is normal size, and he is bad man."

Sam's lips tightened. "Ask him what sort of shoes his boss wears, please."

Waleed looked at Sam and wondered if he'd had too much sun but turned and posed the question. The hand gestures said it all: Big Suit used his thumb and forefinger to demonstrate something small, as if he was brushing his nail through hair.

"These are strange shoes," said Waleed. "Not laces."

"Fuck," said Sam.

"Is problem?" asked Waleed utterly perplexed.

"I saw him. I *think* I saw him. At Nuweiba. Picking up boats wrapped in carpet."

Waleed looked bemused. "I think we need to talk, Meester Sam," and gestured to the door.

The confusion was continental. In the heart of Libya's new intelligence agency information was filtering in from multiple sources. Contacts in America confirmed that they'd been monitoring unusual activity related to a phone in Egypt. Their interest seemed legitimate given it had been sparked by an attempt to track the phone made by an employee of a US social media company. The Americans wanted to know what was going on. They were further confused that their employee was trying to locate the phone from her workstation in Dublin, Ireland.

This made next to no sense to the Libyan analyst who was pulling together a briefing paper for his boss.

Then from Britain came a communiqué suggesting that a former British naval officer had landed in Egypt. On the face of it there appeared to be no connection until the analyst took it upon himself to look at the officer's phone activity. It seemed he'd been in contact with a number in Dublin, Ireland.

Curious, thought the analyst, but why draw this to the

attention of Libya if this man and the tracked phone are actually in Egypt?

The British appeared to be getting their information from the Egyptians because they were also able to establish that the former British officer had been arrested and that the phone he'd used was being transported to a military intelligence outpost in the eastern Sinai Desert.

So far, so unclear.

Then came the most confusing element of all: the Americans had issued information for the eyes of senior staff only. The analyst had to request a code and clearance to access the file in preparation for the briefing. That document stated that an Egyptian military intelligence chief seemed to have the former naval officer in his personal custody; at least their phones appeared to be travelling together. Further to that, and of interest to the analyst at least, was that the Egyptian military intelligence chief had entered coordinates into his phone – and those coordinates pinpointed a position in the middle of the northern Libyan desert.

And so, finally, there was a connection. Sort of.

The analyst compiled the report and sent it up the chain.

"What do you mean?"

"What part?" asked Sam.

Waleed stared at him as if he was being deliberately obtuse. "The part where you see this man with strange shoes in Nuweiba!"

"Well, I can't be sure, but when I was nicking a car—"

"What is *nicking a car*?"

"When I was stealing a car at the port to get me to the hotel in Taba—"

"I see, I see, I see," Waleed whisked the story on.

"I saw a van and a lorry. The lorry had come off the ferry from Jordan, I think, and there was a man in the van who fits the description of the boss of the big cop."

"Coincidence," tutted Waleed. "Nothing more."

"Normally I would agree with you, but he was definitely shifting boats – rubber dinghies. I saw them. I know boats, Waleed."

The Egyptian thought for a while, his arms stretching out his spine against the back of a chair. He gradually lowered his head between his arms and spoke to the floor.

"I wish for him to be gone."

Sam wasn't sure exactly who he was referring to.

"The man with the tassels?"

"No. Yes, him also. I wish for him," he raised his head, "big fool here in cell – to be gone. Vanished. He is trouble for me."

"Is there something else going on here, Waleed?"

There was a long stare, a kind of silent assessment, and then Waleed answered.

"Meester Sam, please take out your phone and passport and empty your pockets. Please place everything on this table."

For a moment Sam thought he was about to be arrested again until Waleed also emptied his pockets and dumped two phones and even his handgun on the table.

"Is all?"

"Nothing else." Sam held his hands up a little.

"Come with me."

The two men strolled out into the ferocious white sun. Waleed kept his head lowered and strode towards the perimeter of the compound. At the gate he nodded to the sentry to open the huge steel-shuttered doors and then led Sam round a corner. One glance confirmed to Waleed he was in a blind spot from the cameras and to all intents and purposes the men were in open desert.

"Are you believe-ed in God, Meester Sam?" he asked.

That wasn't really a question Sam was expecting. "Probably not the same way you do," said Sam, "but, yes, I have a faith. It's not ... conventional though."

"You are Christian, yes? Catholic? Ireland is Catholic?"

"No, well, yes, Ireland is a Catholic country, but I'm not a Catholic. I'm not really a Protestant either. My wife, she was a Catholic. My daughter, she's a Catholic. I was brought up Protestant, I suppose, but I'd say I'm a bit more ecumenical than that."

"Ecumenical," said Waleed slowly, as if working out what it tasted like.

"Look, Waleed, I'm on shaky ground here. I believe in God, yes, but not in everything the Bible says – which I know makes me someone who thinks he can pick and choose, but there are bits I have problems with."

"What problems you have?"

"Well, some people use the Old Testament to justify the death penalty. I have no problem with knocking the odd person off when it is justified, but that doesn't mean I think the state should be strapping people into electric chairs and frying them or hanging them."

Waleed nodded.

"And I don't think God is going to punish gay people. But that's just me."

"Your wife, she is dead?"

Waleed was nothing if not disarming.

"How do you know that?"

"You say *was*, not *is*."

"Fuck, Waleed, you haven't got a tense correct since I met you and that's what you pick up on?"

"Tense?"

Sam looked at him in wonder for a moment then gave up.

"Yes, she died."

"How she is dead?"

"She was murdered."

"And you do not believe killer should hang?"

"He did worse than hang, Waleed. I imagine he died roaring but that was not the job of my government to do that."

"You did this?"

Sam just looked at him.

"What's this all about? Are you trying to convert me?"

"Convert?"

"To Islam?"

Waleed chuckled.

"This is problem, Meester Sam. I am not Muslim. I am Christian. Like you."

"Right," said Sam, yet still none of this was making sense.

"Fat cop inside interrogation suite," he nodded to the compound wall, "he knows secret."

"So it is a secret?"

"Yes, is secret! Christians, they not pier-mitted to be intelligence in Egypt. They not allowed to be in position like this."

"I see. So how does he know? Did you tell him?"

"He is knowing me long time. When I arrest him out here I find out what he is doing in Sinai. I press him too hard. He is thinking, why my friend has turn-ed on me. Then he is thinking to time in academy. Then he is thinking why I never go to mosque or pray."

"So he guessed?"

"Yes. For years is secret – no problem. Then most stupid man in whole of Egypt, he guess. Then – is problem."

"Fuck."

"Yes. Fuck."

"At least you're not gay. I hear the government here really doesn't like gay people."

Waleed just stared at Sam, not appreciating his attempt at levity, and Sam began to wonder if he was gay.

"So I have problem," Waleed repeated after a moment.

"What would happen if your bosses found out you're a Christian?"

"Discipline. Jail, maybe. Not in job, for sure."

"So what are you going to do?"

"I help keep-ed you out of jail. Pier-haps you hel-ep me keep out of jail. You hel-ep me with big cop, maybe."

And suddenly for Sam things became a little clearer.

The Libyan intelligence analyst waited nervously for his boss, a tall, thin man in traditional garb, to finish reading his summary.

"What is at these coordinates in the desert?"

"I do not know, sir."

"What do the satellite images show?"

"Nothing, sir. Just a kind of rock formation."

"Is there any water there – any oasis?"

"Not that I can see."

The analyst pondered. Perhaps the Egyptian military chief had simply been testing his phone or its GPS. Perhaps the coordinates had been random, but that seemed unlikely. Random numbers could land anywhere in the world and these had plotted the country next door.

"I cannot take this upstairs. There is not enough information. Ask the Americans for more. Ask the British too."

Sam and Waleed sat back down inside the compound. Sam had thought through his next moves on their return walk.

"I assume you can monitor phone signals?"

"Of course," said Waleed.

"Well, if we want to find this Libyan people trafficker, we

would do well to track calls made by the big cop's boss with the funny shoes. If he has struck up an arrangement with the trafficker, that could be a quick way of finding him."

Waleed nodded.

The doctor seized the phone greedily from the guard.

"Five minutes, this is all. More time, more euros. Understand?"

"Yes," said the doctor. He dialled his cousin's number from memory.

The analyst opened the new file from the Americans. There was no need to summarise the contents – it was brief:

Egyptian military chief has requested monitoring of phone of mid-ranking police officer in Alexandria, Egypt. Police officer has received a call from an unregistered phone located at a refugee detention centre in Libya.

The analyst copied, pasted and hit send.

Waleed sat up with excitement.

"He's had call."

"The cop with the tassels? That was quick," Sam said.

Waleed read from his phone. "It's from a refugee detention centre in Tobruk, Libya."

"I'm familiar with Tobruk," Sam said.

"Really?" said Waleed.

"Long story," Sam replied.

"Well, you have plenty of time. Is fifteen-hour drive from here."

"I don't have much time, actually," Sam faltered.

"Why?" Waleed was suddenly suspicious.

"I need to be back in Ireland by the end of the week," he said, thinking about Isla's return.

"Then we better leaving now."

The doctor pressed the red button – it was nearly as red as his face. He'd never been so angry. Never.

His cousin had actually laughed aloud. Not just a chuckle, but a belly laugh that went on and on.

"What can you do for me?" he'd asked when the guffaw had subsided.

"*Do for you?*" Tassels had asked. "I'll say a prayer, how's that?"

"Will you not help me?" asked the doctor.

"Help you!" laughed Tassels.

"Remember, cousin, I've information about what you've done – your corruption, your beatings and torture."

"The information you have is *nothing* compared to the information I have! This is the best news I've heard in months. You are in a refugee system that will keep you in Libya for years. Help you? Ha. I will give you advice, though, be careful in the showers – if there are any showers!"

Tassels had laughed and laughed until the doctor cut the call.

"You think-ed you would complete jobs in one week?" asked Waleed, sceptical.

It was three hours into the journey and the first time Waleed had spoken. Sam was driving and Big Suit was trussed up in the back.

"Well, I got half of it done in two days."

The ship, thought Waleed, who pouted his lips. I suppose you did. "Is possible to go Alexandria first," said Waleed, musing. "Deal with big fool's boss, then with traffick man."

Big Suit remained oblivious to their conversation. Even if it had been conducted in Arabic, his ability to follow it might have had its limitations.

"I've been thinking about that," said Sam, "but, ideally, I was thinking you might like to leave your friend in another country."

Waleed's eyes made the slightest move towards Big Suit before a small smile cracked across his face. "Yes, I think yes."

"So provided we don't get stopped or detained or held up, let's just keep going for Tobruk."

"We will not be stopped," said Waleed smiling. "This is my authority. I cannot be stopped in my own desert in my own country."

"Libya could be a different story," Sam said, half questioning his new colleague.

"I am thinking about Libya," said Waleed. "There is way I can contact person same as me in Libya. We can pier-haps make way clear to Tobruk, but highway is dangerous for every pier-son on road. Libya is very, very dangerous."

"So we deal with the bent copper later?"

"What is this?"

"The cop in Alexandria – we will do that after?"

"Yes, you leave to me. I will arrange-ed that."

Waleed smiled his crooked smile again and they barrelled west.

The Libyan analyst referred the encrypted file to his boss. His boss read the contents with wide eyes before lifting the phone to his own superior.

"One of our allies wants to know what is at the location of the coordinates."

There was silence while the boss listened to his orders and then relayed them to the analyst.

"Get one of the long-range units to take a look. Tell them to hurry up."

CHAPTER 24

The road was relentless but at least the car was nice, a relatively modern saloon with air conditioning. Big Suit was crumpled sideways in the back. How his position was conducive to sleep was a mystery but his snoring endured for hours. Waleed and Sam found themselves talking as people on a long haul often do when there's nothing else to distract. Some of Sam's deepest discussions had taken place like this – on the rail of a racing boat while crossing a sea or ocean, or in the bunk of a troop carrier on the way to or from an operation. Perhaps it was to do with the lack of eye contact.

Waleed had talked a little about his family and its dispersal from a town not far from Alexandria.

"We were one of the last," he mused. "Last Copt families in my area. Coptic Christians."

"Were there many? Copts, like, before?"

"Yes, very many. Christians are oldest in Alexandria. Coptic – it is meaning Egypt. Egyptian Christians."

"So what changed?"

"Many years, we are left alone. Even under Mubarak – he is

not for religion, not really. Later things change-ed. Churches with bombing and attack at homes."

"Were you affected?"

"When I was in army. Far away from my family."

"What happened?"

"Joining army was accident really. I mean to be a police. I not telling any pier-son at academy I am Christian. I pretend I am Muslim, but I do not pray and I do not go to mosque. Under Mubarak is acceptable. Nobody care very strong."

"Why did you cover it up, though, if joining the army was just an accident?"

"Is making life easy. This is only reason."

Sam could understand that. He'd always been an outsider in the British military where most claimed to find him barely comprehensible. So to make the going smoother he'd adopted an accent just for being in England and only reverted back when at home. It was purely functional even if it felt like a tiny betrayal, but when you're in your late teens and early twenties small things make a big difference and standing out from the crowd isn't always the best way to get along. Sam learned early that sticking in the middle of the pack made falls shorter and rises quicker. He'd stood out at Lympstone nonetheless, for being quieter than most, for being capable and for having reserves in his character that eventually drew him into even bigger things.

"So how did you go from the police to the military?"

"I never join-ed police," said Waleed. "At end of academy, military approach-ed me and say we wish for you to come with us. Then they train me again."

"In intelligence?"

"Later intelligence. First they train-ed me in military. Unit is name-ed 777. Is antiterrorist unit."

Sam had heard of it. "Special forces."

"Yes."

The pair remained quiet for a few miles before Waleed broke the silence. "You also?"

Sam knew what he meant. "Me also."

"Special sailor?"

"Special Boat Service," Sam said.

"Ah-hah!" said Waleed, suddenly remembering the name.

"Briefly," Sam clarified. "Quite brief, really."

"Why?"

Sam found himself opening up a little about Shannon and how they'd collided in Gaza. He didn't elaborate on anything operational, just that he'd been on a job. Sam made a vague allusion to getting into trouble as a result of something he'd done for her and then deflected attention back onto Waleed.

"You said your family had been affected by the persecution of Copts?"

Waleed hadn't married, in part because he hadn't known how to unravel his lie about his religious background. He explained how difficult it would be to become part of a wider Muslim family given that he had no point of reference. Sam could identify with that and his less than basic knowledge of the sacraments in the Catholic Church, and how awkward he'd felt going through the motions with Shannon despite their religions having the same origin. He had no idea how Christians and Muslims could find a way to unite in matrimony in an increasingly tricky environment like Egypt.

"Did you never meet a Christian girl?"

"If I meet Christian, I cannot marry and stay in job unless she become Muslim, which is crazy as I not even Muslim!" He laughed at the ridiculousness of what he might have to ask a future partner to do.

Sam warmed to Waleed enormously.

And then from the laughter came a sad note.

"There was a woman back home," he said, "but we lose-ed contact."

"Deliberately?"

"How you mean?"

"Did you lose contact on purpose?"

"She is asking me, do not join-ed police. Is dangerous."

"She was right."

"But I think, how can change Egypt if good people not joining police? So much corrupt in Egypt. Is no good."

"What happened to her?"

"I try to find her, one year."

"One year?"

"Yes, one year pass-ed."

"One year ago?"

"Yes."

"Why?"

"I think, maybe is no use. Sinai is lost. Maybe she is right. We cannot defeat jihadist. They will come and come and from everywhere – Iraq and Syria. This is where they will settle."

"You think they're going to win?"

"One year pass-ed I think maybe. Now, not certain."

"Did you find her?"

Waleed fell into an awkward silence. "I think, yes," he conceded after a period. "Some of her family killed in bomb at church. Suicide bomb."

"But she was ok?"

"Yes, I think. Police did good job that day." He shook his head in wonder. "They stop-ed suicide bomber outside church."

"Yet some people were killed."

"Yes, many," Waleed said.

"So what became of her?"

"I believe she leave Egypt."

Sam had a sinking feeling as to where this was going. "I think I can guess how," he said.

"She cross-ed to Libya," Waleed said. "I believe she take boat to Europe."

"Did she make it?"

"Nobody know."

Sam found himself trying to give Waleed hope. He described his night with Isla and how they'd rescued the women in the water. Waleed listened with a solemn resignation and appeared to take no solace in the story.

"Tell me about your daughter," he said instead.

Against his better judgement Sam found himself talking about Isla and what they'd been through. He confessed that she was the reason he had to get back to Ireland quickly.

"One day, for me, pier-haps, children. I would like very much," Waleed said dreamily.

"I reckon you'd be a great dad," Sam said, and he meant it.

"I hope," said Waleed.

The long-range team set out from Benghazi twenty minutes after the order had been issued. The estimated journey time was fifteen hours. The terrain looked lumpy, the destination nondescript.

The eight men couldn't understand the point of the exercise. Their vehicles were aged, the fuel they were burning would be costly and they stood every chance of blowing out more tyres and wheels than they could replace. Besides, such journeys were brutally uncomfortable.

There was nothing else for it, though, but to lie as flat as possible in the big wheeler and try to rest until it was their turn to drive. The lower a man managed to get onto the bed of the vehicle, the less the strain on the neck from the judder and spring of rubber on rock.

Something was going on.

The analyst hadn't seen as much interest from *friendly* intelligence agencies since Gaddafi had been killed. Every hour there was an update request. The analyst had decided against making his boss aware of every demand – it only brought wrath upon the messenger. He opted instead to answer himself with polite courtesy: the team is on its way. We shall advise as soon as we know anything further.

"Why did you want the big cop's phone and GPS destroyed?" Sam asked, the notion occurring to him as the road rolled by.

"I do not want police to know I arrest him," said Waleed. "I think they may be tracing phone."

"Why didn't you want them to know?"

"I have no reason to arresting him. My job is intelligence. Jihadi information. Is not my business to arresting police officers."

"So why did you arrest him?"

"Is good question," said Waleed. "He once friend at academy."

"You said before."

"He call-ed me from desert. He tell me he see fire in front of him. I thinking maybe he is looking at ISIL camp or some jihadi, so I track-ed his phone and I see I have unit of soldier one mile close to him. So I send."

"You were doing him a favour?"

"Pier-haps. Then I question him. Hard. I threat him. Is not

normal for policeman from Alexandria to be in Sinai. He tell me he on way to pick up boat for traffick people. Then I get mad and I leave him in compound."

"So you didn't want the police to come sniffing around your area?"

"Sniffing?"

"Hunting for him, looking for him."

"Exact. Sinai is already dangerous. No need for police also to be cause problems."

"I'm not going to kill him, Waleed," Sam said, rushing out what had been on his mind for miles. He didn't know what Waleed expected of him but he hoped it wasn't that.

"Good, Sam Ireland," Waleed said. "I like-ed that big fool very much, long time ago. He is idiot, but he is like hammer. It is carpenter is real problem."

―――――――――

The doctor watched with horror from his shared mattress as the guard he'd paid for the use of a phone was shackled and slapped and led away.

Of course his concern wasn't the guard's welfare, but his own. Had someone seen their transaction? Other inmates had no doubt spotted him using the mobile phone but surely such transgressions were commonplace – this was a kind of prison after all.

The doctor lay back and tried not to panic but he knew it was only a matter of time.

―――――――――

Sam had literally sailed through many borders but the ease with which Waleed negotiated the Egyptian–Libyan checkpoints was impressive. He'd made a number of phone calls well ahead of time. When they came to the militarised zones he simply redialled a number he'd stored on his handset and handed the phone to the soldiers as they stooped down to ask for ID. Each heard whoever was on the other end of the line issue brief instructions before the mobile phone was respectfully handed back to Waleed and the car waved on.

"Your counterpart?" Sam asked.

"Yes," said Waleed, his mind focused on the road in front, wary of what lay ahead.

The doctor turned to find a boot testing the spring of his mattress. His head was being gently coaxed up and down. He shuddered when he saw the boot belonged not to one of the centre's guards but to a solider who was flanked by another. Both were armed with rifles.

They've got me, he thought. My cousin, the dog, has told them what I did in Egypt.

"Get up."

The doctor was a bleeder not a fighter. He was never going to resist. He rose meekly and with his head hung in guilt was escorted between the two soldiers to the door.

They made their way through a warren of corridors but all the doctor could do was stare at the heels of the solider in front. The boots halted and moved to the side, another door was opened and he was propelled inside by the shoulder.

He was astonished at the first person he set eyes on. Big Suit, a shadow of his former self, sat in an ill-chosen plastic chair with all the ease an adult might sit in a primary school chair.

Exhausted as Sam and Waleed were, they noticed the mutual recognition.

"I see you know one another." Waleed tested the detainee's English.

A flicker from the doctor showed he'd understood. Big Suit looked as vacant as ever.

"Sit down, please," Waleed remained polite, and the doctor settled nervously into his seat as if convinced it would be whisked from behind him by one of the soldiers.

"I am head of Egyptian Military Intelligence in the Sinai region. This gentleman is from Europe," he gestured with his thumb over his shoulder. "And you know this man." Waleed pointed to Big Suit. To his amazement the doctor nodded to confirm their acquaintance.

Waleed's anticipation grew as the dynamics of the situation ricocheted around the room like a pinball. He decided to coax out the story by giving the impression he knew what was going on.

"I will be very clear. We do not have lot of time. For you, is good if you tell us truth fast. Understand?"

The doctor nodded vigorously.

"You tell us truth, we try to hel-ep you." It had crossed Waleed's mind that this refugee might simply be some unfortunate victim of the trafficking ring. "Tell us how you know this man."

The doctor looked at Big Suit and then at the ground. "I used to do work for him. For his boss, really."

Waleed tried to hide his surprise and remain collected. Sam was taken with the man's obvious grasp of English.

"What work please?" Waleed asked.

"They ... they used to torture people in the jail. I am a doctor. They used to hurt people and I would help them."

"Hel-ep them hurt people?" Waleed asked.

"No!" said the doctor. "Help the people they injured. He was dangerous," he nodded to Big Suit. "I'm amazed he is still alive."

"Why?" Waleed asked.

"Because the last time I saw him he was donating blood to one of his own victims. Too much blood."

Everyone looked at Big Suit who had no idea what they were saying and was rather abashed to be observed in triplicate.

"Continue," said Waleed, eager not to betray his ignorance.

"He had cutters for breaking chains and locks." The doctor made a motion as if pruning a hedge.

Big Suit sat up a little straighter suddenly understanding what the doctor was saying. A look of alarm crossed his face.

"The last man, he cut him terribly. I had to seal the wound."

"Cut him how?"

"He snipped off his toe and then ..." the doctor spoke more softly, "his testicular area."

Both English speakers scrunched up their eyes and tightened their lips.

"He is an animal," said the doctor.

Sam leaned forward and whispered in Waleed's ear.

"What was name of victim?"

"Habid," said the doctor.

"Bingo," said Sam.

The analyst ran through to his boss with a piece of paper fresh from the printer.

"Message from America, sir. The two men – they are here!" he spluttered excitedly.

"What men, where?"

"The British naval officer and the Egyptian chief," he said. "They are in Tobruk."

"I know," said his boss.

"You know?"

"I secured their entry at the border," said the boss.

"Why?" asked the analyst, keen to show he was eager to learn.

"Because it is useful to know where people are. If they tell us, then it is easier to track them and see what they are up to."

"I see," said the analyst, but he didn't see at all.

To the minute, it took one hour to empty the doctor's head of all he knew about Habid's trafficking route. He gushed out the details – how the rat had a list and biographies of wealthy Gaddafi insiders. How he'd hidden them somewhere and how he rationed their departures. He told them about his evil little cousin and how the rat had outfoxed him to make him a labourer in the scheme rather than the leader of it. He issued dire warnings about the rat's cunning and intelligence. The doc described the route as best he could – the different border crossings and the pickups performed by his cousin with the help of some corrupt police officers.

"So," said Sam, still pinching himself that they'd made such progress, "where can we find him?"

For the first time the doctor looked blank. "I do not know," he said, mildly shocked at his own answer.

"Then we cannot hel-ep you," said Waleed almost regretfully.

The doctor began to panic. "You have all the information. Everything. This is all I know. You must be able to find him from what I have said!"

"All you have told is that he keeps people in desert. Do you know how big desert is?"

The doctor was truly lost for words.

Waleed nodded to the solitary soldier. The man rose and made for action.

"*Shukran*," Waleed said, and then the screaming and pleading started and the doctor was hit a thump and dragged from the room.

Waleed turned to Sam who shrugged.

"I think we know where he keeps them."

"Yes, I think we do."

"Wonder if there's room in the desert for a large one?"

Both men looked at Big Suit who was utterly zoned out.

"No," said Waleed. "I have enough of dragging him around behind us. We have just heard from doctor what this man has become. He was prepar-ed to send peoples to drown – to make refugee. Let us now make *him* refugee. We will leave him here."

Áine was more than halfway to blind drunk when Sinead got the text:

Am low on battery. We know the trafficking route. Going to try to track down the man that sent Alea to sea. Does Áine know any more about why she was sacked? Could be important.

"Áine, it's Sam. He's asking do you know any more about the hack, or who it might have been?"

Her twin turned to her and enunciated her vowels very clearly for a woman so smashed.

"Tell Sam to go an' fuck himself," she said.

Not really, Sam, Sinead typed. Then she thought a while. Then typed again.

Take care, let me know.

"So now we have problem," Waleed said to Sam.

"How to get into the desert? I know," said Sam.

"No. Other problem."

"What?"

"Libyan intelligence know where we are."

"Sure they've known since we came into the country. You told them, didn't you? That's how we got through the road-blocks, aye?"

"Yes, they also know *why* we are here."

"How?"

"If I have Libyan intelligence in my country, I bug room. Also, we have phone in pocket. You have phone in pocket. They know."

Sam reckoned he had a point.

"Is big problem, really," said Waleed, who seemed remarkably relaxed given the magnitude of what he was about to describe. "We take a walk."

They led Big Suit like a bear on a chain at a circus, opened the door into the warehouse at the end of the corridor and pushed him inside with all the other refugees. They then left the way they'd come, emerging onto a not very busy street. Waleed took his phone from his pocket and placed it on a windowsill, Sam followed suit and they both walked thirty yards up the road.

"New government in Libya," Waleed said.

"Yes."

"Not like Gaddafi or Gaddafi people."

Sam was following the drift. "They will want to find Habid themselves."

Waleed shook his head. "They will not care about rat. They will want Gaddafi's people – his circle. They will hang them in the streets."

Sam could see that. "Then we need to get there first."

"They will follow us."

"Does that matter?"

Waleed swayed his head. "Maybe, maybe not."

"It's worth a go," Sam suggested.

"Ok. We will need map, GPS. Good vehicle."

They looked at Waleed's Mazda.

"Better vehicle."

"Yes," said Sam.

"Easy way is to do with Libya."

"What do you mean?"

"We tell them what we plan."

"But we only want Habid?"

"So we make deal."

"They give us Habid and what they do with the others is their own business?"

"Yes," said Waleed.

Sam thought of Alea and Sadiqah. "No, Waleed. There are women and children there. Wherever *there* is."

"Ok," shrugged Waleed. "What is plan?"

"We hedge."

The analyst scribbled the information from the long-range desert group with widening eyes. His skin stretched around his skull as more and more detail was relayed. He hung up the phone and ran through to his boss's office.

"I have the latest from the team at the coordinates you gave me."

"Sir," barked the boss.

"Yes, sir. Sorry, sir."

"What is it?"

The analyst began to read his own scribbles.

"Twenty-two people, sir, living underground, sir. They are surviving in a wadi, sir."

"Hurry up," barked the boss.

"Yes, some have papers, sir, in preparation for leaving Libya."

"Who are they?"

"The captain says they are what remains of Gaddafi's inner circle and their families, sir."

To the analyst's amazement the boss simply nodded.

"Thank you. Let me know if you hear anything else."

"Do you not want the names, sir?"

But the boss was already reaching for his phone, so the analyst gently set the piece of paper at his side and tiptoed out of the room. He didn't even get to tell him that a small group had recently left the bunker.

Sam had done his desert training. He could navigate, he could drive and he could hike. He had suffered the Brecon Beacons and all Wales could throw at him during the height of summer and the harshest of winter. That was what special forces training was partly about: endurance, but it was also about guile, wit, sense and knowing how to crack the toughest of nuts. The Libyan desert was one such nut.

In classrooms he'd learned about the exploits of the original SAS, the pioneers who'd cut their teeth on this very terrain. His own personal hero, Blair Mayne from Northern Ireland, had been one of the toughest SAS troopers the force had ever seen. They'd conducted incredible attacks on Italian and German airfields throughout Libya during World War II, ferocious fighters doing the bravest of work. They'd ranged into unmapped territory aboard failing vehicles with crap kit and only the sun and stars to guide them. It had taken weeks, sometimes months.

So Sam flew.

It had taken a sizeable withdrawal from Waleed and a few

goes at the ATM for Sam to gather the funds but the rest was relatively straightforward. Tobruk airfield didn't offer day trips or flying lessons but it had helicopters and a few would-be pilots. For the cost of heli-hire and fuel they appeared only too keen to up their air miles ahead of qualification. Sam didn't inquire too far into their *actual* ability but within two hours he was airborne and headed towards the coordinates on Habid's GPS in his hand.

The pilot was excitable and irritating, keen on swooping and showing off. Nine miles out Sam had to bark at him over the hubbub to stop fucking around, but his voice was outstripped by the boom of two fighter jets screaming far overhead.

Sam's heart sank as he suddenly realised what was about to happen.

"Turn!" he shouted, sending his skipper into what was almost a tailspin. "Calm down, sorry, son. Calm down. Get the aircraft steady and turn around. Go back now. Tobruk, yes? Tobruk."

The young man got his shit together and cut a steady curve to head back north-east.

"You are about to hear something shocking, ok? It will be ok. Just get us back to Tobruk, do you understand?"

The pilot just kept nodding.

"Get us there as quickly as you can, ok?" Sam's voice had lowered to a soothing but authoritative register, coaxing the kid to keep his head and get them back safely.

And then came the explosions.

"Eyes front, son," he said, using two fingers on his right hand to gesture to his own eyeballs and then point ahead. And then Sam turned to catch the remains of the fireball that had been generated in the middle of nowhere.

He closed his eyes and prayed that what had just happened wasn't as a result of what he and Waleed had done, but he knew deep down that was the most likely reason Habid's flock had just been cremated.

Sinead was trying to sleep when she got an encrypted message on the app:

Áine correct about hack. Any danger now passed. They have what they wanted. Sorry. Really. Sam.

CHAPTER 25

Sam had three days – and enough anger for three decades.

Waleed hurtled across the highway, this time convoyed by two open-bed jeeps each equipped with a general-purpose machine gun and two armed soldiers in the back. Whatever deal he'd struck with his counterpart in Libyan intelligence, it seemed they wanted rid of Waleed and Sam just as much as Waleed and Sam wanted to get out of Libya.

Big Suit had been left on a mattress at the detention centre wearing the same clothes he'd had on for three months. There'd been some initial resistance but the soldiers had become incredibly agreeable with the handover of cash.

Neither man said anything for a very long time. They were of the same mind – the law of unintended consequences. Both understood that they'd miscalculated, that they'd become involved in matters that had wider, perhaps even global, implications. Both now understood that of course there were people who wanted Gaddafi's insiders incinerated. The new Libyan administration weren't fans, for sure, but there were others too – those who had managed or run informants within the regime, those who manipulated the leader in from the cold to the benefit of the west.

Both Sam and Waleed knew they'd started a chain of events that had led to the identification of the hideout. They'd have to live with that and therefore the deaths of whoever had been stashed in the desert.

And that brought silence, but it also brought determination. This seedy business in human exploitation had to end.

Close to exhaustion, they rolled into Alexandria where the final touches needed to be applied to Sam's hedge.

Sam hadn't seen Waleed in full fight but it was worth a watch.

Tassels was ripped from his bed at three o'clock in the morning. His face forced into the screen of Waleed's phone.

"Your cousin," Waleed screamed in Tassel's ear.

"Who are you—"

"Waleed Ahram."

Tassels evidently knew the name because he began to urinate inside his blue pyjama bottoms.

"You have group arriving from Libya."

"Yes," Tassels bleated.

"Today."

"Yes, how do you know this?"

"The Libyans told me."

Which was true. Waleed's counterpart had got round to reading his analyst's handwriting.

"What do you want?"

"Your cousin, he has sold you out."

Waleed was gripping Tassels by one ear and twisting hard, while whispering and spitting into the other.

"He has told us you collect the boat captains."

"Yes," mustered Tassels. "Later."

"From where?"

"From train."

"My friend here," he twisted Tassels' neck to allow him to see Sam for the first time, "will go with you. Understand?"

"Yes, yes," panted Tassels.

"Where is your phone?"

"By the bed."

"We will be staying with you until this is over. If you want to avoid execution, you will do exactly what we say. Understand?"

"Yes, yes. Understand."

Sam didn't understand. The whole hissing, pissing, growling conversation had been conducted in Arabic, but he imagined the hedge plan had been explained rather eloquently.

Tassels loitered on the platform smoking furiously. He'd spent the night between two exceptionally angry men as instructions were relayed in English and repeated in Arabic, confirmed and refined.

He had an A4 piece of paper to identify himself that he held up each time a new train arrived. He swore blind to Waleed he was never told what train the sailors would arrive on. Three carriages came and went before he was approached by a swarthy man in jeans and a plain blue shirt. Ethnically the match with Sam was far from ideal – the man could be Turkish or Lebanese, and size-wise they'd have to find Sam some new kit because the boat captain was tiny.

He got into the back of Tassels' car and was bookended by Waleed and Sam. Before long he was tied to a chair in Tassels' apartment and was explaining his arrangement with Habid in broken English.

"How did you get this job?" Sam asked.

"Agency."

"What agency?"

"In Romania."

"There is a seafarers' agency in Romania? There isn't even sea in Romania." Sam had scoffed.

"Not shipping agency," the man explained. "Transport. Internet. For get to Europe."

"Trafficking, in other words," Sam said.

"Where did you come from?" Waleed asked.

"Abkhazia," the man said.

"Black Sea?" Sam was surprised.

"Yes, Black Sea."

"So you are Russian?"

"Nooo," stressed the man. "Not Russian."

Sam couldn't be hassled with the politics. He knew there were issues in the Caucasus, a lot of the area craved independence, but it wasn't a primary concern.

"What are you supposed to say to the man who has hired you?"

"Nothing. Strict instruction. Say nothing. Not speak to no one."

"What are you supposed to do?"

"Take boat, start engine, bearing is north-west. When ship approach, light flare, go to Europe."

Made sense to Sam. It fit with what the doctor and Alea had said. He rooted through the man's haversack and withdrew a bottle of water, a handbearing compass, a set of decent oilskins and a woolly hat. There was also a small Magellan GPS. Sam packed it all back in apart from the oilies, which were too small to be of any use.

"No phone?" he asked the man.

"No," he said.

"Search him."

Waleed stood the unfortunate sailor up and emptied his

pockets. In his sock he found a small Nokia in a plastic sealable bag. Under the insole of his shoe Waleed withdrew a slim wrap of euros.

"Papers? ID?" Sam asked.

But Waleed was already on it. In the lining of the oilskin he found a passport – presumably to get the man as far as Egypt, and some sort of certificate written in a language they couldn't understand.

"Is this all the money you have?" Sam waved the cash in front of his face.

"Employer must pay before departure," he said, forlorn.

"Ok," said Sam. "We," he pointed between Waleed and himself, "are police. You have been involved in people smuggling. You have been caught. You will not be going to sea tonight. You are lucky. If you had gone to sea, you would have died, for sure."

And they left him there, bound with knots from the muscle memory of a seasoned sailor. Waleed would deal with him later, once he had dealt with Tassels.

Sam longed to see the man he'd travelled thousands of miles to hunt. It had taken five days and enormous good and bad fortune, but when the moment came he was disappointed.

Tassels, observed at a distance by Waleed, had done his job and ferried the migrants to the bank where monies had been exchanged. That night Sam took up his station by the shore as the tiny tribe approached carrying their heavy bundle between them. Each was bearing a fraction of the load in one hand, and in the other hand four of the travellers each swung a small fuel can.

Tassels beckoned Sam forward to meet the group. He stood and glared at Habid who barely acknowledged him. He was smaller than Sam had anticipated but sprightly given his injuries. Sam wondered if he'd be as resolute if he had only one toe and one testicle. The grisly figure bent to peel off a few fifty-euro notes, which Sam accepted and stuffed in his pocket before taking a handle on the dinghy and helping the group down towards the sea. Habid didn't appear to doubt the proceedings for a moment.

Habid stepped aside from the group and looked around him. Apparently happy, he motioned the others to set the boat down. Then he stooped into it and threw Sam a foot pump. Dutifully Sam set about unscrewing the valve caps and began bellowing air into the inflatable. As he did so he appraised his crew.

There were three other men, three women and two children – a boy and a girl. None of the women were covered as Alea had been. Each wore headscarves but beyond that there was nothing hindering his view. Two were in their thirties, the last was perhaps fifty. He assumed she was the wife of the oldest man, who was at least sixty. They appeared to have great affection for the children and stroked their heads at times, reassuringly. The younger men were wary, watching everyone, particularly Sam. They obviously had no idea who he was or what he was there to do – Habid explained nothing. Sam regretted that things were about to get tough for the kids.

He bent down to test the spring in each tank and, when satisfied, replaced the valve cover and moved to the next. When the boat was fully inflated he reached in to lift the two-stroke engine and attach it to the aluminium board at the transom. He then inflated the floor and stood up, slung his bag over his shoulder and nodded at Habid.

The little man then began gathering documents from the men who each handed over a sheaf of paper with obvious reluctance. One looked regretfully at his wife but parted with the bounty nonetheless. Habid snapped a few commands in

Arabic and the group gathered around the boat once more to drag it the final few feet towards sea. Not one of the migrants had been offered or wore a life jacket. Things were evidently getting tight on the safety front, thought Sam. When the boat was afloat Habid gave instructions for the people to climb in. The sea was washing gently up the beach, catching the women by surprise as the cold water rose higher with each wave. The men helped the children and women in before turning expectantly to Sam.

Habid stood a few feet behind him. He could see the silhouette of Tassels in the near distance and beyond that the unmistakable outline of Waleed ready to secure his prey.

Sam closed his eyes for a moment, thought through what he had to and lashed round with a full hay baler knocking Habid's remaining few teeth ten feet up the beach. He heard the women gasp, not scream, then he leaned over Habid and with his open palm hit him in the sweet spot of the jaw, confirming his unconsciousness.

Sam turned towards the boat with his palms facing downwards in a gesture of calm. He spoke for the first time.

"Do any of you speak English?"

"Yes," said one man.

"I do," said a younger woman.

"Good. I am here to help you. Do you all know one another?"

"Yes," said the man.

Sam looked to the woman. "Is that right?"

She nodded.

"I need to make sure. Were you underground together?"

"Yes, yes," nodded the woman.

"For a long time or just recently?"

"For almost one year," she said.

"Everyone here?" Sam asked.

"Yes, yes," she said. Why?"

"Can the children speak English?" he checked.

"No, they are too young."

"I need to be sure because this man," he pointed at Habid's carcass, "has placed people in boats before and then killed them. Are you sure you know all these men?"

"He is my husband," she pointed at one of them, "he is my sister's husband," she pointed to a woman and the other younger man.

"What about them?" Sam asked, gesturing to the old man and woman.

"They are known to us. They have been underground as long as we have."

Sam had to be sure, so he leaned into the boat and patted the old man down, felt his trouser legs down to his socks and nodded.

"Ok."

He turned and picked Habid up from the beach and tossed him into the base of the boat.

"If he wakes up, make sure you tell me. He is one evil little bastard. Now, you can take your papers back from him – try and keep them as close to your body as possible."

There was a minor scramble from the men as they shook Habid's torso down and sorted the papers between them. Then Sam pushed the boat out a little, dropped the outboard, attached and massaged the fuel lead and ball and ripped the cord. It took almost twenty tugs but the engine coughed into life and Sam gave it some throttle in neutral. Once he was convinced it was pumping water to cool it and that the fuel was drawing correctly, he turned to face Waleed and gave him a long salute of a wave. Waleed returned the gesture with both hands. Sam leapt in and knocked the engine into gear.

A mile offshore he checked Habid for life signs and showed the men how to bail the water out with their shoes. He withdrew the Magellan GPS from the Abkhazian's haversack and switched it on. He motored due north straight into the swell until the shallows became depths and the sea state moderated. Then he turned north-west and ran the engine until empty. The migrants just stared ahead expectantly.

It took three refills and four hours before he was close to the position he wanted: forty-two miles north-west of Alexandria. He allowed the engine to idle while he drew the backpack towards him again and lifted the most valuable weapon he'd held in years.

Waleed had sourced the VHF – a very high frequency radio, from an Egyptian naval colleague in town. Better than that, he'd managed to obtain the planned transit line of a ship familiar to Sam. He fired up the VHF, turned the dial to channel sixteen and began the call, willing it to be answered.

"*LE Niamh*, *LE Niamh*, this is a migrant vessel in need of assistance, over."

There was a hush in the boat as the Libyans gazed up at Sam, confused, curious, hopeful.

"*LE Niamh*, *LE Niamh*, *LE Niamh*, this is a migrant vessel in need of assistance, over."

A full minute passed before the radio snapped into life.

"Station calling *LE Niamh*, say again, over?"

The sound was beautiful. An Irish woman answering an Irish man forty miles north of Libya. Sam could barely contain his relief.

He looked at the GPS. "*LE Niamh*, *LE Niamh*, our position is twenty-six degrees, thirty-three minutes and fifty-one north, and seventeen degrees, twenty-two and eighty-three west."

Sam repeated the coordinates and braced himself for a reply.

"Migrant vessel, this is *LE Niamh*. Transmission received. Hold your position. Over."

"*LE Niamh*, this is migrant vessel. Holding position. Listening sixteen."

Sam turned his attention to the people in his charge. "I need you all to look forward – look for the ship. It is an Irish naval vessel. It is patrolling these waters to rescue migrants. Do not look into this boat or you will get sick. Keep a lookout for the navy ship, do not look into this boat. Keep the children looking forward. Understand?"

The woman spoke to the children and hunkered them down, facing front. The men too all peered into the darkness. The women had gathered at the front of the boat and were transfixed on the horizon.

Sam reached out and pulled Habid towards him by the foot. His body was small enough to bundle behind him while he kept a hand on the tiller and throttle of the outboard. One of the men turned to look at what Sam was doing but Sam pointed at him to look ahead again. The man did as he was bid. Then with a sweep he scooped Habid's waist up with one arm and levered his head and shoulders over the side tank. He gave the engine a little blast of throttle and leveraged the moment of the boat forward to flick the rat's legs over. The noise was no more than a seal might make slipping into a rising tide. Only the oldest man in the boat noticed what he'd done but if he disapproved, he said nothing.

CHAPTER 26

The Irish navy treated the Libyans with total respect. They were corralled on a deck at the stern of the ship and processed, prepared for a wash and given food. Sam had produced his Irish passport and set about the necessary explanations. Initial suspicions were that he'd been part of the trafficking racket. He had remonstrated during an interminable interrogation and had eventually been obliged to make a call he would rather have conducted in private.

"How are you?" Sinead answered immediately.

"I'm grand. We're on an Irish navy ship.

"We?"

"Eh, yeah."

"More waifs and strays?"

"Actually, as it happens—"

"Really?"

"Really. It's a long story."

"Sure, what's new, Sam," she said, more in admiration than admonishment. "There's a few things to fill you in on this end too."

"Really?"

"Really."

"Anything serious?"

"Depends how scared you are of my sister."

"That's quite serious."

Sinead didn't laugh. "When will you be back?"

"Well, that depends. I could do with a favour," he said sheepishly. He looked up at an officer who was listening to every word.

"Like I said, what's new?"

"I need you to explain to some of the officers on this ship what I'm about."

"Oh? That's a bit of a break from the norm, Sam. You're usually pretty protective. You want me to divulge the whole works?"

"If you could just explain some of the work I do for you," he looked again at the officer, careful not to lead the witness, "hopefully they'll understand."

"So not the whole back catalogue – not that I'd be able to tell them much about that, frankly," she nipped.

"And then, could you ask, ehm, the woman you met in Dungarvan to give me a call?"

Sinead coughed out air testily as if to say – are you fucking kidding me?

"Not like that."

"No," Sinead relented. "I know, I think."

"Here's the officer."

He handed the phone to his observer and listened to one end of the conversation.

"We have a man here claims to be Sam Ireland," he began, but with the skill of an investigator he paused hoping the gaps would fill themselves with useful information.

Sam could hear the buzz of dialogue from the other end.

"I need to be satisfied that this man poses no threat to my crew or to the people he was rescued from the sea with."

More chat.

"Over how long?"

Sinead was obviously doing her bit.

"And was this work legal or licensed in anyway?"

Sam heard her pause, then chat, then the man's eyes locked on his own. The officer leaned across and scratched Sinead's name on a Post-it and beckoned forward an NCO. The note was handed over and the gesture clear – check her out.

"These women, they were brought into the country illegally. Why did they not seek asylum?"

Sam's tiredness began to coast over him like puffs of breeze. His confidence in Sinead was absolute, so his cares began to fall away.

The NCO returned with a printout that the officer read as he listened.

"Ok, thank you for your time," he said, and handed back the phone to Sam.

She had hung up, which he tried not to take to heart. "So?" he said, looking at the officer.

"You're ex-navy."

"Yes."

"I suspect you're more than that."

Sam said nothing.

"Your record is limited in detail."

Nothing.

"You will be given quarters and confined to your deck. You appear to be who you say you are but we'll let the authorities deal with that when we land."

"Where are we headed?"

"Catania," came the reply.

"Where is that?"

"Italy, Sicily," he was told.

Sam closed his eyes and gave thanks. "Can I make another call?"

"It's your phone and you're not under arrest," the officer said.

Sam found the name and number and tapped the green button.

The answer was slow and the phone all but rang out.

"*Buongiorno?*" He'd obviously been woken.

"Luca, it's Sam. Father, I could really use your help."

He'd slept soundly for three hours when the handset buzzed at his ear. He longed for it to be morning in the UK so he could hear the voice he craved but the screen revealed an Irish code.

"Hello?"

"Is Sam?"

He closed his eyes, straining to think through what he could say so it would be understood without betraying him to anyone who might be eavesdropping.

"How are you," he began. "How are you both?"

He was keen not to use their names on an unsecure line.

"Fine," Alea said. "How is yourself?"

Sam noted how the vernacular was already creeping into her English.

"I wanted to let you know that the man you told me about, he is gone."

There was a silence for a while, then her voice cracked. "How about the people under the ground?"

Sam paused for a moment not having anticipated the question.

"Some are with me on their way to Europe. They are safe."

"Some," she repeated.

"How many were there?"

"Ten. Sometimes. Twenty. Sometimes more."

Sam closed his eyes. "Some of them are safe and the rest are no longer in danger." The truth has many interpretations, he thought.

"Thank you, Sam," she said.

His phone bleeped as the battery began to give up. He pressed the red circle and dialled again. His mother-in-law had read the tea leaves and immediately put Isla on the line.

"Hallo, Daddy." She sounded sleepy. She'd obviously been woken.

"Hello, wee darlin', how are you?"

"Good. What ya doing?"

"I'm working, wee love, what ya doing yourself?"

"I love it here, Daddy," she said. "It's really fun on all the rides."

"Brilliant, darlin'. Listen, I can't talk for long but will you tell Nanny I'll be a few days late getting back from my job?"

"Ok." She was all but drifting back to sleep.

"I love you so much."

"I love you too, Daddy-o."

AFTERWORD

Thanks a million for reading.

I can't overstate how helpful it is for writers to obtain reviews - no matter the verdict. I'd be enormously grateful if you could drop a rating or even a few words about the book on the outlet from which you bought it, or ideally - on Amazon.

Thanks a million,

Finn.

ABOUT THE AUTHOR

Finn Óg lives and works in Ireland. He is surrounded by rogues and the sea. This book is the second in a trilogy. Part three - Too Close to Home - will be available soon.

twitter.com/@fiercelyprivate

facebook.com/finnbarog

ACKNOWLEDGMENTS

Thanks, always, to the women - tall and small - whose words and ways litter this text. To my pal in stroke city for always being the first eyes across. To Stuart Bache for the covers, to Victoria and Emma for editing and to my belter or a family for absolutely everything.

Printed in Great Britain
by Amazon